NEVER THE SAME

OTHER TITLES BY BRITTNEY SAHIN

Stand-Alones

Until You Can't

The Story of Us

Falcon Falls Security

The Hunted One

The Broken One

The Guarded One

The Taken One

The Lost Letters: A Novella

The Wanted One

The Fallen One

The Wrecked One

Dublin Nights Series

On the Edge

On the Line

The Real Deal

The Inside Man

The Final Hour

Becoming Us

Someone Like You

My Every Breath

Hidden Truths Series

The Safe Bet

Beyond the Chase

The Hard Truth

Surviving the Fall

The Final Goodbye

Stealth Ops Series

Finding His Mark

Finding Justice

Finding the Fight

Finding Her Chance

Finding the Way Back

NEVER THE SAME

BRITTNEY SAHIN

Published by Montlake, Seattle

www.apub.com

Amazon, the Amazon logo, and Montlake are trademarks of Amazon.com, Inc., or its affiliates.

EU product safety contact:
Amazon Media EU S. à r.l.
38, avenue John F. Kennedy, L-1855 Luxembourg
amazonpublishing-gpsr@amazon.com

ISBN-13: 9781662534744 (paperback)
ISBN-13: 9781662534751 (digital)

Cover design by Caroline Johnson
Cover image: © Joseph Cannata

Printed in the United States of America

NEVER
THE
SAME

PROLOGUE

Hollis

Charleston, South Carolina; June 2027

"I could've been naked. What the hell are you doing in here?" Reed lingered in the bathroom doorway, a towel slung low around his hips, water still beading along his collarbone. I'd been waiting a good ten minutes for him to find me on his bed, petting his dog.

"And what would be so bad about that?"

His jaw flexed. "You're just lucky I didn't pull a gun on you like the last time you broke in."

"From where, beneath your towel?" I asked with a laugh. "Besides, that home invasion ended just fine, didn't it? I walked away without a single bullet hole."

"Traitor," he said to Ranger instead of acknowledging me, then motioned for him to get off the bed. I followed the order and stood as well.

Ranger sat protectively at my feet, as if worried his dad might bite me. I mean . . .

Wouldn't be the worst thing in the world to happen.

"Not his fault he didn't give you a heads-up I was here. He loves me."

"No clue why," he grunted.

I ignored him, opting to take a moment to not-so guiltily check out his physique, because a girl's gotta do what a girl's gotta do.

Reed tore his hands through his dark hair, trying to tame the wild, wet strands with only his fingers. All he managed to do was free more water droplets, and they cascaded down to his broad chest.

I zeroed in on the tattoo scrolled across his rib in fancy black script and blurted out, "What's that about?"

"You've known me for months, which means you're well aware of the fact I don't talk about myself." He shoved away from the doorframe, and Ranger howled a little warning at him to behave. "Why would I start now?"

I continued to key in on what was written across the one rib, ideas percolating as to what it meant. "As someone who keeps their walls so high they might touch the stars . . ." I forced my eyes back up to his. ". . . I can respect your unwillingness to share."

For whatever reason, my answer only seemed to annoy him more. He stopped before me, close enough that our Belgian Malinois barrier began whacking his tail against his daddy's shins.

I did something both bold and stupid. I let my hand act on its own accord. Instead of tracing the tattoo, I went for his hair.

Reed immediately snatched my wrist, as if I'd left behind a trail of insults with that quick touch.

His jaw muscles stopped working themselves to death, and his gaze softened. "What happened to you? Why is there blood on your ear?"

Shit, is there? I jerked my hand back to deal with flyaways from my French braid, a lame attempt to hide what had happened at zero five hundred.

"Where were you before you came here?" He nudged his chin in the direction of his bed, now spotting the package I'd left.

I twisted to the side. "That's a baby shower gift for Audrey. I was hoping to stash it here until her party."

"Which isn't anytime soon."

"I know, but I had it with me, and I don't want her finding it in my rental when I pick her and Chase up. We're going for brunch in the city."

Audrey was my best friend, and she had a nine-year-old son, Chase, who was my godson. Audrey had recently remarried, and her husband, Alejandro "Alex" Rodriguez, worked at Delta Shield Security with Audrey's brother, along with Reed.

"What is it?" He stepped around me, picked up the package, and opened the lid. "A baby rattle. Is this thing made of real gold?"

"Of course." I grabbed the blue box, closed the lid, and went into his walk-in closet, taking it upon myself to hide it. I bent over and set it on a shoebox. When I stood and whipped around, he was now bracing each side of the doorframe, trapping me in there.

"Tell me about the blood." The demand slipped narrowly between his lips, the words painted in a cool, dark tone. If a voice could be described as a color, his was blue. He had a way of mellowing me out while also making me feel lost at sea with the waters rough and wild.

I kept quiet, trying to ignore my body's response to his carved and cut one.

"Hollis," he said like a protest.

"Jason." I hit him back with the same moody tone, locking my arms over my chest.

"*Reed,*" he corrected, detesting whenever I used his first name. "The blood. How? Why?"

I closed the gap between us. "I get blood on myself all the time. It's rarely mine. Why is it a big deal? You know what I do." I freed my arms from across my chest and poked his pectoral muscle. "I also know you were in Papua New Guinea three days ago getting blood on yourself, too. Tell me about your mission, and I'll tell you about mine. Fair is fair."

"My op was classified." He walked into his room, nearly colliding with Ranger right at his heels. "Was your op local?"

"Close enough, yeah," I admitted, joining him back in the bedroom.

"Why didn't you ask for an assist?"

I arched my brow. "What makes you think I needed one?" I knelt alongside Ranger, who rolled over so I could rub his belly. "Fine, fine," I relented. "It was an easy op. You know, girl meets rich guy who promises her the world. She gets swept off her feet, marries him, only to find out he's a corrupt and dangerous asshole who makes his fortune smuggling antiquities. Enter me: saves her from the jerk and highly encourages the dick husband to rewrite his will before the Feds show up."

"Let me guess, he stole one of your family's rare artifacts?"

I laughed. "You really think someone could ever get into one of our vaults and steal something?" I patted Ranger's belly twice, then stood. "Anyway, that basically sums up the plot to a romance novel, yeah? So, there you go. Easy in and out."

He shot me a funny look. "More like a thriller."

"What do I know?" I shrugged. "I usually don't have time to read for fun these days. But you like to read, right?"

"How would you know that?" The man nearly brooded me into tomorrow with that tight-eyed look of his.

"What, you don't think I know about the books you're hoarding?"

"I'd hardly call keeping a nice collection of hardbacks 'hoarding.'" He squinted, then tore his hand through his hair. "Wait, they're all in cabinets, behind closed doors. How do you know they're in there?"

"You know what they say about doors?" I smirked. "Made to be opened."

"And breached without an invite, apparently." He gestured toward the hallway.

Remembering I had blood on me and needed to rinse it off, I walked around his muscular body to get to the sink. The blood *may* have belonged to that woman's husband. In my defense, he should have known better than to try to kill me. It didn't end so well for him.

"I wasn't done in there, but sure, go ahead . . . help yourself."

Faucet on, I caught his eyes in the mirror. "I'll be out of your hair soon so you can get dressed. Well, unless you plan to lounge around naked all day. I've been known to do that on occasion at my place in the South of France."

"Remind me never to barge in on you if I'm ever hanging out on a yacht I'll never be able to afford in the French Riviera."

"Mm-hmm." I splashed some water on the side of my neck and ear and scrubbed the evidence clean. "You and I both know you wouldn't mind walking in on me." I turned off the water and dried my hands.

"In . . . your . . . dreams." He slow-rolled those words before I faced him. "And are you taking your time here because driving me crazy is your favorite pastime, second only to saving strangers in distress?"

"Not trying to get a rise out of you, promise." I lowered my gaze to his towel, praying for a slight twitch. Something to indicate he didn't really hate me. At the least, wanted to have sex with me. Not that we'd be doing that, but still.

"No risk of that, don't worry," he said in a low, husky voice that was quite the contradiction to his words, right along with his biceps straining as he braced against yet another doorframe like he was trying to will himself not to set me on the counter and have his way with me.

We shouldn't. The rational side of my brain knew that. My body? Not so much.

"Just keep the gift for me until it's time for her baby shower, 'K?" I waited for the muscular obstruction to budge. When he didn't, it took me staring at his tattoo for him to stop playing chicken and move. "I have ten more minutes to spare before I'm due at Audrey's." *And she only lives down the street, so.* "I'll hang out in your living room until then."

He turned toward me while readjusting his towel. "You asking for permission or . . . ?"

"That doesn't sound very much like something I'd do, now, does it?" I took a moment to commit to memory this man's glorious body, then left with Ranger before he could respond. "Maybe I'll take a closer look at your daddy's books and see what he likes to read, what do you think?"

In the hallway, Ranger went up on his back legs and pawed the air.

"I'll take that as a yes." I wandered into the living room, stopping at the built-ins flanking his flat-screen TV. Each had closed-door cabinets below, the kind of neat symmetry that was very Reed.

I went to my knees, sitting back on my heels as I opened the first door. Rows of hardbacks greeted me. Mostly science fiction (no surprise there), but there was also a solid lineup of nonfiction, too. I reached for one, curious, but froze when a sheet of paper slipped loose and fluttered to the floor.

Shit. I didn't want to look. I *really* didn't. It was one thing to break into his house and poke around. It was another to read something he'd clearly hidden.

But I'd already seen the letterhead, which had my pulse stuttering. The logo at the top was one I recognized, and dread prickled the back of my neck. A low hum filled my ears, and I could practically hear Reed's voice telling me to leave it alone.

Ranger pawed my arm like he agreed, but it was too late. The guilt was already coiling in my gut as I read the first line. I now knew something Reed wouldn't want me to—and no way could I unknow it.

CHAPTER ONE

Hollis

Two months later

What was it with this man and doorways? He was constantly standing in the middle of one whenever we faced off. In his defense, I had broken into his house and *was* sitting in his kitchen uninvited.

Reed kept the door propped open with his shoulder, a faint chill sneaking around him.

He let go of the leash, and I patted my jeaned thighs twice, giving Ranger permission to prop his paws on me. He bopped his face against me. His nose was cool and wet against mine, his fur carrying the faint smell of wet dog I wasn't a fan of, but for him, I'd ignore it.

"Hey, boy."

"That 'hey, boy' for him or me?"

He truly exemplified *grumpy old man* without the *old* part, and he seemed to enjoy owning that personality quirk.

"Both," I teased, slowly lifting my eyes to find him still hovering, allowing the doorframe to cocoon all six-two of his muscular sexiness.

I unclipped Ranger's leash, and he ran over to his water bowl for a drink.

"And you're here because?" The low rumble of his voice matched the storm outside.

"I did warn you over our last text I'd be in town, didn't I? I recall you were in need of a good eye roll. I'm here to help."

The little crinkles around his eyes tightened as he stared at me. "So glad I have that to look forward to."

"I knew you would be." I sat back in the chair and gestured to the bottle of bourbon and the two glasses I had ready to go. I knew he drank it neat like me, so no need for ice. "I come bearing a gift." I added two fingers of bourbon into both, and he let the door shut behind him and walked farther inside. "Audrey's not home, so I came here instead."

He dragged his fingers through his damp hair, giving himself a sexy just-showered look, then wiped his palms on the sides of his jeans. "Bourbon isn't exactly her go-to, and she's pregnant."

"It was for Alex." And he totally knew that.

"For what? Putting up with you?" He jutted his chin forward. "And did *you* just roll your eyes at me, ma'am?"

Why did I find his ma'am'ing me sexy instead of making me feel old? Also, that flash of teeth with a quick grin sent a shiver up my back.

I hadn't been in a good mood before he opened that door, but within a matter of seconds, he had me forgetting all my stress.

I didn't get how he calmed me, but it was becoming an addicting feeling, since this wasn't the first or even fifth time his mere presence gave me peace.

I'd be lying if I said I'd only dropped into town to see my best friend. I was myself around Audrey more than anyone else—well, until this man came along. Whenever I hung out with either of them, I could be Hollis, girl next door. Not Lady Celeste Hollis Avery Wyndham d'Aragon, heiress to a legacy cloaked in secrets and shadows.

"Cat got your tongue, darlin'?"

I blinked my way up from my glass to the man who'd now darlin'ed me out of nowhere. Perhaps parallel universes were real and I'd tripped into one. Because no, Mr. Tough Guy never used terms of endearment toward me unless he meant them as an insult, like with *ma'am*. Nor did he let his accent slip through when talking to me—not ever.

I may have done my research on him back in February, along with digging into the backgrounds of the rest of his teammates at Delta Shield. Not to be nosy and invasive (mostly not), but to ensure they were safe, since they were new to Audrey's life. She'd only learned she had a half brother at Thanksgiving, so I had no choice but to protect her.

"On second thought," Reed continued since the proverbial cat still had my tongue, "I like you this way. Stay quiet. It works for you."

Ranger came over and curled up on top of my feet beneath the table.

I nudged the second glass Reed's way, and he glared at me as if I'd asked him to play a game of Russian roulette.

"This B and E habit of yours is starting to concern me," he added wryly. He took a seat, stretching out one long leg, trying to pull off casual, when it was clear the man was anything but comfortable in my presence.

"I'm sure that's the least offensive thing you find about me."

The side of his mouth hitched at my words, but he didn't respond. Instead, he brought the lip of the glass to his nose and inhaled.

The bourbon caught the kitchen light as I raised my own glass, a swirl of amber and oak that smelled like old wood and quiet nights. The scent alone nearly tugged me backward in time.

"This will be the most expensive thing I've ever had in my mouth."

That was almost too easy for me to make a joke, so I held off and stole a quick look toward his living room, remembering the last time I broke in and went through his books, and now . . .

"Pappy Van Winkle's Twenty-Year Family Reserve," he said on a sigh. "Damn, this is good."

I set down the glass and cupped it with both hands, resting my forearms on the table. "My grandfather used to drink this brand," I said somberly. "I called him Pappy because of it."

Memories flooded in like smoke under a door. My grandfather's manor smelling of leather and peat, his voice as warm as the heat from a hearth fire.

"Pappy, why'd you decide to adopt a son? Because Mum had already moved out and Nanna died? Were you lonely?"

My grandfather had slid the book he'd been holding back onto the shelf and turned toward me while removing his glasses. *"He needed someone to take care of him, and he's our family now."*

"You doin' okay?" Reed's words blindsided me, rougher and more sincere than I'd ever heard from him, drawing me out of the past.

I opened my eyes, lifted my glass as a shield, and forced my mouth into a smile before he could see through the cracks and discover there was more than one layer to me.

"I'm fine." I tossed back my drink, letting it burn my throat and chest, then added more bourbon to the glass.

He didn't call me out on my obvious lie. I rarely let my mask slip and fall like I'd nearly done now.

Instead of pressing me to talk, which wouldn't be like him to do anyway, we sat in silence and drank. Just us, the ticking of a wall clock, and the slight breathy sounds from Ranger filling the space.

It wasn't until my phone vibrated that I finally spoke. "It's Audrey."

Audrey: I'm home and Chase is asleep. Where are ya? ☺

Me: At the Grump's house.

Audrey: That's your SUV I saw when I drove by? 😮 I got my hopes up he was finally on a date or something.

Audrey: Unless you're his date? 😉

I looked over my phone at him. He was skimming his index finger around the rim of his glass, his eyes set on the bourbon and not me.

Me: Definitely not. I'll be over shortly.

Audrey: Take your time. 😈

I started to put away my phone when a notification buzzed. My spine went stiff at the message, even if it was the news I'd been waiting on for days.

Nothing I could do about what I'd just now learned, so I did my best to shove my emotions into the Do Not Disturb box where I usually kept them.

Maybe I'd steal one more drink with him before heading to Audrey's to act like my world wasn't about to spin off its axis this coming week.

I leaned forward to stow my phone in my back pocket, and I couldn't help but clock Reed's dark eyes journeying over my body for a brief moment.

He sipped his drink, acting indifferent, as if I hadn't caught him checking me out in my fitted white tee. "Are you finally leaving?"

"Nope." I refilled our glasses. "You're not done with me yet."

CHAPTER TWO

Hollis

Rome, Italy; a few days later

The Secret Garden was on the third shelf, fourth book in. The second I pulled it forward, the bookshelf groaned and began to shift to the side, like it did this morning before the opening hours when I'd tested it out.

Gunfire cracked behind me. Short bursts of suppressed rounds, the kind that still rang in your skull even with the DJ continuing to blast music.

Splinters of wood stung my cheek as a bullet ripped through the shelf above my head.

I wasn't alone. My six was covered, but I hated leaving him. No other choice, though.

Heart hammering, I hesitantly slipped into the tunnel and yanked the panel shut. The muted *thud-thud-thud* of rounds on the doorframe was the last thing I heard before silence swallowed me.

I flicked on the tactical light mounted beneath my Glock barrel and took off down the tunnel. The next sixty seconds passed in a blur of sprints and sharp turns as I navigated the ancient labyrinth beneath the city, the echo of my boots smothered by centuries of old dust.

When the tunnel narrowed, I dropped to my hands and knees, crawling through a choke point so tight my ribs scraped the walls. The air grew colder, damp enough to cling to my skin, with the faint reek of mildew mixed with something older. Rot, incense, and candle soot.

I emerged into the Capuchin Crypt. A thousand hollow eye sockets stared back at me from the walls, skulls stacked as neatly as books in a library.

My light swept the chandelier made entirely of pelvic bones, then moved over to the femur crosses and vertebral structures—a cathedral built by death itself. My throat tightened as I breathed in holy bone dust, tasting history on my tongue.

I forced myself forward, to the stairwell that would lead to a store, my boots whispering across the stone like I was trespassing on consecrated ground.

I ran up the steps and shoved open the door, only to have the breath knocked from my lungs. The butt of a rifle connected with my chest, and I lost my balance, wig, and gun.

Someone's fast reflexes saved me from falling down the stairs. A man hauled me into the room before throwing me onto the ground like a doll.

I was David up against Goliath, breathing hard while scrambling backward on my ass, peering up at the huge jerk hovering over me in the shop.

As two other men flanked him, I let instinct kick in and shifted upright and into a fighting position. But all my training was ineffective with the three of them pressing in on me. Every strike was deflected. Every maneuver countered and blocked.

Aside from the hit to my chest with the butt of the gun, they didn't hit back.

Two of the men forced me to my knees as a fourth man approached.

I continued to squirm, to try to break free from their hold, but then both shock and relief hit me like rounds to the chest.

What are you doing here?

I turned to the man at my right, expecting him to let go of me and fight his new opponent, but he didn't budge. Neither did the other two men.

Oh God, no. No, no, no.

The dim lights of the shop flickered around us, casting shadows across a face I'd known my entire life.

The world tilted. The smell of gun oil and incense clung to the back of my throat.

My newfound hope that everything would be okay because he was here was gone now that he was quietly crouched before me.

I couldn't wrap my head around this. It made no sense.

"Why?" I pleaded, fighting back tears of betrayal.

He remained silent, and I flinched when something pricked the side of my neck, my body swaying within seconds.

A rush of heat flooded my veins, turning to ice. My fingers tingled, useless. My tongue became thick. My throat squeezed, fear taking over.

The shop light wavered like a candle flame, and the edges of my vision bled to gray. Everything became blurry, and every ounce of resistance slipped away as I closed my eyes.

Someone began talking.

Who was it? *Him?* I was being given instructions and . . .

"Hurry up and finish. We need to get her out of here," someone else said close to my ear. His breath ghosted over my skin, the sound already stretching, distant, like it came through water.

Another jab hit me, this time at the base of my spine.

Pain flared, then dulled to a throb I couldn't quite locate.

As the drugs flowed through me, I did what I was told to do, keeping my eyes sealed shut as images filled my head, ones that brought peace and comfort. Happiness.

Gone was my mum's tough-as-nails daughter as I fell into a pair of familiar hands and did something I've never done in my life—surrendered.

CHAPTER THREE

Reed

Charleston, South Carolina

Yesterday, I was in Panama, securing the canal after terrorists tried to wreak havoc there. And this morning? In my kitchen doing a crossword puzzle.

The whiplash between adrenaline-fueled missions and domestic downtime never got easier. One day, I was getting shot at. The next, I was wondering if seven down was *gallant* or *valiant*.

I scratched my jaw with the capped pen and hung my head as I reminded myself why I was doing this.

I was all for the daily workouts when I wasn't operating, but sweating my balls off in a sauna, followed by brain exercises? That was taking some getting used to.

After listening to countless podcasts and reading a dozen books on my father's condition in the last four months, I'd resigned myself to trying to help him, even if my old man didn't deserve it. I also decided to make a few changes in my life to hopefully prevent the same outcome from happening to me.

Would I give up bourbon and beer like some medical sites said I should? Probably not.

Or stop putting my head in positions where it might get knocked around or even blown off? Not anytime soon.

But the other stuff? I supposed I could do.

As long as my head stayed attached to my body, I'd like to remember who I was. Though I wouldn't mind selectively Control-Alt-Deleting a few memories. Like my entire childhood. Next, I'd eliminate the other dark and painful years from my past that were of my own making.

I lifted my head, tossed the pen, and stood. "How about we see if Chase is home?"

Ranger's ears perked up. That was a yes.

"Get your leash."

He eyed my chest, wise beyond his puppy years, signaling to me that I was shirtless.

"Right, right." I smirked. "You. Leash." I patted my chest. "Me. Shirt." Great. Now I was grunting like a caveman, like he'd answer the same way.

I went into my bedroom in search of a clean shirt since I'd only put on new workout shorts after my post-sauna shower. When I returned to the living room in a white tee with my sunglasses hooked to the front, Ranger was sitting there waiting for me, his leash on the floor in front of him.

"Good boy." I clipped it to his harness and shoved one of those doggy-shit bags into my pocket, and we went outside and walked to Alex and Audrey's home.

Every house in our community was either a brick ranch or a two-story with a wraparound front porch sitting on at least a half acre of property.

Oak trees, southern magnolias, and crepe myrtles made up the landscape. Kids were already outside, laughing and playing in front yard sprinklers to escape the early-morning heat. This was a sharp contrast to the environment I'd grown up in, and I wasn't sure I'd ever get used to it.

Ranger took a piss on the neighbor's mailbox next door to Alex's house just as Chase came running down his front porch steps.

"Ranger!" Chase called out, acting as though he hadn't just dog sat the last two days while I was in Panama.

"Feel like going to the park with us?" I asked Chase as he scratched Ranger behind the ears before he flopped over to get his belly rubbed.

"Of course." Chase patted the side of his leg, and Ranger switched to all fours at the order.

"Where are your parents?"

"Doing something in their bedroom. I don't know. Hanging a picture, maybe? Heard some banging."

I about choked on my own saliva, knowing exactly what the newlyweds were doing. "Let me text them that you're coming with me."

I handed him the leash, but before I had a chance to send a message, both Alex and Audrey came outside and started our way.

"We're going to the park," Chase told them, and I subtly signaled to Alex that his fly was down.

"Get that picture hung?" I removed my shades from my shirt and hid my eyes.

Alex zipped up his cargo shorts and cleared his throat. "We did."

"Nailed really good?" Chase turned to his stepdad, and Audrey patted her chest as if she needed to restart her heart at her son's question.

Yeah, I didn't envy being a parent. I'd also probably never find out what it was like to be one.

"Picture is up. Yup." Alex held Audrey's hand. "We'll join you."

"How's the morning sickness?" I deflected instead of making a joke since Chase was there.

"Gone, thank goodness," she answered as we headed for the park, which was just outside the neighborhood. "And before you ask, like you normally do every week . . ." She chuckled. "No, we haven't changed our minds about knowing if we're having a boy or a girl."

I shot Alex a look before facing forward, knowing that *we* was more of an *I*.

No Tier One operator wanted to go into any situation without every detail mapped out. Being prepared for everything was an understatement when it came to us.

Though I doubted Alex had ever prepared himself for marrying our team leader's sister—a sister Ryder had only found out existed this past Christmas.

"Anyway." Audrey glanced at me once we'd entered the park and winked, letting me know to change the subject. "How's your dad?"

I immediately turned to face Alex, because there was only one way his wife knew my dad wasn't doing well. "I told you about his condition in passing, not wanting anyone to know."

"In passing?" Alex's brow furrowed. "You can't be serious."

"This is why I never talk about myself." I hadn't meant to say that out loud, but it was the truth.

It was my life. My past, full of ugliness and regret. No one else's.

"She's my wife. I didn't think—"

"I'll remember to keep my mouth shut." My bitterness and anger had nothing to do with him, but I needed a target for my frustrations, and he was right in front of me.

"Let's talk about something else, okay?" Audrey placed her hand on Alex's forearm, a quiet directive to back down.

I looked around them, realizing we had company. All the more reason to do what Audrey had suggested and drop it. "Trevor's here with Eden." I folded my arms over my chest as I watched Chase with his father. He was showing off Ranger as if Trevor hadn't met my dog a dozen times before.

Trevor and Chase's aunt, Eden, lived in our neighborhood as well. She was pregnant, so she was bunking with her brother for now. The father of her baby was rotting in a CIA black site half a world away, which meant she'd be raising her daughter with the support of her brother and the rest of us. We were basically the tactical version of a modern-day *Brady Bunch*.

Thankfully, my team had been lucky enough to snatch up new-construction homes in the neighborhood around the same time. It definitely made things easier when it was time to spin up.

With Trevor still having that operator itch after retiring from twenty years in the navy, we gave him room to scratch it. He worked with Delta Shield as part of what would eventually be a three-man attachment unit once we recruited two more veterans to replace the new hires who had barely lasted three weeks. Truth was, we probably didn't need to hire anyone else. Trevor more than pulled his weight, and despite the fact he outranked us all when he retired, he never minded deferring to Delta One.

Trevor stopped petting my dog and removed a ball from his pocket as if somehow knowing this meet and greet was bound to happen. He offered it to Chase to throw.

Seeing the two of them together had me wondering what it would've been like to have a normal childhood. You know, with a dad who pitched a baseball instead of threatening to break a bat across your back for spilling milk. Maybe if I'd had a dad like Trevor, or a stepfather like Alex, I wouldn't have—

"How are you feeling after Panama?" Alex asked Trevor as he joined us, effectively drawing my head from my dark past.

"Ready to spin up again if the opportunity presents itself." Trevor scratched the side of his neck where he had three crosses tattooed.

"Maybe if you had someone to come home to, then you wouldn't be so eager to spin up all the time." Audrey nudged her ex-husband in the side, and Trevor glared at her. "That goes for you too," she added, eyes sharp on me now.

"I have Ranger. He has his sister," I shot back defensively. "We do have someone to come home to."

Audrey waved the back of her hand my way without making contact. "Not what I meant and you know it."

"You gotta tell your wife to knock it off with the dating stuff," Trevor grumbled, a laugh catching in his throat.

Somehow, Alex managed to get along with Audrey's ex, which I supposed was for the best since Trevor was very much in his son's life. It was almost inspiring to see how they all co-parented.

Alex faked zipping his lips and shook his head.

"Yeah, I know where your loyalty lies." Trevor smirked. "As it should." He looked over at his sister standing off to the side of us, a phone to her ear.

"She okay?" Audrey asked.

"Talking to our mom. She calls every five minutes to check on her. Surprised she hasn't tried to move in with me, too."

"Give it time, she just . . ." Audrey let her words trail off at the steady *whup-whup-whup* of rotors breaking through the late-summer air.

Wrong airspace, and the wrong altitude.

Ranger stopped running after the ball Chase had tossed, ears alert. He let out a howl, eyes fixed on the sky.

The all-black unmarked chopper came in fast. Muscle memory took over, and I started to go for my Glock, forgetting I didn't have it on me.

Thankfully, it wasn't needed anyway. A group text arrived from Secretary of Defense Chandler letting us know we had incoming. A friendly. A.k.a. don't shoot.

"Maybe it's your best friend making a grand entrance like she's been known to do, and she gave Chandler a heads-up about it," I remarked as the helo hovered outside the park boundary, searching for a clear spot to land.

Audrey gestured for Chase to come over to us. "It shouldn't be Hollis." Friendly or not, she quietly pulled Chase between her and Alex, and Ranger parked himself in front of Chase. "She's with a guy in Italy, or so she said."

A guy? Before she'd bailed after kicking back a few drinks with me on Saturday, she mentioned she had to go out of town on Tuesday, but she left out the location and the with-a-dude part.

I set a hand atop my chest as my heart tried to break free. *What. The. Actual. Hell?* Why did that response feel like . . . *jealousy?* I was practically allergic to her. That's how I acted around her, especially whenever she broke into my house. She made my skin itch. Crawl. Eyes burn. All of it."

My fingers curled into my palms as I tried to settle down the raging beats happening beneath my rib cage, but I couldn't shake the image of Hollis in Italy with some rich dick Casanova. Probably an Italian. Born and raised there, and I was only third-generation Italian, so that didn't count if she wanted to be with—

I had to put the brakes on those thoughts. Pronto.

Nope, I should be happy for her. She could finally leave me the hell alone if she connected with someone. He was probably in her league of absurdly rich, too.

Good. Great. Fucking perfect. This is what I want. Only, my chest tightened. "Well, uh, if it's not her, then who the hell is it?"

The aircraft kicked up a cloud of debris while setting down. A man jumped out before the rotors even slowed. He was clearly either trained in the art of not giving a fuck or knew how to expertly leave a running helicopter. He also didn't appear bothered by the heat in his all-black clothes.

"Anyone recognize him?" Trevor motioned for Eden to come closer. "I assume he's from the State Department or works for the secretary."

Eden rejoined us, slipping her phone into her crossbody bag.

"No clue who he is," I said as the man walked our way like he owned both the air and the grass beneath his shoes.

When he stopped a few feet in front of us, just out of arm's reach, he removed his shades. "I'm Celeste's brother, Gideon."

I hadn't seen photos of her family, but I knew she had siblings. And now it made sense why the helo bothered me. Wrong sibling inside it. Same reaction, though.

"What are you doing here?" Audrey asked him. "How'd you know we'd be at the park?"

"I was planning on walking to your house. Couldn't land in your front yard, now, could I?" Gideon slipped his aviators back on. "I'm here about Celeste."

"She prefers Hollis now," Audrey corrected him. "And what about her?"

"Well, she's been Celeste to me all her life, but sure, fine." He shook his head. "When was the last time you spoke, and what'd you talk about?"

"Why?" I asked as Chase went to his knees, latching on to Ranger.

"My sister went to Rome on Tuesday."

"Right. For a guy," Audrey responded before Gideon could continue.

Gideon's jaw locked tight. "What guy?"

So, that's news to you, too?

"I don't have a name for you because she didn't give me one. But she said they planned to hang out in Rome. Maybe hit the Amalfi Coast after that." She removed her phone from her back pocket and handed it to Gideon. "She hasn't texted since she landed in Italy."

I did my best to remain calm for Chase, but my pulse was flying at the fact Hollis's brother wouldn't be here if there wasn't a problem. My only saving grace? Her brother gave off asshole vibes, so she had more than likely ditched him for some reason and was fine. "Why didn't you hack her phone, read her messages that way?"

"Her messages were digitally scrubbed."

She could easily do that herself. I held back that forced optimism and instead uttered a backhanded compliment. "Thought your brother Julian was good at recovering the unrecoverable?"

"Not everything can be salvaged. When some things die"—he briefly looked at me as if sending a message of some kind—"they actually stay that way."

"Isn't that how all things are supposed to stay?" Chase asked, his voice innocent.

You shouldn't be listening to any of this.

"You're right." Gideon surprisingly managed to soften his tone for Chase's sake. "As for *your* texts, your phones are protected by the DOD, so for now, we've refrained from hacking them." He handed Audrey back her phone. "This isn't helpful."

"Please tell me she's ignoring your calls and texts because you pissed her off, and she deleted her messages knowing your hacker brother would've read them. And that's why you're coming to me instead of talking to Hollis yourself." Audrey switched from rock steady to slightly panicky, and I was close to joining her there.

Every muscle in my body remained tense as I waited for his answer, and the grim facial expression as he shook his head sent me back a step.

"Her tracker went offline at zero one hundred Italian time. It's proprietary tech our family uses."

I did the math, and with the six-hour time difference, that had to have been about fourteen hours ago. Acid pushed up into my chest. *Nope, she's fine. She has to be. Probably shut it down herself.* My normal cup-is-half-empty mentality was taking a back seat with Hollis's life on the line. No other option. I couldn't stand around a park feeling helpless if she was in danger.

"Mommy, is Auntie Hollis okay?" Chase broke the eerie quiet that'd been sitting between us as we worked to grasp what Gideon was suggesting. The kid had been through enough this year. He deserved a break.

Alex shifted to the side so Trevor could get to his son, and Trevor took a knee next to Chase and rested a hand on his shoulder, whispering something in his ear.

I waited impatiently for Gideon to continue. What I didn't expect was for him to begin unbuttoning his black dress shirt.

He pulled the material back, revealing a tattoo in the shape of a shield with four quadrants, a different image in each section. A crucifix was at the top of it, and a phrase I couldn't translate was beneath it.

"This isn't just a tattoo. The ink's laced with nano-tracer filaments we can monitor anywhere in the world. The tattoo constantly transmits a faint baseline signal, like a biometric heartbeat." He fixed his shirt and removed a silver chain from his pocket with an oval-shaped pendant attached to it. "This is the disruptor. When it's active, it syncs with the lattice in the ink and creates a localized interference field. Masks the signal completely and makes the tracker look dead."

"And Hollis has this tattoo? Chain?" I shouldn't have been surprised her family had their own built-in spy gear. *Rich-people shit.*

"She does," he confirmed. "Her tattoo is on her back."

"Well," I began, "clearly your sister put the chain on to keep whatever she was doing a secret from you. Sounds exactly like something she'd do."

Gideon pocketed his chain. "She'd never go dark without giving us a heads-up. And she *doesn't* run solo missions. Not ever."

His rejection of that idea flatlined my heart.

"When I tell you my sister is in trouble, I damn well mean it," he hissed, and his words were the final nail in the coffin of what was left of my wishful thinking. "Is there anything else you can tell me? Anything that may be helpful that I should know so I can figure out what in the hell happened to her?"

When I checked on Audrey, it was clear the fog of denial had lifted, and she was currently stuck in worry mode. And now I was about to join her—on a runaway train, going headfirst into worst-case scenarios. But I hit the brakes when an important detail slammed into me: *Hollis isn't just anyone, she's a force to be reckoned with. A Category 5 hurricane. She'll be okay. She still may have gone dark on purpose.*

"Um, well, she showed up on Saturday acting a little off. Already had a few drinks before she came over." Audrey stole a quick look at me, clearly knowing Hollis had had those drinks at my place.

"Maybe she was stressed about something." I barely recognized the sound of my gravelly, strained voice.

Hollis was like me when it came to open books. One page turned. Not even to the copyright section. She as much as admitted that to me. So it was hard to know what was going on beneath the surface when it came to her, and the truth was, I was worried she'd think I gave a damn if I—

Gideon derailed my thoughts, pressing, "And how do you fit into this night my sister had?"

"Audrey wasn't home, so she showed up to visit my dog." I motioned to Ranger, and he lifted his head as if vouching for me. I decided to leave out the fact Hollis had broken in (like always).

Gideon removed his shades and tipped his head. His assessment was slow and controlled. Inch by calculating inch as he observed me.

"I've been out of town since Monday. Arrived home before sunrise this morning." I leaned closer. "In case you plan on asking where I was, I sure as hell wasn't in Italy."

"And the night she was drinking?" He kept his glasses in his hand as he waited for me to answer.

"Your sister has good taste in bourbon. Offered it to me. We spoke barely five words. About four more than I'd have preferred." That may have been an exaggeration, but he'd get the message that I wasn't close to Hollis.

Gideon put on his glasses. "So, you don't like my sister."

I kept my mouth shut because now wasn't the time for this—not with Hollis out there somewhere.

"Why would she lie to me about being on a trip with a guy after finally opening up to me this year?" Audrey asked softly. "I—I just don't believe it."

"I don't know anything, or I wouldn't have flown here, now, would I? All I know is she checked in to a hotel in Rome under an alias, and that was the last place the signal on her phone pinged before it was shut off." He ran a hand over his mouth, jaw twitching, like he wanted to say more but chose not to.

Audrey asked what I'd been a second away from asking him myself. "Are you going to Italy to look for her?"

"Of course," he grunted as if offended.

"Then my husband and his team are coming with you. We're in this together, and she has to be okay, you hear me? I can't be mad at her for lying to me again if she's not. So bring her back safely so I can hug her before yelling at her. Don't argue with a pregnant woman, and—"

"Why do you think I came here instead of picking up the phone to talk to you? As much as it pains me to ask, I need help. Most of my team is currently off-grid." Gideon jerked a thumb toward his helo. "My younger brother is on our plane at the airport. Meet us there in an hour. We should make it to Italy before the sun sets." He started to turn, then paused and tossed out, "And yes, Secretary Chandler's already aware you're joining me."

Alex's phone rang just as Gideon took off. "It's Ryder," he said before stepping aside to take the call.

"Are you okay?" I asked Audrey as Chase quietly distracted himself with Ranger.

"I—I can't go through this again."

Lies. Betrayal. Secrets. People she loved in danger. Yeah, I got it.

"I need to hear you say that you'll do whatever it takes to bring her back to us," she whispered.

"I promise we won't come back without her." I did my best to smile. "Besides, you know your best friend. She's a stubborn pain in the ass. She won't let anyone knock her down. *If* someone did take her"—I lightly squeezed her shoulder—"she's probably driven them so nuts they've already let her go."

CHAPTER FOUR

Reed

Rome, Italy

From inside Hollis's hotel suite, I removed the gold cap of the perfume bottle and raised it to my nose, inhaling the scent of Baccarat Rouge 540, clearly losing my damn mind. I wasn't Ranger. I couldn't track her that way. But I knew this fragrance; I'd smelled it before. She'd been wearing it the night she dropped by with bourbon.

I capped the bottle, returned it to the marble vanity, and surveyed the rest of the bathroom. The suite she'd checked in to was upscale. Modern, but with an old-world feel. Fitting for Hollis's bank account and way outside the capabilities of my own.

"Anything in here?" Ryder's voice caught me off guard, and I quickly spun away from the shower and toward my team leader.

"More of her stuff left behind, like she planned to come back. And no aftershave, cologne, or sign of any dude staying with her."

Ryder remained in the doorway, arms crossed. "Her weapons' case was in the living room closet. Gideon knew the code. It was empty." He motioned with his head, a silent command to exit the bathroom.

I followed him into the bedroom I'd already checked out and glanced at the king-sized bed. Hollis's designer clothes and lingerie were haphazardly thrown on top of it. Her suitcase was open and sitting on the bench at the end of the bed. A knife had been taken to it.

I nudged the bag, doing my best to stay in operator mode to combat the worry piling up inside me, but it was becoming harder and harder to act unaffected about her disappearance. "They were looking for secret compartments." This was all the evidence we needed that Hollis didn't go dark on purpose. Gone was any hope I'd clung to that she'd gone off-grid on purpose. "Someone clearly beat us here. Either Hollis told them where to find whatever it is they were looking for, which is doubtful—"

"Or she's on the run, so they can't ask her themselves," Ryder interrupted.

"She's resourceful. She'd have made contact somehow if she managed to get away from whoever had her." I dragged the back of my hand up and down my jawline as I ran through scenarios in my head, none of them good. All of them ended with me losing my mind.

Realizing I was staring in a daze at a black silk bra on top of the pile of clothes, I turned toward the doorway, finding Gideon now joining us.

He seemed far too okay, given his sister was missing. It irritated me to no end how unbothered he seemed to be. Ryder would be losing his mind if Audrey had gone off-grid.

"Anything?" I asked when Gideon remained scrutinizing me as if I'd been the one to butcher the Prada.

He straightened, hands sliding into his slacks pockets. Because why wouldn't he wear a suit on a mission? Why wouldn't he continue to act like he was going to attend a board meeting instead of rescuing his sister?

Did I care more about this woman than he did, even though she drove me crazy? Or was this family incapable of showing their emotions? Did it get bred out of their DNA?

He finally spoke up. "Not much. She was scheduled to check out tomorrow. I just talked to the hotel manager. She remembers her since she'd checked in to their best room. She said she'd been alone and didn't recall ever seeing anyone with her in the time she'd been here."

"I assume you're having the manager discreetly ask more of the staff about her, too?" I followed up.

Gideon nodded. "My brother also checked hotels throughout the rest of Italy. No rooms booked anywhere else under her name or any of her aliases. It appears Rome was her only scheduled stop." He gestured to the living room, and Ryder and I followed him out.

Alex and Julian were the only other two in there. Gideon had ordered his cousins, along with Trevor, to chase down leads in the city—talking to contacts their family personally knew.

Julian was tapping away at his wireless keyboard like he was casually cracking into the Pentagon. I mean, *hell*, maybe he was.

I went to the open balcony doors as my phone buzzed in my pocket. I didn't know why, but I found myself stupidly hoping it'd be Hollis.

Not her. A group text from Ryder.

I looked up at him sitting on the burgundy velvet couch, and he gave me a subtle nod.

Ryder: Got the dossiers from C. Sending the decrypted files now.

Ryder had put in a request to Secretary Chandler to have Gideon's and Julian's operator files sent to us so we'd know a little more about who'd have our sixes out here.

I turned from the room when a screenshot came through from Ryder.

Gideon Eduard Avery Wyndham d'Aragon

Nationality: Dual (UK/US)

Branch: SAS, later NATO Tier 1 Black Cell (not formally recognized). Honorably discharged at 34.

Clearance level: Classified Access

Known Aliases: Gideon Wyndham, Gideon Avery, G. d'Aragon, The Gravedigger (internal use only), The Enforcer

Confirmed Sanctioned Missions: 33

Kill Count: Redacted

I discreetly glanced at Gideon. He was near the suite's main door, speaking rapid-fire Italian as if the man was native born. He'd mastered more than one language, and from the looks of his file, more than one way to kill a man.

Another buzz. Julian's file this time. Not helpful, either.

Julian William Avery Wyndham d'Aragon

Nationality: Dual (UK/US)

Branch: Redacted

Clearance level: Cryptologic Umbra

Known Aliases: Redacted

Confirmed Sanctioned Missions: Redacted

Kill Count: Redacted

Expertise: EMPs, biometric hacking, nuclear grid override, anything cyber-related

Status: Presumed dead—no remains recovered

I had news for the powers that be who'd created their files: Julian was very much alive, which Secretary Chandler also clearly knew, and now we needed to keep his sister that way.

Alex: A whole lotta nothing we didn't already know. Guess we just trust them?

Ryder: I'm sure they feel the same way about us. We're the outsiders this time.

Trevor: True.

Alex: Can you do that, Reed?

I stole a look at Alex hovering behind where Julian worked.

Me: I'll do what I have to.

I pocketed my phone, not in the mood for a lecture via text or in person.

I opened the doors wider to take in the evening view of the city. The Spanish Steps were in my line of sight, along with several Vespas buzzing in the street below. The hum of chatter outside echoed off the ancient stone. The city looked timeless from here.

I'd never been to Rome before, but I'd always wanted to visit one day. *Not* for this reason, of course. *Where the hell are you?* I clenched my teeth, trying to keep it together. Spinning out wouldn't do Hollis any good.

When a conversation in another language started up, I turned toward the two speaking. It was no wonder I had trust issues with this family.

"What language is that?" Because I had a damn-good ear for languages and didn't recognize it.

Gideon's scowl, or whatever the hell broody look he'd outmastered me at—which was saying a lot—landed hard. "Aramaic."

"I thought that language was dead." Alex scrutinized me, waiting for answers I happened to have.

"It's a Galilean dialect. Mostly replaced by Arabic over the centuries, but it's still in use. Borderline extinct, though." I really did know a little too much about way too much.

Maybe I didn't need puzzles after all since my brain was already fairly active with how much reading I'd done all my life. *Or* maybe my genes would get the best of me no matter what, so there was truly no magical prevention to keep my memory intact as I aged.

"Care to share *why* you were speaking in that language, and, from the sounds of it, so passionately?" Ryder stood, swiveling his hat backward as if ready to throw down if he heard something he didn't like.

The look exchanged between Julian and Gideon, followed by their rapid back-and-forth in Aramaic again, didn't exactly do wonders for building trust.

"We're here to help. We can't do that if you don't tell us what's going on," Alex reminded them.

"Someone rewrote Rome's digital history from the moment Hollis left the airport after her arrival up until two hours after her tracker went dark," Julian shared in a hesitant tone.

"Remember what I said back in Charleston?" Gideon asked, eyes on me. "Some things that die stay dead. Well, someone nuked half of Rome's CCTV grid. Wiped it totally out, and it's not coming back. Including the feeds from the hotel." He let that information sit for a few seconds before continuing. "Then they patched in archived footage to mask the loss, probably before anyone knew it was missing."

I had no idea how they even knew that or could verify it, but they clearly weren't guessing. "And who could pull that off?"

"Only two people on the planet," Julian said grimly. "You're looking at one, and a thief who stole my source code is the other."

"I assume you have enough firewalls on your laptop to make the Pentagon jealous," Alex said, and that was undoubtedly not an exaggeration. "So how'd they steal it?"

"There's no way anyone hacked my hardware to get to my program. It's just not possible. Someone had to have gotten close enough to my laptop to mirror it with some pretty powerful tech. A device more advanced than anything MI6 or the CIA have."

"Since it seems much of the world thinks you're dead," Alex spoke up, "I take it you don't hang out with the living all that often."

"I keep my friend circle the size of a dot. Family and a few other teammates only. Even that's pushing it, which means someone I trust mirrored my laptop."

"Someone you trust," I said bitterly. "The kind of person that'd know about your trackers and the chain."

Gideon kept his eyes tight on his brother. "I can think of someone who was at your place in Singapore last month that has the ability to do this."

"Not possible," Julian shot back. "He'd never hurt Hollis, and you know that."

"Who the hell are you talking about?" I demanded.

Julian's eyes slowly cut my way as he revealed, "Tristan." He shook his head while tacking on, "Our half brother."

Another brother? I immediately pivoted, attention shooting to Ryder in question. *How come we don't know about him?* We'd been operating under the assumption there were just the four siblings: Hollis, Julian, Gideon, and Lyra.

Now I couldn't help but think back to Gideon's comment from yesterday in Charleston. He'd said *younger* brother when referring to Julian. Most people didn't add qualifiers unless they had more than one, and it hadn't dawned on me until this very moment.

"Hollis never told Audrey about a third brother," Alex said, breaking through the quiet. "And there's no mention of a Tristan in our files."

I didn't miss the daggers Gideon was shooting Julian. We weren't part of their secret society, so he clearly wasn't a fan of us knowing about their fifth sibling. Too late now.

"We didn't know he was our brother until later in life." Gideon peered at Ryder, clearly knowing his backstory with his sister, assuming he could relate.

Doubtful the circumstances were remotely the same.

"What if Tristan was the one Hollis was meeting up with, and she lied to Audrey because Audrey doesn't know about this half brother yet?" Alex suggested when everyone remained quiet—but that wouldn't explain why Tristan would steal Julian's program and use it to alter the CCTV footage in Rome.

"Do you think it's possible Hollis was working with Tristan?" I asked.

Before I could continue with my theory, Julian yanked the laptop toward him. "Her tracker just went active."

And my heart was going to explode from my chest. "The chain was removed?"

"Must have been." Gideon quickly rounded the desk to view the screen. "She's in the Czech Republic."

"At a monastery," Julian shared, typing fast. "It's abandoned. Seized by the government fourteen years ago."

Gideon braced both hands on the desk. He said something in Aramaic to his brother, but all I could catch was Tristan's name. "We no longer need your help. This is clearly a family matter."

Is he out of his mind? I started his way, stabbing the air. "I made a promise to his wife"—I motioned to Alex—"to bring your sister home. And that's exactly what I'm going to do." Maybe because I also cared a lot more about her than I'd ever admit to myself or out loud.

Julian kept working like none of us existed, so I was surprised when he stepped up to bat for us. "Let them come with us. You and I both know Hollis didn't go behind our backs to work with Tristan, which means she's in danger. She needs us. *All* of us."

I knew I liked you for a reason. "Does Tristan have one of those trackers, too?"

"No, but he knows about ours." Gideon pushed away from the desk, standing tall while rolling his shoulders back. "But *if* he's somehow connected to what happened to her, we'll find him."

"How?" I asked. "If your brother is the one who stole Julian's program, then he can vanish off every digital mainframe on the planet and become as dead as Julian's been pretending to be."

And here I thought our team was done fighting dead men and ghosts after the op involving Audrey.

"There's also a chance Hollis's tracker was reactivated as bait," Alex pointed out. "To draw you two out. What if whoever took Hollis is also hunting the rest of your family, and that's why they removed her chain when and where they did?"

"In that case, it wouldn't be our brother. Tristan could walk into any of our houses and put two in our heads before we'd ever see it coming," Gideon grated in a low voice. "So if he's tied to this somehow, it's not to bait and kill us. *Or* our sister."

"Fair enough," I grunted in frustration. "Maybe it's someone else you *mis*trusted. Either way, we stay on guard when *we* get there."

"Obviously," Gideon hissed, but at least he didn't push back on the *we* in my statement.

From where I stood, if there was even a remote chance Hollis was in the Czech Republic, then that was where I was heading, and no one could stop me.

Not waiting for orders, I went over to my weapons' bag in preparation to go after the only woman in my life who'd ever managed to get under my skin—the same woman I knew damn well I never wanted to live without, not even as the pain-in-the-ass friend of a friend she was now.

CHAPTER FIVE

Reed

Česke Budějovice, Czech Republic

"This is Delta One. Eyes on the target. She's in a gray hoodie and black pants. Going eastbound. Appears solo," Ryder reported over comms.

"Copy that," I said, weaving through the late-night crowd of people spilling out of a tram station, probably heading to bars and clubs.

Hollis's tracker had stayed stationary just outside the city at the monastery. Then, ten minutes before we were set to breach, it'd started moving, leading us to where we were now.

Was I relieved to see Hollis alive and mobile? More than I could put into words. *But* we weren't out of the woods yet, because she was clearly running from someone, and we had to intercept her before they did.

From my vantage point, though, no one else appeared to be following her. No sign of this mystery half brother of theirs, either.

I moved in carefully, not wanting to startle her or draw eyes from anyone else potentially hunting her, then told my team, "Making contact."

"This is Delta One, I've got you covered."

"Roger," I confirmed as I crossed the street to get directly behind her. "Hollis, it's Reed."

She didn't flinch, not even a backward glance. Instead, she kept walking, even shouldering someone so hard she sent their takeout drink flying.

I said her name a little louder as I continued to follow.

No response again, so I set my hand on her shoulder, and she flew around fast.

The nearby streetlamps cast shadows across her face—and was that dirt on her cheeks?

She stared at me, unblinking and breathing hard as if . . . *shit*, as if she didn't know who I was, and then she came at me swinging. I had nowhere to go with so many people around, so I was forced to take it in the jaw.

"Dammit." I caught her next wild punch in front of my face. "I'm here to help."

She attempted to hit me again with her free hand, forcing me to quickly grab her other wrist, and we stood there in a gridlock.

"Not. Trying. To . . ." I enunciated each word while slowly lowering her arms to her sides the best I could without bruising her. "Hurt. You."

She went dead still as people knocked into us on the sidewalk, and she narrowed her eyes, slightly angling her head as if something was starting to click.

"I'm going to let go now." At least she hadn't kneed me in the balls, but there was still that possibility. "Don't run, okay?" I gently released her wrists, and she spun around and took off.

I tapped my ear, breathing hard. "Are you seeing this?"

"Affirmative. Keep on her," Ryder responded in a sharp voice, probably as stunned as I was. "She must be confused."

"More like she doesn't know who I am." I didn't have time to process what that meant. For now, I had to catch up with her.

I located her in a plaza as she ran between two street performers and vaulted over an open guitar case. I halted when one of her cousins changed the plans without alerting us.

The scene unfolded and went sideways fast. She hit him a hell of a lot harder than she'd hit me, then clocked him with a flying kick to the jaw. After, she looked right at me. For a split second, she hesitated, before running down a lit-up alley flanked by shuttered cafés.

"This is Delta Two," Alex transmitted. "I've got her. She's heading for the river walk. There's a parallel alley to cut her off. Delta Three, you see it?"

I scanned and clocked the target location. "Roger. On it."

"This is Delta Four," Trevor announced. "I'll swing wide from the south. We'll trap her before she gets to the bridge."

My boots hit the slick stone as I hurried down a narrow street. When I rounded the corner, I nearly collided with Hollis. Her hood slipped back, revealing her tangled and messy hair and those same wide, startled eyes.

I held up my hands, palms out, so she could see I wasn't armed. "It's me."

Her lips parted, like recognition was dawning on her, but before she had a chance to say anything, her cousin, with his poor timing, tackled her. They crashed hard to the pavement, and she twisted around, driving an elbow into his ribs.

I stepped forward, offering my hand as an olive branch to stand, but she jerked around and kneed her cousin in the abdomen, then rose on her own.

Before I had a chance to intervene, Gideon did it for me. He closed in fast, locking his arms around her.

She bared her teeth, fighting to squirm out from the prison of Gideon's arms, and it took every ounce of my control not to fight him to free her as a crowd swarmed and gathered.

Hollis slammed her head backward, catching Gideon square in the chin. He grunted but didn't release her.

"She's in a full adrenaline dump," I said. That was the only thing that made sense. "I don't think she recognizes any of us. Must be drugged."

Gideon kept a tight hold of her. "Sedate her," he ordered, presumably to his cousin, since I didn't have anything on me. But wouldn't that make an already-drugged person worse?

Before I could reject the idea, Foxtrot Three moved in, pulling a field injector from his kit. Hollis was still thrashing, her entire body coiling in panic, as her cousin jabbed the needle into her thigh.

Seconds passed, then her limbs began to sag. She went down in slow motion, and Gideon sank to his knees with her in his arms.

I stepped in front of them, arms open wide, doing my best to block the raised phones recording everything.

"Initiate media scrub," Gideon ordered over comms. "I want every CCTV, every phone feed, every digital record in a five-block radius gone."

Julian knew how to do that, too, apparently. Make this all disappear for good, never to be found again. The only problem was, someone else out there who had Hollis before now did, too.

"On it," Julian answered, his voice crackling in my ear. "But is she, uh, okay?"

Gideon kept his eyes on his sister as her breathing began to slow down. "I don't know," he told his brother as Foxtrot Three began offering cash to people for their phones and silence.

"Could be a dissociative drug," I guessed, taking a knee alongside them. "A compound of some kind. God knows what. But . . ." My voice trailed off as something darker settled in my gut. I lifted her hand to get a better look, discovering dirt beneath her fingernails. "What if she was buried in that monastery and she had to dig her way out?"

Gideon gestured with his head, signaling me to help. "I don't know what to think, but we have to get her somewhere safe."

"And where might that be?" I lifted her while standing tall. Her head lolled to the side as I cradled her between my forearms.

Gideon scanned the crowd, squinting with the streetlamps in his face. "I'll have a medical team meet us at my plane. We'll fly her to my parents' place in Surrey." He stepped forward to take his sister, but part of me wasn't ready to let her go. "We need to find who did this to her," he said in a strained voice as I finally handed her over to him. "And figure out why the hell she didn't recognize any of us."

CHAPTER SIX

Hollis

Unknown location

My fingers twisted in the heavy gold-and-cream-colored bedding as I considered trying to make a run for it again. Unlike when I woke up for the first time, I was alone. No strangers claiming to be doctors poking and prodding, asking questions I mostly couldn't answer.

It was a special kind of horror, not knowing where you were and why you were there. But even worse, not knowing *who* you were.

The sedatives the doctors pumped into me had dulled my senses and made my legs and arms feel heavy. There also had to be narcotics buzzing around in my system, because my fist didn't hurt after connecting it to the steely jaw of one of the men who'd been in my room earlier. I had my doubts he was another MD, but at least he didn't fight back after I punched him. Just growled and backed up as one of the "doctors" doped me up.

I had no idea how long it'd been since they'd sent me to Nothing Land, but I was awake now and anticipating round two.

I glanced at my hands fisting the covers. No restraints around my wrists, and I wasn't chained to the bed. Apparently not a risk in my captors' minds, despite my best efforts to break free before.

Chills started to bulldoze their way beyond the barriers of the sedatives, and my pulse went to war with the drugs in an attempt to push my body into fight-or-flight mode.

My teeth lightly clicked together, and I needed to get this shakiness under control *if* I was going to map out an exit strategy. It was a strange feeling, to have my body and brain in disagreement on what to do. One side warning of danger, the other crying out to remain calm.

Who the hell am I? Knowing that might help me choose which direction to go. But the fact I couldn't answer that probably meant whoever was watching me on the other end of the camera on the ceiling had done this to me.

The second the double doors slowly opened, the tug-of-war happening inside me came to a halt. All I could focus on were the two men striding in—one was familiar and the other wasn't.

I shivered as I took in the sight of the men parting ways to stand on either side of the bed.

"Have you calmed down yet? Ready to talk?" the not-an-MD asshole I'd hit earlier asked.

"I don't know. Plan on giving me a reason why I should hit you?" I hissed back.

"I don't recall giving you one," he steadily remarked, his dark eyes boring into me as memories from before waking up in this room battled their way forward.

A coffin that was at least six feet down in the ground.

The earth had yet to cover it, but I had to claw my way up out of the hole.

Then a lot of running and bumping into people before—

"You tackled me," I blurted out. "Not here, but somewhere else."

I scooched farther upright, sitting against the headboard as I converted my hands to weapons, preparing to swing. "Who. Are. You?" I enunciated each word as my mind also screamed, *Who. Am. I?*

"I restrained you last night, but I had my reasons. I didn't do anything to provoke you today." He held up his palm. "So easy with the fists, all right?" He slowly lowered his hand to his side. "I'm Gideon." He lifted his chin. "And *you're* Celeste."

My mind circled around the names like Earth rotating around the sun. Seeking and searching for connection, trying to draw on the light for the truth. Nothing came, just nerves. "That's not my name." *It can't be.*

"Hollis, does that sound better?" the other man asked. His green eyes held a lot less *burn the world down with one look* than Gideon's dark ones.

"Are you picking names from a hat and testing them out on me? Did you two abduct me without even knowing who you were taking?" Had I bonked my head somewhere as I tried to escape, and that was why I couldn't remember who I was?

"You're *Celeste* Hollis," Green Eyes said, then he added a string of surnames I couldn't track. "You go by both, and we know who you are—and no, we didn't abduct you."

From where I was sitting, they sure as heck did. My chest constricted, frustration piling on top of the anxiety that neither the men nor the names they offered as mine were familiar. "If you didn't, how'd I get into this bed?" I pointed at Gideon, remembering his big arms wrapped around me on a street somewhere. "Free will wasn't involved, that much I know."

Gideon's haunted eyes slipped to my face, looking at me as if I'd offended him somehow, like I'd alerted him to being knocked down to a lower tax bracket. "We rescued you. Well, after you escaped the monastery where we first tracked you down." His clean-shaven jaw flexed as he added, "I'm your brother, and he's your *twin*."

I immediately guffawed, a little taken aback by my body's natural response to fake a laugh at a time like this.

"We *are* your brothers. We're in England. More specifically, Surrey. At our family's estate, Rothvale Park," Green Eyes said, and his words came off a little too "trust me, bro" for my liking.

It was also irritating that I could spit out slang and random facts without a problem but not know anything about myself. What kind of head trauma would cause that?

"Sure, sure," I muttered. "You emphasizing words doesn't make me believe them—you get that, right?"

The two men exchanged looks as if they were uncertain what to do with me.

While they shared a quiet moment, I took one myself to check in on my body, hiding my hands under the covers. I stretched out my fingers, testing their strength for punching. Then I wiggled my toes and shifted around as discreetly as possible to see if my legs were a little less dead in case I needed to run or kick.

My energy was coming back, which meant the sedatives weren't as potent, so that was a step in the right direction. The fact I was able to mentally map out an exit strategy from the room had to mean something. *Whoever I really am, I'm not weak.*

"Are you done?" Green Eyes asked. "You know, with devising your escape plan?"

"How'd you—"

"Because you're one of us, and it's what I'd do if I woke up in a strange place." A smile ghosted Green Eyes's mouth. "Good to know you're still *you*, even if you don't remember that for some reason."

My body relaxed a little as I processed what he'd said and *how* he'd spoken. His voice was much more soothing than Gideon's deep one. He could probably hypnotize me with it, which was no doubt a red flag, given my present state of apparent amnesia. I didn't need him hijacking what was left of my mind to convince me I was his sister if I really wasn't.

"I know this must be scary, and you're not used to being afraid of anything, but—"

"That's the first thing that's made sense to me since I woke up in this nightmare," I said, cutting off Green Eyes just as a thought dawned on me. "Wait, I don't sound English, and neither do you two." I brought a hand to my throat, checking if my vocal cords had been damaged at some point.

"We haven't lived here in over thirty years," Green Eyes explained. "We only visit from time to time. We grew up in the United States. Are you familiar with—"

"Yes, of course, I even know the name of the US president." I lifted one shoulder. "Isaiah Bennett. But ask me if I voted for the guy? No clue." My shoulders fell at the absurdity of all this.

"So you have some memories, just not your own," Green Eyes said under his breath.

"Yes, but why am I not freaking out?" My voice broke on that question, contradicting what I'd said. "Part of me wants to, since I don't know you *or* me. That me wants to act like a hot mess express." I glanced back and forth between them, my stomach wrenching. "The other half is strong. Stubborn too. Wants to fight you both and run."

"Any chance you'll settle somewhere in between?" My alleged twin quirked a brow. "Maybe worry about not remembering anything *but* believe we're who we say we are and not swing at us?"

I peeked at Gideon to get a read on him. He was rolling a shirtsleeve to his elbow, exposing a corded forearm. *Preparing for a fight, are ya?* He paused mid-roll, eyes flicking to mine, offering me that offended look again. "The only time I've hit you is when we spar in the fighting ring, and you're in head-to-toe protective padding." He moved on to his next sleeve. "I also go easy on you in the ring, by the way, which pisses you off."

"*Pssh.*" Green Eyes waved a dismissive hand. "Don't mind him, he's just grouchy and unsure how to handle you like this." His forehead tightened. "Actually, forget what I said. He's always miserable."

I didn't miss the sneer-scowl from Gideon, aimed at my supposed twin.

"Any chance I can get your name so I stop calling you 'Green Eyes' or my 'supposed twin' in my head?"

"Ah, yeah, of course, that'd help." He smirked. "Julian William Avery Wyndham d'Aragon." He rested a hand over his heart and tipped his head in greeting. "Your honest-to-God twin. You're more of the set-fire-to-it kind of sibling, and I'm the one who hacks the building to get you inside to do it."

"Prove you are who you say you are, and we can talk without me putting up a fight," I decided, because what choice did I have?

"I don't carry an ID. It's a whole thing. People outside our family and close friends think I'm dead. Prefer to keep it that way. Can't really go to a DMV, you know?"

"Not the best way to get me to believe you." I turned to Gideon. "What about me? You?"

"Your purse was stolen from your hotel room before you went missing, so I don't have your ID." Gideon produced his license. He walked around the bed alongside Julian and offered it to me.

"Gideon Wyndham," I read out loud, hating that my hands were still slightly shaky. "No other names like the two of us have?" I handed him back the Montana ID, somehow doubting he truly resided there.

"It's just one of my aliases," was all he gave me.

"I'm still not convinced you're my brothers. You could be serial killers." I searched for the camera again, and it was still active.

"We don't have photos of us together on our phones. We're not the selfie types. It's hazardous to our health," Julian said in a humorless tone, then flipped over his forearm to show me a tattoo, as if that was supposed to mean something. "Our family crest."

"Are you about to tell me I have one of those on my body?"

"On your lower back," Gideon let me know before he began speaking to Julian in another language as if I wasn't there, and I rapidly translated everything in my head with relative ease.

While I still didn't know if I could fully trust them, at least I didn't pick up on any back-and-forth that suggested they'd done this to me. "You do realize I know what you're saying?"

Julian brought his hands to his hips, the corners of his mouth lifting into a semi-smile. "You still remember Aramaic?"

"Apparently." I shouldn't shrug. I should be hysterical. But I wound up settling in between, like Julian had suggested. I went with nervous-*ish*. Apprehensive-of-them-*ish*. Annnd still a little panicky-*ish*, too.

"You're fluent in seven languages." Julian swiped the locks of his unruly hair away from his face, then sat on the edge of the bed and began testing me.

I responded back to his first remark in Italian.

Spanish? No problem.

French? Almost sounded like my mother tongue.

He tried out three more, but on the next, my brain put up a wall. "Sounds like Mandarin, but I don't speak it, do I?"

"I was just testing you." Julian held open his palms. "This is . . . interesting, to say the least."

"You mean *terrifying, devastating,* and a bunch of other words that end in *ing*?"

Julian eyed Gideon as if searching for the right thing to say.

"Repeat what you were just discussing, this time in English."

Julian stretched out his neck, rotating it around like he'd been the one stuck in a box. "Our family, well . . . we're cautious people."

How long had I been in that coffin before they found me in the streets? Not long enough to die from a lack of oxygen, clearly. But still. The whole thing was a nightmare from start to finish, and if I could wake up anytime now, that'd be great. "Are you planning to add details to that statement, or just leave it hanging in the void?"

Julian brought a fist to his mouth, hiding a dark chuckle. "I'm sorry, really. I don't handle this kind of shit in normal ways."

"Like a nervous tic? Laugh-at-a-funeral kind of thing?"

He nodded.

"I'll take the laughter over the brooding," I said, unable to contain the jab at Gideon.

"That's another very *you* thing to say." Julian rested his hand on his lap. "That's why I keep smiling. You're in there somewhere—we just need you to follow the light and come on out."

"Yeah, well, right now I'm Alice falling down a rabbit hole, and it feels like it's never-ending. So maybe you could throw me a lifeline here and help me out. Tell me what happened?"

"Alice, eh?" Julian raked a hand through his hair. "Well . . . our tattoos themselves are trackers. Yours went offline while you were in Rome. Unfortunately, we don't know why you were there."

He kept talking, his voice all code words and science while discussing signals, nano-somethings, and a chain. Somehow most of it didn't go over my head, which was saying a lot, given my situation.

I waited for chills to break out across my skin. This would be the perfect time for them. But nothing came. Not yet.

"We went to your last location, which was a hotel room in Rome. While we were there, your signal came back online, which means your chain was removed," Julian said, his tone growing flatter. "We thought it might be a trap, baiting us to the location. We showed up in the Czech Republic, prepared to infil a monastery, but you took off just before we got to you."

And hello, anxiety, welcome back. Even my hands were becoming clammy. My palms went damp, goose bumps crawling up my arms.

"You were alone and running when we caught up with you," Gideon added to the horror-story recap. "You didn't know who we were, and you attacked us."

I closed my eyes. Memories hurtled back to mind from that showdown. "That's why you tackled and sedated me." *You held me but didn't hit me. Didn't fight back, just like you didn't fight when I hit you today.* "I remember waking up in a coffin, but it wasn't locked. No dirt covering it." Wood had pressed against my palms; a sweet, varnished smell had assaulted me. "If someone wanted to kill me by burying me alive, why not actually bury me?"

"For that matter, why remove your chain so your tracker would come back online?" Julian murmured, and I opened my eyes.

I needed that fearlessness back, or at least the meet-in-the-middle attitude, because *this*? This shaky feeling was gut-wrenchingly horrible. "So, someone scrubbed my memories. I didn't just hit my head?"

"The doctors checked you. No head injuries," Gideon said. "No substances they could find that'd cause memory loss, either. But something undetectable was clearly used. Aside from the sedatives we gave you, they only found remnants of another tranquilizer, which is probably how they kept you asleep while traveling, and why your first memory is waking up in that coffin."

Julian slipped a hand beneath his shirt and showed me a chain around his neck. "We're all wearing ours to remain dark for now since we don't know if someone has access to our signals. We put your backup chain on you as well."

I smoothed my fingers over the thin metal chain, the coolness grounding me.

"Someone clearly knew about the tattoo and the chain, but as to who did this to you and why . . . ?" I preferred Julian emphasizing words than abandoning his sentences.

"How long was I missing?"

"Less than twenty-four hours. We found you last night, which was Thursday. You woke up here this morning. Now it's midafternoon." Julian let me process the timeline before adding, "We'll find who did this to you, and your memories *will* return."

"This could be just a temporary thing happening in response to shock, right?"

"There are fast-acting drugs that wouldn't show up on any tox screening that can make someone forget things," Gideon said, his voice as grim as his expression. "We've used them on subjects before, so I'm more inclined to believe that's what happened here than this being a result of shock."

"How soon do they wear off?" I asked, feeling a flicker of hope.

"It can vary." Gideon's eyes locked on mine. "But we've never encountered a drug that can selectively delete your entire identity while leaving the rest of your mind intact."

And there it is. The reason for his brooding, and why Julian's smile had been nervous. They were worried I wouldn't return to them in the way they'd last seen me. They'd be stuck with this empty shell of a woman who only remembered random facts, and what good would knowing those languages be if I didn't recognize the people I'd once spoken them to?

My shoulders bowed forward, and for the first time since I woke up in that coffin, liquid gathered in my eyes.

"I, uh . . ." Gideon walked back, like my impending tears were contagious. "Mum and Dad are on their way here to see you. Should arrive in two hours or so. Our younger sister as well. Maybe seeing them will help."

Help how? I had no idea who they were. "Are they doing okay?" I abandoned holding the chain and swiped away the first tear to break free. "Freaked out?"

Julian mussed up his hair with one hand while standing.

Thanks for the tell. I should be worried about our meeting.

"We're not really the freak-out type." Julian winced. Maybe he was embarrassed by the lack of human emotion from our family? Well, unless you counted a dry laugh or a dark scowl as emotions.

"So what type of family are we?" I pointed at the ceiling. "This estate. The tracker and chain. I speak seven languages and can clearly fight." I waited for an answer and, when I didn't get one, asked, "Are we Mafia or something?"

Julian with that smile again—and I had to say, it really was preferable to panic. "Quite the opposite."

"So we're good guys?"

"The two of us are usually good." Julian gestured to Gideon and back to himself. "You?" He started as someone rapped at one of the double doors. "Always."

"Yes?" Gideon called out, voice flat yet still piercing.

The doors slowly opened, and it wasn't one of the doctors from earlier, but instead, someone who immediately stirred something inside me.

My body reacted, like a hum under my skin. Each step closer he took, my nervous energy waned and a sense of calm filled the void.

What in the world? I set my hands on either side of me and sat taller, curious about my body's strange reaction to him.

The man had broad shoulders, and from the looks of it, a strong body hidden beneath his jeans and tee. Slightly wavy black hair that was just long enough to run your fingers through. He had a killer face, too. Masculine features. A hard jawline covered in stubble with deep, dark eyes that were currently captivating me into some type of trance. I'd thought Julian could hypnotize me with his soothing voice, but this man could hold me prisoner with just one look.

Why do you feel so familiar if I can't even remember who I am? That also reminded me, what did *I* look like?

"How are you?" He broke the quiet, standing at the end of the bed, never losing sight of me. Like he was worried if he blinked, I'd vanish. Maybe disappear for good down that rabbit hole.

"How do I know you?" My question back probably just answered his in a roundabout way.

He couldn't mask his concern, or his sadness, the way my brothers had. It was sharp and distinct; his worry bled into me. When he quietly peered at my brothers, they shook their heads, confirming I was still an empty vessel of random knowledge and skills, and that was it.

"Wait," I blurted out when it dawned on me, and I lifted my hand to try to propel myself into the past with a gentle push. "I hit you on the street, didn't I?"

The man touched his jaw, nodding. "You did."

"You didn't hit me back."

"Never," he breathed out.

I dropped my hand to my lap, hoping and praying he answered *no* to my next question. "You're not another brother, are you?"

"*Definitely* not related to you."

Thank God. My memories may have been MIA, but I was attracted to him.

"I'm relieved you're safe, but I'm, uh, sorry about . . ."

"Forgetting everything?" I finished for him, shocked that I smiled. Maybe I was a little like my twin?

The side of the man's mouth pulled to the right, fighting a smile before he lightly nodded.

Who are you to me? "Your name?" I whispered.

He retrieved a wallet from his back pocket and walked around Gideon as if he wasn't even there and handed it to me. I appreciated the proof without having to ask, but the moment our fingers made contact, a little jolt of *something* hit me, and he subtly cleared his throat and pulled away.

"Jason Reed, but I go by Reed," he said as I noted his place of residence and age: Charleston, and thirty-eight this October.

I handed him back his ID, and he took it without touching me. "And how old am I?" I asked.

"Thirty-five at the end of September, which is next month," Julian answered while standing, and now a line of three men stood protectively alongside my bed, but I only had the urge to hug one.

"Which name do you call me?" Why'd it also feel like we were alone in here, that we didn't have my brothers hanging on to our every word?

Reed returned his wallet to his back jeans pocket. "Hollis, because that's what you prefer."

"Hollis," I repeated, waiting for it to fit somewhere in my mind. "Any chance I could see what I look like?"

"I set a mirror on the nightstand in case you needed one." Julian walked around the bed, picked it up, and handed it to me.

I lifted it slowly, a little nervous about meeting myself, but the woman in the mirror was pretty. She (*me*) had a symmetrical face. High cheekbones. Full lips with a determined tilt. Skin that was almost annoyingly perfect and either money-bought or genetically blessed. Long dark-brown hair with a few dyed-red strands at the front framed my face. And I had the same eyes as Julian, but unlike him, I had a small scar cutting through my right brow.

"How'd I get this?" I pointed to the mark, eyeing my twin.

"You wouldn't believe it if I told you," Julian said as I handed him back the mirror. "But don't worry, it'll come back to you."

"I feel betrayed by my brain, that's all I know." I slumped back against the headboard, lightheadedness starting to set in. "Anything else super important I should know?"

"One more sibling we didn't mention," Julian said slowly. "A half brother, Tristan."

"Julian," Gideon said in warning, "she doesn't need to know about that now."

"What don't I need to know?"

Gideon dragged a palm down his face, shaking his head. He hissed a low, deep breath.

"We haven't been able to reach him," Julian revealed in a raspy voice, no humor to hide his worry this time. "But it's normal for him to be off-grid."

"You're sure he's not in danger?" I asked Gideon instead, since something told me he was calling the shots. "Was Tristan with me in Rome?"

Gideon quickly dismissed my concerns with a blanket statement. "We don't know anything right now." He began addressing his sleeves as if that were a more pressing matter, rolling the left one down. "You should rest. The doctors said not to overwhelm you. Let's let the drugs wear off, and we'll chat tomorrow, okay?"

"Wear off so you can tell me we have a brother out there that could be in trouble, and my memories might be the key to unlocking where to find him and how to save him?" I held my chest, finding a spot there sensitive to touch, as I searched for a deep breath I couldn't seem to achieve.

When neither brother made eye contact, I redirected to Reed, hoping he'd calm me again as he had before.

Reed grimaced, and his throat muscles went visibly taut. Not the best indicator everything was A okay with my half brother.

"Tell me what you know," I requested.

"Don't," Gideon ordered, and I assumed that command was for Reed.

"No, please *do*." Not that I had any freaking clue what information was being held back from me.

A troubled look passed over Reed's face.

It was wild. I didn't even know who this man was to me or why he was there, just that he'd been part of my rescue and my brothers were allowing him in the room with me.

"Your half brother could be in danger, yes," Reed answered despite Gideon's death stare, then closed his eyes. "Or, uh . . . Tristan could be the one who did this to you."

CHAPTER SEVEN

Hollis

I'd spent the last two hours tossing and turning, flipping through blank page after blank page in my mind, only landing on movie plotlines and random facts in a slew of languages. Gideon had shut down the conversation about our half brother and kicked everyone, including himself, out of the room so I could sleep. Rest was as elusive as my memories, so I tossed the covers off and swung my legs around to the side of the bed.

Once my feet made contact with the honey-hued hardwood, I looked up at the camera and stated the obvious: "I can't sleep." I drew my hand beneath my chin, a command to kill the feed. My patience wasn't tested, because the light turned off a few seconds later.

Satisfied to be alone-*ish* now, I stood with relative ease, grateful the effects of the drugs seemed to have worn off, which meant I should be able to walk unaided. Or *run*, if the tattoo of the same family crest Julian and Gideon had wasn't there.

I walked across the ballroom-sized bedroom (only a mild exaggeration) to the full-length mirror wedged between two floor-to-ceiling windows.

The stranger I'd expected to find was staring back at me. Even when I lifted my hand, it was as if someone else was waving, not me. I curled my fingers around the wood frame to get up close and personal with myself.

My pupils were slightly dilated, fighting for space with my forest-green irises. The whites of my eyes were a little red, and my under eyes had a purplish tint competing with my otherwise tan face. Drugged, tired, and hungry were the probable causes.

I lifted my free hand to the curve of my cheek, then skimmed the line of my brow's scar as if touching it might draw me back to the moment it happened.

Nothing came. Not a damn thing. I let go of the mirror and shifted my thick mass of dark hair out of my way, unsure who'd changed me. These clothes smelled and looked too clean for my coffin escape.

Also, talk about a reason to hyperventilate—waking up in a box. Yet my first instinct had been to fight. To get the top open and climb out of the six-foot hole I'd found myself in. My saving grace had been that the coffin hadn't been sealed with a lock or by dirt.

Someone clearly had gone to a lot of trouble to take me, only to hand me right back over, and it made no freaking sense.

I smoothed my hands up and down my forearms at the goose bumps gathering as a result of my thoughts.

Arms to my sides, I abandoned my mission to eradicate the little bumps, remembering I was here to check for the tattoo.

I had on a white fitted tee that clung to my curves. *Avery* was printed in black script on the front pocket—and wasn't that one of my many names? I peeked down my top, where my breasts were fighting against a too-small sports bra.

Thankfully, my black leggings were more comfortable and not riding up my crotch. I had long, toned legs. My feet were bare, toenails painted a nude color, which was a little boring for a woman who climbed out of coffins and ran down dark alleys like it was just another Thursday.

I checked my fingernails. Same color, but chipped. No sign of dirt under them after yesterday's struggle, either. *Someone both cleaned me and changed my clothes.* Hopefully a female nurse and not one of those male doctors from this morning.

"Tattoo," I reminded myself, becoming concerned at how forgetful I was.

I only had a few memories to cling to from the last twenty-four hours, and I couldn't afford to lose those, too.

Shifting to the side, I lifted my shirt, my pulse quickening.

The so-called family crest was there.

It was real, like a brand, and I belonged to a secret society I didn't remember joining.

What had initiation been like? Did it happen via the birth canal, or did I have to go through a series of tests to prove myself worthy?

I was getting ahead of myself, trying to fill in the blanks to the story of my life. If I wasn't careful, I might mix up reality with movies I could frustratingly still remember.

Shirt back in place, I dropped my head into my hands, my temples throbbing. "Get it together." *Get what together? You don't know who you even freaking are.* My inner voice hit me back with enough sass to send my head upright, hands falling. Talk about feeling split in two and not recognizing either half.

I needed answers. *Something* to click. I also needed to get out of this room.

I didn't make it down the hall too far before I heard voices.

The carpet runner was thick beneath my feet, the scent of lemon oil trailing behind me as I tracked down whoever was talking.

I stopped outside an open door and listened in. There was a woman speaking, but she didn't sound physically present. Over speakerphone, maybe.

I peeked around the corner, locating only one of four men I recognized. Jason Reed. The man who'd defied my broody-grouchy brother and also managed to steady my pulse with his presence.

Reed noticed me within a second and set his laptop on a coffee table and stood. "Hi," he mouthed, brows slanting with the same concerned expression he'd hit me with in the bedroom.

A guy on the phone slowly turned around as if catching on to the fact Reed was distracted by someone or something. "I'm going to have to call you back. Love you." He ended the call as the two other men in the room redirected their attention my way.

"Come in." Phone Guy waved me over.

I scanned the space, uncertain whether it was the best idea to be alone with three strangers, even if the fourth man in the office was oddly familiar for some reason.

"It's okay." At Reed's words, I took my first hesitant step across the threshold into the space, which appeared modern in comparison to the rest of what little I'd seen of the home so far.

Sleek furniture, smooth lines, and minimalistic black-and-gray everything. Even the book spines on the shelves were color coded and divided into three categories: gray, grayer, and grayest.

"Hi." That awkward hello was for Reed and him alone. *How do I know you aside from punching you on the street?* He smiled while running a hand through his hair.

"I'm Alejandro Rodriguez." Phone Guy broke through my staring contest with Reed while offering his hand. "You can call me Alex."

"And who are you to me?" I folded my arms, remaining close to the doorway since there were still three obstacles in my way to the only one I seemed interested in talking to.

"I'm married to your best friend, Audrey," Alex said as if that'd explain everything.

Nope, it explained absolutely nothing.

Another man stepped up alongside Alex and tugged at the brim of his black ball cap. "Audrey's my sister. I'm Ryder Lawson."

Okay, maybe we were getting somewhere now, but I kept my guarded position. "And you are?" I asked the only one with visible tattoos.

"Trevor Sloane." A slight smile cut across his mouth. "I'm Audrey's ex-husband, and the father of our son, Chase."

"So Audrey connects you all, and she's my best friend, so that's why you're here—because I was taken?"

Ryder nodded. "Quick study."

More like still playing thirty-four years of catch-up. "What about you? What's your relation to Audrey?" I peeked around the wall of three men, searching out Reed.

"The four of us operate together. I have no relation to Audrey." Reed gestured with his head toward the others. "Outside of being her friend because of these guys."

Huh. My shoulders slumped. Not the answer I'd hoped for or expected, given my strange feelings. "My brothers didn't have any photos of me. Any chance you do?"

Alex produced his phone and closed the space between us. "Photos from the wedding. You were the maid of honor."

"You also attended my wedding this year as a guest," Ryder remarked as Alex began swiping through photos on his phone.

One after another, the pictures blurred together, making me a little dizzy. The woman in the photo with the bride matched the stranger from the mirror, but it was jarring to see her smiling, dancing, and so *real.* So not *me* right now.

At the tilt-a-whirl feeling happening in my stomach, I held up my hand. "That's good, thank you."

Alex turned toward the room and went over to the others, standing alongside Audrey's ex-husband. "You two get along?" I had no idea why that was relevant, but out the question came.

"We do," Alex confirmed, pocketing his phone.

I walked back a step, needing the doorway for support in case my legs embarrassed me and gave out. Shoulder to the interior frame, I crossed my arms, scanning the four men, waiting and hoping for something to click. "And you all work together. How so?"

"US military, but not in the traditional sense." Ryder's response was about as vague as my brothers' not-the-Mafia answer had been. "Delta

Shield Security. All formerly in the Unit, except Trevor," he added. "He was a SEAL."

Unit? Is that another name for Delta Force? "What about me? Did I serve? Is that why I feel like my body is a weapon in itself?"

Ryder smirked, then took the lead as everyone quietly hung back, which had me assuming he was in charge. "No, not military, but you do take on missions for the government. Not just for the US and the UK."

Missions? I didn't bite the bullet and ask for more details. At least their story seemed to be in line with Julian's "we're the good guys" remark. "And you helped my brothers locate me yesterday?"

"We did." Ryder again, when I wished it was Reed answering.

"Do you believe Tristan is in danger, or that he did this to me?" I bit the bullet on that one, unable to keep the question at bay any longer.

Ryder turned to the side, eyeing the camera in the corner of the room. The light was on. "We don't know anything about your brother to offer our opinion," he said steadily, turning his face to mine again. "We only learned you had a half brother while in Rome yesterday. Apparently, you didn't know about him until later in your life, either. Well, so Gideon said."

I wasn't sure what to make of that last bit of news. I stood unassisted by the doorway as I tried to read between the lines of what else Ryder had said. "You don't regularly work with my brothers, then, do you? Not part of their, uh, club?"

"Aside from this week, once in February." Reed spoke up that time, and the sound of his voice somehow relaxed the tension in my body I'd been riding like a wave while waiting for the inevitable crest and crash to follow.

"And the government let you take on my case because you're Audrey's—"

"Our commander in chief values your life," Ryder interjected, offering an almost diplomatic answer.

"We'd have come even if he didn't ask us, though," Reed added in a no-nonsense tone, eyes tight on me like he had a million things he wanted to say but no plans to say any of them.

"How long have we known each other?"

I'd only meant that for Reed, but Alex answered instead. "You've actually known Audrey longer than any of us. Well, aside from Trevor, of course."

"Wait, even you?" I asked Ryder, since didn't he say he was my best friend's brother?

Ryder rested a hand on his chest. "I only found out I had a sister this past Christmas. I met her and her son, Chase, then."

"Oh, wow, that, um . . . *sucks*."

"You met my sister while you were undercover eight years ago. You gave her the name Hollis and didn't tell her the truth about who you were until you had no choice on an op this past February. You started preferring that name to Celeste, as well as the person you tend to be around her instead of, uh—"

"I lied to my best friend about who I am for *that* long?" My gut twisted with guilt.

"You had your reasons." Ryder opened his palms to the room. "Like to try and keep her safe from this world of yours. But when Audrey was placed in danger this February, you helped us keep her safe. You had no choice but to tell her the truth then."

I opened my mouth to respond, but an intruder to our get-to-know-you conversation beat me to talking.

"They're about to pull up." The deep, growly-ish voice behind me had to belong to Gideon. "And as for you four, you shouldn't be discussing the case with her, especially not without my presence."

I turned to face Gideon, my spine tingling and right-hook fingers itchy to swing. What was with the compulsion I had in wanting to slug my own flesh and blood? "I'm not a prisoner, correct?"

"Of course not." He propped his hand up on the doorframe, eyes sharp on me. "But they're outsiders."

I crossed my arms, feeling a bit stronger standing my ground with four elite operators behind me. Something told me they'd have my back.

Gideon lifted his head, straightening his posture while tossing out the order. "Do me a favor and don't bring up Tristan to Mum or Dad yet. Let me talk to them first."

I didn't even know what to say or ask them, because I barely knew a thing myself.

"The only person I want you focused on is yourself, got it?" His tone of voice that time was as layered and complex as I suspected he was.

"And what will you do next?"

"Kill the bastards who did this to you . . ." He paused for a beat, his gaze flicking to the operators in the room. "And leave a trail of bodies behind so everyone knows never to screw with my family again."

CHAPTER EIGHT

Reed

From the second-floor window, I watched Hollis outside as she stiffened when her sister hugged her. She remained like a statue, arms slightly raised and locked at the elbows. She didn't hug her back, but she didn't shove Lyra away, either.

Her parents approached next, the duke and duchess. Her mother rested her hand on Hollis's forearm and gave her a small squeeze. Her father offered a nod and a quick hug. Neither lingered. It was depressing, and that was coming from someone with shitty parents.

Never, in all the months that I'd known that woman—whether she was busting my chops or not—had she looked at me like she had today. Staring at me not as a stranger, but someone who gave a damn about me. She even had me feeling off, almost drunk. Oddly warm in my chest and throat, a little lightheaded, wanting to word-vomit shit I knew I shouldn't . . . So yeah, out of it, for damn sure.

I let go of the drapes and turned, finding Alex dragging a leather armchair over to the corner of the room. He began screwing around with the camera. "Don't like being watched?"

"Who does?" he grunted in response, then hopped down from the chair. "We can talk freely now."

Trevor checked his watch. "I'll start a timer. I'm sure you only bought us a minute before her brothers come barging in."

"Then talk fast." Alex winked.

Ryder set his laptop on the coffee table and stood, waiting for someone to speak up with theories or news during the precious seconds Alex had given us.

"I got nothing," I surrendered, and Alex nodded his *Same* right back at me.

We turned to Trevor next. He rested a hand under his chin, cracking his neck. Probably slept as bad as I had. We'd been exiled to a small place at the back of the property, forced to sleep in bunk beds where the stablehands used to sleep thirty-plus years ago.

I'd slept in much worse, but it was more a slap in the face that we were outsiders in their family's trust circle. I didn't totally blame them, since the only time we'd worked together, Hollis had been an intermediary. But still.

"This is probably not too helpful, but I remembered my cousin had her memories wiped a few years back." Was Trevor kidding? That was the definition of something akin to a possible lead. "*But* she remembered who she was, just not what happened to her during the time she'd been taken. No way the same person's responsible." He'd shot down what little optimism I had. "I can still talk to them. See if Tessa ever got those memories back. Or find out if they know what drugs were used on her."

"Make the call outside where you don't have ears and eyes on you."

"Roger that." Trevor left the office, and Ryder turned our way as if waiting for us to pull another possible lead out of thin air.

I held open my palms in apology at the nothingness still there. "I'm sure she'll be back to herself soon and can tell us what happened."

"Well"—Ryder glanced at the camera, which was still off—"what about any other cases involving memory loss and operators?"

Alex stepped forward. "Only ones I can think of involve traumas to the head."

"I'll call Secretary Chandler," Ryder offered. "See if we can get help putting together a list of possibles. Anything even close to what happened to Hollis could be helpful to take a look at."

Don't leave me alone with Alex.

Too late. Ryder took off to make the call before I could object.

I checked the camera, and it was my bad luck that it was still inactive, which meant Alex would be safe to harass and annoy me like I knew he was about to do.

"Don't," I begged, holding up my hand, as if that'd do any good.

"You've conveniently done your best to avoid me since we realized she lost her memories." He parked his hands on his hips, shifting into dad mode, which was the last thing I wanted or needed. "Talk to me, man."

"Hollis is alive, and your pregnant wife can now sleep because of it. Her memories *will* come back."

"Not the kind of conversation I'm talking about." He glanced at the camera, and whatever magic shit he'd done to it was still holding up.

"Well, her case is the only thing I'm up for discussing."

The man doubled down on not dropping this and closed the space between us to hiss in a low voice, "Your dad doesn't remember who you are, and now we're dealing with a mission about *this*, and Hollis—"

"Hollis isn't my dad," I snapped back. "Her situation is temporary." I motioned to the hall as if she were there. "His memories, on the other hand, aren't coming back." I'd already said too much and needed to shut up.

I turned away from him and went back to the window to look outside. Hollis was no longer there. Just her parents' Brabus G-Wagon, an enhanced version of the Mercedes-Benz G-Class.

"I'm not going to drop this, not when I know your head has to be off right now for more than one reason."

"Oh yeah?" I sputtered, half losing it as I pivoted back around. "What's the other reason?"

"The woman you've spent half the year pretending to hate was in danger and now going through this, and you weren't—and still *aren't*—scared shitless?" He scoffed. "You can lie to yourself and act like you're fine, but I see right through you. You've been keeping yourself together with prayers and maybe a little duct tape."

"I was fine before. I'm *still* fine." I bit down on my back teeth and hissed, "And *she'll* be fine."

Because I believe in her.

"That's a whole lotta lies for someone who hates liars." His jaw muscles tensed as he hit me with his tough-love bullshit.

"She *will* be all right." That was the only acceptable outcome. She was safe, and soon she'd remember everything, and we'd find the assholes who did this to her. I squeezed my eyes closed, unable to look at one of my closest friends and do exactly what he said I hated: lie. "As for me? I'm good already. Perfectly fi—"

"Dammit, Reed." His voice was rough with emotion, grating across my skin like sandpaper as he tried to get *under* my skin. "You and I aren't at war here, I'm only trying to help. But I also need to know if you can work this mission, given what's happening back home and—"

"Back home?" A dark laugh loosened free from an equally dark place inside me as I opened my eyes. "You mean because my father doesn't remember the hell he put me through my whole life? And I can't stop hating the man even though he has no clue what a bastard he is?" I brought my hand to my chest, worried my heart was about to fly right out of it. "Does it suck?" I nodded, no sense lying now. "Yeah, it does. But that's not going to stop me from doing my job. Operating is all I have."

He held up his hands like a possible white flag, like he'd fall back, but I wasn't done. The beast was already out of its cage and running straight for the target he'd opened himself up to be.

"And as for why else I'm upset? I'm just plain angry at the evil in this world. Why couldn't that evil have come after me instead of her? Done me a solid by stealing my memories? She doesn't deserve what happened to her." I slowly looked up at him. "But my life is one giant clusterfuck of failures I wish I could forget—and to make it worse? I'd been hoping to lose my own memories the day she went missing."

And I hated myself for it. *Blamed* myself. Was terrified this was my fault and I'd willed this sick reality into existence.

Alex muttered a string of curses, probably shocked I'd actually opened up and also unsure what to say back.

"Can we be done talking about me now? I promise that duct tape is holding me together," I rasped, still a little pissed off at his accusations about my feelings for her (that were possibly correct). "Just talk to—" I immediately dropped my words the second I realized we had company.

So much for that duct tape, because as soon as Hollis met my eyes, I could feel myself unraveling like I had last night when reality caught up with me on the plane.

Now there I was, on the verge of losing my shit again, but she was awake and in front of me. The battle happening inside me had nothing on what she was going through, so I'd man the hell up for her.

"Am I interrupting?" she whispered, and that sweet innocence dragged my ass forward two steps, somehow even poking a hole in some of my pent-up frustration.

"No, we're done here." I glanced back at Alex, my shoulders falling at the fact I'd been an asshole to him when all he'd done was give a damn. "He needs to call Audrey anyway—don't you?"

I wasn't so sure whether being one-on-one with her was the best idea with how she'd been looking at me earlier, but it was too late now, because Alex nodded and left us alone.

"Redecorating?" She pointed to the armchair beneath the camera while taking a seat on one of the couches.

I smiled. God help me, I did, and I even meant to do it.

"Our temporary solution for privacy from your older brother, who doesn't have the best manners toward guests." I sat across from her, deciding it'd be best to keep some distance between us. I leaned back, holding the arm of the couch, hoping my pulse might drop out of tachycardia range soon so I could survive our talk.

She wrung her hands together on her lap, her nerves as unexpected as my opening up to Alex. "Gideon's a bit much, isn't he?" She faked a smile—or maybe it was partially genuine. I wasn't sure of anything at this point.

"That's putting it mildly." I angled my head, staring at her long lashes as she slowly lifted her eyes to my face. "Your meet-and-greet not go well? Rather short."

"It was stiff and awkward, like they didn't know how to handle me being like this. I gave them an out by saying I was tired. My sister seems nice, though. She's throwing snacks together."

"Good. You should eat."

She patted her thighs twice. "So."

Yeah, I don't even know how to handle this version of you being this nervous, awkward, and . . . well, sweet.

"I'm, um, glad we're alone."

My damn heart rate was never going to slow down. "You are?"

"Mm-hmm." She stood, then sidestepped the barrier of the coffee table between us and offered her hand.

I was probably scowling as I bit out, "What are you doing?"

"Asking for a favor. Will you do it for me?"

"Depends."

"I was hoping you'd touch me." Red crawled up her throat into her face.

Never have I ever—a game we used to play in high school, and I had no idea why I was thinking about that now, but never had I ever witnessed Hollis blush or get tongue-tied.

She's not herself, genius. I forced myself to stand so she wouldn't feel alone in whatever she was going through. I even held out my hand—no idea what she planned to do with it, but if she wanted it, she could have it.

She gently rested her hand on top of mine. The second contact was made, it took all my energy not to pull away at the electric current passing from her fingers into my skin.

"See?" she whispered.

"What am I supposed to see?" I was using the sense of touch, not eyesight right now.

"Sorry, I meant . . . do you feel that?"

I eyed our clasped palms, then let my gaze wander up to the length of her still-pink neck to the most beautiful face in the world.

"Do I feel your hand? Yes." I played dumb because I didn't want to lie to her. Because yes, I felt a little too damn much, and that was a problem.

"You mean something to me, I just know you do," she said as if in a daze while locking our fingers together so we were now holding hands. "Are we secretly sleeping together?"

Sleeping together? "Hollis," I choked out. I hated to destroy whatever peace she was feeling, and even giving to me, but I had no choice but to be honest. "We're not sleeping together," I said as firmly as possible. "In fact . . ." I exhaled. "This is the first time we've ever even held hands."

Her eyes flashed open, narrowed and sharp in disbelief. "No, that doesn't make sense."

Shit. "I don't know why you feel this way, but we don't even"—I hated myself for this—"like each other."

She pulled her hand away, and it was a punch to the gut I deserved. "What are you saying?"

I dragged both hands through my hair, trying to find a way through this with minimal damage while also shutting down this ridiculous idea that we were together. "We have an unconventional friendship."

"Unconventional," she echoed, her mouth drawing tight around the word.

"You're Audrey's friend, not mine. I mean . . . we"—I faced the camera, checking if Alex's Houdini work held up—"hate each other, actually." *And I'm an asshole.* I slowly turned around as she dropped down onto the couch. "Well, uh, more like you do your best to get under my skin." *This is going great.*

"Wow, um, okay." She cupped her chin, and I lost her eyes to the floor. "So it really makes no sense why I feel like this?"

"Exactly." I clearly needed EQ training, because I sucked at this. "We do hang out from time to time, though," I admitted, going for my phone. "You love my dog." I sat next to her, keeping a little space between us, then swiped through my photos to find a few to show her. "Audrey's son is always stealing my phone to take pictures. You've been in some of them."

"Surprised you didn't delete them, if we don't like each other," she said while taking the phone from me. "What's his name?"

"Ranger. Not creative, I know. Some of my best days were when I was still a Ranger before I—" My throat jammed up, blocking the ugly truth from falling free. "Anyway." I'd just hijacked Audrey's favorite subject-changing word, and I didn't even care.

"Well, he's adorable." She expanded one image that was of her standing next to me while I held Ranger.

"Chase made us take that photo at the park." The same park where Gideon had shown up and killed me with the news that she was in trouble.

She smoothed the pad of her thumb across the screen. "Why are you grimacing? Your puppy can't be that heavy."

She checked out the arm closest to her, and I nearly flexed to give her a better show. *What is wrong with me?*

"You can easily hold him even if he's full grown."

Was I grinning? I wasn't used to her being so . . . well, nice. Not that her typical smart-ass, teasing self didn't do a number on me, too.

"You were standing next to me. That's why I made that face." In truth, that moment was too picture perfect, like we were posing as a family or something, and for whatever reason, my whole day had been messed up because of that one photo.

"So, what you're saying is, you really can't stand me that much?" She playfully elbowed me.

"There you are." The words came out like a gutshot, on autopilot.

She lowered the phone, waiting for me to explain myself.

"Sorry, I just . . ." I cleared my throat and took my phone from her. "You and I have this thing where we joke around, and that's something you'd, uh, have said to me before. Right along with the jab to my ribs."

"Ah." Her face lit up with a bright smile that met her eyes. "So . . . is the hate thing also a joke?"

Shit. I wasn't sure what to say to that.

Julian and Lyra walked into the office, and I'd never been more grateful to see her siblings.

Julian had a tray of food, and his gaze flicked to the camera in the room as he set it down. "Nice work."

"The honor isn't mine, but I'll pass on your regards." I stood and placed some distance between myself and Hollis.

"You must be Reed." Lyra took me by surprise and flung her arms over my shoulders, hugging her hello.

I reacted the same way Hollis had with her outside, arms stiff at my sides, unsure what the hell was happening. The fact I'd never hugged Hollis and now I was doing that with Lyra wasn't lost on me, and for some reason, it bothered me.

"Forgive her," Julian said as she untangled herself to sit by Hollis. "She's the only one with emotions in this family. Well, the good kind of emotions, at least."

"We can't all be broody and terrifying." Lyra pulled the coffee table closer to where they were sitting, a plea for Hollis to eat. "Though it does get a little lonely being the only one who doesn't play spy games."

Hollis glanced at her sister. "You don't . . . ?"

"Nope. I'm the innocent one." She shot her sister a playful wink.

"I should go check on my team." I didn't feel right staying in there.

I started for the door, only to stop when Hollis called out, "Jason?" She quickly corrected, *"Reed?"*

I set my hand on the doorframe and glanced back at her. "Yeah?"

"Sorry for the misunderstanding."

For thinking we slept together?

"Also for punching you on the street yesterday. And I owe you for helping get me to safety. Thank you."

She could punch me all she wanted, as long as that meant she was safe. "Water under the bridge." My chest constricted as I struggled to act calm and collected about all this. "No need to thank me, just doing my job."

I let that lie hang in the air, then went off in search of my team and that metaphorical damn duct tape I'd be needing to survive being around this woman much longer and not explode.

CHAPTER NINE

Hollis

The next morning, I half expected the fog in my head to lift when I woke up. For my memories to return and my identity to come back if I could sleep through the night. But there was nothing there. Just yesterday's fragments and last night's one and only dream, floating at the surface as the doctors performed a vitals check on me per big brother's orders.

After getting the okay, I escaped into the shower—*alone*, because I refused to let anyone help me. And last night's dream snuck back up on me, clinging to me like steam, curling into the corners of my thoughts even as the water rushed over my skin.

I kept my eyes closed, palm on the tile, and bowed my head, allowing the dream to unfold as if it were happening in real time.

Sunlight filtered through partially opened blinds. Comfy sheets. Coffee abandoned on the nightstand.

Jason Reed had been naked next to me. We'd been in a different bed than the one I'd slept in last night, and we'd just had sex. Too bad the sex part hadn't happened in my dream.

But after we'd dressed, he made breakfast as our *three* children sat at the kitchen table, joking around. They looked to be about three and eight. The eldest was our son, and we had twin daughters.

The dream wasn't just vivid—it seemed *real.* So real, in fact, it was like I'd lived it. Could even taste the bacon on my tongue. *But* Reed had said we weren't together, and no way did I have kids. So maybe this was my brain's weird way of trying to build something familiar out of the chaos.

I finally shut off the water and got out of the shower. I towel-dried in front of the massive vanity that a family could easily brush their teeth at. You know, that family I was still clinging to as the only "memory" I had—one that was just a figment of my imagination.

Steam covered the glass, which meant I'd been in the shower too long. I wiped my pruny fingers across the glass, finding that same green-eyed memory-less stranger watching me.

She looked like me, but she still didn't *feel* like me. I caught sight of a bruise on my chest, which explained why it'd been sensitive to the touch yesterday. No clue how I got it, of course.

"You're in there somewhere, aren't you?" Great, now I was talking to myself. Well, to the self I was supposed to be. Celeste. Hollis. I'd take either of them right now. I didn't care. I just couldn't handle being so empty on the inside.

Unable to continue a confrontation with these black hole eyes of mine, I stared down at the marble as if fixating there would do any good. All that did was take me back to that dream, and a pulse of heat rolled through me.

The dream hadn't even been erotic. More sweet and safe than sexy. But there I was now, wanting to add in details that hadn't been there while I'd slept. To actually experience what it was like to have him make love to me.

Would his mouth drop between my thighs? How would the weight of his body over mine feel? Would it be raw and unfiltered, or soft and slow?

And am I that lonely and scared that I'm standing here creating a false reality to feel grounded and connected to someone who doesn't even like me? Probably.

Palms on the counter, I tried to tether myself to this world and not to the fantasy one.

I was growing exhausted with this physical and emotional war happening inside me, and it was only day two of this.

"You alive in there?" my mother called out while knocking, and that was one way to greet me, I supposed.

I'd only spent a handful of minutes with her yesterday, same with my father. This all had to be too hard for them to handle, even if we were apparently a family of badasses.

"I'm alive," I confirmed. "Be right out."

I dropped the towel and put on the full-body robe while mentally preparing myself to talk to the woman who raised me.

When I joined her, my mother—and it just dawned on me I didn't even know her first name—was in the middle of drawing open the drapes for one of the floor-to-ceiling windows at the back of the bedroom.

"I can't imagine you'll want to be cooped up here too long. You've always hated this bloody place, and I can't say I blame you. Bad memories."

Unlike my siblings, she still had an English accent. Same with our father. Though I had no idea about Tristan. Where was he raised, and who took care of him?

"I have clothes in the closet for you to wear—not sure if your brothers brought any of your things with them. This is normally my bedroom when I visit."

She crossed the room to the other side and began opening the curtains at the front to let in more light. I hung back by the bed, just watching her, waiting for her to face me.

When she was done, she slowly turned, swiping her fingers across her lips before subtly clearing her throat and starting for me.

She had dark hair like mine, but it only met her shoulders. Hazel eyes, sharp cheekbones, and a killer jawline. She was in a black sleeveless jumpsuit, showing off sleek and toned arms. The woman looked like a runway model, not a grandmother to my three kids.

No, I don't have kids. Rewind. That was a dream. Maybe even a strange amnesia fantasy, or a movie memory. Not *reality.* I needed to do some research on my situation so I'd know what to expect between now and whenever my memories returned.

"Age really is just a number when it comes to you, huh?" I spoke my thoughts out loud, which had her giving me a no-teeth smile. "Lady . . . ?" I waited for her to fill in the blanks for me.

"*Duchess* Catalina. Aleric is your father, the Duke of Rothvale."

My father's a duke? What in the Bridgerton? And why'd I know that show but not recognize her touch when she held my wrists?

"I'm glad you're okay." Her voice was stiff, the emotion seemingly forced. "I didn't tell you that yesterday, but of course I am." As quickly as she'd grabbed me, she let go, like that was that, conversation over.

I had no idea what to talk about, so I searched for the first thing to come to mind. My hand skated around to the small of my back, which reminded me: "Do you and my father have a tracker as well?"

"Of course." She adjusted her necklace, her eyes sweeping to the oval-shaped diamond. Quite the upgrade from the chain I had on. "But I'm sure Julian explained we're all masking our signals currently as a precautionary measure."

"And you're also in the same line of work I'm apparently in, right? A spy. Warrior. Whatever we're called?"

"Yes, just as my mother was. And her mother. Your father and his. Our families were united to merge two powerful bloodlines. The Wyndham d'Aragons and the Averys." She rested her hand on her chest atop the pendant. "I'm an Avery. I'm an only child, unlike your father."

"Do we also own businesses or something?" I thought back to the T-shirt I'd been wearing yesterday with that name on it like a logo.

"We do." She didn't elaborate, and so I didn't bother pressing. I'd find out eventually—or even better, actually remember my past.

"Any more questions?" She smiled, and it was as forced and fake as that hate thing Reed and I allegedly had going on.

Gideon had said not to bring up Tristan yesterday so he could talk to our parents first, but I assumed I was in the clear to do it today. Tristan was also the only other important topic on my mind at the moment. "My half brother, tell me more about him."

She immediately checked the camera in the room—no blinking light. She began fiddling with her bracelets and revealed, "He's my firstborn child. A by-product of an operation. I did what I had to for the sake of the country, and your father understood. I did *not* have an affair."

By-product? The sake of . . . What? And which country?

"I also don't believe Tristan had anything to do with what happened to you, and we will get ahold of him soon so he can clear his name."

"So you're not in the least worried he's in danger, or that he was taken along with me?" Before she could answer, I pressed, "And for that matter, why in the world is he on the suspect list to begin with, since he's my brother?"

No one had explained that to me, and it was clear Delta Shield had to be careful what they said to me because of my brothers.

A knock on the door saved her from having to continue, and she was quick to take that reprieve, lightly calling out, "Come in."

I fidgeted with the belt of my robe while waiting to see who it was. Gideon and Julian, of course.

Gideon looked like he was about to dominate a board meeting in a three-piece suit. As for Julian, I'd expected him to resemble the kind of hackers I recalled from shows and movies, but he ruined that stereotype in his dark-wash jeans and black tee beneath an open black button-down shirt paired with what looked like designer sneakers.

Julian's sleeves were rolled to his elbows, so when he brushed a strand of his longish hair away from his forehead, I caught sight of the crest tattoo we all shared. "How'd you sleep? How do you feel?"

I skipped over sharing the details of my one and only dream and surrendered a small, "Okay," as an answer to both of Julian's questions.

I mindlessly walked to the back of the room to look out the window, not up for eye contact with either brother at the moment. I set my hand on the windowpane, my stomach flipping in response to who was walking up to the house.

Reed was talking to his teammate, and he must have sensed he had eyes on him, because he jerked his head up toward the second floor and stared right at me.

Trevor noticed me next and waved, then nudged Reed in the side as if to get a move on.

"Celeste?" At my mother's use of that name, I slowly peeled away from the object of my strange affection and turned to face her and my brothers, who remained quietly hovering by the door, watching me.

"Where'd Reed and his teammates sleep?" I looked to Gideon for an answer, but when he remained quiet, I shifted to my mother. To staring down the woman I'd surely have become one day, or maybe already was, if my memories hadn't been stolen.

"The men are staying in the bunkhouse where the stablehands used to sleep when we kept horses here." Before I could ask her why, she plucked an answer from her ice-cold universe and delivered it to me with quite the punch, so much so her words sent me to the bed to sit. "They're not one of us."

"Just because they don't share our laundry list of names doesn't mean—"

"It does, in fact, mean they're outsiders." She doubled down on her tone, then hit me with some major side-eye, as if saying, *How dare you think otherwise.*

I clearly inherited her spine of steel, refusing to back down. "Well, I feel more connected with the men out there than I do with you three. And why, *pray tell*, do you think that is?"

She didn't seem amused at my attempt to throw Old English back at her. The sneer haunting her lips was as hurtful as the look in her eyes. "You have a weakness, my daughter, and that's wanting what you can't have." She leaned forward and had the nerve to cup my chin like I was a small child in trouble. "I blame your father for that. Treating both his daughters like priceless artifacts, giving you two whatever you want, not always what you deserve."

My insides shook, insulted by a woman I didn't even know. Something told me our relationship had always been superficial and rarely more than skin deep.

"That's enough, Mother." That was the first time I'd appreciated the sound of contempt from Gideon's voice. "She's—"

"This is her fault, and we all know that. Don't make excuses for her. She's always chasing after some new thing, wanting what she can't have, and once she finds what she's looking for . . . she gets bored."

Well, when you put it that way. Damn. I wouldn't like me, either.

"We don't know what happened to her, but this is *not* helping." Gideon to my defense, again.

She stared at me, unblinking, continuing to hold on to me, and I hated that I remained stuck in some stupor, not fighting back.

"So help me, I won't set a hand on you, but if you don't back away from her, Hollis *will* remember who she is, and you know damn well the daughter you raised. She hasn't lost to you in a decade." Gideon's threat lingered in the air—but what in the world was he talking about?

"My daughter's name is Celeste, not Hollis." She gave me a firm squeeze and let go. "And calling yourself that name, playing pretend as some normal girl with your friend Audrey"—she smoothed a hand over her bracelets, righting them in place—"just proves my point. You only want that life because it doesn't belong to you. It's *beneath* you."

Beneath me? Rage burned up into the back of my throat. Who was my real enemy here?

She flicked at the last bangle. "You only want that soldier out there because he's not interested in you—isn't that right, Gideon? He said that man can't stand you, which is one reason Gideon's not comfortable with Reed sharing a roof with you." She casually lifted a shoulder. "At least Reed has some good sense, knowing he could never be—"

"Stop," I cut in this time, my stomach turning with disgust. "You can talk shit about me if you want, but leave everyone else out of it." I abruptly rose, standing my ground, as I should have done a few insults ago.

"Don't listen to her." Julian circumvented both obstacles in his way to get to me. "She's trying to bait you. Get you to fight. See if you'll snap back to yourself that way."

Well, she did have me up on my feet, hands balled into fists at my sides. The fighter in me was awake. My memories? Not so much.

"You two spar. Fence. Train together. And as Gideon said, you haven't lost a fight to her in ten or more years, and it's destroying Mum to see you so—"

"Weak," she interjected, hitting me right where it already hurt.

I may have been a shell of a person, just the ghost of who I once was, but something told me she believed what she'd said about me.

"I already know Jason . . . um, *Reed*, doesn't like me. He told me last night." I didn't need to tell them how I found that out, though. "He was honest with me from the get-go." As for the other stuff she said about wanting what I couldn't have? I had no defense without any memories to fall back on.

"And you still trust him?" Julian asked me.

"I do," I whispered, then zeroed in on the woman who'd apparently picked a fight with me in the hope that I'd wake up from this nightmare. "You win this round," I surrendered. "As for the next one?" A light grunt left my barely parted lips. "You better hope I stay living in the dark for as long as possible, because I'm guessing the real me won't forget or forgive you for this."

She flicked her wrist like a command toward Julian. "When you three are done here, take her to the vault. Remind my daughter who she is." She glared at me. "Until then . . . I'll go clean up whatever mess I'm sure you got our family in."

CHAPTER TEN

Hollis

"Was that planned? Good cop, bad cop?" I asked my brothers once our mother was thankfully gone and I could breathe now that the air wasn't so heavy. "She, uh, switched up on me real fast. Came in kind of nice, then turned into *that* real fast."

"No, it wasn't." Julian aligned himself with Gideon as I sat back down. "Mum can't handle not being in control, and she has no clue how to deal with you being helpless like this. It's probably a fate worse than death for her, you forgetting all of us."

"Her death or mine?" I grumbled, unsure whether she'd rather have left me buried in that box. In her eyes, probably a more dignified way to go.

Neither brother bothered to respond to my slightly metaphorical question. They just swapped uneasy looks.

"What about the other stuff she said about me?"

"Don't we all want what we can't have?" Julian gave me a sly grin, and nope, that didn't work. "And what daughter isn't the apple of, uh, her dad's eye?"

"He has Lyra for that," I said bitterly.

"Dad never wanted his youngest daughter to follow in Mum's footsteps. Mum disagreed, so she's a little resentful at him for winning her over to his side. Now she's probably worried she lost another." If Julian ever wanted a career change, he'd make a decent therapist.

Unfortunately, his words didn't undo whatever damage our mother had left behind with her words.

"Do me a favor, will ya? Let the guys sleep in the house tonight."

I finally garnered big brother's attention. Gideon heaved out a deep exhalation, and something told me he was stuck on the same page as mummy dearest about Delta Shield being outsiders.

Julian spoke before Gideon had a chance to presumably reject me. "You really think Mum is going to let them spend another night on the property, even in the bunkhouse?"

"What's that supposed to mean?" I knew exactly what that meant, but I needed them to spell it out for me so I could adamantly refute it.

"How about we table that conversation for now? Mum is right—you should see the vault. Maybe it'll help," Julian said, another deflection attempt.

"Fine." I folded my arms. "But first things first, I'd like an update on Tristan. Is he still on your suspect list? In danger?"

Gideon immediately turned and walked over to the windows facing the front of the house. One hand went to the glass pane, the other into his pocket. He was much more reserved today compared to how he'd been last night, ready to commit murder and all.

"Someone wiped out half of Rome's CCTV footage while you were there. Like from the time you left the da Vinci airport up until a few hours after your tracker went dark. The source code used to do that was mine, and no one else outside of me could've done it." Julian's words slammed into me harder than I thought they would. "*Unless* they were ever in close proximity to my computer and stole the code that way."

"I assume you're about to tell me Tristan is that someone?"

"Could he pull that off?" Julian lifted a shoulder. "Maybe. He visited me in Singapore last month. I was distracted enough that he could've done that. I haven't seen or talked to him since that visit, but that's the norm with us."

"Any chance I stole it to cover my own tracks and he has nothing to do with this?" I winced at the idea, but our mother seemed to think this was my fault somehow, so. "Maybe I was working with someone who knew about my tracker and they stabbed me in the back?"

"Everyone who knows about your tracker, *and* that your protector is off-grid in South America, is on our suspect list." Gideon's hand dropped from the window, and he turned back to face the room. "And no, I don't believe you did this to yourself."

"My protector?"

"There's a bloodline of trained men who've been guarding our family for hundreds of years. Nowadays, we consider them teammates, but we each still have one protector assigned to us. But right now, they're all in the Andes for a training exercise," Gideon steadily explained, remaining by the window. "Which is why I allowed Delta to help me locate you in the first place. Needed more bodies."

"Your protector isn't due back for five more days, and the only way we can contact him, or any of them, is by flying to Peru and climbing a mountain, which we'll do if we need to," Julian added, drawing a hand to the back of his head, threading his fingers through his hair. "But I don't think your protector knows anything, because he was due to leave the day before your trip to Rome. *That's* why we think you chose to go to Italy when you did, so you could avoid him following you and finding out what you were up to."

Great. "You said you didn't know why I was in Rome, so I kept that hidden from you for a reason." I hated that my mother was potentially right about me. Partially, at least. "Looks like I could be complicit in what happened in some way, shape, or form."

"You told your best friend you were meeting up with a guy," Julian said in a hesitant tone. "No names on the flight manifest we recognized, and we didn't see you with anyone at the airport before we lost sight of you on surveillance. The hotel staff also never saw you with anyone, and I can't recover the CCTV footage from the city to see *if* you were with someone."

"Something tells me you don't think there was a guy—or if there was, I wasn't there to have some romantic rendezvous." *Clearly, not with Jason Reed.*

"Maybe Tristan asked you to meet him there? I don't know why or for what, but he could've said to keep it a secret, and it was a trap," Gideon said in an anguished tone, like the mere idea our brother might be involved gutted him to his core. "Or, hell, it could've been a contact or friend you trusted, and they flew into Rome on a different day and stayed elsewhere."

"Regardless, I just don't believe you'd choose to go dark without giving us a heads-up first," Julian noted with conviction in his voice. "*Or* allow someone to dope you up and delete your memories. Let alone bury you in a coffin. You're not a fan of being in tight spaces."

"Are there people who are?" I let a small smile come and go quickly, and Julian did the same. "Any chance this possible friend or contact of mine was someone I was secretly dating and I knew you wouldn't approve of him? What if I let him know about the tracker?" My pulse picked up as I let my mind wander into Theory Land. "Maybe he was using me to get to our family, and he—"

"That exact thing happened to you in college. Well, minus the tracker and source code part. But you haven't been in a serious relationship since," Julian remarked, brows pinched, eyes sharp on me, as if in apology to be the one to be the bearer of that trauma dump.

"What happened?" Nerves fluttered from my stomach to my chest, all the way to my throat, forming into a solid lump.

"Your boyfriend used you to get to Dad. Dad killed him first." Blunt and to the point. I wouldn't expect anything less from Gideon, even if this me barely knew him.

Got it.

"Dad took Lyra to check out your place in London," Gideon shared a few seconds later. "She knows you the best of all of us, even though she doesn't operate, and if you left behind any clues about why you were in Rome, she'll find something."

"And when was I last there?"

"About two weeks ago. You took one of our planes to the city and flew to the French Riviera after that before heading to the States," Julian answered before turning to Gideon. "Maybe I should reach out to Gwen Montgomery? She's as good as me, if not better. If anyone can help, it'd be her."

"Mum will never approve of that and you know it." Gideon tipped his head toward the back window. "She won't even let those Tier One operators in on anything."

"Who's Gwen?" Did they forget I wasn't exactly briefed on my own life?

"Gwen's a cyber genius like me." A wicked smirk cut across Julian's mouth for some reason. Did he have a thing for Gwen? Or was that a touch of cockiness about his own skills? "Her father's a Navy SEAL sniper who leads a team that works for President Bennett. And Gwen's grandfather is the US secretary of defense, Admiral Chandler. Delta Shield also works for the secretary and president in an indirect way. We do sometimes as well."

"Yet you don't trust them enough to share a roof with us?" I jutted my chin forward, arms flying over my chest in defense mode on Reed and his teammates' behalf.

"I do, I suppose." Gideon grimaced, like that was painful to spit out.

"But we got our asses handed to us by Mum last night when we let her know we told the team about Tristan," Julian tacked on. "She called

President Bennett and ordered their secrecy." I didn't hear sarcasm there, so that was . . . well, not great.

Chills spilled down my back in a dramatic fashion as the reality of my situation struck me all over again, along with the reality of who I was before waking up in that coffin. I came from a family that had the American president on speed dial, which meant our family was a hell of a lot more important than I'd previously realized. "Who are we? For real?"

"Get dressed. Shoes on, too." Julian nudged his chin toward the closet. "And I'll do what Mum told me to and show you."

CHAPTER ELEVEN

Hollis

I peeked around Julian, staring down an eerie stairwell that looked like it led straight into the depths of hell.

He flicked on a series of sconce lights that lined the stone walls. "You sure you want to do this?"

"Well, when you put it that way . . ." At least with the lights on, I wouldn't fall to my death in the dark. "Something tells me this is a regular occurrence in my life. Creepy tunnels, hidden rooms—that kind of thing. And if I'm ever going to learn who I am, I have no choice, do I?"

He frowned. "There's always a choice."

"Just, um, lead the way."

His mood lightened, and he winked. "Roger that."

Two things hit me at once: the wink and the military-style response. Both seemed out of place for a cyber guru. I didn't know how or why I knew that. Maybe it was just leftover movie trivia rattling around in my head.

"Were you in the military?" I couldn't seem to picture him serving behind anything other than a keyboard, even if, based on the fit of his clothes, he clearly hit the gym.

"Surprises me, too, that I ever wore a uniform or took orders." He held my arm, steadying me as we took the first step. "I was a sniper.

Only after I proved myself did Dad put in the request for the military to use my other skills." He glanced over his shoulder at me. "I am a decent shot, though. So don't let my appearance fool you, *or* Gideon's cockiness have you believing he's the best of us. In truth, you're neck and neck with him."

I paused on the next step. "Are you saying I'm on *his* level of terrifying?" I mean, apparently I could go head-to-head with our mother, but Gideon? No way.

The man had to be at least six-four and was as broody as he was intimidating—*even though that didn't stop me from swinging at him yesterday, I suppose.* Still, most definitely not someone to bump into in a dark alley. Or, heck, in the light of day.

"Your kill count is right up there with his," Julian laid on me.

I thought back to Gideon's serial killer-y comment about leaving a trail of bodies behind. *Great, and I'm like him.* I checked my palms, ensuring they weren't stained with blood even now. "Hard to believe I've killed anyone with these things." I lifted my hands between us like they were weapons in themselves.

"You usually use a firearm. Knife, sometimes. Rarely just your hands to take someone out."

Rarely implied it had happened.

"We're not psychos, I promise," he said quietly, urging both my arms down. "We're not even red flags. More like yellow lights."

I cracked a smile, surprising myself with that reaction. "And that means?"

"We always give warnings." He smirked. "If someone chooses not to listen, then—"

"I get it." *A little too much, in fact.* I gestured for him to start walking again, and we took baby steps into my literal past until we made it to the end of the corridor, stopping before a domed chamber.

Without thinking twice about it, I moved in front of a retinal scanner and punched in the access code.

"Muscle memory. Your fingers knew the numbers, even if you didn't."

I stumbled back in surprise as the door clicked and began to creak open, scraping against the stone floor.

"Come on," he said when I remained stuck at the threshold, unsure whether I should take the plunge. "It'll help."

"Not so sure about that." But I did as he asked, and a burst of goose bumps prickled across my skin as I walked into the chamber.

The room was encased in smooth gray limestone laced with obsidian veins that shimmered under the soft golden glow of the lanterns.

Forgetting for a moment why I was there, I just took it all in. I ran my fingers along the edge of a marble bust, absorbing the sight of the artifacts lining the walls. Swords, scrolls, framed maps—each preserved in glass or reinforced metal casings.

"Recognize that?" Julian pointed to a painting on the wall. "Our family crest."

I stepped closer to the oil painting, an exact match to our tattoos.

It was divided into four quadrants. A crown in the right-hand corner. A chained lion, a falcon holding a scroll, and a phoenix wing rising through fire in the other three. A crucifix sat at the top, and beneath the shield was Latin script: *In tempore veritas.*

In time, there is truth. I assumed I'd correctly translated that.

"Tell me about the crest," I requested, my voice soft, like I might disturb the dead while stepping into the past. "What do the symbols mean for us? For our family?"

"Well, uh, the scroll represents knowledge we've protected under our wing. And it's a falcon because they don't rule from the sky. They hunt. Silent and precise. They don't wait for war. They end it before it begins."

"And that's who we are? What we do?"

"That's who we were trained to be."

I focused back on the sword and crown. "This is a classic heraldic symbol?"

"Yeah, but what makes ours different is that the sword is in *front* of the crown instead of behind it like normal. It means truth *over* sovereignty. Truth above loyalty to any king."

"So we don't serve the crown?"

A nearby sconce light flickered against his pupils, giving them a brief golden sheen. "No, we defend the truth."

"And the lion?"

"He's chained to represent restrained strength. That just because we *can* do something doesn't mean we should." He traced his stubbled jawline with his knuckles while continuing. "Power can corrupt, and we have to be careful we don't let it corrupt us."

"So truth over ourselves, even." I turned to face the final quadrant. "The phoenix. I recognize that symbol. From a movie, maybe?"

"That's Audrey's doing. She's been catching you up on a lifetime of movies you missed whenever you hang out."

Audrey, the one I'm using to feel normal? Eight years was a long time to play pretend, though, wasn't it? Maybe my mother didn't know the real me—or at least, only the one she wanted to see: Celeste, the warrior.

"Our phoenix is different from what you may remember in the movies." He lifted his chin as a directive toward the painting. "Only the wing is in the fire, not the whole bird like usual. It represents a transformation still in progress. Not a full rebirth. Just . . . *survival*." He turned away from the painting. "Once it was safe to visit England again, you'd always spend your time down here exploring."

"Why wasn't it safe to—"

"An enemy of our parents tried to kill Gideon. He was seven at the time, and that's when they opted to move to the US."

I was less shocked by the story and more surprised at the outcome of it. "So what you're saying is, she cared about us at one point?" My shoulders sagged with regret almost immediately. "Sorry, that was rude."

He rested his hand on my shoulder and gently squeezed, and thankfully, his touch didn't bother me. "No, it's just untrue." His dark brows slanted as he stared at me. "Mum is a hard nut to crack. She's got walls higher than the one our parents helped dismantle in Berlin in 1989. She has her reasons, I swear."

"Sure." I rolled my eyes, then huffed out a deep breath. "What if Tristan is responsible for what happened? Gideon said he'd kill whoever did this to me."

He was quiet for a moment, taking longer than I thought he'd need to answer. "He'd never kill Tristan. Not even if he did this."

"Just lock him away?" I raised my brows.

"Maybe." His gaze slipped over to a case that held a leatherbound book with bronze-capped corners, as if searching for a distraction.

Books in cases—why does that feel so familiar? I closed my eyes, trying to summon a memory. I even tightened my lids as much as possible, as if the action would produce something. The only thing that came to mind . . . a husband I wasn't married to and kids I didn't have. *What in the world?*

"You used to read this all the time." Julian's words returned me to the present, which was ironically also my past. "*The Avery Wyndham d'Aragon Codex.* It's one of the records of our bloodline—from Iberia to our Vatican ties. This isn't legend, it's documentation."

Iberia? Vatican? "So we're not just—"

"No," he cut in. "We're far from being just British aristocrats."

"Our mother mentioned she's an Avery and our father is a Wyndham d'Aragon." *What a mouthful.* "Why does he have two last names?"

"Dad's mum's side is the Wyndhams—another powerful bloodline. Our grandparents were matched together just like our parents were."

Matched? Like . . . arranged marriage?

Julian typed in a code, letting that subject go as if it were no big thing. The case hissed and unlocked, opening with a click. He tried to hand the codex to me, but I hesitated, because something told me a book that needed special sealing shouldn't be touched.

"That's okay." I waved him off. "Just tell me what I need to know."

He opened it, revealing pages of illuminated script. Handwritten Latin, intricate diagrams, and gilded edges.

"It's a history of war and peace. Influence and legacy. Family secrets, too." After gently turning a few more pages, he closed the book, resealed the case, and returned it to the shelf.

A hopeful feeling of familiarity pulled at me, but I didn't bother to shut my eyes this time. No point.

"Our bloodlines have advised the Medicis. Funded some of da Vinci's work. Have long-standing privileges with the Vatican. Helped launch MI6. And that's barely scratching the surface."

"So what you're saying is, we've been there, done that. Been around a while."

This should have produced a lot more shock and awe inside me, but my pulse remained fairly steady. And as long as we weren't discussing lives I'd taken, I didn't feel the need to upchuck. I supposed that meant the badass me was front and center, not the shaky, sad *who-the-heck-am-I* version my mother couldn't stand.

"Pretty much," he finally said, doing a three-sixty as if to admire the place himself. "This room is one of six. We have vaults like this all over the world, protecting knowledge and secrets. Dangerous truths." He went over to a framed oil painting and angled his head toward it. "That *was* vault seven. It was located on the back of the property where our pops lived. You called him Pappy."

Pappy, huh? I read the inscription beneath it out loud. "Destroyed in a fire in 1992." There were two side-by-side canvases in one frame: before and after the destruction.

The first showed the exterior rising from a mountainside like part of the stone itself. Narrow arched windows that caught the light, glinting like shards of ice against a darker facade. The terraced steps led up to heavy doors bound in black iron. It looked like a fortress cloaked in snow and silence.

On the right side, a scar carved into that same mountain. A collapsed roof in jagged sheets, leaving exposed blackened beams jutting skyward like broken teeth. No longer windows reflecting light, just hollow sockets rimmed in soot. Empty and broken.

"Arson?"

"Doubtful. No foul play was detected, so it was assumed to be an accident."

"Well, it's too bad it's gone. It looked beautiful."

He nodded. "We used to call it the library. It held all of our family's mission archives on Mum's side, along with other important documents and books. Well, outside of the codex kept here. Whenever you visited Pops, he used to share stories with you all the time, including . . ." His eyes abruptly flew to the floor, and he staggered back, bumping into me while cursing.

"What is it?"

The war of indecision in his expression didn't bode well. "Let me talk to Gideon first. And Mum and Dad. I don't want to say something I shouldn't and—"

"No secrets. Please. I'm drowning in questions. Just talk to me. Do you think that's why I was in Rome? Something to do with that burned-down vault, and that's why I lost my memories?"

He dragged both hands through his hair, messing it up. He began muttering in another language, and of course, he chose one I didn't know.

"What is it?"

His jaw and neck muscles strained as he lowered his hands to his hips. "Not sure how I could forget this, but you brought up the library to me a little over two months ago." He blinked a few times, and every second he kept me in the dark had me losing it. "I didn't think much of it then, but you told me all the books and archives may not have been destroyed in the fire, and there was one you were looking for."

"I was looking for a book?"

He backed up against a statue, nearly knocking it over before spinning and catching it just in time. "Pops's father was a brilliant scientist. He created weapons for those who fought on the front lines instead of going out himself. He was always doing experiments. He was even involved in different nuclear programs during the Cold War."

He really needed to spend more time with people instead of computers, because his slow roll of information in suspenseful fashion would have me unhinged and snapping in 2.5 seconds if he didn't hurry.

"One of the books destroyed in the fire belonged to Pops's father, and it held a collection of formulas that'd prove dangerous in the wrong hands. Well, so we were told, at least. But you shared with me Pops hinted at the fact that it may not have been in the library during the fire, because he liked to go over his father's work from time to time. You said he'd been cryptic like always, but you wanted the book because there was . . ." He swallowed. "A formula to erase our memories."

Chills crept across my skin like a thousand little blisters pricking me all at once. "I'm sorry, but *what?*"

He closed his eyes like he was mentally retrieving a folder of information to share. "The compound requires our blood to activate it. It was *allegedly* invented by our great-grandfather in case of an emergency. It was supposed to be a way to safeguard secrets without having to kill yourself. It was meant to wipe only your personal memories while leaving your imagination and skills intact." He slowly opened his eyes. "In case someone captured and questioned you, you couldn't reveal anything, because you didn't know anything. *But* you could still fight your way free, if possible."

Shock propelled me back, and it was my turn to bump into something. Julian was faster, and he saved the heirloom from crashing as I tried to process what he was saying. "How in the world could you forget we had that conversation?"

"I know, I know. Shit." He held up his hand, patting the air. "I never believed it was legit, even if you did, which is probably why Pops didn't waste much time talking to me or Gideon about it." He palmed his jaw, eyes lost to the ceiling as if in deep thought.

I took a calming breath, trying to dial down my pulse. "I'm literally a testament to the fact it is real and it did work. It's not weird science, but *real* science. That book has to exist, and I must have found out."

"I'm sorry, I just don't believe it."

How could he not when I was standing in front of him like this?

"For argument's sake, let's say it is," I rushed out as worry battled its way forward, triumphing over any lingering state of calm. "Why would I want a drug to take away someone's memories in the first place?"

"*If* it's legit, then it wouldn't work on anyone else. It was designed only for our family. Gotta have our DNA to activate it *and* for it to work on ya. It was never meant to be weaponized against people. Well, so Pops said."

"Then what if I was planning to use it on myself?"

"No damn way. You'd never." He set both hands on my shoulders, waiting for my eyes to meet his. "And I know that because I know why you were after the book."

What else was he holding back from me, and what was with all the slow reveals? Was he making all this shit up for some reason? I had no idea what to believe at this point.

"You hoped if the book was still out there and the drug was real, you could reverse engineer the formula to give someone back their memories, someone you knew who'd lost them."

This is all just . . .

"I've been so wrapped up in my own thing lately, and then you were taken and someone used my source code . . . and I'm sorry I didn't think of this sooner."

"Does Gideon know I was looking for it?"

"No, you asked me not to tell him. You said he'd brush it off as a waste of time. A mythical unicorn thing or whatnot. Like me, he thought it was BS. And Mum and Dad? They won't even talk about the library. It's an off-limits conversation when it comes to them. Before you ask why, I don't know."

I let my hands fall like lifeless limbs to my sides. Liquid burned my eyes, but no tears came. "This seriously *can't* be a coincidence that I was looking for that drug and lost my memories."

"What's going on?" Gideon's deep voice jarred our attention to the entranceway. He was casually leaning in the doorway. When neither of us answered, he straightened, his expression changing from calm to grim. "What is it?"

Julian walked around and blocked me like a shield as he quickly shared what we'd been discussing.

I remained quiet as I searched for the backbone I'd temporarily had against our mother upstairs.

Gideon's already strong broodiness developed a severe case of brood*ier* with every word Julian said.

"It all adds up now," I said once Julian was done talking. "The tracker. The source code. The knowledge of the book and that drug. You were right about something, that only someone close to our family could have pulled this off, and possibly"—I swallowed—"this is somehow my fault if I was chasing that book and left you all in the dark for some reason. Our mother is right about me."

Julian abruptly turned and faced me, but he couldn't deny that last part, could he?

"I don't think I can stay here, I'm sorry. I—I feel partially responsible but also afraid, because someone close to us had to be involved."

I didn't know who to trust when it came to my family, including my brothers, but I did know where my gut said I belonged. With Audrey, and most of all, with the man I couldn't stop thinking about, even if he didn't like me.

I stared at the painting of our family crest. *"In tempore veritas."* A tear escaped as I translated in a hoarse voice, my mind made up about what to do. "In time . . . there is truth."

CHAPTER TWELVE

Reed

"I need to talk to you." Hollis latched on to my forearm and tugged. "Alone."

From inside the office, I surveyed my teammates, preparing myself to say no to her, but she squeezed her request right into my flesh, her nails digging in.

"Guess it's urgent?" I said like a question as Alex gave me a funny smile and shrug. "I'll follow ya, but mind letting go?"

She glanced at my arm and cursed, releasing me. "I left a mark."

You always do. I waved off her apologetic expression, forcing a smile. "Where would you like to—"

"The bedroom." She didn't wait for my objection and took off, clearly assuming I'd do as promised and follow.

Great. Perfect. Just where I want your murderous older brother to find me alone with you. I dragged a palm down my face, muttered an, "I'll be right back," to the team, then did what I was told and met up with her in the bedroom.

It was my first time seeing her today; I'd only caught her staring down at me from the window this morning, and that was it. What happened that had her needing me ASAP and alone?

Hollis shut both doors behind me, then whirled around and declared, "I'm coming to Charleston with you and your team. With the time difference, if we leave soon, we can make it before nightfall."

"Whoa, slow down." I held up my hands like that'd do any good. I knew damn well once Hollis made up her mind, she became an in-motion human wrecking ball, swinging away. And I was currently her target.

She stepped in front of me like she was ready for a face-off. "I can't stay here, and my family plans to kick you out. You know too much already. They won't even let you sleep under the same roof as me and—"

"We know absolutely nothing. Neither do you, unless something changed this morning." I folded my arms, doing my best to stand my ground so she wouldn't knock me over, or the wind out of me.

"Tristan—you know about him. That's apparently too much." She flung her arm wide, narrowly missing whacking me in the jaw. The woman was dangerous for my physical and mental health.

I walked back a step, free and clear of her hands. I didn't need to be punched again, or have nail marks in my skin like a brand. Not that I wouldn't mind her—

Shit.

Another step back was needed. Unfortunately, I had nowhere else to go but up against the doors.

"We have contingency plans if they try to force us to leave. Gideon already tried that in your hotel room in Rome."

"You were in my hotel room?" she asked, her voice softening a touch.

"Of course."

"And?"

"No sign of any dude having also been in your suite," I said, assuming that was what she was asking, that her family had raised the whole "off with a guy" story to her at some point.

"Apparently, I haven't dated since college, and the only guy I seem to think I, um . . ."

My hand went up, begging her not to finish that dangling thought.

She discarded a pent-up breath. "I'm sorry. Julian overwhelmed me in our family's secret lair, and I learned some things, so I don't feel"—she began unbuttoning her gold blouse as if this were the most normal thing to do right now—"like myself. Crazy, since I don't know the real me, but you get the idea, right?"

"And you're taking off your shirt because . . . ?" I had no choice but to close the gap between us and take hold of her wrist, halting her.

The glimpse of that nude lacy bra that couldn't contain the swell of her breasts would live rent-free in my head forever.

"Oh my gosh, I didn't even realize I was doing it." She clutched the fabric. "This is my mother's, and it feels wrong to wear. I just wanted it off."

I unhanded her, but I wasn't ready to back up, worried she might reopen her blouse and kill me.

"Someone tossed your hotel suite and took a knife to your Prada, but I threw all your clothes back in it. I brought it here." I hiked a thumb over my shoulder. "I'll go find it if you promise to keep your top on in the meantime."

"Someone searched my hotel room?"

"So, no one told you that?"

She shook her head.

"Your gun and purse were missing, and if you had a laptop or tablet—gone too." I turned to the side, ready to exfil and hunt down her suitcase.

"I *really* didn't do this to myself, did I?" she whispered as if that'd ever been a possibility and it had finally hit her that she was innocent.

She lost hold of the silk while stumbling backward, sending me forward yet again to keep her shirt and my shit together.

By the grace of God, I got to her in time before I got another eyeful of her gorgeous body. "What are you talking about?"

"I, um." Her lip slipped between her teeth. She was acting like a lost sheep, scared and alone, waiting to be rescued.

"How about I get your clothes first, then we talk after that?" I suggested, painfully aware of how close we were standing and also how it might look to anyone who walked in with me clinging to her shirt for dear life.

I closed my eyes, let go of her top, then turned for the door. "Be right back. Don't move." I hightailed it from the bedroom and made my way downstairs to the bag still in the hall where I'd left it.

Back to her room fast, grateful for no awkward bump-ins, I hurried and closed the doors behind me, only to go dead still when facing her.

Her back was to me, but her shirt and bra were on the bed. Her low-rise jeans were snug on her hips, showing off her narrow waist and tight body.

I cleared my throat, signaling I was there, since the closing of the doors hadn't alerted her. She had to be lost in her own world.

"Can you bring it to the bathroom? I'll change in there."

"Good idea." I went in and out fast, ready to get this over with. "All set," I announced, shutting my eyes to keep my sanity.

"Never seen a naked woman before?" A feminine huskiness slipped past her anxiety as she spoke.

And you're still with us. "No comment," I grumbled, catching a whiff of her as she approached. A different perfume than I was used to. More flowery, and probably her mom's.

I didn't open my eyes until I heard the door click shut. Didn't breathe until then, either. I went over to the window she'd watched me from earlier and propped my hand on the wall by it.

There were two security guards roaming the property while a gardener worked nearby. Quite the contrast. Rifles and flowers.

At the sound of the door opening, my back muscles flexed. "Decent?"

"Yes, and I'd apologize for not being myself, but then we'd just be beating a dead horse—and wow, I hate that expression. Remind me never to use it again."

"Noted." And why was I smiling? I dragged my free hand across my mouth, not ready to turn around. "So, back to what you were saying."

"About me joining you in Charleston?"

"Not happening." I faced her, finding her in black jeans and a fitted black tank top. She only needed her hair in a French braid like normal and to be in combat boots instead of flats, and she'd look like herself. I wasn't used to seeing her hair down around her shoulders like this, and the urge to tangle my fingers in it was pissing me off. "I was talking about the 'you really didn't do this to yourself' part." I even pulled out air quotes.

"Ah, that, yeah." She stared at my arm, the one that still held evidence she'd sunk her nails into my skin. "I was searching for my great-grandfather's book. Inside it were formulas. One of them, well . . . was designed to wipe our memories. He created it during the Cold War in case there was a need to protect secrets."

I tried to digest what she'd rushed out as if it were a completely normal conversation to have.

"I was trying to find that book for *that* specific drug, a drug that was never actually tested out, though."

What in the world? "You're saying your family had a drug that can do to you what happened to you?"

"I'm saying we did have it. The library-vault the book was allegedly stored in was burned down in 1992, but I told Julian I believed the book wasn't there at the time of the fire." She quickly added more details involving the vault and book, finishing with, "But I'm proof such a drug is real, aren't I?"

I didn't know what to think. "Why didn't Julian bring this up before now? It's kind of important."

"He said I asked him about it two-ish months ago, but he forgot all about it. Plus, he's been busy and distracted with something." She lifted a shoulder, a touch of defeat in her eyes.

She went to one of the two dressers in the room and rested her hands on it, bowing her head.

"All I know is that I can't be here right now. Julian's not telling me something about that book, and I think it's because Gideon doesn't want him to. Apparently, I didn't even want Gideon to know I was searching for it. Talk about a red flag."

What the hell?

"So nope, I don't trust anyone here. Why stay? Plus, I only feel safe with you."

Why'd I feel familiar to her when no one else did?

She pushed off the dresser and turned to face me. "I can't do this without you. If they make you leave and I have to stay here? I'm doomed. I can feel it in my gut."

"Hollis." That was the best defense I had. *A real winner, I know.*

"You're working this case even if they kick you out, yeah?"

I kept my distance, not trusting myself to be closer to her, and nodded.

"Wouldn't you rather be near me while you figure things out?"

"Of course." Shit, that came out far too fast.

"Good. It's settled."

What did I just walk into? Right, an ambush. "You can't stay with Audrey. She's pregnant and has a nine-year-old at home. You don't want to endanger them."

"She's pregnant?" Her eyes widened. "Well then." She massaged her chest with the heel of her hand. "Then what about staying with one of your other teammates?"

I gave her the reasons why it wouldn't work for Ryder and Trevor, and that left us with one option, and something told me she knew we'd land there eventually.

Well played. But also, no damn way would she be staying with me.

The fragile life I'd barely kept together for five years, nine months, and some change would collapse with her under my roof. Each piece would crash into a single, irreparable mess. All that hard work . . . gone in a flash.

"No, it's not possible. I'm sorry. I have no clue why you feel the way you do around me, but you can't bunk with me."

"Not *with you* with you." Her hand skated around to the back of her neck. "Spare bedroom?"

"Yes, I have one. No, you can't sleep in it." A hotel, maybe? Safe house, more than likely, *if* I were ever to agree. But my place? Absolutely not.

She had the audacity to close the space between us and touch me again, and my body had the *audacity* not to stop her this time.

Her fingers curled into my biceps, and she lightly squeezed her plea straight into my muscles.

"Hollis." Her name cracked from my lips like a broken sound yet again, regret buried tight into the two syllables, because I could see the future, and I was going to give in to her. And if she stayed with me—I knew myself, I'd screw up. I could barely be alone with her here, and we had her family and their arsenal down the hall. What would happen if she wandered into my bedroom at night and asked me to hold her hand again, and it turned into more?

"I need answers, and I'm worried my family won't just lie to your team, but to me, too. Looks like they already are. My mother, for sure. Now my brothers." She visibly shivered. "Who needs a physical vault when they seem to be one." She licked her lips, immediately drawing my eyes to her mouth. "My gut says that the book is the key to everything. How could it not be? From the sounds of it, someone beat me to finding it and they used the drug on me."

"Your brother say why you were looking for the drug in the first place?" If we could believe anything he said.

"While the drug is only supposed to work on our bloodline, I was hoping to use it on someone else. Well, to reverse engineer the formula so someone could get *back* their memories, not lose them."

My body went cold, and I set my hands on her wrists, ready to back away, because no . . . *No, it's not possible.*

"What's wrong?" she whispered as I released her, my stomach free-falling.

I didn't have a chance to answer because both doors flew open, and Catalina blew in like a storm, announcing, "You're not leaving." She pointed at me. "But your team is. President Bennett should be calling with marching orders any minute."

Hollis stood in front of me like a shield, not that I needed one. "If Jason leaves, I leave." She glanced back at me, hitting me with an apologetic look, then quietly added, "I mean Reed. If he leaves, so do I."

"You're choosing *him* over us?" The rage from her mother may have been concealed, but I could see a crack in her armor. A small one, but it was there.

But also, did I actually agree to her leaving with me?

"Yes, I'm sorry. While I don't think I did this to myself, it's clear that—"

"Of course someone betrayed you, and no, you didn't do this to yourself. And this has nothing to do with that bloody book, so just drop that nonsense," she cut in.

I couldn't help but align myself alongside Hollis, offering her my support even if I was still confused over how I wound up in this position. Was I going to let her stay with me in Charleston? *Shit.*

"You don't even want me here, do you? You want your daughter back, and at the moment, I'm not her." Her voice broke. "And if what happened to me *is* because of that book—"

"You have got to be kidding me." Catalina scoffed and looked up at the ceiling as if yelling at someone in her head. "So help me . . . my father and his love for telling stories." She lowered her gaze to Hollis. "Everything was destroyed in that fire. *Nothing* survived."

"But he may have—"

"No, he didn't." She wouldn't even hear her daughter out. "Just. Let. It. Go."

All I could hear and see were red flags whipping in the wind at her remark.

Hollis stepped forward, not backing down. "You really think someone else created a drug just like the one in that book and used it on me? It's some big coincidence?"

"I do," her mother quickly responded, her tone tight. "Now, drop it."

No chance would Hollis let anything go. I knew that part of her was still there, even if she didn't remember herself.

"Just tell me one thing." Hollis eased her volume down slightly. "Did Tristan know about the library? The book?" There was no question who was facing off with her mother right now. The woman with a steel spine who could kill a guy with a broken champagne flute. "He knows about our trackers. He was at Julian's place last month and could've stolen the source code. So . . . what about the formulas in that particular book?"

"Yes," Catalina said through barely parted lips. "Because your grandfather is the one who raised Tristan in secret as his adopted son until he was eighteen, since I couldn't."

CHAPTER THIRTEEN

Hollis

"Who's Tristan's father? Why couldn't you raise him? Is my grandfather still alive?" Something told me I was pushing my luck in asking my mother those questions, but I had to try.

"My father died years ago." My mother's hazel eyes flicked to Reed standing quietly off to my side. She'd likely clam up in front of him; she'd probably already said more than intended as it was. "Once you were all eighteen, I told you the truth—that Tristan was your brother, not your grandfather's adopted son. And I didn't tell you who his father was before, so why in the world would I tell you now?"

"Are you really saying I grew up knowing Tristan, just not that he was my own blood?"

"I am. No one outside your siblings and father know the truth," she said calmly. "Well, and now your team," she added bitterly. "The less anyone knows about Tristan, the safer it is all around. That holds true now, just as it did last week, last year, and last bloody . . ." There was a slightly exasperated expression parked on her face, as if she was annoyed to be wasting her breath and time. "You get the idea."

"You're kidding me." Reed stepped forward. "Your son's father's identity is a secret even from your other children?"

"You're no one to judge," she deflected while looking him up and down. From his sneakers to his dark denim on up to the snug fit of his sleeves around his biceps. "We're done with this conversation, along with the idea my daughter is leaving here with a high school dropout."

"Excuse me?" The words burst fast from his lips, but his body remained locked tight and rigid.

"I don't know who you think you are," I interjected before she could spew any good cop, bad cop venom toward the man who was only there to do his job, "but I—"

"It's okay," Reed cut in, even going as far as to reach for me. His fingers skimmed down to my wrist before he held it, urging me to face him and ignore her. I could easily do that, no problem. "If she doesn't want you to leave with my team, then that's all the more reason why you *should*."

Relief loosened the hard knot in my stomach, untangling my nerves a bit at his words. *Thank God.* Before I could verbalize my gratitude, my brother strolled in.

"You can't be serious about leaving with them." Gideon peered at Reed's hold on my wrist before aligning himself with the woman he'd just protected me from pre-vault visit.

"I am serious." I swallowed, and Reed unhanded me so we could face the two problems in the way of my escape.

Reed may not have liked me, but he clearly wouldn't be bullied by my family and took his assignment to help me seriously. I owed him for this, especially after placing him in an awkward position last night with the whole sleeping-together question.

Gideon's jaw flexed as he approached us. He bent his head down, eyeing me while trying to rally, to get his breathing under control. This was the first time I'd seen him unhinged. I didn't recall him even being so bullish back on the street. "You can't leave. We're stronger together. You're in this mess because you went to Rome without me. So do you really think—"

"You don't know that for sure." Reed came to my defense and even went so far as extending his arm between my brother and I, then protectively guided me behind him. "You have no clue why she was there, and maybe she didn't tell you for a good reason."

"The threat is still out there, and—"

"That threat let her go, did they not?" Reed wasted no time in interrupting Gideon again, and when I peeked around Reed's hard frame, it was clear Gideon wasn't used to anyone confronting him like this. "Why take her and release her?"

Million-dollar question. Or, in my family's case, a multi-*billion*-dollar one.

"I have no damn idea, but neither do you. No guarantees they won't come after her again, and she's safer here." My brother attempted to get by Reed, but he moved right along with him, blocking me with his body.

"I have no plans to argue with you," Reed said steadily, lifting his hands. "Hollis is *not* your prisoner, but if you try and make her one, I won't hesitate to do what I do best, which is hostage rescue."

I still couldn't believe we'd gone from arguing about letting me leave with him, to him being a champion for exactly that.

When neither my brother nor mother spoke this time, I hesitantly rounded Reed's guard. The second Gideon's eyes connected with mine, it was easy to see that my decision was hurting my brother more than my mother.

"We don't know if you went missing because you were searching for a book that no longer even exists." The corner of Gideon's mouth lifted into a partial sneer, clear contempt for my twin at sharing that information with me. "Julian shouldn't have put those ideas in your head when you're currently . . ."

Yeah, best not to finish that sentence. "And it's better to leave me in the dark?" I set my hand on my chest. "I'm already deep in that dark place in my head, and I'll never escape if you keep secrets from me." I stared at our mother next, because those words were mostly for her after our brief conversation before Gideon breezed in full of vinegar and animosity toward the hero at my side.

"No one in this room did this to you." Gideon crossed his arms, the vein at the side of his neck visible. "You can trust me. All of us here."

"What about our cousins?" I challenged. "Uncles and aunts? Heck, what if one of them stole the book in 1992 and then burnt the place down themselves?"

"I'm looking into everyone, believe me," Gideon remarked.

"Until I can clear you from my own list, then your family and anyone who operates with you all remain a suspect," Reed said. "My team will run our own investigation free and clear of any potential interference from you and your family."

"Looks like I need to make another call to President Bennett," my mother warned, lifting her chin like he was beneath her, and after her heinous comment to him a few minutes ago, it was clear she believed that.

So help me, if I was ever like her before, then maybe I—

"Go ahead," Reed said, interrupting my thoughts. "Once we're off your premises, you have no say or authority over us or what we do."

My mother had no response to that. *Good.*

Reed turned toward me, clearly not intimidated by the two power-houses trying to control the situation. "This is what you want?" He went so far as to take hold of both my wrists as if he didn't despise me. "You're sure?"

"*Stay,*" Gideon said in a clipped tone, like a plea, before I could answer Reed. "I promise, I will find who did this to you."

"I believe you will," I forced out as Reed unhanded me. "But if they can't be here with us, then neither can I." A slight tremor moved through me as I finally peeled my eyes away from the man who was becoming my rock, and shifted to my brother.

Gideon rested a fist over his heart and ground out, "I may come across as ruthless and heartless to you, but I'd go to hell and back for you. Tell me you know that, that you believe me. I've only ever tried to keep you safe, to protect you."

I couldn't get the words out because I didn't know what to believe. I didn't want to hurt him, but I also didn't know him.

He tore both hands through his hair, something I'd only seen Julian do since waking up here yesterday. He was . . . rattled.

Catalina gripped his forearm and squeezed. "If your sister doesn't want to be with us, then so be it." She let him go, gave me one last look, then muttered on her way out, "Just like my father, I swear . . ."

Gideon faced forward, eyes boring into Reed now as he stroked his cheek and jawline with his knuckles. The man looked like he was contemplating murder. Target acquired.

He erased the space between them as if ready to start his trail of dead bodies here with Reed.

"If something happens to my sister under your watch, so help me . . ." Gideon's voice dropped so low and deep that it even scared me as he grated out, "I won't hesitate to slit your throat and cut out your heart."

CHAPTER FOURTEEN

Reed

Charleston, South Carolina

I waited for Secretary Chandler's text message to finish decrypting so I could see if we had new marching orders. There was a chance POTUS would reroute us to a safe house instead of returning home.

We were already closing in on the last two turns for my street in our gated community, and it'd be too hard to reintroduce Hollis to Audrey, Chase, and the others only to pull her away five seconds later.

Though maybe a safe house would be better? I wouldn't have to live alone with her, only having Ranger as a barrier between us. Of course, ever since she woke up in Surrey on Friday, she'd been a lot less "bane of my existence" and far too something else I couldn't yet identify. I just knew it both worried and scared me.

"Text come through yet?" Ryder glanced at me as he slowed down, going over a speed bump.

"Finally, yeah." I read the message, shaking my head at the mission name Chandler had assigned it. "Operation Return the Crown," I muttered.

"But I *have* been returned." Hollis unbuckled and leaned forward, bracing the back of my seat. "And why am I being called a crown?"

Because you're a royal pain. I held back the joke I'd have said if she were herself. *Old you was a pain, at least.* Until she was herself again, I had to behave and monitor my tongue. It was known to unleash ugliness. I also had to do my best to stop touching her. I'd set my hands on her too many times already.

"I assume it has something to do with your family bloodline," Alex said when I'd yet to wrestle open my jaw and speak.

I'd done a decent job in keeping my distance from Hollis on the flight over, but we'd had an entire cabin of space between us. Now? About four inches, give or take.

"Yo, you good?" Ryder swatted the back of his hand against my chest, forcing me to face forward and drop my thoughts. "What'd Chandler say?"

That I'm screwed because she's staying with me. "The orders are to stick to the plan. Our neighborhood for now, and to be on standby in case we need to head to a safe house. He's concerned her family will intervene if we try keeping them in the dark by going into hiding. They may have let us leave without a fight, but that doesn't mean they're not monitoring our every movement." I could feel Big Brother, in the very literal sense, watching us.

"Sounds about right, and I don't even know them," she said softly. "I assume Chandler agrees it's safe for me to be here, though, because if someone went to the trouble of ensuring I was found, then why come after me again, right? You, um, alluded to that back in that face-off with my brother this morning."

"Right." I'd also discussed that with my team as to why it was okay for her to leave with us. They'd stared at me with shocked expressions over the fact I was volunteering to have Hollis live with me. Yeah, well, I'd clearly lost it.

"Am I also bait? Do we *want* someone to come after me so we can finally get some answers?"

"Not bait, no." I stupidly turned and put eyes on her, because I was a glutton for punishment. "You're not a damsel in distress. If someone does show up, you can hold your own."

"I don't know about that." She slumped back in the seat. "Sometimes I feel helpless and even understand why my mother can't stand the look of this weaker version of me. Other times?" She lifted one shoulder. "I feel like if it was me against the world, I'd actually have a fighting chance."

"The second one," Alex said before I could find the right words. "That's you. The first?" He side-eyed her. "That's just normal to feel that way, given your situation. Ignore whatever your mother said, will ya?"

My sentiments exactly. And now that I'd met Hollis's mother and siblings, I was pretty sure I understood why she enjoyed pretending to be normal and hanging out with Audrey so much. It was an escape from not only the pressure of her family but also probably from having to carry the weight of the world on her shoulders. I knew that feeling all too well.

"Anything else from Chandler?" Alex asked.

I reread the text. "Same orders as we had in the UK. Find who took her, and if her memories don't return naturally, then figure out a way to get them back."

"So, you all have to be scientists along with being operators to help me?" There was a touch of both guilt and frustration there.

"We'll be whoever you need us to be," I promised without hesitation, but my tone was huskier than it needed to be for a man speaking to an off-limits woman I supposedly couldn't stand.

Alex shot me the look of the century, too. He'd heard what I said and *how* I'd spoken, and now I couldn't shake our conversation from the office in Surrey. I *had* lost it when she was taken, then lost it a second time when learning her memories were gone.

Prayers and duct tape may have held me together before, but I'd need an intervention by God to get me through the rest of this mission with Hollis living at my house.

Ryder broke the silence while adjusting his rearview mirror toward Hollis. "Tonight, let's just get some shut-eye so we're fresh to go over everything tomorrow."

She slid farther back in her seat, and I turned myself around again, just in time to see Audrey, Chase, and Ranger waiting for us outside my house.

"We'll swing by your place tomorrow and get started on the case," Ryder added while parking in my driveway.

"I take it I'm rarely at the center of a case, more like the one helping solve them." Her voice was softer that time. I hated this for her. Hated it so damn much I couldn't put it into words.

"You'll be okay and back to kicking ass in no time." Trevor joined the conversation for the first time from the third row, which had to be a tight fit for him back there.

The back doors opened, and I was surprised Hollis didn't take a minute to steel herself before facing off with people she was supposed to remember but couldn't.

"Hold up," Ryder said as I unbuckled and returned my phone to my pocket.

He waited for the others to clear out, and I could feel a lecture coming. Already got one from Alex yesterday, I sure as hell didn't need another from my team leader.

I kept my eyes on the window, watching Audrey clinging to Hollis, and Hollis shocked me by returning her hug.

"You really okay with this?" Ryder finally asked after letting me stew a little too long.

"Of course I'm not. You know how I feel about her." Well, how I wanted everyone, including myself, to *think* I felt about her, at least.

"You're not a people person, man." He followed up with a quick, "Sorry," to what I didn't take as an insult; he was only telling the truth. "*But* she's going to need you to be one, so are you—"

"I'm not sure of anything." I left behind the calm mental state I'd somehow been in when facing off with Gideon a few time zones ago.

Ryder removed his ball cap and tossed it on the dash. "Is there something you're not telling me? You've seemed off these past few days."

"Nope," I said through clenched teeth, going for the door handle. "I'll do what I have to do for the sake of the mission. Survive living with her for a few days, or however long I have to." I forced a tight-mouthed smile. "Have I ever let you down?"

He angled his head, scrutinizing me like I'd gone mad.

I mean . . . maybe I have? Because my house was a short walk away from where we were parked, and I was starting to sweat bullets now that we were actually here. It was a reality, not just some wild idea she'd proposed back in Surrey.

"Your wife is waiting for you. Go to her, will ya?" I gestured with my head in the general direction of somewhere else, hoping he'd change his mind about riding my ass. Because yes, there was a problem. But no, he couldn't help. "So, if you'll excuse me, I have a woman to babysit that is more than capable of protecting herself." I shoved open the door, but he parked his hand on my arm in a request not to get out.

"Your mood went from zero to sixty the second we pulled into the neighborhood, but you've been acting cagey since England. So if you plan to continue working this mission, then you better tell me what the hell is going on, and right damn now."

Great, this really was turning into Alex 2.0 when it came to questioning my ability to operate with a clear mind.

Now I had no choice but to tell him *part* of why I was so out of my head and hope he'd accept it.

I released the door handle as hot air filled my lungs. A deep breath later, I rushed out, "My father has dementia, and he doesn't remember who I am."

My heart was speed-racing as I stared at Hollis petting my dog and smiling as if her world hadn't turned upside down, and she wasn't turning mine that way right along with hers.

I slowly turned to face him, to share a secret fear I'd been hanging on to ever since this morning. My voice was raw as I forced out, "I'm terrified she learned somehow about my dad's condition, and she was searching for a cure to help him."

CHAPTER FIFTEEN

Hollis

The moment I crossed the threshold, it was as if Reed physically wrapped me in his arms. He hadn't actually touched me, not even a brush of the hand, but his presence was impossible to ignore. Silent, solid, and steady. Like gravity itself keeping you grounded.

The security system beeped as it armed, and he dropped our bags by the door. For whatever reason, the sight of worn-out boots, sneakers, and a leash hanging up made me smile. Maybe because it was much homier than that mansion in Surrey. It was also oddly familiar, which didn't make sense.

"You okay after all that hugging out there?" he asked in a slightly teasing tone as he began filling Ranger's water bowl.

"The kid is cute. The best friend? Not so bad herself. Seraphina and Eden are nice, too. Well, from what little I gathered."

He added kibble to Ranger's bowl next and washed his hands. "They are."

I expected him to offer me some food, too, but he probably didn't know I hadn't touched either meal served on the flight here. He'd avoided me like the plague on the private plane they'd borrowed from some Irish billionaire friend of a friend. Sebastian-something sent his regards, because apparently *I* also knew him.

Reed turned toward me, resting his hands on his hips, an uneasy expression crowding his face. He was clearly uncomfortable now that we were alone.

Considering that the last time it was just us I'd absentmindedly taken off my shirt in front of him, I didn't blame the guy for worrying what I might do next. In my current state, his guess was as good as mine.

"So," I breathed out, just as nervous. "How about a tour?" I'd never asked for one at Surrey, but in my gut, I was pretty sure I knew I wouldn't be staying there for long.

"Yeah, uh, sure." Reed began walking, and Ranger stayed behind to scarf up his food.

I trailed after him until he stopped and opened a door.

"I converted the garage into a gym and added a sauna." He flicked on the light. "You're welcome to sweat it out when you're up for it." He motioned to the stand-up wooden box tucked beside his equipment.

"Is the sauna big enough for two people?"

"It is. You know, if you want room to stretch out." He caught my eyes, only to quickly look away, jerking his head back like he hadn't meant to do that, then he killed the lights before I could better examine what appeared to be an armory in there.

"So, am I the sweat-it-out type? Do I like saunas? Working out?" I asked as we continued with his tour.

"You are," he confirmed as we passed by a closed door. "My bedroom." He motioned to the next door on the same side of the hall. "And the guest room is here."

"I feel like most single guys wouldn't have a guest room, so I'm lucky you do."

"What makes you think I'm single?"

"Something tells me you wouldn't let a woman stay with you if you were in a relationship, but what do I know?"

The side of his mouth lifted, like he was fighting a smile and to call me a smart-ass.

"Well, with your room next to mine, I guess I'll have to do my best not to keep you up at night." I winked, because you know, why not keep making things awkward between us every time we were alone together? It was like it came second nature to me, and that thought had me realizing: *Maybe I really am in here somewhere, trying to wake up and claw my way back to the surface.*

"And what do you do at night that'd be loud and might keep me awake?" Either he hadn't realized I'd been joking, or he was slipping into normal default mode and acting how he would've around me pre–memory loss. Regardless, the rich huskiness in his tone struck a nerve, but in a good way. It delivered a bolt of heat to my stomach that kept on going down.

"Pretty sure I was teasing, sorry. Old me hijacked my voice. There's a good chance it'll happen again." I innocently lifted one shoulder. "I assume that means I'm moving in a positive direction of remembering who I am whenever that happens, though."

"The real you showing up from time to time might make it harder for me to follow Ryder's orders." He clasped the door handle. "I'm supposed to be on my best behavior and play nice with you."

"Right. I, uh, keep forgetting we don't like each other. Won't be easy to live with me."

"You have no idea how hard it'll be." His voice shouldn't have slid across my skin like silk, continuing to warm me up in places that had no business being warm right now, *but* it did.

I licked my lips, and he tracked the movement without missing a beat. We remained like that, just stuck in the moment, and all I could think about was our conversation in the office.

"Your bedroom," he prompted in a low voice, shaking his head as if trying to pull both of us free of a silent but dangerous storm. He opened the door without another word and turned on the light.

There was a queen bed with a plain gray bedspread, nightstand, and dresser. Simple, but it'd work.

"Audrey ordered the furniture, insisting I might have a visitor one day. Picked out the bedding and the picture, too."

A little *hmph* noise left my lips as I mindlessly fidgeted with the tail of my French braid that I somehow muscle-memoried my way into pulling off on the flight here.

I let go of my braid to chase away the goose bumps pebbling my skin as I studied the photo of a desert sandstorm over the bed, feeling caught up in the harsh winds myself.

"You'll need to use my bathroom for a decent shower, unless you want to use the one in the hall where I give Ranger his baths."

"While I don't mind sharing with Ranger, something tells me he likes his space. But does his dad? How are you at sharing?"

"Horrible." A wolfish grin crossed his face, and he immediately brought his hand over his mouth to physically wipe it away.

At the embarrassing growl coming from my stomach, I startled free of my thoughts.

"You not eat on the plane?"

"I was too stressed out about the whole turning-my-back-on-my-family thing, even if this is where I want to be."

"You need to eat." That sounded very order-like, and I didn't even mind.

"Well then . . . are you cooking, or are we ordering in? In my dream, I wasn't a good cook, and something tells me that's true."

He grimaced as if I'd somehow offended him. "What dream?"

Shit, I wasn't ready to talk about that yet. It'd only make him ten times more uncomfortable than he clearly already was. "Nothing, just nonsense." *Now I'm lying, so this is going great.*

He closed the space between us and started to reach for me but stopped himself. "You okay?" he asked while curling his fingers into his palm at his side.

Nope. I coughed up a plausible excuse to avoid the truth. "Jet lag."

He checked his watch. "I need to keep you up for another hour or two so you don't screw up your sleep too much."

Something told me the old me would tease and joke, *Keep me up, how?* while lifting my brows a few times. "Might need a shower to wake me up, then."

"Wash up while I fix dinner." He caught me off guard, taking a knee by the bed. He retrieved a black metal box from under it. "There's also a gun safe like this one in my room if you need to access a weapon." He told me the four-digit code while punching it in, then stood and offered me the weapon.

I didn't feel any hesitation to accept it. It was familiar. Painfully so. Part of me wished it didn't feel so natural to hold such a thing. *I've killed people with these things. Close kill count to Gideon's, even.* That last part was still hard to digest.

"Remember how to use it?"

I shivered, handing it back to him. "Unfortunately."

"At my old place, I used to sleep with a Glock under my pillow. With Chase living down the street and coming over so often, I have to keep everything locked up." He put it away and returned to stand before me. "I have a lot more weapons in the garage. I'll show you tomorrow, just in case."

"I figured those were gun safes, not tool chests," I teased.

"What, don't take me as handy?" He smirked, then quickly washed that smile away with his hand once again, as if pissed he kept having that reaction around me.

"Mm. Something tells me you're also good with your hands." So help me, I even followed the length of one slightly visible vein down his forearm and to his big, masculine hand.

"You really can't help yourself, can you?"

Neither can you, mister, I wanted to hit him back with, because why the sexy rasp and hooded eyes?

"Don't answer that," he said before I could summon a worthy response. "Just go. Get naked." He cursed. "Shower. I mean, shower." He pinched the bridge of his nose and hung his head, muttering something incoherent. "I'm jet-lagged, too. Forgive me."

I waited for his eyes before whispering, "You're forgiven."

He gave me a tight-mouthed nod, like he was trying to soldier forward. "I'll grab your luggage and put it in my room for now." He breezed around me in a hurry to get to the hall, and I quietly followed him. "I'll check with Audrey to make sure you don't have any food allergies before I cook."

I paused in the doorway, and when he turned, he nearly slammed into me. He snatched my wrist as if worried I'd fall over.

Why was it that anytime he touched me, even the slightest bump, an unexplainable zing of connection hummed under my skin? I didn't believe my mother, that I wanted this man because he didn't want me. No, that wasn't what this was. It was innate. Natural, because I couldn't remember who I was, but the feeling was still there just as I knew God was real.

Reed's thumb skimmed the line of my wrist as if desperate not to let go, before releasing me.

"That's thoughtful of you to check for any allergies. I forgot about that possibility."

"Of course." He backed up two steps, like he was worried he might accidentally touch me again. "Can't go into anaphylactic shock on me. Gotta keep you alive, right?" A lopsided smile came and went fast. "I, uh, should also have another look around the property and ensure it's secure before I cook."

"Good idea." I pointed to the ceiling. "You think my brothers hacked a satellite to spy on us?"

He quietly nodded, then tore his hand through his dark hair, which was thick enough to tangle your fingers in. "My room is all yours." He quickly tacked on, "For now," then whistled, and Ranger came barreling down the hall, nearly flying into us from excitement. "Stay with her." He turned back to me, shooting an apprehensive look. "Not going to fall in the shower and hit your head, are ya?"

"Only if you think that'll help knock my memories back into place?"

He rolled his eyes but was fighting another smile.

"And unless you plan to keep an eye on me every second, which means watching me shower, sleep, and—"

"I get it," he agreed. "Just be safe, okay? Last thing I need is to come rescue you while you're—"

"Naked?"

He propped his palm on the wall at his side, his attention moving to Ranger wagging his tail between us.

"You're sure there's no us?" The words tumbled free of their own accord, and I had no one to blame but Sleeping Beauty somewhere deep inside me.

"I promise you, there's no us. And there's one thing you're going to learn about me while here . . . I'm not a liar."

"So when you say we don't like each other, that means you were being honest?" I'd meant to save this confrontation for another time, but here we were anyway.

His mouth tightened around whatever words he wanted to say; he just quietly stared at me as if fighting an invisible enemy with the power of his mind.

"I'm sorry. We don't have to do this. You had my back with my family, and you brought me here. I should just be thanking you right now, not giving you a hard time."

He pushed off the wall, jaw strained beneath sexy stubble as he remarked in a low, even-toned voice, "If you weren't giving me a hard time . . . then I really would be worried about you." He turned and left after that, and I waited until he was out of my line of sight before Ranger and I went into his bedroom.

I kept the door unlocked so he could drop off my bag, then went into the bathroom.

After my shower, I was sadly still the same. Confused and a little brokenhearted at how things had gone with my family as well.

Aside from my bra, panties, and perfume, I couldn't find anything appropriate to sleep in. Silk nightgowns that barely covered my panties would give the man an ulcer. On a whim, I decided to invade his space and check out his clothes for something comfortable to wear.

I caught Ranger staring at me as I rummaged through a drawer, head tipping left, then right.

"I know it looks like I'm being a bad girl, but I promise, I'm trying to be good," I said defensively, landing on a T-shirt that looked big enough to pass for a nightgown. Hopefully, it'd be Reed- and Ranger-approved.

The tee smelled like fresh linen, *not* sexy man, which was probably for the best. I was already intoxicated with him as it was, for reasons I didn't understand. Breathing him in all the time, too? Bad idea.

Barefoot, my French braid still intact from the body-only shower, I went over to the door, mentally preparing myself to face him. "Ready to have my six in case your daddy gets upset about me wearing his shirt?" I asked Ranger, smiling.

He yelped, going to his hind legs to use his front paws to pat the air.

"I'll take that as a yes"—I went for the door—"and not a warning that I'm about to get myself in trouble."

CHAPTER SIXTEEN

Reed

The kitchen was too damn quiet. Just me, the boiling water for pasta, and the faint crackle of the stove as I heated the sauce.

I grunted at the silence and grabbed my portable Bose speaker, pairing it with my phone as a new notification popped up on my work cell. A group text.

Ryder: I called in a favor to the Costas to see if they have anyone they trust in Italy to check with the staff at Hollis's hotel. Constantine was already in Italy with his family, so he's personally heading to the hotel tomorrow morning.

We'd relied on help from the billionaire family a few times before. I was relieved they could be of service now. Not only were they rich and connected, but they were also former operators themselves.

Ryder: Constantine's checking in with his contacts there. Enemies, too. If anyone there knows anything, they'll tell him.

Me: Good. What about X-Man?

We had orders from above not to mention Tristan's name via text or over the phone, not even through encrypted messages, so we'd settled on an unoriginal code name.

Ryder: Hard to ask Constantine about X-Man when I'm not allowed to talk or text his name.

Shit. Jet lag was messing with me. Or I was just off because the woman I'd been telling myself I hated the last four months was in my shower.

Alex: You talk to the secretary yet about pulling in FFS on this too?

Falcon Falls Security had helped us on cases before, and they had direct ties to not only Secretary Chandler but also the president himself.

Ryder: FFS is already aware of what's happening since Trevor reached out to his cousin about when she was taken and lost her memories. Falcon is ready to join if they get the greenlight from Chandler.

At least we had a few more heavy hitters in the world of special operations on our side. Both Falcon Falls and the Costas *also* worked with a secret organization known as The League that battled criminals on that side of the globe.

The Irishman that was pretty much in charge of The League fortunately had a private jet in London and had lent it to us today so we could make a rushed exit without too much pushback from Hollis's family. We'd also brought him up to speed on the situation, and if he heard any chatter tied to our op, he'd let us know.

If we were going to go up against one of the wealthiest and most powerful families in the world—Hollis's own flesh and blood—in a race to get to the truth, we needed all the help we could get.

Me: And for now, what do you want me to do?

Ryder: Just keep an eye on her. Keep her comfortable.

Yeah, she was comfortably naked in my bedroom.

Trevor: Your wife coming to church in the morning? Eden and Chase are asking.

Ryder: Yeah. Could you keep an eye on her while Alex & I work some leads at Reed's?

Trevor: Of course.

I set aside my work phone, trying to remember what I'd been about to do before the group text. A strange twinge of fear shot through me that I was becoming forgetful. No, this wasn't some sign I'd be like my dad one day, dammit.

I shook my head, guilt hitting me for having that concern when Hollis had lost her entire life overnight.

Music. Right. I opened Spotify on my personal phone. Audrey had confirmed Hollis had no allergies and liked Italian—which made sense, because I'd never met anyone in the world who didn't love it—but I hadn't thought to ask what kind of music she preferred. *I guess we'll figure that part out together.*

I hit shuffle on my repeat-worthy playlist as a solo text from Ryder popped up on my personal line. He was checking on me since I'd unburdened half my issues on him thirty minutes ago.

Me: I'm fine. Worry about her, not me.

Me: And before you remind me, I'm being as nice as possible, so relax there, too.

I ignored his incoming response and went for a beer, needing something to take the edge off. The last thing in the world I wanted to think about right now was my father, or the possibility there was even a remote chance Hollis had been trying to help him.

I nearly choked while guzzling the beer when I spotted Hollis on approach, walking cautiously into the kitchen. I slowly set down the bottle and braced myself on the counter, worried I was hallucinating. Though that'd be preferable to her physically being in front of me.

"What are you . . . ?" I couldn't finish my line of thought, because she'd stolen my damn breath.

Her cheeks were flushed, hair still in that sexy braid thing, and she was wearing one of my old army T-shirts that barely skimmed her mid-thighs. Hopefully, she had shorts under it. And a bra.

Ranger flopped down on her bare feet, tail thumping like he expected a treat. *Or* forgiveness for letting her dig through my dresser without warning me first.

"I was in the mood for pajamas after my shower." She rolled her shoulders back, casually shrugging. "Unfortunately, all I had to sleep in were things that'd be inappropriate to wear to dinner."

My hand slid to the edge of the counter's overhang to get a grip, and fast.

"Hope you don't mind." She didn't give me a chance to address her wearing my shirt as a nightgown. She glanced at the stove, then back at me. *"Italiano?"*

"Me? Or the food?"

She smiled. "Both?"

I let go of the counter and dragged a hand down my face as if I could literally scrub away the visual of her standing in my kitchen like this. "Yes and yes," I finally answered while emptying a box of ziti into the boiling water. "Sort of. The food is an Americanized version of Italian. And I guess you could say so am I. Third gen. Barely qualify anymore."

"Mm." She hovered just behind me as I set down the spoon. "Well, I learned I'm a mutt. There's a lot going on in this package."

And that package is perfect. Too damn perfect, which was why I needed to keep my back to her.

I jolted at the feel of her hand coming down to rest on my shoulder, but I didn't dare turn around.

I squeezed my eyes closed, inhaling her scent. She must've sprayed herself with that Baccarat Rouge 540 perfume, the one I'd found in her hotel bathroom in Rome.

I sucked in another deep breath, the pasta sauce battling with the sexy fragrance. The perfume was a clear-cut winner. Now I'd never want to wash that shirt.

"I don't think anyone's ever worn my clothes before," I said under my breath—and shit, that thought was supposed to remain in my head.

"Oh." That sound had my eyes opening, and I stupidly turned to face her because I had to know if her mouth was still rounded into the same shape of that sound.

There was no shape or sound, just green eyes sharp on me that were capable of ripping me apart, and I wouldn't know how to put myself back together again after she had her way with me.

"Want me to take it off?"

"Funny," I grunted.

"I didn't mean in here." She came over and stirred the pasta. It took all my restraint not to stand behind her, trail my hands up her silhouette, and nuzzle my face at the side of her neck.

"No, it's fine. Wear it." I had to find a way to survive my time with her, knowing damn well this was the tip of the iceberg of things that'd get under my skin.

If I could do things I hated on the regular, like jump from planes and talk to people, then I could get through this woman being here.

"So, you've never had a girlfriend wear your stuff? Never borrowed a hoodie from you?" Spoon down, she turned around, and there wasn't enough space between us for me to think clearly. "Jason?" she prompted when I ignored a question I had no intention of answering. "I'm sorry I keep accidentally calling you that. Feels like second nature. I don't even know why you don't prefer it but—"

"It's my father's name. I'm technically a junior." My jaw locked tight at the fact I'd just shared that with her. She'd asked me about my name before, and I'd brushed her off and changed the subject. Why on earth I hadn't done that now was beyond me.

"Oh." There it was again, and this time, I managed to catch the O shape of her mouth hanging around for a second. "Would you like to talk about—"

"No," I snapped, and she gave me a small nod of surrender.

"How about I set the table?" she offered.

I nodded, still stuck in my head and not up for chitchat, especially while she was in my shirt and my father's name lingered in the air.

She went to work, softly humming along with the music while opening each of my cabinets in search of dishes.

I continued cooking, praying she wouldn't talk again or press me as to why I didn't like carrying my father's name as my own.

Once she had the table set, she surprised me by picking up my beer, taking a small sip like she was taste-testing it to see if it was her thing. I wasn't sure if she should be drinking in her condition, but I wasn't about to tell her what to do.

She winced and set it back down.

Doesn't like beer. Check. At least not the cheap stuff.

While I drained the pasta and mixed it with the sauce simmering on the stove, she made herself at home in the living room open to my kitchen. She went straight for my bar cart, snagging the bottle of Pappy Van Winkle.

Muscle memory?

I did my best to ignore her as she returned to the kitchen in search of a glass, but it was impossible *not* to notice her. She pushed up on her toes to reach my highest cabinet where I kept my whiskey and wineglasses, and her shirt lifted higher, revealing the fact she didn't have shorts on. I caught sight of the curve of her ass cheek and a hint of black satin—then forgot how to breathe again—before turning around to snatch my beer.

I lowered the lip of the bottle from my mouth just as Ranger shot me a funny look.

I'm only human. He didn't need to be a mind reader to know I was struggling here; who could blame me with Hollis strutting around in my shirt?

I carried the pan over and dished out some pasta with the sauce into our bowls. "More to your liking?" I asked as she took her first sip.

"Much." She sat opposite of where I set my bowl at the four-person table in front of the bay window, blinds closed.

"Makes sense, since it's yours." I grabbed my beer and joined her. "You brought it here last weekend. It was originally meant for Alex, but we wound up drinking it together instead. Right here at this table, in fact. You insisted I keep it here for the next time you break in and—"

"Break in?" she echoed.

"That's your thing. You never ring the bell. You like to sneak in to—"

"Drive you crazy?"

I nodded, fighting a smile at the memory of the one time she'd broken in and found me in only a towel.

She eyed me over the rim of her glass as she sipped. "Well, I have excellent taste." She traded her glass for a fork. After a few bites, she asked, "Where'd you learn to cook? For Americanized Italian, it's still fantastic. Not that I remember what *Italian* Italian tastes like." She licked some sauce from her lower lip.

"I had to learn to fend for myself as a kid or starve," I admitted in a stone-cold voice, hating opening up, sitting there shocked that I'd done it again. "Went for option one."

She studied me for a handful of seconds, then swept the pity under the rug as if understanding I'd hate that, too, and drank the bourbon and left well enough alone.

Thank you very much.

She even let us eat our meals in peace without another word, which I'd be eternally grateful for. She finished every last bite, seemingly satisfied with my food, which shouldn't have made me so damn happy, but it did.

She leaned forward, grabbing the crossword book from the other side of the table. "Valiant." She flicked the page with her finger. "The last one you didn't fill in, that's it." She grunted a breath of frustration. "It drives me crazy I know that and not anything about myself."

I honestly couldn't begin to imagine what that was like.

She swapped the book for her bourbon. "You have a lot of country on your playlist," she said as I left the table to pour plain pasta in Ranger's bowl before beginning to clean up.

"I do." Hopefully, she'd stop with the comments and questions and just let this night end as smoothly as possible.

But then she had to go and bend over to place our dishes in the bottom rack of the dishwasher.

I bit down on my back teeth and was a good boy and immediately looked away.

Ranger lifted his head from his bowl, and I swear, he was smiling. Loving every minute of my pain. "Payback, dude," I mouthed. *See if I give you any treats tonight.*

"So, where'd you grow up?"

I turned around, hating how much I didn't hate seeing her in only my shirt, standing there with a dish towel over her shoulder. Frustrated at myself, I went the asshole route in answering her. "You don't need to know where I'm from."

I removed the dish towel from her shoulder and tossed it on the counter. The woman was an heiress to wealth and power; her mother would have a coronary seeing her like this in my home.

"Well, did I know before?"

I stepped around her to close the dishwasher, then chucked my empty beer bottle in the recycling. "Nope."

"Did I ever ask?"

"Negative."

"You don't like talking about yourself because we *supposedly* dislike each other, or you don't talk about yourself in general?"

"We're just two different people. We'll never understand each other. There's no point in trying now." I thought back to her mother's words. The fact she'd done her research on me. Considered me beneath her. Beneath her daughter. "This situation is temporary. When you remember who you are, you'll walk away, and . . ." I cleared my throat. "I won't stop you."

She cast her eyes to the floor, forehead drawing tight. "Got it," she said in a strained voice, then turned and left me alone like I deserved.

Ranger rushed by me to go after her, whacking his tail against my leg in the process.

Yeah, I was a jerk.

But I couldn't go after her. No amount of chasing that woman would ever do any good.

When she remembered who she really was, she'd never want to be with a man like me.

So why the hell would I let myself fall for her and risk losing everything I'd worked for, only to get my heart broken?

CHAPTER SEVENTEEN

Hollis

I peeled off Reed's shirt and flung it onto the bed, fighting back tears as Ranger scratched at the door.

I hesitantly opened up, worried Reed might be out there, too. The coast was clear, so I let Ranger in and shut the door.

He sat by the bed, eyeing it as if waiting for permission to jump up. "It's okay, come on." I plopped down on top of his dad's shirt, and he curled up next to me, resting his head on my bare thigh.

I patted around in search of my phone and finally located it. Before I'd left my family's estate, Julian had given me a disposable cell with his number, our parents', Lyra's, and Gideon's programmed in it.

Lyra: You doing okay? I miss you.

I stared at her words, my chest aching at the fact I didn't miss her since she was a stranger to me.

Me: It's late where you are. Go to sleep.
Lyra: Well, I'm up. Talk to me.

In that case, I did have a question.

Me: Any chance you can tell me what happened when you went to my flat in London with Dad? Find anything?

Me: Or are you sworn to secrecy about all things related to me since I ran away?

Lyra: I don't trust Julian's not reading our texts for Grumpy Gideon. 😠

Grumpy? More like terrifying. Also, talk about an invasion of our privacy, but since the phone came from Julian, I shouldn't be surprised he'd be monitoring my conversations. Also my every movement, more than likely.

Lyra: Your flat was tossed. Your place in the South of France, too. Dad sent someone to check it since you were here and there two weeks ago.

Lyra: And, Julian, if you're reading this: 😀

Me: So, someone went through my stuff at the hotel and my two places over there. What were they searching for, and why not just ask me if they had me? Something doesn't add up, right?

Lyra: That's what I heard Dad say to Gideon. Unless they wiped your memories first before asking, assuming you wouldn't talk, even if interrogated.

Lyra: Right, Julian/Gideon? 🙄

Me: He's probably asleep, like you should be.

Lyra: None of us can sleep, you kidding?

Lyra: I wish you didn't leave, but I kind of get why you did. You wanted to be near your best friend (I'm a little jealous of her btw) and you've really grown close to those Delta operators this year, so … Nope, not toooo shocked you chose them over your family even though everyone's a stranger.

Me: I'm sorry.

That was the best I could do. I didn't know how to explain why I knew I was safe with Reed. Though, after his little speech to me in the kitchen, maybe I needed to rethink this living situation. It was possible he did hate me and I'd been misreading things, since I wasn't exactly in my right mind.

Lyra: It's okay you're closer to someone else. I'm still number 2 & Julian would give anything for that precious spot, wouldn't ya, J? 😑 He thinks because you're twins he should be your #1, but the man can't get his head out from behind his screen, so it's his fault.

Me: You're making me feel a little better, btw. Thank you.

Lyra: I'm here for you, always. Just worried about you.

Me: Something tells me we're not a family of worriers. Apparently, Julian smiles/laughs when nervous. Gideon, well . . . broods harder?

Me: What am I like?

Lyra: You pretend that everything is fine. No nervous laughter though. Fake it until you make it kind of thing.

Lyra: Sometimes you can't hide your feelings. It's rare, but it happens. Gotta be pretty bad for you to show any signs of . . .

Me: Weakness? That's what our lovely mother would call it, right?

Lyra: More like show signs you're actually human. Mortal. Sometimes I wonder 😀

Me: What about you? How do you handle things?

Lyra: Pretending everything is good, just like you do. Also, insomnia, which is why I'm up now. You went missing for a day, and I can't stop thinking about what happened to you while you were gone. Makes me sick to my stomach. So glad you're back, of course. But . . .

When she put it that way. *Missing for a day.* Why'd those words hit me like I was being stoned to death by them? Fear trickled in slowly before whipping me hard and fast, propelling me to the floor to stand.

No, no, no. Chills beat down my bare skin, and my teeth clicked together. I cupped my mouth as liquid gathered in my eyes while Ranger jumped from the bed to stand next to me, offering his paw and support.

It was Reed I needed, even if he could hardly stand me. He could calm me down, I knew it. Anything to stop the what-if scenarios playing in my head as I imagined what may have happened to me during those missing hours.

Me: You should try and sleep. I will too.

My teeth chattered and my hand trembled as I texted her.

Lyra: Love you.
Me: ♥

That was the best I could do for now. I tossed the phone on the bed and rushed to the door. I flung it open, only to stumble in surprise that Reed was there, hands braced on the doorframe.

"You're here," I sputtered, catching a tear with my tongue before launching myself into his arms.

He went stiff at the contact as I crushed myself against his hard frame, my cheek pressing tight to his chest, truly breaking down for the first time since I'd woken up in that coffin.

A few seconds later, he wrapped me in his arms, a hand to my bare back, another cradling my head.

Our first hug, apparently.

"I got you," he promised in a hoarse voice as I trembled, sobbing. He kept hold of me, letting me unleash every ounce of sadness I'd held back before this point, while whispering, "I'm not going anywhere."

My ugly cries mixed with the sounds of Ranger's worrying whimpers as he pawed my leg.

I wasn't sure how long we stayed like that—seconds or minutes—but when the tears slowed down, I lifted my head to look up at him.

He framed my face between his big hands and stared at me like I was the light at the end of *his* tunnel.

"Twenty-four hours gone," I said softly, hiccupping. "It just hit me that they . . ."

"They *what?*" His fingers gently pressed into my damp skin, and his thumbs caught more tears. "Do you remember something?"

I lightly shook my head. "I'd know if they did *that*, wouldn't I? Or made me do something, right?"

His eyes immediately tightened on mine, understanding what I was trying to ask without spelling it out.

I'd swear the blood visibly drained from his face as he processed my questions.

"No," he gritted out, lowering his hands to my bare shoulders and then to the sides of my arms. "I don't believe that. We don't know why you were taken, but it's most likely someone who you'd let in your own house. They knew you, and I . . ." His words trailed off, like he didn't have it in him to lie to me.

Memories or not, I was well aware that sometimes the people you knew the best were the ones to cause you the most pain. A gut feeling, at least.

"I don't hurt anywhere." *Just my chest.* "But I have a million horrific ideas from A to Z that could have happened flying through my mind." I stepped out of his arms and swiped the backs of my hands across my cheeks.

I supposed even warriors could have their hot mess moments. I didn't have to be one or the other. Julian had told me to hang somewhere in between while I worked through this, and maybe he was right. Also, now I was feeling bad for turning my back on my twin. My whole family. But . . . I still had questions.

"I, um, was so distracted by waking up without my memories I didn't stop to think about those missing hours." Ranger slipped between us and plopped down on my bare feet, and I forced a smile, not wanting him to worry about me. "People don't deserve dogs."

"I say that all the time." His gravelly voice had me peering at him, but I couldn't meet his eyes because his were pointed at the ceiling, throat muscles taut, a vein visible.

I shivered, realizing I was covered in chills for more than one reason. I was only in a bra and panties, and that was why this man was respectfully looking anywhere but at me.

"I'm sorry. I was mad and took off your shirt. I'm clearly not acting like myself." I stepped away to grab his shirt from the bed.

"Not your fault." His voice was steady. Calming, even. "Also, I'm sorry I upset you in the kitchen."

"Not your fault, either." I swallowed. "I pushed you, which is probably one reason you didn't like me before."

He didn't reject the idea. Didn't say anything at all. Just remained quietly standing in the hall, hands on the doorframe, head bowed, and eyes closed.

Shirt on, I dropped on the bed and patted the spot next to me, signaling for Ranger to join me. "I'm dressed."

Reed slowly looked at me, dispensing a deep breath before crossing into my room. "You're going through a lot right now. The least I can do is be, uh, cordial while you're here."

"O-okay." *You really don't like me, but based on how I'm feeling, I was only pretending to dislike you before.*

I stroked Ranger's head, finally calming down, but that oddly opened my mind to new what-if ideas, and a movie memory popped up and had me rushing out, "Wait, what if they *Jason Bourne*'d me?"

He frowned and cupped the back of his head at the base of his skull. His arm muscle flexed, temporarily drawing my eye to his obvious strength. "You mean—"

"Used my skills to do something for them." My heartbeat pulsed up into my ears at the new theory percolating. "They didn't need to super-soldier me because I'm apparently already that girl, but maybe they brainwashed me into committing a crime, then wiped my memories so I wouldn't remember I did it." I stopped petting Ranger and stood. "Anyone get assassinated while I was missing?" *Did I really just casually ask that?*

He grimaced. "Not that I'm aware of, no."

That's a relief. "What if they needed me to access something that only someone in my family could, and then they wanted me to forget afterward and used the drug on me?" I proposed next before my eyes went wide as another idea lanced my mind.

He closed the space between us, and his warm, rough palm slid down my forearm and to my wrist. "You'd never talk. Too stubborn—I mean, strong."

"I—I don't know. If they threatened people I cared about . . . ?"

"Maybe now's not the best time to make guesses." He let go as if just realizing he was holding on to me. "You're scared and overtired."

He was right. I'd had a good cry and a welcoming hug. Sleep was needed, and with any luck, tomorrow would be the day answers would come.

"Get some rest. I'm going to check in with my team, then do another perimeter sweep. You know, make sure your brothers see me from those satellites they've probably hacked so they know I'm not dropping the ball."

I couldn't believe it, but he had me cracking a smile.

He surprised me when he leaned in and slanted his mouth over my ear. "I gotta keep my heart in my chest." He paused for a moment as I recalled Gideon's words to him. Then he pulled back to find my eyes and added in a husky voice, "I can't risk having it cut out . . . now, can I?"

CHAPTER EIGHTEEN

Hollis

I startled awake, bolting upright. I slammed a hand over my chest, trying to catch my breath as Ranger crooned in response.

"It's okay, boy. Not a nightmare." I reached around in the dark room for his head. "The same dream. Always the same." *But why?* "Same bed and . . ." My words faded as something dawned on me.

I threw my legs over the side and stood. Ranger flew off the bed on alert.

"No bad guy, sorry. But we gotta wake up your dad." I nearly tripped over him on my way to the door.

Out in the hall, I waited for my eyes to adjust to the darkness, then slid my hand along the wall to get to Reed's room. I didn't bother knocking and tested the handle.

Running on adrenaline with the fog of sleep now lifted, I flung open the door with a little too much excitement and flipped on the light switch.

"What the—" Reed cut off his curse the second he realized it was me, not an intruder. Though I probably deserved a gun pulled on me for waking him like this. He sat upright and threw the covers aside. "You okay?"

"Nope. Yup. Don't know," I said in a daze, taking in the sight of him. I *shouldn't* have checked out his near nakedness in only his light-gray boxer briefs, but it was a challenge not to notice his hard body and his hard-*on*. *Wow, okay. Damn.* I really had to stop staring. *Why am I here, again?*

"Shut your eyes," he ordered while standing, cutting off my dirty thoughts, "or turn around, will ya? Give me a second to put something on."

"Right, yes. Sorry." I slapped both hands over my face.

"You're good," he said about thirty seconds later. I lowered my hands but kept my eyes squeezed shut. "It's okay," he added, his voice drawing closer.

I hesitantly parted my eyelids, slightly disappointed to see him in a gray shirt and black loose-fitting shorts since he'd been naked in my dream, and I'd guiltily enjoyed him that way.

"So, what's going on?" He whistled to Ranger, and he hopped off his bed.

"Your bed," I blurted out. "I know it."

His face scrunched in confusion. "What?"

I pointed at the crumpled bedding as if that'd clarify things. "Even the bedspread. Same one."

He lifted his hands up, palms facing out. "Walk me through this like I'm someone who was just woken up from the dead so I can meet you halfway here."

I rested my hand on my chest, still needing to dial down my pulse. "I keep having the same dream."

"Where you're not a good cook?" he asked in a low voice, still utterly lost.

I'd forgotten I'd mentioned that part to him last night, and only that part. "No. I mean yes."

He pushed his hands into his pockets, jaw set as he stared at me with weary eyes.

Poor guy. "I've been having a dream, and it's always the same. Your bed is in it." I clutched the hem of the shirt as if that might help ground and steady me, but when his eyes shot to my thighs and he walked back a step, I realized I was showing too much skin.

"You were saying?" His question came on the tail end of an exhausted breath as I let go of the shirt.

"I keep having a dream involving you. I thought the dream started Friday after we met in my mother's bedroom. Even questioned if it was a memory, not a dream, which is why I asked you if there was something between us."

I'd expected his body to relax at this news, but I was pretty sure he tensed up even more than I thought possible. His muscular arms were tighter than tight, a vein visible down his forearm.

"The dream always starts with us naked in bed after we've had sex, never during." Talk about awkward, and now the hardwood had my attention so I could get through this. "Then our three children yell out for food, and we all sit together and eat breakfast, the five of us." Heat built up in my cheeks. "But Friday wasn't the first time I had that dream."

I slowly looked up at him, finding his lips parted and eyes narrowed.

"The coffin. I just remembered . . . I woke up in there to that dream before realizing where I was, switching to escape, panic mode." My heart wouldn't stop working double time, making my speech a little breathy. "How is that possible? That was also before I hit you on the street." There was more, too. More that made no sense. But I wanted to give him time to process this first.

"I don't understand," he said in a rough voice, drawing his palm to his stubbled cheek, eyes on the floor.

"Reed?" It took all my energy not to call him Jason. "We were in this bed. Not just any bed, but this one. Same covers. Same nightstand." I closed the gap between us and held his wrist. "Come with me." I gently tugged, then let him go and quietly left his room, assuming he'd follow.

I turned on the lights in the hall so I wouldn't stumble and made my way to the kitchen and flicked on the switch.

"We ate breakfast with our kids at that table." I glanced back to find him standing behind me, staring at me, not his table. "It's just missing the fifth chair." My voice broke as I went over, the echoes of their adorable laughter surrounding me. "Why am I dreaming about being married to you? Having three kids together? Why does it feel like a memory and not a figment of my imagination?"

He came up behind me and rested his hands on my shoulders, and I peeked at him. His eyes were fixed on the table, like he could see our kids there.

"Tell me how I'd know this table and your bed. Know *you*. But not myself." I turned toward him, forcing him to let go of me.

His deep inhalation had his chest brushing against my body. He exhaled through his nose, staring at me. "I don't know."

I closed my eyes, my skin pebbling from chills. "Maybe I saw a similar scene in a movie, but that doesn't explain why—"

"Why you remember me and my home," he cut in. "And you're sure it was me in your dream in the coffin? You're not mixing me up with an actor? This house, too—it's a dime a dozen in design."

"Sure, I guess that could be true," I hesitantly agreed, opening my eyes. "Maybe?" I wanted to cling to the hope that I was remembering something, though. "I, uh, know we've never had sex and we're not married." I half smiled, embarrassment kicking the surprise to the side now. "No kids, either. It just feels so real, but maybe you're right. I mean, you have to be." I turned and held on to the back of one of the chairs. "I'm probably confusing things. Making things up. I—I don't know."

"I'm not dismissing your dream or what you think you remember. It's just a lot to process. You've been through quite a bit, so I don't want to . . ."

I turned again, nearly bumping into him at the fact he'd abandoned his words.

He cupped his chin, eyes shooting to the floor. "That op in February . . . we were undercover as a couple. We even checked into a hotel room together. It was all an act, and nothing happened between us."

"So maybe I *am* remembering things, just mixing stuff up?"

He slowly met my eyes. "Possibly."

Of all the people, though, why was my brain circling back to him? Still, it gave me an ounce of hope.

"Your memories *will* come back." He held out his palm, and it took me a second to realize what he was doing. I rested my hand on top of his, and a warmth filled my chest the moment contact was made.

A sense of peace took over and settled my nerves.

"Thank you," I whispered a few seconds later, letting my hand fall to my side.

"Least I can do after being such a prick at dinner."

"You were hardly that bad. I'm just sensitive right now."

"Not used to you being any type of sen—" He cut himself off, shaking his head. "I'm going to stay up. Make some coffee." He backed away from me, clearly deciding it was time to abandon the conversation. "You want any?"

I checked the time on the microwave. Five o'clock. "Sure. How do I take it?"

"Black. You don't like it sweet."

I wasn't sure why my coffee order disappointed me, but it did. "Of course I wouldn't, since I'm apparently nothing like Lyra." If she was daytime, I was night. Maybe if I'd chosen the life she had, I really would be married with three kids.

"You're perfect the way you are." Reed's kind words pierced my *what-if* thoughts.

"A perfect pain in your ass?" I forced a smile.

His dark brows slanted. "Not always," he said in a low, husky voice that had my stomach flipping and me starting to wonder whether that dream was based on a *fantasy* I'd had before I lost my memories.

"Well then, maybe I can be different now." I shrugged. "How about making my coffee sweet?"

He quirked a brow. "You sure?"

"If there were ever a time for a change . . ."

He turned on his coffee machine, then set his hands on the counter and glanced at me as it warmed up. "Out of curiosity"—he cleared his throat—"those, uh, kids in your dream?"

I leaned my hip against the counter, palming it for support. "Twin girls and a son," I answered what I assumed he was asking.

"Sounds like we had our hands full in that dream of yours." He pushed away from the counter and placed a pod in the machine and a mug in place.

I sighed, a little overwhelmed, in a good way, at the peace that dream gave me whenever I had it or even thought about it. "I don't know, you made being a dad look easy."

His back muscles flexed, and he cupped the nape of his neck and squeezed like I'd hit a nerve. "Guess that's why they call 'em dreams, not reality."

There was a sadness to his tone that broke my heart, but I behaved and didn't push this time.

I let him make our coffees in peace, and when he handed over my sweetened one, I nervously took a sip.

Dammit. "I hate it," I admitted.

He quietly took the mug and gave me his untouched one, as if he'd assumed that was bound to happen.

"Guess some things really don't change, memories or not," I said softly, worried that was going to hold true in other areas of my life.

He emptied the drink into the sink. "At the end of the day, we are who we are." A bit of a drawl slipped through as he added in a somber tone, "And unfortunately, sometimes there ain't no changin' that no matter how hard you try."

CHAPTER NINETEEN

Hollis

Later that morning, I curled up next to Audrey on the couch in Reed's living room, all my senses waking up at the sight and smell of homemade banana bread on my plate. "I take it I like that?"

"I always make it for you whenever you're in town. It's the reason you put up with my chattiness when we first met. Stuck around for my baking skills, wound up stuck with a best friend."

I frowned, thinking back to what I'd learned about our relationship before flying here yesterday. "Something tells me it's the other way around. You got stuck with me."

She picked up the iced tea I'd already rejected in the kitchen and balanced her own plate on her thighs. "No one I'd rather be stuck with."

Sweet and undeserved. I'd lied to her for eight years about who I really was. The guys had said I did it to protect her from my world, but did that make me any better than my mother?

I took a bite, and a soft moan slipped out before I could stop it. "Is this better than sex?" I joked, drawing a laugh from Audrey.

I could feel Reed's eyes before I saw them. When I checked the kitchen, he was holding his laptop in one hand, standing between Ryder and Alex, staring at me instead of the screen.

"It's not better, I can assure you." Audrey's amused tone didn't pull me back to her—not yet. Not with Reed still pinning me in place with those dark eyes that could've coaxed another moan out of me.

Nothing between us.

Nothing between us.

I had to keep reminding myself of that fact, especially with that dream rolling around in my head, feeling more honest than anything else currently in my life.

Reed arched his shoulders back, lightly shaking his head before Ryder nudged him to pay attention.

As I watched the three men work and talk, it only just occurred to me—where was Chase? Trevor? And why hadn't I thought to ask about them five minutes ago when she came over with her husband and brother? *Some kind of friend I am.*

Maybe it was because I'd been a little bummed by the intrusion. I'd just been getting into the show Reed had me watching all morning, *Mad Men.* We'd sat there on the couch with Ranger asleep between us as if it were the most normal thing for us to be doing.

Reed was probably just happy I'd kept my mouth shut and hadn't brought up the dream again, or asked questions about his personal life.

"So, where's Chase?" I finally managed to get the words out after taking my last bite.

"When Trevor is in town, he works security at the church. Chase, Eden, and my brother's wife, Seraphina, are with him." Audrey took my plate from me and slid it beneath her barely touched one, setting both dishes on the coffee table alongside her tea.

She folded her legs underneath her, twisting around to better face me, propping her elbow on the back of the couch, resting her other hand on her stomach, hiding a tiny burp with the back of her hand. "Sorry, baby's fault."

"Congratulations, by the way. I'm sure I said that before, though." I stole a quick look at Alex. "He seems like a great dad. Trevor too."

"They are." She smiled, some of that nervous energy hopefully waning.

I didn't want her to be awkward around me, even if I was that way around her. Maybe if we had something to fill the—

"Music?" she offered, reading my mind. "I heard it can help trigger memories." She grabbed her phone from the table.

"I'd love that, thank you." I glanced at the built-in cabinets on each side of the TV for a brief moment before looking into the kitchen. I hated being a useless fixture on the couch while they worked my case without me.

Reed was now sitting at the table, in the same chair I'd swear was from my dream. He casually looked over at me while sipping what had to be his third cup of coffee this morning.

"She's pulling together a list for us," Ryder said, and Reed set down his mug and eyed his team leader's screen just as faint notes from a piano reached my ears.

"What do you think?" Audrey asked as the music played from her phone sitting on top of the pillow between us. "If you don't like it, don't tell me, though."

I closed my eyes and listened. "It's beautiful," I whispered. "Sounds familiar. Do I know it?"

"You've only heard it when I've played it for you. It's not been released yet."

I opened my eyes, curious. "How do you have it?"

"Well, the piano you heard in the background? That's me playing. As for the guitar and singing . . . definitely not me. That's Calliope Costa. Well, she goes by Callie."

I let the last note fade, taking it all in, right along with my best friend's talent. "You're a musician?"

"Pianist." She hitched a noncommittal shoulder. "Wild story, but back in February when I was in danger because of my ex—"

"*Trevor* placed you in danger?" I couldn't imagine him being a threat if he was such a great dad and still in their lives.

"No, no." Audrey lowered her voice and clarified, "Different ex." She rested her hand on her stomach. "Anyway, um, while you were helping keep me safe, this Italian family, the Costas, watched over Seraphina. After, I got to know them, and one of their wives is a country singer. She won an award for her hit 'Not Mine to Keep.' Asked me to play the piano for her next single, and that's the one you just heard. It'll be out later this year."

I peeked at her screen and hit play again. "It says 'Untitled.'"

"Callie called last week to discuss song titles, but we didn't decide on one yet."

"'Never the Same,'" I said as the song came to a close. "That's what I'd call it, and it's wild how much I can relate to the music, like it could've been written about what I'm going through."

"No, because you *will* be the same again. You'll get your memories back." She paused the music and leaned forward to grip my forearm. "And if that book exists, and that formula was used on you, then there has to be an antidote."

"Reed told you about the book?"

"Well, Reed told the team, and Alex isn't so great at keeping secrets from me." She patted my arm, then let go. "When two people get married, they become one, right? So, in his defense, he told his other half." She trailed her fingers over her baby bump in light strokes, and I couldn't help but think about my dream yet again.

I'm a mother in my dreams. Why?

"I just know you'll find your other half, your 'the one' when the time is right for you," she said with air quotes and a small smile.

"So I really don't date, huh? My brothers said that, which was why they didn't believe I was with a guy." *And that reminds me.* "Sorry for lying about why I was in Italy. If only I told you the truth, then maybe I wouldn't be in this position now."

"Maybe you were there for Tristan, so it wasn't technically a lie. It's not like you said you were romantically involved with the guy you were going there with."

She was too good to me, truly. "Alex tell you about Tristan, too?"

She nodded, pulling her mouth off to the side as if suppressing something.

"Another apology I owe you. For not telling you about him, especially when you discovered you also had a half brother," I added, tipping my head toward said brother. "I suck."

"Nope, no feeling bad, not on my watch." She took hold of my arm again, gently tugging it in a request to look at her, so I hesitantly surrendered.

"You're way too patient and forgiving."

"Years of being tested by an energetic kiddo will do that," she said with a light laugh, but something told me what she really wanted to do was cry.

"Everything okay?" Alex asked, coming to his wife's rescue.

His timing was perfect. I had no idea how to make things right. Not even a little better. For her. Me. For anyone.

Audrey pulled her hand away and answered, "Of course."

At the sight of Ryder and Reed heading over now, I stood and faced everyone. "Anything?"

"It's almost like it never happened." Ryder lifted his hand as if to say, *I know it did, don't worry.* "The source code Julian created and was allegedly stolen from him . . . it's like nothing the Department of Defense or CIA has ever seen."

"Well, um, Julian mentioned a name yesterday." At least my new memories were still there. "A Gwen someone? He said she might be able to help, but Gideon said my parents would reject the idea."

"Gwen's already been pulled in, per orders of the secretary of defense," Ryder said flatly.

"Along with a few other teams," Alex added while helping Audrey stand. "Falcon Falls Security, for one. Secretary Chandler's son, Gray, co-runs Falcon."

"Let me guess, I've worked with them before, too?"

Alex smirked and nodded. "Don't suppose the name Carter Dominick rings any bells, does it? He co-runs the team with Gray."

I shook my head. "Not a one." The only one who managed to ring my bell was standing a few feet away, pinning me with his broody stare, and my cheeks were about to heat up as I remembered our five a.m. moment when I'd startled him awake, finding him in only boxers and stiff.

"Falcon Falls has a lot of resources even our government can't access. Connections to other powerful people and organizations that work outside government red tape to get results," Ryder continued, intruding on my dirty thoughts.

"What about the Costas? Did Constantine find anything?" Audrey asked, then quickly explained to me he was Callie Costa's brother-in-law, and his family was also assisting with my case.

"The hotel manager gave him the same answers he provided Gideon. You appeared to be traveling alone. No one saw anyone with you—not at the hotel, at least." Ryder explained what I'd expected to hear: that there'd been no hookup happening. "Constantine has contacts all over Italy. Someone had to have seen something."

"There's one other lead we're following," Alex said before I had a chance to digest the Constantine news—or, well, lack thereof. "Someone we know had her memories wiped a few years ago. Trevor's cousin, actually."

My stomach tightened as I rounded the couch to draw closer to them, the sweetness of the banana bread turning to lead in my stomach.

"His cousin Tessa was also taken," Alex went on. "Woke up in a hospital with no memory of what happened to her while she'd been missing, *but* she remembered who she was."

"We figured it was worth looking into." Ryder rocked back on his heels, quietly assessing me. "Her husband's team never figured out how it was done. They assume it was a combination of drugs and hypnosis."

"Tell me she eventually remembered what happened to her," I said like a plea as Ranger came over to sit next to me.

"Unfortunately not," Ryder responded while I crouched to pet Ranger. "But Gwen's building a program to compile and cross-reference any memory-loss-related cases. Should have the list by tomorrow at the latest."

"But there's no guarantee the same drug used on them or Trevor's cousin was the one used on me. Doubtfully by the same person." My thoughts drifted back to that mystery book and formula. There had to be a connection—how could there not be? "There's just no way it's a coincidence I was searching for a cure to memory loss, and then this happened to me."

"Wait, what?" Audrey stepped closer. "You were looking for the book for a *cure*?"

I clocked a surprised look from Alex, but Ryder turned to the side and palmed his jaw like this wasn't news to him. Why hadn't Reed told them both the whole story?

I kept quiet, unable to answer Audrey, too busy reading everyone's body language.

Audrey shot Reed a wide-eyed, questioning look, and he subtly lifted his hand and patted the air while lightly shaking his head, as if telling her to back down.

What was that all about? "Yes." I finally broached the awkward quiet while standing tall. "Julian said I was planning to reverse the formula once I found it. *Save* memories, not steal them."

Audrey walked backward, right into her husband, and he caught hold of her arms.

"Anyone want to tell me what's going on?" I cut to it, trying to fend off the return of anxiousness. I was currently comfortably sitting between panic and calm, and wasn't in the mood to let the pendulum swing all the way over to the shaky side.

"Now's not the time," Reed said in a low voice, eyeing Alex, not me, who was staring at him as well. "Please," he tacked on, now studying me with a somber request in his gaze.

There was so much hurt and pain in his eyes that all I could do was nod and agree.

"Do we, um . . . know anything about my grandfather? My mother said he passed, but he's the one who raised Tristan until he was eighteen. Maybe he's the key to figuring out more about this mystery brother and that book."

Reed visibly relaxed at the reprieve I'd given him by changing subjects.

"If he really raised Tristan, there's no legal record of it. No evidence of anything relating to your brother, in fact. Gwen did the digging, too, so if she couldn't find anything, it's more than buried—it's nonexistent." Ryder removed his hat, squeezed both sides of the brim, then put it back face forward. "And we confirmed your grandfather did die back in 2012."

I mindlessly petted Ranger. "From what?"

"Heart attack. Home alone at the time," he answered.

I waited to feel grief. To feel something.

"You okay?" Audrey asked as I stood, resting her hand on my forearm. "Shoot, sorry, of course you're not. Maybe rest?"

To stay put or run? I was torn, but went with a "Probably a good idea," in response.

"If you're up for it, maybe tomorrow we can watch a movie or something?" she suggested.

"Sure." I peeked around Audrey to locate Reed. He was in the kitchen now, hands on the breakfast bar, muscles tight and spine stiff.

Now wasn't the time to ask him if he was okay—not in front of his friends—but he was clearly far from it.

"Come on, Ranger." I patted my leg. "Thank you for your help." I took off, only to stop walking once in the hallway. I set my back to the wall and shut my eyes, my heart slamming hard against my rib cage. *Get a grip. Be strong.* I issued a few more commands to myself, but none helped loosen the sadness now festering inside me like a disease. I couldn't pretend my way out of what I was feeling.

"Did you tell her about my dad?"

I immediately opened my eyes at Reed's words, snapping me from sad to alert within a second.

"Alex told you, so . . . did you tell Hollis?" Reed asked someone.

"Of course not," Audrey responded, her voice low but audible enough for me to still hear. "Do you think she was trying to find a cure for your dad?"

"Just forget I said anything, please," Reed rushed out. "I'm going outside, and for the love of all that's holy, no one follow me."

Now I knew why Reed was so on edge. *You think I was trying to help your father.* I wandered to my bedroom, gently closed the door, and dropped down on my bed. *The question is . . . was I?*

CHAPTER TWENTY

Reed

I dropped my dumbbells, and they slammed down onto the mat. Ranger startled, bolting straight between Hollis's legs as she stood in the doorway to my gym. *Some guard dog you are.*

"You okay? How'd you sleep?" I scanned the room for the shirt I'd tossed somewhere mid-workout. "I made you lunch earlier, but you were knocked out, so I didn't want to wake you."

I looked back at her, curious why she wasn't speaking. She was just standing in the doorway as if in a daze, holding open the door with her shoulder, a statue of kill-me-now sexiness in her gym outfit with her hair in a tight ponytail.

I resumed searching for my shirt while she kept up with the quiet act. I spotted it, but so did Ranger. He ran straight over and turned it into his bed. *Of course you did that.*

She finally broke the silence. "Any updates?"

Not so fast. I set my hands above the waistband of my black gym shorts. "You didn't answer my questions."

She joined me, letting the door swing shut behind her. "You know exactly how I slept and what happened while I did." She inhaled a deep breath and kept hold of it, and she had me wanting to hold a breath captive myself.

"I don't, actually. Not a mind reader."

"If only you were, then you could figure out what happened to me, since the memories have to be somewhere in my head. I just don't have access to them."

Her semi-sad response forced me to remember she wasn't in my house to drive me nuts in those short shorts. Never thought I'd see the day when Hollis needed me.

"I slept fine."

I quietly snorted my rejection of her response, hands falling to my sides.

"Do you actually want the truth?" She carefully avoided the equipment to face off with me.

"That'd be an excellent start."

Her gaze flicked down my bare chest and back up again. Still couldn't believe she'd walked in my bedroom at 0500 and discovered my morning wood. I'd been dreaming, too, and mine had been a hell of a lot less innocent than hers. X-rated and filthy.

She poked at my pec muscle, and my jaw muscle ticked as I looked between our bodies in search of her touch, only to get distracted by her nipples, hard and visible through her sports bra.

"I woke up feeling at peace because I had that same dream yet again, only to slide into a state of confusion because of it. Not to mention . . ."

She abandoned her words, so I did something stupid. "Finish what you were saying," I grated out, growing increasingly tense with her being technically shirtless like me. "Don't be shy now, you've never been before."

She hit me with the sass that I loved while retracting her finger from my heated, slick skin. "You seem like a smart man—figure it out."

Smart for a high school dropout? Yeah, her mother's words had become a chip on my shoulder. "Genuinely no clue what you were planning to say." I backed up, bumping into my bench. "But if you're in here to work out, absolutely not."

"You told me during the tour yesterday I could use the space anytime."

"You've barely eaten today. And no, coffee and a slice of banana bread doesn't qualify as nutritional enough for you to lift." I really wished there was a better barrier between us other than air. "And to answer your question, no updates from Constantine, or anyone working the case, for that matter." *Unfortunately.*

She peered over at my squat rack.

Oh, hell no. "Nope, not changing my mind." I gestured to the door, signaling for her to get her ass to the kitchen.

"I'll grab a snack *after* I work out. Something tells me I'll survive." She stubbornly stood her ground, locking her arms over her chest, which only further accentuated her breasts in that tight black sports bra top she had on.

I forgot her defiance for a moment, because I couldn't help but notice a bruise on her chest. How'd I miss that when she was practically flashing me the other day? "How'd you get that?"

"Get what?" She tucked in her chin, locating the mark. "It was there when I woke up on Friday in my mother's bed in Surrey."

Now I couldn't help but think about our conversation last night. What *had* happened to her during those missing hours? If I were to examine possible ideas, I'd lose my shit, and no amount of duct tape would hold me together. No, she needed me to remain of sound mind until her head was once again jam-packed with her memories.

"Still hurt?"

"Barely." She shrugged. "But back to the problem at hand . . ."

"That you should eat first, burn off some steam later?" I was stubborn, too. Did she think she was the only one?

I waited for her to agree with me, but then she went and wrecked me again by reaching out, dragging her finger along my rib cage. She'd spotted my tattoo. It wouldn't be the first time she'd asked about it, and hell would have to freeze over before I'd talk about it now.

"Any other tattoos aside from this one?"

I caught her wrist and guided her hand away, my pulse thrumming fast at the side of my neck with her so damn close. "This is the only one."

"Why?"

I let go of her before I changed my mind and decided to hold her somewhere north of forever. "Why just one?"

"No. Why *that* one?"

Here we go. Some things never change. "I'd rather talk about literally anything else." The truth bled through, right from a place of shame.

She made a little noise of dissatisfaction, but she didn't push. Thank the Lord.

"I'll eat first, you win. After I work out, I'd like to use the sauna."

"After you eat *and* digest your food first."

"You really think you can tell me what to—"

"I do." I smirked. "My house, my rules."

She rolled her eyes. Typical. I had to admit, it was nice seeing her flair for dramatics return. Part of me always liked that she was still capable of humor and being a little bratty despite also having to be Wonder Woman. It made her human. Mortal. The other part of me hated it because, of course . . . it turned me on.

Hollis turned to face my equipment, and now I was forced to see her ass in those high-waisted short shorts that outlined her glutes.

I looked up at the ceiling, trying to pull myself together. I was currently on the verge of taking a one-way train to that place that just might freeze over if I wasn't more careful around her.

"Come on, I'll make you a sandwich," I grumbled, needing to get out of here before I did something stupid. Like let her trace my tattoo with her finger. Let her touch me wherever else she might want to explore. "Let me clean up first. I'll meet you in the kitchen in five. Just promise you'll behave while you're out of my sight?" I should have said "*in* my sight," too.

She tipped her head, her tongue caressing the line of her lips as she eyed my bare chest.

If she showed her tongue one more damn time, so help me . . .

"I'm not trying to be difficult. I don't even know how to be. Just doing whatever comes naturally."

Which is being difficult. I thanked myself for keeping that retort in my head.

"I read online on the flight here yesterday that movement is good for your brain."

"It is." I knew that from my own research when looking into my dad's condition. "But food first."

Her attention snagged once again on my tattoo, and that was my cue to take off. I needed a mind-numbing cold shower before I burned alive from lust.

The second I was alone in my bathroom, though, she was all around me wherever I looked. Her perfume on the counter. Her hairbrush. Floss. Toothbrush.

I had to remind myself her being here was temporary.

All of it.

Her in my sphere.

Me in hers.

I'd never fit into her universe of wealth and power—all I'd ever be was some small-town high school dropout with a mountain of baggage.

CHAPTER TWENTY-ONE

Reed

When I walked into the kitchen after my shower, the last thing I expected was for Hollis to be preparing food for both of us. Also . . . "You changed," I breathed out, knowing there was some type of double meaning there I couldn't tackle right now.

"You seemed to be uncomfortable around me in what I had on." She turned toward me, armed with a butter knife covered in mayo. "I assume you're not allergic to anything in your kitchen, or you wouldn't have bought it, right?"

My shoulders relaxed, but my heartbeat didn't seem ready to calm down. "No allergies." I gave her a hesitant smile before stepping behind her, looking over her shoulder at what she was up to with my food.

She'd butchered the homemade sourdough bread Audrey had dropped off this morning, clearly using the wrong knife to cut it. Slices of turkey and cheese were on top of the bread. She was currently adding the mayo to the meat, instead of to the bread like I'd have done. That would've normally bothered me, but for some reason, it didn't. She was trying, and the effort did something strange to me, like making that useless muscle in my chest—only good for keeping me alive—beat even faster.

"You didn't have to change," I said a few internal curses and two skipped heartbeats too late (I probably needed medical attention).

"I didn't technically change. I just put on a shirt." She looked back to catch my eyes. "Proper etiquette to wear a top while we eat together, yeah?"

"How about you always keep your top on when we do anything together?" My voice remained surprisingly measured despite the blood rushing from one head to the other, with her tongue now sliding across the seam of her mouth, just waiting to be caught between my teeth.

"You're going to strain a muscle if you keep looking back at me." Against my better judgment, I brought a hand to the nape of her neck. My palm slid up and around her soft skin to the front of her throat, skimming her sharp jawline, before gently urging her face to point toward the tragic sandwiches and away from me.

She dropped the knife and braced herself against the counter, slightly tilting her head like an invitation to keep my hand on her.

For the life of me, I couldn't pull away. I set my other hand next to hers on the counter, then dragged my knuckles over her cheek before cupping her chin, resting my thumb over her mouth. She arched back, and that ass I ached to grab hold of went flush against my body.

At that moment, I forgot who I was. Forgot I was supposed to keep my distance and not fall for her. We were two souls in each other's orbits. Her forgotten past and my horrible one were yesterday's news. They didn't exist. Just the here, the now.

"What are you doing?" *To me.* I left off those two key words from my question as my desire poured from my lips, my body, from every part of me. Melting right into her.

She couldn't possibly get any closer with our clothes still on, but God help me, she tried. Wiggling her ass, like she was trying to absorb everything I had to give her, realizing I was in rare form.

She flicked her tongue out at my thumb. I kept it there anyway, wanting to feel the vibration of her words thrum into my skin when she finally answered me.

"I'm, um, just making sandwiches," she finally answered.

My arm remained looped around her as she angled her head, offering me better access to her throat.

I held her just under her jawline, lightly squeezing, trying to stop myself from turning her head toward me again. To kiss her. Taste her. Have sex with her right here on this counter.

She trailed her fingers along my forearm down to my hand before squeezing like a request to hold her tighter.

When she covered my other hand on the counter and rotated her hips, she nearly obliterated what was left of my brain cells. I pressed my erection against her and growled a curse under my breath.

"Hollis," I warned. Begged. Pleaded. *Also*, didn't let go of her throat. I didn't grip harder, either.

"This feels . . . *right*," she whispered between breathy pauses while shimmying against me, her warm hands still covering both of mine. "You. Me. That's all that makes sense."

Don't do this. Don't. My conscience hollered out even more demands, and I ignored every single one of them, feeling like a man possessed.

She was never going to believe me now when I told her there was nothing between us. Why would she? I was about to take her in my kitchen, all because she looked so damn sexy making us sandwiches.

"Hollis," I tried again. It'd probably help if I stopped holding her throat like I owned the words that came out of her mouth. The problem was? Old me could do exactly that. Make her cry out in ecstasy with my hand, tongue, or cock.

But she wasn't herself right now, and more than ever, I couldn't be my old one.

She lifted her hands, probably about to reposition them, and I took that as my chance to fight with everything I had in me to remove myself from temptation.

I unlocked my hand from her throat and staggered back, tearing my fingers through my damp hair, trying to regain some sense of control.

She slowly turned, forest-green eyes narrowed, a swirl of confusion there. I was damn grateful I hadn't left a handprint on her throat. What had I been thinking?

"I'm sorry. I don't know what just happened," I gritted out, knotting my hands at my sides so I wouldn't haul her against me. Swoop her into my arms and cart her off to my bed, where she'd dreamed we'd already made love as husband and wife. We could go ahead and turn fiction into reality.

She blinked her way up from my dick still filling out the crotch of my shorts to my face. "I'm sorry, too."

"You don't owe me an apology. What I did was out of line." I hung my head, drawing my fingers to my temples. "I have no idea why I did that."

"Well, I wanted you to touch me. It's all I seem to want, even if it doesn't make sense."

The vein throbbed at the side of my neck as I worked to rein in my desire, her words not helping at all. I remained stiff and ready to go. It was more than that, though. She was slowly resuscitating me in other ways. Like pumping blood to my heart.

"You don't remember who you are," I shot back, trying to put up a guard and dismiss her feelings right along with mine.

She let the words simmer between us for a few seconds. "Maybe I'm confusing you because I told you about my dream, and that's why you touched me." She bypassed my last remark and addressed my other comment.

She was also being too good to me. She had no idea who I really was. Who I used to be, at least. I'd been a prick to her since we met in February. I was well aware this very thing might happen if I wasn't, and that'd been a fear of mine since day one, after meeting her in person.

"You, um, may hate me . . . but your body doesn't seem to."

I followed her gaze to my raging hard-on. "You're gorgeous, Hollis. That won't ever change." I let go of a gruff breath. "I'm a dude with eyes, so." I did my best to act like whatever happened was purely physical, when I damn well knew better. "Just stop being so gorgeous whenever you're close to me, will ya?" I stepped around her to assess the mess she'd made on my counter. "Otherwise, I just might have to gouge out my eyes," I added in a lighter tone, hoping to switch gears here from lust to how we rolled before: banter and mild insults.

"That's a little extreme." She chuckled, and it was the best sound in the world, and I hated how much I craved hearing it again. "I could just not wear shorts that make my ass look so good and always keep a top on." She playfully elbowed my side as I tried to salvage the sandwiches and turn them into something edible.

"No, you wear whatever you want." I glanced at her. "It's a man's responsibility to control himself." And if I had to seal my eyes shut and maintain six feet of distance from her at all times, then so be it. Whatever kept me sane and her out of my bed, I'd do it. I had no choice but to, because she wasn't my "the one" as much as I wasn't hers.

She gave a half-hearted shrug, then began swiping the crumbs into her palm.

"Let's just eat, okay?" I plated the sandwiches and went to the breakfast bar.

Ranger was asleep in his bed in my room, which explained why he wasn't trying to steal our food now and why he hadn't barked up a storm over me touching her.

She sat on one of the three backless barstools, and I scooted mine farther away from hers. The memory of her ass tight against me with my fingers curled around her throat was still too fresh in my head.

"Am I crazy for being turned on and thinking about sex when I don't even know who I am? Don't even remember what sex feels like or how I even like it?"

I honest to God choked on my food. She hopped off the stool and wasted no time wrapping an arm around me.

"I'm guh-good," I said, finally swallowing my food before she cracked a rib.

She poured me a glass of water and handed it to me like a peace offering.

"Just went down the wrong pipe." I was making a real liar out of myself today, because nah, she'd nearly choked me to death with her words. "And I thought we were done talking about—"

"You're right." She waited for me to drink up before sitting. "I feel like I'm constantly apologizing for making things awkward, only to do it again five seconds later." She picked up her sandwich, which was falling apart at the side. "I think I have a problem."

Don't we all? "Don't be so hard on yourself." I also had to keep reminding myself of that. "I can't imagine what it's like not remembering . . ." I let my words trail off because thoughts of my father popped into my head.

"Can I ask you something?" She set down her sandwich and swiveled on the stool to face me.

I finished my water, hoping it'd put out the fire inside me as I waited for her question to come, one that'd surely make me uncomfortable again. She'd been on a roll the last few days. "You will anyway even if I say no. So go ahead."

"I don't want to be—"

"You are. Always were." I crooked my lips into a partial smile, side-eyeing her. "I reckon come hell or high water, you always will be a pain."

"Not Southern, but every so often, I hear a little twang of something there."

Did I really just . . . ? Shit, I did. What was she doing to me? How could I make it stop? "Oklahoma. There. You satisfied? That's where I grew up. Haven't been back since I was eighteen." *Nothing to go back to.*

"I wonder if I've ever been in a tornado. That state is known for them, yes?" She hooked her ankles around the stool legs and set her hands on her thighs.

I pointed to her food. "If you want to work out, *eat* and talk." *And stop staring at me like you're hungry for me, not the sandwich.* "And I have no clue if you've dealt with a tornado before. It's doubtful. Feel like they rarely hit Boardwalk and Park Avenue."

"Look at you, with the jokes now," she teased.

I waited for her to turn her ass around and answered a question I knew she would ask, "And yes, I've been in some. Two big ones. A couple smaller ones."

"Oh. Um, was everything—"

"Nope, it wasn't." Without looking at her, I stabbed a finger in the direction of her plate, a plea to give her sad sandwich her sad eyes instead of me.

"I can't do this, I'm sorry," she blurted out.

"What? Eat?" I shook my head, confused. When was I *not* confused when it came to her? She gave me as much whiplash now as she used to.

"No, I can't sit here and act like I don't know something."

My stomach dropped, and I shoved my plate away and twisted around on the stool, resting my forearm on the counter to brace for Hurricane Hollis to make impact.

"Your dad," she said softly, like she was terrified of how I was going to react. "I know about him. I heard you all talking after I left the room this morning. Something about a cure."

I had no words. Not a damn one.

I curled my fingers into my palm, biting down on my back teeth as I switched to staring at her barely touched sandwich instead of her.

"Do you really think I may have been searching for that book to help your dad? I can't be that much of a pain, or that bad of a person, if I was trying to—"

"You trying to help my dad and get up in my business is exactly the kind of pain-in-the-ass thing you would do, yeah." I shifted around to stand, not trusting myself not to blow a fuse while discussing my father, and she didn't deserve to be on the other end of my anger.

I was pissed at the man who'd raised me, who now didn't recognize me, while in the presence of a woman who could *only* seem to remember me. Was this some sick joke? I raked my fingers through my hair, trying to calm down before I met her eyes.

"I'm sorry, I shouldn't have said anything. Here I go sticking my foot in my mouth yet again, but I feel guilty I eavesdropped."

"You're not the problem, I am," I admitted, lifting my hand as a plea for her to not object to that. "I just hope you didn't get hurt because you were trying to help that man. He doesn't deserve saving by you." I slowly looked up at her, swallowing. "He's my own flesh and blood, and I don't even want to help him."

"Oh, Jason." She blinked, sympathy pouring out of her I didn't want, deserve, or need. "Sorry, um, Reed." She slowly rounded the barstools in an attempt to get to me.

I raised my other hand while backing away as if she had an M4 in hand and I was only armed with a water gun.

Survive tornadoes and war? Just another Tuesday.

Handle her being in my personal space and not explode? I'd have to be carried out on top of my shield, because I'd surely die.

"You're in my home because of what happened to you. Not to talk about me. Not for anything pertaining to me." I had to get us both back on track here. "You're my mission."

"Two things can happen—"

"Negative." I kept my arms extended as a barrier, not trusting her. Trusting myself even less. "While we're at it, maybe we need to establish some ground rules. Three feet. We, uh, should keep that much space between us at all times."

Her brows shot up, and she folded her arms like a guard. Good, that was a start.

"I'm being generous here. Would prefer six."

"Anything else?" she asked coolly.

At least one of us was maintaining a healthy blood pressure.

"No more questions about my personal life." My hands slowly fell to my sides as I exhaled. "I refuse to believe this happened to you because of my dad. My past is mine to keep, not to discuss." I gestured to her plate. "Now, eat. Work out if you want. But no sauna today. I can't be in there to babysit you. To make sure you don't faint on me."

"Why can't you—"

"Because I have to go find somewhere in this house where you're not so I can breathe," I grumbled, managing not to yell, but I wasn't exactly Mr. Wonderful.

Before I became even more of an asshole, I whistled for Ranger, and he came sliding in and straight over to us. "Watch her. Don't let her out of your sight, got it?"

Ranger howled, then hit my leg. He was clearly sensing I was in a foul mood, and a few paw taps wouldn't undo the damage. I appreciated the effort, though.

I stepped around Hollis, careful of Ranger's tail and making eye contact with her. But then she went and broke rule number one and reached for me.

I dipped my chin, jaw set, as I stared at her long fingers gripping my arm.

"I'm sorry." Those two words from her were fragile and damn near split me in half.

"Please don't do this to me," I rasped, my stomach turning as painful memories from my past hit me hard.

"Do what?" she whispered.

"I don't know how to handle you like this." I met her eyes. "So I'm begging you, just stop. Stop being so nice." I pulled my arm free from her touch. "So perfect. So everything I know I can never have."

CHAPTER TWENTY-TWO

Hollis

So everything I know I can never have. His words kept rotating around in my head, flashing through my mind like ticker tape.

Reed had done as promised and kept his distance after our post-sandwich showdown. Glimpses here and there. A protective shadow keeping me safe without coming near me. I'd been lonely and sad without sharing the same space as him.

I worked out alone. Showered by myself, of course. Ate the sushi he'd ordered for dinner with Ranger at my feet and without his dad in sight.

And now? I was in bed, tossing and turning, plagued by Reed's parting words while also battling being aroused anytime I remembered his hand around my throat and his erection pressing into me.

We'd gone from nuclear hot in desire to nuclear hot in frustration. His dad was clearly his trigger, and I'd hurt him by bringing him up. Something told me I hadn't known he had a bad relationship with his dad before today. Had I risked my memories by trying to save his father's, though?

"I can't sleep, how about you?" My eyes had already adjusted to the dark, so when I sat upright, I could easily make out Ranger on the bed with me. "Want a snack?"

He barked once.

"You agreeing with me, or are you upset I'm disturbing your sleep?" I'd only had Ranger to speak to all day since his dad wanted nothing to do with me.

His little howl told me he was tired, to leave him be.

"Okay, stay put. I'll be right back." I snuck out of bed and the room as quietly as possible and went to the kitchen.

It wasn't empty like it was supposed to be. Reed's presence filled the room from end to end. All six-two, handsome, muscular, and *shirtless* man.

He was parked behind a laptop at the table, and he was not going to be happy to see me invading his space.

His posture was deceptively lazy with one leg stretched out. The glow of the screen lit his sharp cheekbones as his eyes found me, sweeping over the oversized T-shirt I wore. Another one of his, of course. A small logo on the front, and a sideways American flag took up the whole back.

Too late to tuck tail and retreat now.

I came closer, and when his gaze locked back on my face, my pulse stuttered under the weight of that hooded, dark look.

"Why are you up?" Goose bumps raced across my arms as if the air itself carried some type of warning: *Leave him alone.*

"Right back at you." He closed the laptop with an unhurried snap, sitting forward.

I leaned against the counter, folding my arms across my chest at the memory I had nothing beneath the cotton except panties. My skin heated, the movement suddenly less defensive and more revealing as he noticed the fabric shift against my skin. He glanced briefly at my thighs before pulling his eyes away.

The evidence of his frustration at my presence, along with my lack of pants, was obvious in the lines of his mouth and the hard set of his jaw.

"I can't sleep." I swallowed. "You?"

He held the back of his neck and rotated his head, the wall of abdominal muscles tightening from the movement. Now all I could think about was that hand cupping my throat earlier, and I hadn't just liked it—it'd turned me on.

"Gwen made contact earlier than expected." He rested his forearm on the table.

"And?" I straightened, arms returning to my sides, and his eyes shot straight to my breasts like a reflex. A chill whipped up my spine, and I shivered. My nipples were probably poking through the fabric, and I didn't even care. Because he wasn't hightailing it from the room for sharing the same air as him. "Reed?" I prompted, waiting for him to share what Gwen told him.

He slowly locked in. On my face. Then on the mission. "No surprise, but your situation is unique. You're an anomaly."

The last word landed heavy, like a death sentence instead of an observation.

I forgot about my hard nipples and the fact this T-shirt wasn't doing a bang-up job covering much of my legs and approached him. "What about Trevor's cousin? I thought—"

"Not related." His nostrils flared, and a vein became visible at the side of his neck. He was working hard not to snap at my proximity.

I backed up to the required three feet, but he remained tense, every part of him visibly taut.

"Closest match, but still off," he continued, maintaining eye contact, but it was clearly taking everything in him to do so. The man looked like he was trying to fight the laws of gravity and was losing the battle. "Gwen's program puts it at a four percent probability that the same drug used on you was used on Tessa. And the same person? .002."

My throat went dry, and my stomach hollowed out at the news.

His chair scraped back. The sound was sharp in the hushed quiet of the room. He stood, his black pajama bottoms hanging low on his hips, the navy waistband of his briefs on display.

"We're thinking something new was used on you." He slid his hands into his pockets, leaning his hip against the table, and the casual movement only made his shoulders look broader, his arms more tense.

The man's body was a work of art. Well, the type of art found in a war museum. Bronzed skin that was carved, cut, and strong. Ready to do battle and stand on the front lines as a sacrifice to keep others safe.

"So, what next?" I backed up against the counter, needing its solid edge for support. I was too tempted to run into his arms and violate that three-foot rule. "You've got contacts. Constantine. That Carter guy. The Irishman who let us use his jet."

"I do, and they'll turn something up, I'm sure." He brought one hand to his face and slowly lowered it from his forehead to chin as if trying to steal away the fatigue and wake up. Or maybe *focus* up. "The Irishman—Sebastian Renaud—is talking to everyone in The League to see if they've heard anything, too."

"The League?" It didn't strike a chord of familiarity, unfortunately. "Is that the name of a secret society or something?"

"More like *the* secret society."

My laugh came thin and brittle. "Of course it has a name like that." In truth, I just didn't want to offer up the possibility that one group might be even more secretive than this League organization—my own family.

"There used to be two major players in the world of *criminal* secret societies, The Alliance and The Collective. The League took out The Alliance, and Falcon Falls wiped out The Collective," he continued. "So if there's a group out there tied to what happened to you, trust me, we have the best of the best on our side in this."

"Even if that secret group is my family?" I frowned. "Well, someone from my family or team."

He nodded. "We'll give them forty-eight hours. If nothing breaks—"

"Then I crawl back to my family and demand answers?" The words tasted like acid, and I fought the burn happening behind my eyes. Goodbye, lust. Hello, sick betrayal. "Do I need to force them to tell me everything they know? Do you think they even will?"

"Gwen told me tonight that if she and Julian join forces, maybe they can work a miracle with the footage and salvage the unsalvageable. If we can see what happened to you in Rome . . ." His voice softened, but his message wasn't exactly comforting. "Separately, it's impossible to undo what your brother's source code did. Together? Maybe."

"But we'd need to convince my tight-knit family to let you into their inner circle, and right now, even I'm an outsider." I turned away from him and braced against the counter.

At least Julian seemed on board already when it came to Gwen. I wasn't so sure what to think about the rest of my family. "And if they let us in, what if it's a Trojan horse and we wind up working with the enemy?"

"I don't see a way around taking the risk."

That ache in my stomach returned, sharp, curling me forward slightly. "Is it awful that I'm praying for a lead just so I don't have to admit to my mother I was wrong to leave?" I pushed off the counter and whirled around, finding him breaking that three-foot rule, right in front of me. Like so close he could catch my breath with his tongue.

His mouth curved, a shadow of warmth there. Then he shocked me, setting a fist under my chin, his thumb grazing the line of my jaw. My pulse shot up high and hard.

"You weren't wrong to leave," he murmured as his thumb slipped across my lip in the same way he'd done earlier. "Sometimes you don't know what you don't know until you step away." His brows tightened, and he immediately pulled away and walked back more than three feet. More like six. The man really was scared of me—well, at least, his obvious attraction to me.

I spoke once he seemed to be comfortable again, breathing easier without me being in his reach. "I do know I'm glad to have you and your team on my side."

He shoved his hands in his pockets with too much force, because the movement revealed more of his boxer-brief waistband, and all that did was send my mind to the gutter. Reminded me of seeing him in only his underwear at five this morning, which was about nineteen hours ago.

"We'll figure this out. I've never failed a mission," he said steadily.

"Guess I don't want to be your first."

His lips twitched. "Failure's not an option." He gestured to the fridge as it hummed between us. "I assume you came in here in search of food, not me?"

"Mm-hmm."

"Did I not feed you enough?" He blessed me with a quick, sexy smile.

"You didn't feed me. The restaurant you ordered from did."

He tipped his head slightly forward. "Apologies, ma'am."

The mood bent again, shifting into something lighter, but I managed to refrain from testing him by closing the space.

"I think I'll skip the snack and head back to bed," I decided, unable to be around him much longer, not trusting my mouth wouldn't run away like it had a habit of doing. I gave him a polite nod, then started to leave.

"I should also apologize for earlier." His voice was rough, and his words stopped me in my tracks.

I dropped my hand to the counter for support and closed my eyes, waiting for him to continue.

"If you risked your neck for my old man and this is what it cost you . . ." There was a crack in his armor that was as sharp and unexpected as the intimate moments we kept sharing. "I won't be able to live with that."

I processed his words, his guilt, then slowly stole a look back at him without fully facing him. "We don't know why I was in Rome." I swallowed, hating to see the pained expression crossing his face. "But *if* it was for your dad, that's on me. Not you. After all, one thing I know to be true . . . is that secrets always come with a price."

CHAPTER TWENTY-THREE

Hollis

Monday came and went. Fast, but also somehow slow. Reed had kept his distance most of the day, but it helped that we had a few distractions and obstacles between us from sunrise to sunset: Audrey and her son. They'd kept me busy with movies, baked goods, and even board games while Delta Shield chased leads.

But we were now in Tuesday territory, and that hourglass Reed had tipped over Sunday night would run out soon, and his team still had nothing. Not a single lead to speak of, and the idea of reaching out to my family made me physically ill.

I paced my bedroom, on the verge of spinning out. Gone was the happy middle between fearless and panicky. I was teetering on the edge of full-blown anxiousness. I didn't want anyone to see me like this, not even Reed. I hated when people looked at me like I was a stranger, even if I'd stared at them like that.

I collapsed onto the bed, resting my head in my palms, trying to chill out. I needed to find something to distract myself with while I waited for Audrey to get here with Chase. They were currently at a skating rink. Ryder was taking a brief break from work to spend time with his nephew, because apparently he used to play hockey and Chase loved the sport.

Reed had turned down my request to join them, which made sense. Probably shouldn't leave the house. But then he'd also turned down watching more episodes of *Mad Men* with me.

He had to clean his guns. Sure, sure. He was just too scared to sit next to me on the couch. Worried our hands might brush against each other and we'd violate the three-foot rule he'd broken himself Sunday night when reaching for my chin.

I drummed my fingers on my legs, trying to come up with a plan to still my body.

Maybe the sauna would help? I made up my mind, grabbed a towel from the hall closet, then went into my room and took off my clothes, leaving only the chain on to mask my tracker.

I wrapped myself in a towel and made a hurried rush for the gym. I flung the door open with a little too much force, and remained stuck between the two spaces like I was in limbo.

With my one hand, I held the towel tight above my breasts, every part of me prickling with awareness at the fact I'd barged into his space like this, which was going to wind up on his list of rules, no doubt.

Still, urgency outweighed dignity, so I hovered there, waiting for him to notice me.

He was bent over a rifle, oiling the barrel with surgical precision in front of his wall of gun safes. The steel trapped in those safes could arm a small country.

He lifted his eyes, slow and steady, from my bare feet up my body.

My stomach dropped at the look in his eyes. Dark and unreadable, like he was seeing more than he wanted to. "And you're wearing a towel—why?"

I tipped my chin toward his sauna, feigning bravado while my grip on the terry cloth tightened. "I'm feeling anxious, which I don't like at all, and I'm bored. I think I need to sweat whatever is happening to me out of my system."

Ranger ran around me and into the room, nails clicking on the floor, barking like he already knew the ground beneath me was giving way. *Yeah, me too, buddy.*

Meanwhile, Reed stayed maddeningly calm, wiping oil from his palms.

"The reason I'm spiraling, even though I know that's out of character for me, is because we're going on hour thirty-four of those precious forty-eight." My voice pitched higher, fraying at the end. "Still nothing since you set that countdown. *Cero. Zéro. Sifir. Nada* from that Italian guy who's supposed to be intimidating. *Zilch* from Carter. No info from Sebastian and his secret society." Forget anxiety, I was officially free-falling into rock bottom every second I stood here. "Ughhhh. This isn't me. I know that. I don't pace or freak out. I *know* I don't." I crossed the space to him, Ranger glued to my side. "Make it stop. Please," I begged, feeling a tremor shoot through me.

Reed stayed silent, like anything he said could be used against him in a court of law.

I held my hand up so he could see just how far gone I was. The evidence of my anxiety was right there, my entire body visibly quivering.

He dropped the rag and abandoned his three-foot rule. He slid his warm palm under mine, his fingers steady and unyielding as he cradled my shaking ones.

His hand was rough, and the smell of the gun oil lingered, yet his touch was grounding. Warmth pressed into my skin until the tremor slowed just as it had the last time we held each other like this. My pulse didn't slow, though. It hammered harder, out of sync with the calm he radiated. We stood there, palms locked together, breaths mingling in the narrow space between us.

"Don't focus on trying to act how you think you're supposed to." His voice dropped low, almost intimate. His eyes lingered on our joined hands before climbing up the line of my arm until locking on to my face. "It took years for you to become the woman you are. Your past shaped you and how you respond to the world." He smoothed his thumb along my hand once—absent-minded or maybe not—before he finished. "If you can't remember your battle scars and all that you've endured . . ." He let the words trail off, but the heat in his eyes burned like he'd said them anyway.

I blinked hard, fighting for composure. "I—I feel like me sometimes. Other times? Like an empty shell of nothingness, and it hurts. It's the worst feeling," I sputtered, hating getting emotional on him, but I couldn't stop it.

"You're in there somewhere, I promise." He took me by surprise again, drawing his other hand to my chest, partially over skin and the towel. "They may have taken your memories, but they didn't take your soul. That's the real you. Everything else is just flesh. Your spirit is unchanged, untainted."

Those were the last words I'd expect from a man who claimed to be bad with people. It was like he'd just written scripture right onto my body. I could even visualize the words scrolling over every inch of my skin, calming me down.

"You'll come back to me."

I waited for him to correct the Freudian slip of *me*, but he didn't. He just kept staring at me as if he could see through my flesh to that soul he'd been alluding to.

I squeezed down the lump in my throat and tried to will away the tears. "Okay," I mouthed, unable to get my voice to carry the word. "I, um, still would like to sweat it out, though."

"You really think it'll help?" he asked as he slowly retracted both hands.

My breath snagged at the loss of his touch. "I think so."

He sighed, shoulders falling with that deep breath. "Ten minutes, max."

"Will you stay in here to keep an eye on me?" I half smiled. "I mean, to ensure I don't faint or something from the heat?"

At his hesitant nod, I took that as my cue to hurry to the sauna before he could change his mind. Inside, I shut my eyes and prayed, not just for my anxiety to go away but also for a miracle. For even just one memory to return.

But after ten minutes passed by, I nearly cried when he opened the door and nothing ever came. I did feel a little better, but I was pretty sure that was thanks to him, not the sauna.

"Fourteen more hours left," I muttered, remaining frying on the wooden bench. How hot did he like it in here? This heat was brutal and beyond what a human could tolerate.

"That number's not fixed in stone. We can push it to tomorrow afternoon. Only surrender to your family if we have to and when you're ready. That help?"

Having one more full day? Actually, yeah, it did. "Yes." I lifted my head. "Thank you."

"I'll run it by Ryder and the team when they get back from the rink. I'm sure they'll be fine with it." He braced the door open with his shoulder and offered me his hand.

Breaking your rule again, huh? I stood, and of course, my towel started to slip. I caught it fast before I wound up flashing him. That didn't stop his eyes from flicking down my body, his mouth tensing as if holding back what he wanted to say.

He was probably even more grateful for my fast reflexes than I was. And now, the heat in the sauna had nothing on the heat of his stare when his intense eyes found mine. He remained staring at me for a few quiet moments before letting go of my free hand. He stepped aside, keeping the door open with his body so I could exit.

He shut the door and went for his phone, and I circled him, curious whether someone had texted with an update. "News?"

He shook his head. "My mom." He slid the phone back into his pocket, his dark gaze drifting from my collarbone to my neck.

Was he remembering when he'd held on to me there? Because I was. A rush of desire pooled between my legs at the mere thought of that exchange on Sunday. At least I now had a few new memories flying around in my head to think back on, since I was missing almost thirty-five years of my life.

"Everything okay?" I hesitantly asked, worried about broaching the subject of his parents. I licked my salty lips, nerves tangling me up again.

"She wants me to visit my, uh, dad. She doesn't get that I can't just drop everything whenever she calls."

"Does she know what you really do?"

He frowned, then shocked me by actually answering. "No. Just that it pays much better than the army. I got out because . . ." He propped his hand on the sauna door, muscle flexing.

I didn't press or poke. I remained a good girl. If he wanted to tell me about his past, that was his choice. He'd asked me not to do that, and so I'd behave, even if I was dying to know more about him.

"Bills don't stop," he said, his voice low. "Even when you're overseas fighting someone else's wars. You come home and the battles are waiting. Debt. Family. All of it." He exhaled through his nose. "Ryder offered me a position at Delta Shield a few years back, and so I didn't re-up. Took the job hoping it'd ease the burden of the back-home stuff."

"And did it?" I couldn't help but ask.

He lifted his shoulder, a nonanswer.

"You did it for your parents. To help them despite—"

"Despite hating both of them, yeah." His throat flexed, but instead of getting mad at me for violating his no-talking-about-his-past rule, he continued, choosing to share more of himself. "They've always needed bailing out. Debt. Spending money they don't have. Even before

I was paying for my dad's treatments and his facility this year, they bled me dry."

"You really are a hero, aren't you?" I stepped forward and palmed his cheek. I had to let him know I was there for him, and if I hadn't been before, well, screw that me. *I'm here now.*

His eyes snapped to mine like I'd just rocked the boat and triggered the calm peace that'd been happening between us. "I'm not. Just a guy cleaning up after two people who had no business being parents." The gravel in his voice gutted me.

He caught my wrist, and my thumb grazed his lower lip before he pulled my hand away, returning it to my towel. "Don't let that fall."

I obeyed his request. "I'm so sorry." For what he went through, for asking questions again, for all of it. For not remembering our past, even if it was allegedly a rocky-ish one.

He walked back, his arm returning to his side. He nearly tripped over Ranger, muttering a curse.

"Don't forget, it took years to make you who you are now," I said, unable to tame my tongue. It was like trying to roll a boulder up Everest. Impossible. "Your past shaped you, too." I stepped closer, the towel clinging to me, sweat still dripping down my skin, and I didn't care.

"Don't use my words on me. That's different."

But is it?

"I can't do this. I couldn't on Sunday, and I don't know why I thought I could do it now." He shook his head, body visibly tensing. "You don't know me, not the real me." He brought a hand to his chest for emphasis. "I'm no saint. No hero. Not special. A nobody."

His stare tangled with mine, fierce as he demanded I believe what I never would. His words from Sunday hit me hard all over again, right along with my mother's despicable comment about him.

Oh God, you don't think you're good enough for me, do you? Who made you feel this way? I bit my tongue, nearly drawing blood as I refrained from speaking my thoughts out loud this time.

"But you?" he went on. "You're everything."

His voice was so stripped down and raw, the pain of his past right between us. I couldn't remember mine, but I could feel his like it was something tangible I could reach for.

"I'm not that husband, that father, from your dream. That's just a fantasy, Hollis." His breath fanned across my skin as he leaned closer, our noses nearly touching. "And in the real world? For people like me?" He faked a dark laugh, righting his posture. "Dreams are only an illusion. Just when you think you can have whatever you want . . . it's taken from you."

CHAPTER TWENTY-FOUR

Reed

I let the sun beat down on me, tilting my chin up like Superman soaking power from the rays, hoping a little vitamin D could burn away what Hollis had done to me this morning. Like had me opening up, making me feel things I had no business feeling.

I'd blown my own rules to hell, and it had nothing to do with her being only in a towel. She was irresistible. Always had been, always would be. Fake hate and my three-foot rule didn't change that.

At the sound of the back door opening and shutting, I pretended it was only the ghost of my past coming to haunt me.

"Hey, you good?" My head fell forward at Alex's voice.

"Yup."

"You lying?" He was probably at my six now. Didn't need him to have my back or be anywhere near me.

"Nope." I cracked open my eyes, making sure Ranger hadn't escaped.

He was a few feet away, sunbathing on his back, belly exposed, tongue lolling, as if the world wasn't falling apart.

"Let me guess: She's ruffling your feathers?"

Seeing as he wasn't letting me off the hook, I faced him, jaw rigid, body strung like a trip wire. "I'm not a bird."

Of course he pressed and called me on my bullshit. "Could've fooled me, with all the times you fly away. You know, whenever shit gets real."

The guy had a psych degree, and I had to be reminded of that at every turn when he tried to use it on me. Not that it ever worked. I was a steel trap, at least before Hollis went missing and turned up only remembering me.

"Come on, man, talk to me."

"I'm not looking for a repeat of what went down in that office," I warned. "That duct tape is keeping me together just fine." The lie was almost comical, considering everything that'd happened with Hollis since we'd arrived at my house.

"And the prayers? How are those?"

I rolled my eyes and stepped forward, untucking the chain I knew he had hidden under his tee, revealing a cross. "Why don't you go pray for us both, how about that?" No way God wanted anything to do with me at the moment anyway.

Alex glared at me as I let go of his cross; I wasn't in the mood for judgment, so I searched out Ranger to look at.

"Just tell me if it's her that's got you in such a foul mood, or the case. Your father?"

"You're as bad as her, I swear." I hung my head. "Just don't know when to stop."

"I don't abandon a brother, and you should know that by now." Alex remained locked in, not bailing the way I'd once wished my parents would. That one of those times when they ghosted me for days on end, they'd just stay gone for good. I was better off alone at thirteen than cleaning up after them. So I'd begun to believe, at least.

Before I had a chance to continue battling my way through this with Alex, the back door opened.

"I have Constantine on the phone," Ryder said, holding the door open without coming out. "He might have something."

I'd never been so thankful for an interruption.

Alex shot me a *You're not off the hook* look I ignored on our way inside, Ranger leading the way.

I expected Hollis to be waiting there already, but she was nowhere in sight. After our towel talk earlier, I'd barely spoken a word to her. Saved by Audrey and Chase showing up a few minutes later, thankfully not finding her in only a towel.

"She's on the phone with Gideon," Audrey told me, beating me to having to ask.

My pulse grew wings and took off in flight at that news.

"Hollis texted Lyra, asking her to send a photo of Tristan so she knew what he looked like. She was hoping it'd spark something for her," Audrey explained as Seraphina joined us in the kitchen. "Gideon called before Lyra could even answer, pissed off."

"Why?" Alex asked, clearly not in the know about this, either, which meant it had happened while he'd been playing shrink with me outside.

"Not a shocker, but Julian and Gideon have been reading her texts." Audrey held up her hands as if to say *Don't shoot the messenger.* "Her asking for a photo set him off."

"She must've forgotten her mother's orders not to mention Tristan over the phone," Ryder remarked—and shit, I'd nearly forgotten about that and our code for him because of it, X-Man.

Audrey jerked a thumb toward the hallway. "I'll go grab her."

"If I didn't have safety measures in place," I said as Audrey left, "I wouldn't be surprised if they were listening to us."

"Sure they tried." Ryder grimaced. "They're taking Big Brother to another level."

Tell me about it. "Where'd Trevor go? Chase? Eden?" We'd had a full house when I went out back.

"Decided to take them to the park while we took this call. Didn't want Chase hearing anything that could be unsettling," Alex shared before Audrey returned with Hollis a few seconds later.

Her hair was a little messy, as if she'd been running her fingers through it.

"What'd Gideon want?" I couldn't help but ask as she made eye contact with me.

She crossed the kitchen and held out her cell phone. "He asked you to destroy this and get me a new burner. I forgot and, um, mentioned Tristan over text. Julian's scrubbing the messages and data, but Gideon doesn't want to take any chances. He wants a hammer taken to it."

I took the phone from her, careful to avoid touching her, then set it on the counter and placed some distance between us. I could never seem to think straight when she was close enough for me to breathe in the smell of my body wash on her skin.

"After warning me to never mention Tristan over the phone again, he hung up so he could destroy his own device."

"We really need to find out who the hell your brother is. You know, for real." Alex pulled out a chair for Audrey, and once she sat, he rested his hands on the back of her chair.

As Seraphina and Hollis took a seat next, I found myself staring in a daze at the fourth empty chair, my thoughts drifting to Hollis's dream of our family. Part of me wanted to order that fifth chair, and that thought alone was enough reason to send me over the edge.

But for now, I had to hang on for dear life and get through this call.

"Unmuting Constantine. You ready?" Ryder asked Hollis.

Hollis stole a look back at him, then hesitantly nodded before her eyes found mine. There was a story there. An entire saga sitting between us I had no idea how to explain away.

"We're all here now," Ryder said, holding out his phone.

"I think I got a lead. Well, my teenage son did, actually." Constantine's light Italian accent cut through the line. "He heard about a rave that happened the night Hollis went missing."

Was Constantine really comfortable letting his teenage son get in the middle of this mess? Not my call to question him, but damn.

"A rich kid took over the basement of a fifteenth-century library for it. Rumor has it, shots were fired, cutting the night short. Though no police reports were filed. If anyone was hurt or killed, there's nothing in the system."

"Wait . . . a *library*?" Hollis sat taller, shoulders arching back, and I knew exactly where her mind had wandered. To the book. To my *dad*.

I stiffened, keying in on the cross around Alex's neck, and a prayer sat on the edge of my mind that I couldn't seem to let loose.

"They cut the alarms and shut down the cameras inside even before the rest of the city's footage was screwed with," Constantine went on. "I took a look around myself. There was evidence of gunfire, but no shells left behind. It was clean."

Because I was full of bright ideas lately, I rounded the table so I could check Hollis's reaction to all this.

There was a flicker of something in her eyes. It was quick and sharp, like a memory was there waiting to resurface, but she couldn't pin it down.

"I called in a favor to Gwen before I went there to see if anything stood out about the library, including any rumors about something being sold or traded that night." He spoke directly to Hollis next. "Gwen couldn't find anything, but criminals are getting smarter these days about leaving a digital footprint." He paused for a brief moment. "But Gwen did discover there's a system of underground tunnels down there. Found one secret door behind a bookshelf so far. One set of footprints, too. My guess? A woman's. European size 39. They stopped outside a crawl space that led to the *Museo e Cripta dei Cappuccini*. The Capuchin Crypt."

The only Capuchin-anything I'd ever heard of was a monkey. I highly doubted there was a secret burial place for monkeys beneath Rome. After Constantine gave us the quick explanation, I was almost offended that even with all my knowledge, I didn't know about this place. *Monk bones. Really?*

"The trail went cold once inside. Concrete pathway. But there are stairs that lead to a store above. It's possible she ran out that way." He was back to speaking as though Hollis wasn't the subject of our conversation.

At this point, since Hollis had no memory of ever being there, she probably didn't feel tied to the "she" of his story, either.

"I tracked down the kid who threw the rave, and he's working on a list of who he invited to the party so I can personally question everyone to see if anyone can confirm if you were there. He denied seeing you, but he was also rolling on E."

"You believe him?" I asked.

"About the drugs? Yeah. About not seeing Hollis? No." A deep breath curled through the line in a low hiss. "His father is Benjamin Putcheski. He's a businessman from Eastern Europe. Doesn't have the nicest of friends. It's possible if Hollis was at that rave, she wasn't there for a book, but for someone tied to the Putcheski family."

The weight of his words landed hard. *Thank the Lord.* Now we were getting somewhere.

"And we obviously can't check footage to see if Benjamin or another criminal was at the rave because of the CCTV issue," Ryder noted. "What about flights? Do we know if he was in town that way?"

"Benjamin has a boat slip at a marina in Naples. His yacht was docked there the night of the rave. If he went to Rome from there, I haven't been able to get a hit. It's not outside the realm of possibility, but it may just be his son was vacationing in Italy with him and that's why he threw the party in Rome and not Naples—so his father wouldn't catch him. The kid begged me not to speak to his father, terrified of getting in trouble, so . . ."

"This is something, at least," Hollis said, her tone soft and tentative. "If you found this lead, you think my brothers did, too?"

"Probably," Ryder answered. "Did you ask the Putcheski kid if anyone else reached out?"

"I did, but his *no* could be bullshit. I pressed him, but not hard enough that he'd shit in his pants. He's not my enemy. Not yet, at least. Not looking to make one of his father at the moment, either, but I will if I have to." Constantine kept quiet for a few seconds, before adding, "I'll talk to Benjamin if need be as well."

"If you're asking people if they recognize me," Hollis slowly began, "you may want to change up my look a little. Something tells me I'd go in disguise."

"I already thought of that. I had Gwen put together a couple different photos of you. Glasses in one. Different wigs in a few others," he confirmed.

"Red," Hollis said in a hushed voice, lightly shaking her head. "Just . . . try that one, okay?"

"Will do. We'll also try to get our hands on some cell phones from inside the rave. Might be our best bet at seeing footage, since the security systems and CCTV were wiped. Be in touch when I know more." He cut the line without a goodbye.

Audrey rested a hand on Hollis's forearm, supporting her the way I wanted to. "You remembering something?"

"I thought I might, but whenever I try to remember anything, I always go back to that dream." She shook her head. "It feels like a reset point. I don't understand it."

Reset point? I stared at the floor, trying to wrap my head around what this meant. I'd known about her dream, but I didn't know that she also . . .

My stomach wrenched as a sinking feeling hit me, and the truth blasted into me like a round from a shotgun.

It made sense now, and I almost hated that it did.

The dream, the one she clung to like a lifeline, served as a wall. A fail-safe someone had planted in her head to keep the truth buried behind it. And whenever she tried to recall her memories, she landed on me and those three kids.

"The dream, that perfect picture in your head, it's there to stop any real memories from surfacing," I said under my breath, thinking out loud.

Hollis stayed locked on me, eyes wide in understanding. Like she could feel the ground tilting under her, too.

You don't actually want to marry me. Have kids with me. Not before, not now. Someone just used me—the last man anyone would ever expect for you to want—to keep you from clawing back to get to the truth.

"What dream?" Ryder asked, but I couldn't give him my attention.

Hollis pushed her chair back and stood, one hand covering her mouth as though holding something in.

"Anytime you reach for the past," I continued, my voice gravelly, "you land on that dream because it *is* your reset point."

Her breath shuddered, and my chest became raw, like her pain was carving into me. Like I'd just lost her and those three kids that were never mine in the first place.

It really was an illusion. This feeling. It wasn't real, and as fast as the hope for more between us had come—just like I predicted would happen—it was swiftly taken away from me.

"You feel safe with me . . . because someone wanted you to."

CHAPTER
TWENTY-FIVE

Reed

Hollis lowered her hand from her mouth, shoulders trembling. She looked at me like she was standing on a cliff's edge and I was the only solid ground left. "I, um, need a minute alone. Excuse me." She took off before anyone could stop her, and Ranger wasted no time in trailing after her.

"Plan on enlightening the rest of us what that was about?" Ryder removed his ball cap, dragging his hand through his hair.

I glanced at Audrey, curious whether Hollis had told her about this. She read my thoughts and shared, "While we were watching movies yesterday, she pulled me aside out of Chase's earshot and told me about the dream."

"Mind filling them in, then?" I asked, and she nodded.

I picked up Hollis's phone and handed it to Alex. "Destroy this while I'm gone." I left the kitchen, my heart thundering and nerves stretching tight every step closer to her room, torn on how to handle her, the "reset" revelation—all of it.

At her door, I propped my hand up on the wall alongside it, trying to make up my mind. Plan A: rationalize my way through what we'd learned while remaining in operator mode. Plan B: do the opposite of A. Be irrational. Be a civilian. Be like a teen from the '80s with a boom box on my shoulder standing outside a girl's house, about to declare my feelings for her through a song.

What song could I possibly pick to explain what I was feeling, and *why* I was feeling it, though?

I pushed away from the wall as I mentally skipped through my entire saved playlist and went for the door handle. No need to knock. If it was unlocked, that was my invitation to enter. And yes, I was absolutely about to justify my way into her bedroom with that mentality.

The door opened, and the moment I saw her stretched out on the bed, with her back to me and Ranger curled tight against her, I decided to cut straight to a third option. Plan C: wing it, go with my gut, and see where it took me.

"Go away." The words cracked like a whip and yet held no weight.

Even Ranger didn't budge when he heard my steps. He knew she needed more than him.

"Can't do that." Because I was a walking contradiction in the flesh.

"You don't need to be here. I'll be fine." Stubborn woman.

I shut the door and rounded the bed. "You should've locked the door if you didn't want me to come in."

She refused to meet my eyes, and her face was partially buried in a pillow, so her words were muffled when she spoke again. "And you wouldn't have picked it or broken it down if you wanted to?"

"Maybe," I admitted. "But I guess we'll never find out."

Ranger lifted his head, ears perked up as if curious what I was about to do.

Your guess is as good as mine, buddy. I rested my hands on my hips, assessing the situation. From where I stood, my past, common sense, and Ranger were the main obstacles in my way of getting to her and fixing what I may have broken.

Someone may have manufactured her feelings for me with that dream by the power of suggestion and drugs, but that didn't change the here and now. That she was under my roof, which made her mine to protect. Physically *and* mentally.

A half-hearted grunt of frustration sailed from my lips as I removed my shoes and set aside my own issues to get in the bed with her.

"My turn," I told Ranger, and he got the message and jumped off.

The mattress dipped from my weight as I lay down.

"What happened to that three-foot rule?"

"On hold for now. You've had a tough day. I'm just trying to be people-y here for you." I switched to my back and set my hands on my chest, head on the pillow, trying to get comfortable. "*But* my being here doesn't change what I said to you earlier." I could only let my walls down so much. I needed to remain as strong as possible with six inches separating me from the woman I desperately wanted but could never have.

Still nothing from her, just sniffling.

I could be quiet all day, all night. No problem. But hit me back with the kind of silence my old man used to give me as a kid? I'd wind up trying to fill in the blanks, becoming a talker. Didn't make sense, but it was what it was.

"I'm sorry someone did that to you, that they created a false reality with me in it—the last person the *real* you would ever want to be with."

While I'd expected her to challenge me, I didn't expect for it to come in the form of a sudden pillow whacking my chest.

"What the—" The pillow connected with my face this time, cutting me off as Ranger howled. "Hollis," I snapped while sitting and twisting around to catch her next attempt to thrust her pillow at me. I snatched it midair and wrenched it free from her, tossing it to the floor.

Ranger set his paws on the bed, barking. He was coming to her defense when I was the one under open fire. "Down," I ordered before lifting my hands in surrender as she side-eyed another pillow.

She was on her knees, panting, ready to go to war with me in a way I hadn't prepared for. Then she did it. Made her move. She picked up her next pillow weapon and held it like a threat between us. I grabbed the other side.

"I can't have a pillow fight with you." She knew damn well why I wasn't about to wrestle with her in bed. I would most definitely lose on purpose, let her wind up straddling me so I could kiss her.

She kept a firm grip of the pillow, her eyes becoming glossy. "Then stop with that self-deprecating bullshit."

She tugged. I pulled right back.

"I don't want to hear how you're a nobody. Not worthy or whatever nonsense you spewed earlier." A single tear slid down her cheek, distracting me, allowing her to nearly break the pillow free from my grip. "And screw what my mother said. You may have dropped out of school, but look at you now. You became part of one of the world's most elite units. Delta Force," she continued, more tears trailing down her face, hitting her lips.

All I could do was hold on to the pillow with everything I had in me and not jerk it *and* her over to my lap.

"I don't know what happened to you, but you're the definition of *resilient*. It makes perfect sense to me why someone would choose you to be the one they plant in my head as my husband and the father of my children."

My husband and the father of my children had to be the best words I'd ever had thrown at me in my entire life.

"So yes, you deserve a pillow to the face, over and over again, until I can get it through your thick skull that you're good enough. More than good enough," she rasped, voice breaking. Also breaking me in damn half.

"You don't know me," I said under my breath, unable to shake my past.

I'd overcome more obstacles than I could count in my life and struggled every day not to fall back to my old ways. It was a daily battle trying to be a better man. But could I be *her* man? No, no way.

"You're right. My body and mind don't know you." She licked her lips, catching her tears. "But my soul does. Or did you forget what you told—"

"Stop." I shifted off the bed, needing to get away from her. Ranger remained by my feet, his gaze volleying between us. "That 'soul' feeling . . ."—I was a jackass and used air quotes—"it's based on lies someone shoved in your head. The desire? Fake. Your perception of me? Tainted."

She chucked the pillow, ready to go to war on her feet. She rounded the bed to confront me, and Ranger whimpered, as if he hated seeing his mom and dad fighting. "I hate you for saying that, for making me—"

"See?" I bit out, jaw strained as I stared her down. "That feeling right there is the *real* one. Stick with it. Been trying to tell you since the day you asked me if we were . . ." I shook my head and left off the *sleeping with each other* part of my unhinged statement.

She swiped her tears free with the backs of her hands as if those liquid drops had betrayed her.

"You're confused. You don't want me, I promise." I softened my tone that time, remembering why I came here, and it wasn't to knock down someone already in pain.

"Fine, okay," she sputtered, slamming her hands on her hips. "Then look me in the eyes and tell me it's all fake for *you*. It's just desire because you're a man who finds me attractive."

I squeezed my hands open and closed at my sides, trying to get a grip. To do what she said and lie right to her face. "No." I had no idea what I was even saying *no* to. It was the only word I could get out.

She poked my chest, and I gritted down on my back teeth and lowered my chin to stare at her finger, catching sight of Ranger still wedged between us.

"Look at me."

I did as she asked. Eyes clashing with hers. Snarling at her. Baring my teeth. My lungs ached as I felt the weight of everyone's pain and disappointment from all over the world fill up every crack and crevice of my very being. *Fuck*, it hurt.

I couldn't lie. I couldn't tell her I only wanted her body. So I did my best to reroute. Find a new path out of this. "We'll never fit together.

It'd never work." The words tasted like ash, and it was also a scapegoat. The clichéd excuse: poor boy and rich girl, blah-blah-blah, nonsense.

"Good, great." She leaned forward so far she had to grab my forearm to maintain her balance and not step on Ranger. "Now try that again while *looking* into my eyes. And tell me you don't want me."

I'd rather have open heart surgery while I was awake than lie to her. She already had a grip around my heart; I could feel her trying to physically pump life into it, and she had no business doing that. Because the second she came back to us with her memories, she'd leave me there with my chest cracked open, heart bare to the world.

"Can't do it, can you?" She tightened her hold of my arm.

"Why won't you listen to me? What the hell did they do to you to make you want . . ." I closed my eyes, hanging my head. "Are we really standing here talking about *this*? You and me? When there are a dozen things that matter more? Like who did this to you, why they did it, and how to get your memories back?" Dodge and deflect—that was the only ammo I had left to try to win this war.

"The fact we are talking about it despite everything going on must mean it's important. We've been circling back to *us* since the moment you walked into the room at my parents' house. Doesn't that tell you something?"

"Just proves my point." I should have gone with plan A. Even B. Anything but the direction I'd gone. "Someone used me to mess you up." My free hand slid from my chest to my ribs at the memory of what I had tattooed there.

This Hollis may want me, but *Celeste* Hollis wouldn't. I hadn't missed the signs before. Sexual tension? Maybe. But love, and for me to be the father of her children? No, she never wanted me like that before. Not possible.

"Jason," she breathed out.

I had no idea how she managed to redeem that name, but somehow I could physically feel the damage done by my father begin to drift away. Each time that name hit the air from her tongue, it hurt a little less.

"I can't do this." I opened my eyes, rested a hand on top of hers, and gently removed her touch so I could retreat. "You should rest."

God, every part of me felt banged up and broken.

I went over to a pair of boots she had in front of the closet, forcing myself to transition back to operator mode. I picked them up and checked the size. "They're a match. European 39." I set them back down. "As soon as we hear from Constantine, I'll let you know."

I forgot about my own shoes and went to the door, hoping to exfil before she'd try to stop me. Because if she asked me to stay? I didn't trust myself that I wouldn't. One of us had to remain strong, and it had to be me, the one who remembered our past.

I unlocked and opened the door, my heart thudding up into my ears as I went into the hallway, grateful she hadn't called out for me. No pillows thrown, either. I left Ranger with her and shut the door.

My chest burned as I walked away from her, and the house hummed with too many voices. I needed everyone gone, which was what I announced the second I made it back to the kitchen.

"She okay?" Audrey asked after I'd given my order to leave.

I held up my hand, a request not to ask anything. "Please, just . . . go."

Alex closed his laptop, shooting me a worried look, and I prayed with everything I had in me that he wouldn't poke or press.

"Let me know if Constantine learns anything," I managed.

Ryder scrutinized me before relenting. "We do need to talk to her family. At this point, we don't have a choice."

I folded my arms, glancing at my watch. "First thing tomorrow, we'll make the call."

"Or just send them a text about Tristan?" Seraphina suggested. "And then don't answer when Gideon calls fuming. We won't have to talk to them. They'll even come to us."

Ryder peered at his wife, a quick smirk cutting across his lips at her smart idea.

"Destroy the phone after the text, of course, to protect this mystery brother of theirs," Seraphina added as Ryder laced his fingers with hers.

He had Seraphina.

Alex had Audrey.

And what'd I have?

Right . . . Hollis's dream that will never come true.

CHAPTER TWENTY-SIX

Reed

The quiet had been my idea, but after two hours of Hollis being alone in the bedroom and no updates from the team, the silence was officially deafening.

I poured two fingers of Buffalo Trace. It'd be enough to take the edge off, not enough to dull my guard. The bite scorched my throat, but it didn't touch the storm in my head.

Footsteps padded across the hardwood, and I didn't look up until Hollis was in front of me, plucking the glass from my hand. "The three-foot rule is on hold again."

Here we go.

Ranger came in behind her and curled up in his doggy bed in the living room as Hollis raised the glass to her lips.

Her eyes held mine the whole time as she drank. When she lowered the bourbon, her voice was steady despite the slight tremble in her hand. "We have to talk to my family, don't we? Tomorrow?"

She indulged in one more sip, and I tipped my head yes for an answer. I took the glass from her and finished it off, and turned around to add more.

Her short nails skimmed over my shirt and up my spine, and I slowly set down the glass and bottle. "Why are you touching me?" I squeezed my eyes shut, hating how a single scratch could light me up.

"I feel bad about earlier. I pushed you. It's just . . ."

That didn't explain why she was still touching me, causing my entire body to break out in chills. If all our arguments ended in back scratches, then I might have to . . . *Nope, don't go there.*

"You're probably right." Those words would've had to be pried from her mouth in the past. "I'm focusing on us because that dream is all I have. Well, aside from movie trivia, I suppose. But I don't have my memories, so I'm clinging to the one thing I do have."

I kept still, not ready to move with her lightly scratching my back. Plus, if I turned around, she'd undoubtedly notice the bulge quickly forming in my jeans. Damn body, betraying me at every turn.

"I'm useless in helping you and your team, and it's making me a little crazy that my own brain is the key to unlocking what the heck happened to me, and yet anytime I try to remember, I wind up . . . well, going back to that dream," she explained, her voice far more level than it'd been in her bedroom.

As for me, I was about to be no better than Ranger and let my tongue hang out, if she kept up with the back scratches.

"So I guess I keep focusing on that dream since that's all that actually occupies my mind. If only I could remember even one other thing, we'd get closer to the answers."

This was what I'd been trying to tell her two hours ago. Now there she was, admitting it, and I was standing here one back scratch away from telling her, *Screw what I said, I was wrong. I don't know jack shit.*

"I, uh, can't imagine how you feel," I settled on instead, drawing my hands to the bar cart. "It has to be frustrating to not remember anything *but* me and those children that don't exist."

In another life, in another world, maybe they could. All three of them. And I'd learn from the mistakes of my parents and do the opposite. I'd help them with their homework. Teach them values. Raise them to respect their mom and others. Maybe teach them to shoot a firearm (or soccer, there was that, too).

"I'm sorry." Two words I'd never heard my parents say to each other after a fight poured from my lips faster than I anticipated. "I shouldn't have snapped at you earlier."

I supposed I could be a better man in this reality, too. I opened my eyes, checked my crotch to ensure my erection had taken a chill pill, then pushed away from the bar cart to man up and face her.

"Not your fault. I broke your rules."

"I broke them first by getting in bed with you," I said roughly, keying in on her jawline and the throat I'd held the other day. *What had I been thinking?* "This whole situation is—"

"Confusing?"

I went stiff, doing my best to recalibrate, especially with her up in my personal space, smelling like my body wash.

"How can I help you get through this?" That was what I should have asked her in the bedroom. That should have been plan A.

"Distract me?" She angled her head toward the TV, fidgeting with the chain around her neck. "More *Mad Men*, or . . . well, do you have any other ideas for stress relief?"

Yeah, my body had other ideas, all right. I needed my head out of the gutter before my hard-on made a comeback.

I did my best to fake a tight-lipped smile, worried I was giving her *American Psycho* vibes with how off I was right now. Pulled in a hundred different directions with her at the center, tugging my strings. "I think it'd be best if Audrey distracted you, since I'm the one you need distracting from."

She stayed quiet, and so did I, frozen in place. No vortex dragging me into the darkness this time. Just me, rooted in front of her, and my heart had the audacity to question my head, to wonder whether my path to redemption could ever include her.

She released her chain and wrapped her fingers around as much of my wrist as she could grab. I should have walked backward. To hell with the bar cart there. Let the bottles crash. That three-foot rule was needed because she was dragging me tighter into her orbit where there was no her or me, just *us*.

"Can I ask you something that hopefully won't push your buttons?" Her words cracked through the unbearable tension.

"Is it personal?" I dropped my eyes to where her fingers pressed against my skin, the contact humming through me.

"Breaks your second rule, but I figured since we were breaking your first . . ."

I couldn't believe it, but instead of getting upset, a legitimate smile stole over my lips. "You just can't help yourself, can you?" She really did have no control over her tongue, and it was taking all my restraint not to offer her some assistance and take control of it with my own.

"As established." The side of her mouth lifted as she smoothed her thumb along my heated skin where she held me, piercing me with her intense stare. Seeing through my walls and to my *soul*. To the soul I'd worked so hard to get back after bartering it to the devil a decade ago.

Her dark lashes fell like a curtain, but I wasn't ready for that to be the closing act. No, I needed an encore. For her to never stop looking at me like I was someone special to her.

"Go ahead, ask away," I relented, my muscles tightening as I waited for the impact of her question.

She slowly opened her eyes. "I apparently chose to become this person, this warrior." Her chin wobbled as she held back her emotions, as stubborn as me. "So I'm curious: Why'd you choose to be one? What led you down the road to wearing the uniform, serving others?"

"No choice." I didn't want her putting me up on some hero pedestal. "It was the only way." I eased my wrist free of her grasp and sidestepped her, unable to look at her while I got through this. "I didn't join for any righteous reason, I did it to escape."

I rested my hands on my hips and hung my head, surprised I was about to tell her the truth, but there was no more dancing around the fact that at this point, I'd pretty much do anything for her. I didn't even recognize that until this very moment. Those rules were made to be broken when it came to her.

She began touching my back again. Walking her fingers up and down my spine in a rhythmic way that I didn't deserve. I needed to comfort her, not the other way around. And yet she kept pivoting back to my life, and I supposed it made sense seeing as though we couldn't talk about hers.

"I dropped out of high school as soon as I was eighteen and joined the army. I couldn't wait another semester."

I was done with my mother's meth addiction.

Done with my father beating the shit out of me.

I knew if I stayed, one day I'd hit him back.

At least he'd never set a hand on my mother. He'd be dead. I'd be in prison.

I kept that shit to myself. I didn't need her feeling even worse for me.

"Got my GED in the military. I thought if I ran far enough, I could actually get away," I finally finished.

"And did it work?"

"Yes and no." I lifted my head, tipping my chin up, eyes shooting to the ceiling. "But at some point, I discovered all I was doing was running in place. Other side of the world, same demons chasing me. I stupidly thought I could outrun them, wound up only running headfirst into new problems."

Instead of offering an apology or pity like I'd have hated, she hit me with something as unexpected as that pillow earlier. "You think we're different? I actually think we're alike."

"Oh yeah? How so?"

She let her hand fall from my back, and the absence burned a hole in my heart. "Sounds weird coming from someone who can't remember her favorite color, but based on what I've learned about myself . . . well, it seems to me I spent the last eight years trying to run away from who I was. I couldn't even tell Audrey the truth. I wanted to play pretend. Escape. Maybe my mother was right about me."

Her words had me about-facing, unsure what to make of them or how to respond. A tear slid down her cheek, and I caught it with the pad of my thumb, exhaling a shaky breath in the process.

I need to end this conversation while I still can. "Audrey should come talk to you. It can't be me." For reasons we'd already discussed, and I had no plans to go back over them again.

"Any other ideas for a distraction, aside from Audrey?" she asked as Ranger ran over, offering an idea of his own—to pet him. She took a knee, rubbing his back.

Lucky dog. I looked around the room, not able to come up with anything that didn't involve getting myself into trouble and crossing lines.

"Maybe the whole 'remembering stuff organically' isn't what I need." She tossed out partial air quotes with one hand. "Any chance you have some reading material for me? You know, so I can get better acquainted with myself."

"What do you—"

"Texts." She stood, and Ranger whimpered at the loss of her touch.

I looked at Ranger, fighting a smile. *Yeah, I get that feeling. Trust me.* I blinked, pulling my focus back to the woman we both wanted attention from. Only one of us should be getting it, though.

"Did we ever exchange any messages that I could read?"

A chill rolled down my spine, and I roped a hand around the base of my neck and squeezed as the tension ticked up. "Yes, and you'll discover the truth." Then maybe she'd finally stay three feet away from me and stop asking personal questions since I couldn't stop violating my own rules.

"Which is?"

"That we don't work." The truth burned as I said it. "We're oil and vinegar." I went into the kitchen, where I'd left my personal and work phones, deciding this was for the best. Maybe I should have thought of this before. I had clear evidence I could provide her, proving her dream was pure fiction.

When I came back to her with both phones, she was already waiting for me with her hand open. I rattled off the six-digit code for both phones as I gave them to her.

"Eleven, twenty-five, twenty-one," she repeated. "Trusting me with your password, are you?" She attempted to lighten the heavy load I'd literally dropped into her hands with a small smile.

"I have nothing to hide." Not on the phones, at least. "I'll be in the gym, finishing cleaning my weapons." Unable to bear standing before her any longer, I started to leave, but of course she had to ask one more question, stopping me.

"Do those numbers have any significance? Sounds like a date."

It was a date. November 25, 2021. But why'd she have to ask me about it?

I wasn't a liar, but I also couldn't give her the whole truth. The best I could manage was somewhere in between. I kept my back to her as I rasped, "Yeah, the date marks *my* reset point."

CHAPTER TWENTY-SEVEN

Hollis

I bent my legs up underneath me, trying to get comfortable alongside Ranger on the living room couch, preparing myself for a deep dive into our texting past.

Ranger set his head on my thigh, his curious eyes pointed at me like I was doing something wrong.

"He gave me permission. Not violating your daddy's privacy, promise."

I was desperate to ask him what he meant by the November date being his reset point, but I knew better than to press my luck and push him to open up.

"Work or personal phone first?" I peeked at Ranger, and he bopped the work phone with his nose. "Okay, then."

I opened Reed's texts and had to scroll through several other names to get to mine. A group text with Ryder, Alex, and others was at the top. That thread probably had to do with me, but I wasn't going to abuse the trust he gave me and read anything other than our messages.

I spotted my name and opened our exchange. No image of me for the profile, which made sense. Why would he want to look at my face when we swapped texts?

I swiped back as far as it'd allow, landing in late February of this year. I read over the messages, and it didn't take a rocket scientist to figure out why I drove the man nuts. I was *not* easy to deal with, that was clear. My way or the highway when it came to a mission involving Audrey, and my God, what the heck . . . Based on what I could gather from the texts about the operation, my best friend had been through a lot.

I stopped on a string of texts while we were in New Zealand undercover as a couple.

Me: Your suit is on the bed. I didn't trust you to shop for yourself, so I picked something out for you.

Reed: 😑 I can dress myself, thanks.

Reed: And why were you in my room while I was in the shower? You could have walked in on me.

Me: Should've locked the door.

Reed: I did. 😖

Me: Locked it . . . better? 😏

Reed: Why Audrey likes you, beats the hell out of me.

Me: Same goes for why anyone puts up with you, Mr. Grump.

Reed: That's . . . fair.

I smirked at our back-and-forth, reading between the lines, pretty sure we were flirting, *not* hating on one another.

There were a few more texts after that relating to the mission, but that was it.

I switched to his personal phone, my stomach aching at the first name at the top in his messages: Mom.

When I opened our exchange, I was surprised to see there was a profile picture of me in this one. I was outdoors, crouched alongside Ranger and smiling.

Interesting.

I swiped all the way back to our very first message and began there.

Me: It's me. Figured I'd text on your personal line when it's not op related.

Reed: Who is this?

Me: Your favorite person. 😁 Give you three guesses, but you'll only need one: a sexy brunette who kicks ass for a living, drives you nuts just by breathing, and is a sucker for banana bread.

Reed clearly programmed my number at some point after that, since it didn't say *Unknown* with my picture.

Reed: Did Audrey give you my number?

Me: Do you really think it was hard for me to find an unlisted number myself?

Reed: Why are you even texting me?

Me: It's 0300 where I'm at, and I can't sleep. Bored.

Reed: And you thought . . . let me bother Reed?

Reed: Where are you anyway that it's so late?

Me: Russia.

Reed: Why?

Me: Classified 😑

Reed: Bother someone else, will ya? Or you know, sleep.

Me: Well, you have my # if you ever want to chat.

Reed: The idea of talking to you because I want to has never, and will never, cross my mind.

And yet, a few days later, he reached out.

Reed: Just checking to make sure you're home and didn't die. Audrey would hate that.

I didn't respond, so he'd texted the following afternoon.

Reed: You good?

It was as if I were eavesdropping on someone else's life. Reading *their* story, not mine. I was relieved to see I finally answered him four hours later and hadn't died (as if I wasn't sitting right here, very much alive).

Me: Sorry, things went sideways. Let me tell you, Russian prisons . . . 0/10 don't recommend. All good now. My dad made a call and a deal.
Reed: WTH
Me: Sweet you cared. Also, just pointing out the fact you texted first. 😎

He didn't respond back to that, but now I was hung up on the fact I'd been in a prison and my father had to negotiate for my release.

We didn't text again for a few weeks, and it went about the same as before. Next three exchanges after that, too. I poked, he jabbed back.

The next back-and-forth, though . . .

Me: Thought you'd want to know I got back that artifact we had to auction off in NZ. Had to deal with lions, tigers, and bears to get to it.
Reed: You're joking.
Me: The correct response to what I said is: "oh my." Haven't you seen The Wizard of Oz?
Reed: Nope. Why would I have?
Reed: So, the artifact was at a zoo, is that what you're trying to tell me in your typical weird way?
Me: More like at the home of a rich asshole who collects wildlife. Got what I went there for and set all the animals free. Annnnd without getting mauled. Believe it or not, that scar above my brow was when a lion cub almost had me for dinner two years ago. Gideon tranquilized him before he could eat me. Just a scratch.

It was hard to believe I was truly this person I was reading about. I took a few more seconds to digest that—decided I couldn't—and moved on, back to our messages.

Reed: I don't know if you're being serious, but if you are, you're stressing me out.

Me: Thought you don't care about me, why would I stress you out?

Reed: Because Audrey's your best friend. Told you before, if you die, she'd be upset.

Me: Ah, yes. Makes sense. Well, I don't care about you either.

Reed: Good, great, please don't.

Me: You're extra grumpy tonight. What's wrong?

Reed: It's 0200, and I just got back from operating. I'm tired AF, and you're texting me about wrestling wild animals.

Me: You didn't have to answer.

Reed: I'll remember to do that next time. Well, I'm glad an animal didn't eat you. Now go to bed.

Me: Yes, sir. 😊

Reed: I hate you.

Me: 🫶

A text popped up from his mother, interrupting my reading. I quickly discarded the notification so I wouldn't see what she'd texted. Not my business.

I was a little sad to discover I was near the end of our exchanges, though. I wanted to read more. Also, I needed a happily-ever-after; their story—shit, *our* story—couldn't just be left hanging.

Reed: You staying out of trouble?

Me: Just can't help but check on me, huh?

The time stamp was from about two weeks ago. When he didn't acknowledge my response, I sent a follow-up.

Me: In France with my brother working on something.

What had I been working on? And didn't Lyra say Gideon had checked my place in France and it'd been found tossed?

Me: I'm going to swing by Audrey's later this month to say hi. Will you be around?
Reed: I'll plan not to be.
Me: Sure, sure. You wouldn't miss seeing me.
Reed: Haven't had a good eye roll in a few days, you're right.

That would have been the weekend before last, not too long before I went to Italy, right?

Me: See you then. x
Reed: That x supposed to represent a kiss?
Me: Don't you wish? 😆
Me: Why wait until I come when you can roll your eyes now? 😊
Reed: How kind of you. 😐

We had one final brief exchange Wednesday morning of last week.

Me: I heard you're in Panama for an op. Be safe.
Reed: I planned to do the opposite actually.
Me: Smart-ass.
Reed: Only for you.

I had to have been in Italy when I sent that text, and then . . . *I was taken and woke up like this.* No wonder I never checked to ensure he made it home safe from his operation—I'd been MIA by then.

I took a moment to process everything I'd read, my skin flush and warm, goose bumps peppering my arms.

Reed had said our texts would make me understand why we'd never work, but that was *not* what I got from our messages at all.

I gently patted Ranger, letting him know it was time to get up and confront his daddy. Standing, I held both phones and slowly made my way to the gym, my heartbeat quickening every step of the way.

Outside the door, I shifted the phones to one hand so I could open it, then looked at Ranger. He tilted his head, ears up, staring at me as he was waiting for me to turn the knob.

"Need alone time," I told him, gesturing to the hall with my head, hoping the smart dog would understand. He yelped, but he turned and took off.

I took a calming breath, then opened up.

Reed's back was to me, and he had multiple firearms spread out on the table in front of him.

"Your mother texted."

His back muscles flexed, drawing the material of his tee together. "And?"

"I didn't read it, just thought you should know." I finally got my butt moving, and I set his phones on the table near a Glock.

He picked up his personal one, quickly checked the text, then returned it to the table. "Are you done reading our messages?" He slowly turned, drawing his arms across his chest like a guard, probably because I was also violating rule one by being in his personal space.

I visually tracked the vein in one of his corded forearms. "I am."

His throat muscles moved with a deep swallow as our eyes connected. "Now you understand?"

"That I have a death wish?" I half smiled. "The woman I was in those texts would most definitely sneak off to Rome and risk her neck if the cause was worthy. That much I know."

Worry lines bracketed his mouth. "And what did you conclude when it came to you and me?"

That there's supposed to be an us. I kept that to myself, stepped over his rule, and held his hard biceps.

He studied my hand as I lightly squeezed his arm. "What are you doing?"

"Touching you." Nervous, I walked my hands up to his shoulders, then to the sides of his neck. I wanted his hand on me like it had been on Sunday. Cupping my jaw, ass, throat. Taking command of any and every part of me. Just as long as his hands were on me, that was all that mattered.

"I'm well aware." His voice deepened. "But why?"

I hit him with another small smile of surrender. "Those messages read like a love story. It's only missing the ending where the two people confess their feelings."

"What?" His arms relaxed to his sides as his eyes narrowed in disbelief. "No, that's not—"

I brought a finger to his lips, silencing him, and he scrunched his face but obeyed.

"I just want to wake up. I want to remember the woman I was when I sent those texts." My voice cracked as I brought my hand over the sexy scruff along his chiseled jawline.

"And what else do you want? What can I do to help you in the meantime?" The sexy, gritty sound of his voice slid under my skin, sending a shiver up my back.

"You can't wake me up with a kiss . . . but that doesn't mean I wouldn't love you to go ahead and try."

He shut his eyes, and I thought he might retreat. Tell me to go fly a kite. Leave him alone and follow his rules.

Instead, he slowly turned his face into my hand, then flicked his tongue against my skin before sliding his lips across my palm in a kiss, lighting me up inside.

"Hollis," he hissed as if saying my name pained him. "Please don't ask me to set my mouth on yours."

"Why not?" I asked in a shaky voice.

His nostrils flared, and his eyes flashed open. "Because I'm going to snap the second your mouth touches mine," he nearly growled before brushing his lips over my palm again. "You saw what happened in the kitchen. You know what would've gone down had you thrown another pillow at me in your bed. You know I can't . . ."

"Can't what?" I needed to hear the words. That dream may have been implanted in my head, but it didn't change the fact we did have chemistry now *and* before. My feelings were real. *Soul*—not skin—deep. "Reed?"

"Jason . . ." he said on a sigh. "You can call me that if you want to. *Only* for you."

Only for you. That'd been his last text to me before I disappeared, and here we were, and he was giving a piece of himself to me.

"Jason," I said around the knot of pressure pushing into my throat from my chest.

He leaned in, resting his forehead to mine. His guard was slipping. Willpower waning. "Yes?" he responded, voice ragged.

"Go ahead," I whispered, "and *snap*."

CHAPTER TWENTY-EIGHT

Hollis

Jason tipped his head back until his eyes caught mine. The slow burn between us exploded in an instant.

He shoved his firearms aside, then gripped my hips and lifted me onto his bench.

Metal and gun oil bit at my thighs as I instinctively hooked my legs around him, dragging him closer until every hard line of his body pressed flush against mine.

Nose to neck, he inhaled me, his breath hot against my skin, the faint scent of gunpowder bleeding from him, sinking into me. "You smell so fucking good."

His lips skimmed over my skin as his stubble scraped fire down my throat. One hand braced against the table, the other sliding up my side, probably leaving smudges of oil, branding me as his.

Every nerve sparked, my body strung so tight I might shatter, and he hadn't even kissed me yet. I didn't remember sex, but instinct whispered that no one had ever made me feel this way before.

"Oil and vinegar," he ground out, like that was his last-ditch effort to remind us this was a mistake.

"If anyone can make those two mix"—I clutched his arms for balance—"it's us."

His answer was a curse against my mouth, swallowed by the hungry crash of his lips over mine.

His kiss was rough, almost punishing at first, until it softened into something desperate.

My back arched as his tongue found mine. His hand swept into my hair, and he fisted it while drawing his other around my throat as he'd done in the kitchen. This time not to hold me, but to find my pulse, as if needing proof I was real. That *this* was really happening.

He deepened our kiss, and the rumble of his groan vibrated through me. Every stroke of his tongue and his touch pulled me apart piece by piece.

He destroyed me a moment later by tearing his mouth from mine. "This isn't right."

"No, it's—"

"No, I mean, it's too fast." His hands framed my face as his gaze pierced mine, raw and unguarded. "It's been . . . years for me."

Years? How long has it been for me? I really hated I didn't know the answer to that.

"I'm not supposed to . . ." He let his voice trail off, kissing me instead, gentler this time, unraveling me even more than before.

I melted into him, dizzy and drunk on every kiss. We moved together in perfect sync, a dance that was only ours. His mouth guided mine, anchoring me to something solid, something real, which was a blessing after what I'd been through the last few days.

A few minutes later, he hoisted me off the bench, my legs remaining locked around his waist. He carried me through the gym, and I twined my wrists at the back of his neck. Somehow he managed to wrestle the door open without letting me go.

In the hall, he had me up against the wall, his mouth finding mine again. One hand slammed beside my shoulder, and the other gripped my ass as his hard length pressed into me.

I caught his moan with my tongue. He swallowed my breathless cries of surrender.

Paws scratched the floor, along with a whimper. Jason lifted his head, eyeing our company.

"Not hurting her, boy, I promise," he said, a laugh falling under his breath, and the sound was low and sinful. "But I do need her to myself. Now *git*."

"Your bed," I begged after Ranger followed his command. "Please."

He lightly nodded his *As you wish*. By the time we crashed into his bedroom, the world outside didn't exist. Just heat, need, and him.

He set me on the edge of the bed, swept the pillows aside, and pulled the covers back in one rough motion. Then he laid me out like I belonged there, like I really was his wife in that dream.

His shirt hit the floor, and he unbuttoned the top of his jeans but left them on. His muscles flexed in the low light. "I got you dirty," he muttered, shaking his head.

I glanced at the dark smudges streaking my arms and thighs. Probably my face, too. "I don't care."

His grin curved slowly and dangerously before he joined me, and I straddled him, the heavy weight of his erection pressed through his jeans. Heat spiked down my spine. Leaving on my chain, I stripped my shirt and bra off in one motion, baring myself without hesitation.

A guttural sound tore from his throat and his hand closed over my breast, the other cupping my chin to drag me back into the kiss.

I propped my hands on each side of him for support to give him my mouth.

We're in his bed together, not a dream this time. No waking alone. This was real. Him. Me. Us.

My pulse thundered with his every touch, every caress. Every spine-tingling sensation this man delivered.

Time blurred as we lost ourselves in kisses, his fingers teasing my nipples, his other hand tracing my curves as if memorizing me.

Desperation clawed through me. I wanted his hands between my thighs. On every inch of me.

I sat upright on top of him, and he held my hips and stared at me as if I were his everything. And my God, he made me feel like I was. This me, the old me, it didn't matter. Right now, I was his, and he was mine. That was all I knew.

"You're so beautiful." His voice cracked as he cupped my cheek.

"Still drive you nuts?" I smirked.

"Absolutely."

I licked my lips, my eyes falling to his bare chest, longing and desire pulling me apart. I lazily ran my nail across his rib, following the writing tattooed there.

He removed my hand, his eyes shooting to the ceiling. "I . . . forgot, and I—I *can't* forget."

Forget what? "Because I can't remember who I am?" Panic pushed into my throat, forcing my next words to be a little mumbled. "I still want you, that doesn't change anything." I freed my wrist from his hold and rested my hand over that sensitive spot on my chest. "I'm still here, remember? My soul. I'm making my own choices, and I choose you." In a shaky voice, I continued, fighting back tears, "I choose this. Right now, right here."

When he remained quiet, refusing to make eye contact, I rolled off and lay down beside him.

He slid his legs over to the side of the bed and dropped his feet to the floor. His spine bowed, muscles drawn tight as he covered his face with his hands. "You don't understand."

I shifted to sit next to him, rubbing his back, and he tensed from my touch. "Then help me understand."

"It's complicated."

"I'm a walking complication. Then and now. But I'm here with you, and I want to be. Not because of a dream." Well, maybe that dream had led me here, but I was staying because of what we had before, what I knew deep in my bones we had now.

He let his hands fall to the bed on either side of him. He slanted his head to steal a look at me, his gaze clashing with mine, keeping me a prisoner to whatever pain he was feeling with that heavy, somber expression crossing his face.

He broke first, stood and picked up his shirt. "You should shower. Gun oil and all," he said as if in a daze, holding his shirt between his palms, eyes on the floor, like he was ashamed of what happened between us. The opposite held true for me.

I rose and followed his cues and snatched my shirt, hiding my breasts behind the material. My instinct was to argue, to fight back, but I couldn't, not with how distraught he looked.

"Okay," I agreed, then started for the bathroom, unsure how we'd gone from reckless abandon to a cold, hard stop. I tossed my shirt and glanced back at him. "I'm leaving this open."

He was still clutching his shirt like a lifeline, shoulders forward under a weight I couldn't see. He didn't look at me, and I accepted the rejection and went into the bathroom, leaving the door open as an invitation in case he changed his mind.

Shorts and panties off, I stepped into the shower with only the chain on, hanging back, away from the spray, as I waited for the water to warm up.

Once it did, I stood there, numb and confused, only to startle a minute later at a shadow on the other side of the glass.

With a trembling hand, I slid the door open. Jason was leaning against the doorframe, still shirtless, his chest heaving. Dark eyes raked down my body, lingering between my legs, which had my body reacting immediately, a pulse of heat shooting through me.

"Talk to me." I held out my hand, water trailing down my skin. "Or at least . . . come to me."

"There are things about me . . . things you don't know." His eyes drifted back up my body, heavy with both desire and pain. "But I do want you. More than I can put into words. You have no idea how much, which is why"—he shook his head—"I've tried so hard to stay away from you."

I sniffled, my tears hidden by the shower. "I don't need answers if you're not ready to give them." My tongue darted over my lips. "Just come in here with me. That's all."

The muscle in his jaw jumped, forehead tightening, too. "Jeans stay on. If I take them off . . . and *if* you ask me to make love to you, I will. I won't have the willpower to say no."

I knew in my heart we couldn't rush into sex, even if everything in me screamed to do that. I didn't even remember my past sex life, my birth control situation—none of it.

"Okay," I agreed. Anything to have him in here with me. "And as for the jeans—do whatever you need to do. Just be here with me."

He pushed away from the doorframe and slowly came over, denim clinging to the thick outline of his erection.

When his palm met mine, the world stilled. Like something permanent clicked into place.

"So much for my three-foot rule and pretending to hate you," he rasped, fingers threading with mine.

My body trembled, from the cold air and from everything he made me feel. "Well, you said you're not a liar. So what's the truth?"

He leaned closer without joining me, the shower spray bouncing off me to hit him.

His lashes dripped, eyes dark as black glass beneath them.

"The truth?" His mouth coaxed open mine. "That I'll never be the same after today. That I want you, Hollis." His kiss deepened, tender and certain. "And God help me, no matter how much I try and convince myself I can't have you, that doesn't change the fact I know I'll always want you."

CHAPTER TWENTY-NINE

Reed

The spray beat down on my shoulders, hot water masking the chills crawling up my spine. I stepped next to her and rested my palms on the tiled wall, trying to process what was happening. Trying to understand how we got here. I'd been cleaning my guns, and she was supposed to read our messages and see how obvious it was that we didn't belong with each other, and now here we were.

I pushed away from the wall and slowly faced her, ensuring I hadn't hit my head and passed out. I deserved that kind of cruel fate, to wake up to the fact my mind was screwing with me.

My breath caught in my lungs when reality flexed its muscles. *You're here.* And the evidence of what we did was on her body. My fingerprints marked her cheeks, her arms, her legs.

She remained quietly staring at me, her long, wet lashes fluttering. Her tongue catching drops of water when it should have been my tongue doing that for her.

I cupped water in my hands and ran it gently over her face, washing away my handprints, and she quietly watched me with those eyes that made me forget logic. Forget my past, the life I'd run away from.

I soaped up the loofah next and dragged it along her arm, her neck—avoiding her chain—then continued to clean the rest of her upper body.

Hesitantly, and maybe stupidly, I knelt before her. My jeans clung, becoming soaked through as I stayed there, washing my prints from her thighs.

Her hands rested on my shoulders, and when I looked up, the sight of her loosened something inside me. Every instinct begged me to bury my face between her legs, to taste her until she was shaking on my tongue.

I dropped the loofah, resting my hands on her outer thighs, breathing hard as I battled with the desperate urge to make her come.

Her fingernails bit into my shoulders, a plea to do exactly that.

But if I started . . . I knew where that would lead.

I groaned, hating myself, my past—all of it—and forced myself to stand.

"I'm sorry," I mouthed.

"It's okay." She lightly nodded. So understanding. So perfect, and she had no idea just how broken and fucked up I used to be.

What if I still am?

She pressed her lips to mine, and that was all it took for me to forget again. Forget the darkness and the pain.

The water poured over us, and she melted into me. There was an achy need in her touch as she raced her hands over my body, arching into me.

I couldn't handle it, not without snapping. I caught her wrists in one hand and swiftly brought her hands up over her head.

God help me, dominance only seemed to turn her on even more. Her back hit the wall as I kept her arms in the prison of my embrace.

She rolled her shoulders back, breathless, her tits starved for my attention as she breathed heavily.

"Are you allowed to touch me?" she cried out.

"I *am* touching you," I growled, unable to take my eyes off her, wanting to take in every part of her from head to toe.

She wiggled her hips, bucking forward. "I'm trying to behave, I'm sorry. It's just hard." She squeezed her eyes shut, tilting her head to the ceiling, and I loosened my grip on her wrists but didn't let go.

"Can't control your tongue or your hands, hmm?" I asked, my voice rough as lust violently stormed through me, and I continued to fight back with everything I had in me.

"Trying to b-be good for you," she sputtered. "Whatever you want, I'll do it. Want me to behave? I will. We can't have sex, I—I respect that. But if you want to push your fingers inside me and give me the first orgasm I'll remember—"

"Fuuuuck." I cut her off when her green eyes landed on mine, and she annihilated whatever was left of my self-control. I let go of her wrists and grabbed hold of her ass cheeks, guiding her to use my body however she wanted or needed to get off as I kissed her.

I convinced myself this was okay. That as long as I didn't have sex with her, this wouldn't screw me up in the head. I wouldn't have to start over again. No new reset point. I dragged my mouth around to her ear as she whimpered and moaned, her hands flying across my chest, nails scratching me as she searched for relief by rubbing against my jeans.

No, this isn't right. She deserved better than this, even if it'd destroy me. "I'm going to give you my hand, okay?" I pulled back to search for her eyes.

"But if that's going to cause you—"

"You're going to ride my hand, okay? I'm going to"—I swallowed—"put my hand between your legs, and you're going to get off. You need relief. To feel better."

"You're sure?" She was still grinding against my jeans, a hand tangling my hair, the other clawing at my back.

Yeah, this woman needed some tension relief, that was for damn sure. I wouldn't be walking away from her until she had it, either. I back seated my issues, removed my head from the past, and anchored myself to the moment.

My fingers feathered over her clit, and something inside me snapped.

My hand went around her throat, gently holding her steady as I kissed along her jaw, devouring her mouth again.

So much for just letting her use my hand. *I* was going to make her come with it. Dictate the movements. Each stroke. The amount of pressure.

I gave her everything I was physically able to with my touch. And if she wanted the universe? I'd find a way to get that for her, too.

She shuddered hard against my hand, orgasming.

I released her throat, and she pinned my hand between her legs as if not ready to be done yet.

I caught sight of a shadow in the doorway. That shadow launched into a full-on storm of barking before a familiar voice called out my name.

We weren't under attack, but my team leader was about to have my ass.

"Don't move." I pulled my hand away, kissed her temple, then slid open the door to get out, water streaming off me. *"Git,"* I told Ranger, lifting my chin as a second command, feeling oddly protective of letting anyone, even an animal, see my girl naked.

I paused at the thought whiplashing me in the face. *My girl?* I shook it off, not yet digesting what had just happened in that shower and how fast I'd thrown five-plus years of practiced restraint out the window for her.

I snagged a towel and half-assed dried my hair as if my jeans weren't plastered to my legs. "Coming, one sec."

Ranger was waiting alone in the bedroom, hackles raised, still barking his head off.

"Where are you?" Alex that time—just great. I'd get a two-for-one lecture special.

I went out into the hall, Ranger following close behind. "When I said use my key for an emergency," I hissed, "this wasn't what I had in mind."

"You weren't answering your phone," Ryder said, waiting for me at the end of the hallway alongside Alex. "We got worried something happened." He holstered his sidearm.

"Looks like something did happen," Alex tossed out under his breath, securing his Glock as well. Silent judgment, or maybe amusement, was written into every line of his face.

"What?" I scoffed. "You don't take showers in your jeans?" I dragged the towel across my chest. "Why were you calling?"

Ryder propped his hand up on the wall, shooting me an *Are you kidding me?* look.

I walked down the hall, water dripping from me with every step, a dark trail in my wake. I couldn't stop staring at it, following the evidence of what I'd done.

My tongue had been in Hollis's mouth, my hand between her legs, and I . . .

Ah, shit. I checked my jeans, praying my hard-on was gone. *Thank God.*

"What's going on?" At Hollis's soft voice, I froze mid-step, the towel slipping from my hand. She was supposed to stay back out of sight, but of course she didn't listen.

She stood in the hall, damp hair over her shoulders, soaking through her shirt. Bare feet on the slick hardwood floors as she took cautious steps our way.

Her lips were still swollen from kissing, and they parted open in question.

Right. Why were we interrupted? I pivoted around to the reason I wasn't making her come for a second time.

"Constantine called with news," Ryder said, a worried expression crossing his face.

Hypocrite. The guy had once blown his own cover for Seraphina, and now he wanted to judge me?

Hollis stood alongside me, wrapping her arms around herself, shivering. She was cold, nervous, and exposed.

I shoved past the guys to grab a blanket from the hall closet. When I draped it over her shoulders, she looked up at me, eyes apologetic for not hanging back as I'd requested.

Ranger came around between us and planted himself on her feet like a guard, and I forced myself to face Ryder. "So?"

"Three people confirmed Hollis was at the rave in the library and that she wasn't alone." Ryder's words hit me hard. "They wouldn't turn over cell phones, and Constantine couldn't exactly force them to do it."

My spine went stiff, and my fingers curled inward at the sides of my wet jeans as I tried to rally, to get through whatever was about to hit me next, and I could feel it coming. Something that'd knock the wind from me. *Wait, did he say . . . ?*

"I wasn't alone?" Hollis echoed my thoughts, playing catch-up to what Ryder had said. Meanwhile, my chest was splitting in two.

"The crowd allegedly scattered when they realized shots were being fired," Ryder continued, not addressing her question. Not yet, at least. "One witness saw you run to the back of the basement's library and disappear. He said the guy you were with covered your escape. Several men were shooting at you two."

The guy you were with were the only words I could latch on to.

"The kid who threw the rave bought off the police and witnesses, as we suspected. I don't think he asked his father to do it, since he seemed afraid for Constantine to talk to his dad, but who knows. He just said he didn't want to get in trouble. Constantine's still looking into any possible connection between the Putcheski family and who attacked you that night, especially since his father was in Italy at the time," Ryder explained, his voice even-toned, a sharp contrast to how I was on the inside.

"Did anyone see the shooters?" I asked, trying like hell to get back to the mission and out of my own head.

"No. Vague descriptions, and it was dark with flashing lights down there." Alex spoke up that time. "But, uh, one witness believes the man you were with was someone you were . . . well, uh, with."

With? The word detonated in my head. I staggered back, nearly stepping on Ranger's tail from the abrupt movement. My hand went to my sternum as I searched Hollis's eyes for her reaction. She'd gone pale in shock.

"Well, he's wrong," she said a few moments later while recoiling, the blanket becoming a distant memory on the floor. "I wasn't with anyone in that way." She fisted her hand, tapping her mouth while staring at the floor.

You're worried you cheated on some guy with me, aren't you? I *should* have felt bad about that, but instead, I was dying on the inside for my own selfish reasons. That her heart may belong to someone else and that microscopic chance I'd stupidly thought I might have with her just blew the hell up.

But it was one terrified punk's word. He could've easily made a mistake. How well could he see in a rave anyway? But try telling that to the weight in my chest.

"You don't remember, though," Alex reminded her, interrupting my spiral. "And you did tell Audrey you were going to Italy with someone."

I was ready to lay him out for that. I dragged in a breath that scraped my lungs, trying to get back to mission-focused. But I was standing there in wet jeans, after showering with the subject of our operation, and I'd had my hand between her legs and my tongue in her mouth.

"Constantine showed the witnesses some other photos, too"—Ryder was next up to bat to interrupt my thoughts—"to see if we could get a hit on who may have betrayed you."

"Who of?" she asked, her voice as fragile as my current state of mind.

"Pictures of your family. We discreetly took photos of everyone while we were at your parents' place," Ryder shared. "One witness recognized Gideon." He held up his hand as if to say *Hold up.* "It's because he beat Constantine to the punch, questioning the ravers yesterday. Gideon found out about it before Constantine did. Not a shocker given your family's resources and power. But here's the kicker." He leaned his shoulder against the wall. "The college kid who saw you disappear also recognized the guy you were with when Gideon showed his own set of photos."

"Gideon knows who I was with, then," she whispered.

"I'm guessing Gideon didn't name drop who that was during his questioning," I muttered, and Ryder shook his head. "Any idea what he looks like?"

"Just a headshot was shown to him. Dark hair, gray eyes, and tan," Alex said. "No real help."

Dammit. "Any chance Gideon fed this kid a story he wanted relayed to us?"

"It's worth considering. I could think of a few reasons why Gideon would do that," Ryder responded, and I was about to breathe easier because I wanted this witness to be wrong, but his next words erased any chance of possible calm. "But Constantine can be intimidating when he wants answers. From what I hear, people don't lie to him, not unless they have a death wish."

I went quiet, unsure what to say next, when I overheard my phone ringing from down the hall in the gym.

"Expecting someone?" Alex asked.

Nope. I went and grabbed it, careful not to slip. It was my personal cell. Blocked number. "This is Reed," I hesitantly answered.

"Gideon," he responded, and my muscles banded tight at the sound of his voice, ready for a fight. "We need to talk."

I placed him on speaker and returned to the others, holding out the phone. "We're here and listening."

"We need to speak in person," Gideon said flatly. "Neutral territory. I heard you pulled in Falcon Falls, not just Constantine Costa, to help you out."

Ryder set his hands on his hips, standing opposite me, eyes on the phone. "And?"

"We'll meet at Carter's hotel, the one he co-owns with that Irishman from The League. Switzerland doesn't get more neutral than that."

"Works for us," Ryder agreed.

"Tomorrow," Gideon demanded. "Reserve an entire floor." The line went dead after that, and I lowered the phone to my side, checking on Hollis.

Her eyes were downcast and on Ranger pawing her leg, offering her emotional support that I might need myself.

Ryder muttered something about making calls, urging Alex away. But space wasn't what I wanted. No, I needed them close because I was on the verge of losing it.

There was a chance Hollis may have been romantically involved with someone else, and I was assuming the worst and blowing things out of proportion. That was typical of my glass-half-empty self, but what if I was right?

What if someone Hollis cared about was out there waiting for a rescue? Or hell, what if they were already dead?

CHAPTER THIRTY

Hollis

Jason's anger simmered beneath the surface; he was ready to kill. After what Ryder had shared, along with my brother's call right after, who'd blame him for feeling like this?

He hadn't said a word to me after Gideon ended the call. Instead, he'd disappeared into his bedroom and changed, then wordlessly stormed into my bedroom with an armful of my stuff from his bathroom. Why he packed his body wash as if our hotel wouldn't have any was beyond me, but I wasn't going to object. The citrusy scent had grown on me.

After he'd dumped everything on my bed, he'd breezed into the closet and located my trunk. Not the Prada suitcase that'd apparently had a knife taken to it in Rome, but the bronze hard-shell RIMOWA that Lyra had given me in Surrey to use. He'd urgently pulled my clothes off hangers and opened the dresser drawers to help me pack.

I dropped onto the bed next to where he was currently shoving my clothes into the suitcase like they had offended him. Though he had just stumbled upon my sexy nightgowns, so maybe that scowl had to do with the lace and silk tangled around his fingers.

Hand over my heart, I searched for a deep, calming breath. Only a shallow one that offered no relief came. I opened my mouth wide to try to force a yawn, to see if that'd loosen the achy, acidic pain in my chest, but nothing helped.

"Are we ever going to talk?" I broke the awkward silence lingering between us as he returned to the dresser.

He opened the drawer that held his T-shirts before dropping his hands on the dresser, hanging his head as if I'd just asked him to defy gravity. Then again, didn't planes do exactly that with the force of lift? "What is there to talk about?" The bitter edge of his tone triggered my nipples to harden.

Great. Now I was distracted by thoughts of where his hands had been in the shower not that long ago. Though it was nice to have my own memories involving this man to think about instead of the ones someone had manufactured and implanted in my head.

"I'd say there's quite a lot to talk about." I stood and walked over, waiting for him to turn, to make eye contact. To tell me why he was so angry and who he wanted to kill.

Every visible muscle in his body was tense, and his back rose and fell with deep breaths as if he'd just tried to outrun Ranger and failed. That dog was a living missile, from what I'd seen in the last few days. Born to be special ops. I was going to miss him. Miss this place, too. I wasn't so sure I was ready to leave the safety of this home, but I needed answers, and from the sounds of it, my brother now had some.

Jason grabbed his shirts out of the drawer, refraining from looking at me as he brought them over to the suitcase.

"Why are you packing—"

"Because you like wearing my shirts." He began folding them one by one, neat and methodical. "And if it turns out you were with some other guy before . . . well, then you can wear his instead."

Those words nailed me in place, and full-body chills slid over my skin, so much so I started to tremble. "I wasn't with someone." I rested my back against the dresser. "I know in my heart there was no guy—not in that way, at least. Don't forget, you had Constantine double-check with the people at the hotel if I was with anyone, and I wasn't."

"People lie," he said in a clipped voice, closing the trunk.

"Well, something tells me I wouldn't have been flirting with you over text if I was secretly seeing someone. I think I'm the loyal type, don't you? *And*, um, don't you dare lie and tell me that we didn't flirt." I swallowed, then tossed out one more flimsy detail: "Also, my family said I don't even do relationships."

"Yeah, well, I do." He whirled around. "That's all I'm looking for, which is yet another reminder why you and I won't ever work."

I stepped forward, and he shot his hand up, requesting we return to that three-foot rule as if his tongue hadn't been in my mouth and I hadn't gotten off from his hand between my thighs. He'd been careful not to penetrate me, just delicately touched me in the best possible way while I lost control.

My one and only orgasm to date that I could now recall, and it'd been bliss before we were interrupted with news. That news was clearly why he was all fire and brimstone right now. Itching to kill someone while erecting steely walls.

I finally got the synapses in my brain to fire, sending words to my mouth, asking, "What are you talking about?"

"Nothing, just forget what I said." He pushed at the skin on his forehead, hissing something I couldn't fully make out under his breath. "All that matters is figuring out what happened to you and why. Getting your memories back. And if there's some guy out there that you were with, and he's still alive but in danger, well then—"

"This alleged guy is who you want to kill, yes?"

"With. My. Bare. Hands," he snapped back, powering up each word as if they could stand on their own.

Breathing hard, he stared at me with dark eyes, like he was trying to convince me he had an equally dark heart.

"Why do you want to hurt this guy?" I closed the space between us, fingers trembling at my sides, aching to reach for him. To let him know my past was my past and I belonged to him now.

He leaned in, jutting his chin forward. "You know why," he snarled, a possessive need bleeding through his tone, and if that was a red flag, then consider me a bull about to run toward him, because I liked it. I wanted him crazy about me.

I broke that three-foot rule and stopped in front of him, clutching his arm, urging him to lift his hand. He had to help me out. He was too strong.

He surrendered and let me raise his hand, and I brought his palm to my face—four fingers on my jawline and his thumb resting on my throat. I gradually unwrapped my hand from his forearm.

Just when you think you can have whatever you want . . . it's taken from you. I thought back to his words in the gym, understanding what had to be in his head now.

He wasn't angry or enraged. He was scared and hurting, unsure how to cope with all his emotions hitting him at once. First, he'd never thought he could have me, and he did. Almost every part of me in that shower, in fact. Now he was probably assuming he was going to lose me, and he didn't know what to do or how to handle that.

I had to shut down his worries before they spun out of control.

"I'm yours," I said steadily, standing my ground so he'd know I meant it. This me, old me, *all* of me.

His brows drew together as his gaze slipped to his hand holding me captive like I wanted him to. "No."

Sensing he was about to pull away, I snaked my hand around his wrist, a request to stay in place. "Yes."

His eyes narrowed to slits. "No," he ground out.

"Yes." I could do this all day. Never back down. He had to know that. My stubbornness was innate.

"If there's a guy—"

"There is one," I shot back, burying my nails into his skin. "You. I'm falling for *you*. Fairly certain I felt the same way before now, too." I stretched my neck out, angling my head, then guided his hand to travel the length of my throat to my heart.

He closed his eyes. "No, you're just confused, and I crossed the line to make things worse."

"My soul knows the truth even if my head's been corrupted." I threaded my fingers with his, keeping our hands on my chest. "You didn't cross any lines. I pushed you. I left the door open, invited you in. The only one to—"

"I walked in, didn't I?" His eyes flashed open, haunting and full of heat. "I got in that shower with you knowing exactly what would happen. That I wouldn't be able to resist you." He lightly shook his head, some of that anger-pain evaporating before my eyes.

He shifted our palms alongside of us and hooked his other arm behind my back, unexpectedly drawing me flush against him. The weight of his erection pressed into me, and I trapped a moan behind my lips.

He rolled his hips once. I rolled mine right back.

A heartbeat later, he cursed a mild expletive under his breath. "I was wrong. Angry. Maybe even scared." He paused, exhaling deeply. "I take back what I said about the shirts."

"Wait, what?" I blinked, confused myself now.

"If you're going to wear someone else's shirts, then they'll be mine. *Only* mine," he said like a commandment etched in stone. "And *if* there's a guy . . ."

I opened my mouth to interrupt yet again, but he slanted his over mine, catching my lip between his teeth.

He slowly let go and pulled his head back, and a pulse of hot need shot through me. *What were we talking about, again?*

"*If* there's a guy, then I'll fight for you." He freed his hand from mine and brought it between us to cup my chin. "I may not deserve you," he began in a strained voice, "but for the first time in my life, I've found someone worth fighting for. Worth losing everything for if I have to as well." He pushed his hand into my still-wet hair and held the back of my head before setting his lips to my temple. "I have to at least try, or I'll never know. I understand that now."

He didn't have to lose me or lose anything. How could I get him to see that without him questioning me, considering I couldn't even remember what I did last week?

In tempore veritas. *In time, there is truth. He'll see soon. Heck, so will I. Because I* will *remember everything. And this time, no fake hate. Just authenticity. Just love.*

Mouth to my ear, cradling my head as my body shuddered with his breath dancing across my heated skin, he whispered, "I never truly believed I was worthy of a second chance after everything I've done . . ." His voice fractured on his last word. "But if this is God giving me one, then who am I to say no?"

CHAPTER THIRTY-ONE

Reed

I hung back by Ranger, holding his leash while remaining a good distance from everyone as they said their goodbyes.

Ryder, Alex, Hollis, and myself would be taking a military flight overseas, and everyone else would be traveling with Trevor to DC, including my dog.

Charleston International was a civil-military airport—having JB Charleston, a joint base, in proximity to our neighborhood was just one benefit of living in the area. Another? Having a pilot friend able to whisk our family and friends away on a moment's notice. Well, if he wasn't on an operation, but thankfully, Owen York had been home today.

Alex caught my eyes as I hovered near the C-17 as air force operators wrapped up loading the plane with pallets of cargo, coiled fueling hoses, and more. A few airmen in fatigues did maintenance checks, clipboards in hand, ear protection slung around their necks.

It wouldn't be the most comfortable ride for Hollis compared to what she was used to, but it was safe and worked on short notice.

Keeping a tight grip on the leash so Ranger wouldn't launch like a missile outside the hangar and onto a runway, I turned toward the open door. There were two other C-17 Globemasters looking Hulk-ish alongside Owen's matte-gray Gulfstream-style jet. His brother's name was painted on the side, the one he'd lost years back.

At the feel of a vibration from my back pocket, I faced the inside of the hangar, preparing to go for my phone. At the sight of Alex on approach, I held off.

I peered at Ranger as his ears perked up at every slight noise and movement around him. From the radio chatter to the shuffling of boots on the concrete, to the slamming of a hangar door—too much stimulation for him to process and not want to bark up a storm. I was still working on his training.

"Is it weird that my wife's ex-husband is going to protect her while I'm gone?" Alex folded his arms, standing next to me.

"I'm sure Trevor would like to operate with us, but his priority will always be his kid and the mother of his child."

"I don't disagree. I wouldn't let him come with us even if he wanted to. I just feel like *I* should be getting on that plane to DC with them instead."

"I'm sure no one will go after Audrey as leverage to be used against Hollis," I said, doing my best to reassure him. "Hell, they let Hollis go, so why attack now? Audrey and Chase will be just fine while we're gone. Audrey wants you with us, don't forget. She needs her best friend back." I cleared my throat. "You know, her memories back." Those memories and Hollis's past were a sore subject for me after what had happened between us today.

"True, and they're all staying with President Bennett's son, and his wife is Secret Service," he said as Ranger went on his hind legs, barking at something.

I calmed him down, crouching next to him. "They're going to be better protected than we could do ourselves. No offense."

"None taken, it's what I need to hear," he replied, taking a knee to help me with the Maligator, a.k.a. Ranger.

"We're lucky we report to POTUS and the secretary of defense directly now and have their teams of Tier One operators on our side in times of emergency." I stood once Ranger had finally chilled out.

Alex rose, arms back over his chest as he tried to pull off casual and asked, "How are you feeling about this trip, though?" He had to be doing his damnedest not to be direct and ask why both Hollis and I had been wet when he and Ryder had stopped by earlier. I knew he also wanted to ask my thoughts on this mystery guy Hollis had allegedly been with in Rome. I was grateful he was respecting my boundaries for once and not pushing.

"I'm worried about what Gideon learned that spooked him enough to demand an in-person meeting. Also, neutral territory my ass. That's not why he chose The Sapphire." I decided to stick to operator mode, to not give Alex the go-ahead to take a meat cleaver to my mind and mess me up right now.

"You think Gideon needs help? Not just ours, but Carter's? The League's?"

"I don't know what to think," I said as Hollis turned to the side and made eye contact.

I stared at her in a daze, my head landing back in my bedroom, still shocked I'd somehow gotten out of my own damn way in trying to be happy. It had been divine intervention that it'd happened. Or maybe insanity. All I knew was, instead of running, I opened the door wide. *Only for her would I do that.* Was it still reckless to do? Possibly.

She didn't know who she was, and there could still be another guy from her past . . . *but* back in my bedroom, with her eyes on mine and my hands on her, it suddenly hadn't mattered.

I hung my head, looking away from her as guilt caught up with me. "I still have to tell her the truth about my past."

"What about your past?"

Shit. Had I spoken out loud? "Nothing." I went for my phone when it vibrated three more times. *My mother. Perfect timing.* "Do me a favor, take Ranger over to the others? He'll behave for Chase."

"Sure." He nodded, then took the leash from me.

I waited for them to walk away before dealing with my mother's texts.

Mom: Your dad really needs you. He's not doing well.

Mom: I need you, too.

Mom: I relapsed. Stress, you know? Planned to have only one drink last night. It turned into six.

Mom: Come to an AA meeting with me?

I became physically ill at her words. It'd taken years and years, not to mention a small fortune, to get her off drugs. But after only a year of being clean, she'd turned to the bottle as a substitute while I'd been deployed.

I had no idea what to text her. I could only handle so much. I had a new war in front of me. Unresolved battles still lingering in my past.

Me: I'm about to spin up, I'm sorry, I can't fly there right now. But YOU need to go to a meeting.

Me: Text me after you go so I know you went.

Me: And Dad doesn't remember me. How can he need me?

Mom: You know he feels so bad about how he treated you. He's proud of you and who you became. Before he forgot everything, he told me that.

I could upchuck in my mouth at her lies because they were utter bullshit.

Me: Stop trying to atone for Dad's sins. Focus on your own redemption.

Harsh? Maybe. But after years of parenting my parents, I was out of energy. Exhausted from it all.

Me: I have to go. I'll swing by when I'm Stateside. Stop drinking. Go to church. Get help. Just do something.

"Everything okay?"

I went still at Hollis's voice, and my shoulder blades pinched at the realization that she got the drop on me. She was one of the few in the world who could do that.

"My mom." I held the phone between us, blowing out a deep breath, trying to rally. To get my heartbeat out of the danger zone.

"Is everything okay?" She folded her arms, but I knew she wanted to reach for me. To rub my arm. Scratch my back. Just do something. I could see it in her expression and body language. But we had an audience, and she was probably still worried she'd scare me off. Like any subtle movements and I might bolt, changing my mind about what I'd said to her in the bedroom. Didn't blame her for thinking that way; I wasn't so sure I'd trust me, either.

I lowered the phone to my side. "She wants me to visit."

"Where do they live?"

"They're in Houston now," I said as Ryder waved us over.

It was mission time. Another out from having to share too much. Or was I looking at this as an opportunity to fall back to my standard operating mode, avoid and deflect? I hesitated, unsure what to do.

"I guess it's time to leave?" She shrugged, giving me a half smile of uncertainty. "I don't even know what we're about to walk into when we get to this mysterious hotel, but I'm glad we're going together, and without any kind of tension between us."

No tension, really? For me, it was taking all my resolve not to wrap her up in my arms and hijack Owen's plane and steal her away. Take her from a past she couldn't remember and from a past I wished I couldn't. Too bad I didn't know how to fly planes, just jump from them. "Wait." I grabbed her wrist, not giving a damn who was around. "Still remember my phone passcode?" *What am I doing?*

She nodded, mouth tight.

"I'm not good at the, uh, talking thing, as established." I pressed my phone into her hand. "Read my messages with my mother. The ones from my dad, too, before he . . . you know." My damn hand was shaking. I let go of her wrist, buried my fingers into my palm, and hid my hand behind my back. "That'll explain a lot. Not everything, but a lot."

"Are you sure?"

I nearly leaned in and kissed her quivering bottom lip. Sucked it between mine, right in front of everyone.

"No second chances if I keep doing the same shit I always do, right? Like keeping everything to myself," I said in a low voice, emotion ripping through me, my heart trying to break free at how real this was starting to become.

The dark and possibly more logical side of my brain was also hollering, *This is too fast, too soon. It's only make believe; when she remembers who she really is, she'll leave you.*

"So, that's a yes?" She had to be reading the uncertainty on my face. Surely those unsavory thoughts had manifested into a physical reaction there.

"Yeah, I'm sure." Too late to back down now. And while I was at it, why not go *almost* all in with the truth? "There's a folder in my photo app. DGU. Go through that, too."

"DGU?"

My heart was pumping so hard my hands were getting sweaty. I couldn't remember the last time I had such an adrenaline rush that didn't revolve around doing my best not to die while downrange. "Don't give up," I finally shared. "Reminders of all the shit I've survived, so I don't give up when things get hard again."

I may have swiped through the images in that folder a half a dozen times when Hollis had been missing and after she'd been found but woke up lost to everyone all over again. Oddly, I hadn't checked it once when she was at my house.

Her green eyes yielded a glossy sheen as she held back tears. "I know how big of a deal this is for you." Her chest lifted with a deep inhalation, and she held that prisoner for several seconds before releasing it.

It really, really was. *But the only way to move in a direction that isn't backward is by doing something different, something you've never done before.* I had no clue where that thought came from, but so help me, I wanted to stick with it instead of clinging to the negative ones.

She brought the phone to her chest, and there was only one thing left to do before we joined the team and took off for the hotel.

I wordlessly stepped back and unfurled my fingers, offering her my hand. She rested her free one on top of mine as I finally responded to her earlier comment. "We *are* in this together." I swallowed. "No matter what."

CHAPTER THIRTY-TWO

Hollis

In the air

The engines droned like angry bees bottled in steel, a sound that didn't seem to disturb the operators on board. Nor did the intermittent hiss of hydraulics and fans. Because when I surveyed the inside of the plane, looking beyond the cargo pallets and gear strapped down with bright-orange webbing, at least three soldiers were passed out.

Even if I didn't have anything to do, I doubted I'd be able to sleep so easily. I'd been putting off going through Jason's texts because I knew it was going to hurt. Like a thousand little knife pricks into my flesh as I learned why and how he'd become so closed off, broody, and not people-y.

This was a big deal. *Huge.* My knees had buckled when he'd offered me his phone in Charleston. The same happened to me when he told me I might be his second chance as well.

I glanced at Jason at the back of the cavernous cargo plane setting up a nylon-mesh hammock-thing. Talk about improvising comfort.

He'd offered me a "bed," but I'd declined, choosing to stay strapped into one of the red troop seats for now.

Jason turned to the side, slipping on a pair of headphones while catching my eyes. "You okay?" he mouthed.

I gave him a hesitant nod, then he forced a smile and climbed onto the hammock. *Now or never.* I typed in the passcode. My thumb hesitated over his mother's name before I opened the thread. I flipped back as far as I could go. 2019.

Unrelenting shivers banked my skin as I read the messages. The phone became heavier the longer I scrolled, the weight of his past physically with me. He was giving me his memories, and I had none of my own to give him.

Endless requests for money and promises to change from his mother. She'd even opened credit cards in his name using his identity, and when he would ask her about it, she'd casually apologize. He'd pay off the debt, and she'd do it all over again.

Then there was her drug addiction. He'd beg her to get help. She'd agree, then blow the money he sent for treatment on more drugs. Apologies came, followed by his forgiveness. The same cycle of her taking advantage of him and him helping her anyway.

Rehab finally stuck, only for her to switch vices to alcohol when his father started getting sick. *Forgive your father* messages came next. *He doesn't remember hurting you. He doesn't remember hitting you. Forgive him. Help him.*

I had to stop and take a break. Pull myself together before I could finish. My heart broke for the abuse he'd suffered. *No wonder you didn't want me risking my neck for your father's.*

After fidgeting with the ridiculous chain I had to wear, I worked my way to their last text exchange. I may not have remembered anyone from my past, but no doubt in my mind he had to be one of the strongest men I'd met in my life.

I forged ahead to his father's texts next. None had been exchanged in the last year. His texts had been hollow and brief, eventually muddled as his memory declined.

I checked on Jason. His headphones were still on, eyes shut. He had one knee bent, the other leg lazily stretched out with his arm behind his head as a pillow.

You were going through all this with his condition, and now I'm like this.

He'd carried his family like a rucksack full of bricks, and he'd never set it down. Now I truly understood why he didn't talk about himself.

I went to his photo app next, nervous to go through his Don't Give Up folder after everything I'd read. That folder had to exist because at one point he *had* wanted to give up, and he'd found the courage not to and come up with a way to fight through the pain.

The first image was from a newspaper article depicting tornado-ravaged homes from an F5 twister. There was a picture of a boy, maybe Chase's age, standing in the rubble, the foundation of the home all that remained.

Is that you? I read the names in the article, confirming it was, in fact, Jason. I cupped my mouth, a few tears creating tracks down my cheeks. I tasted their saltiness on my lips, trying to keep it together to continue.

More screenshots of news articles from online from when he lived in Oklahoma, including another tragic F5 tornado event, along with an image of a food shelter, which had me assuming he'd had to eat there at some point.

I thought back to the kitchen when he told me he had to fend for himself when it came to food; he'd literally meant that, hadn't he?

I wasn't sure how much more I could take, and this wasn't my life. My face was hot to the touch and puffy.

When I got to the pictures he'd saved from his service time, I lost it. I ignored the stares from the strangers eyeing me and unbuckled and made a beeline for Jason.

Alex met my eyes, his forehead tight with worry, as I rushed past him and Ryder to get to the man who'd opened himself up to me in his own way.

I stopped by his hammock, and his eyes flashed open when I tried to climb in with him. He shifted his headphones around his neck, setting aside his work phone they were attached to, and helped me up.

Still clutching his phone, I buried my face against his chest, and he sheltered me in his arms. I was grateful the hammock could hold our combined weight.

I knew he wouldn't want me to say anything. No pity or apologies. But what this man needed was a hug and to never be hurt again. I had every intention of guarding his heart far better than I was supposed to guard sacred secrets and priceless artifacts.

"I got you," he said into my ear, and the fact he was reassuring me when it should have been the other way around broke me.

I wasn't sure how much time passed as we remained like this, but his heartbeat in my ear while being in his strong arms helped calm me down.

I tipped my chin up, peering at him. I had applied a little makeup before the flight, but I assumed since my eyes weren't burning, my products were top tier and I wasn't a total disaster. "What were you listening to?"

"My DGU playlist."

I definitely wanted to listen to that at some point. I rolled my lips inward, fighting another ugly cry, when an idea suddenly hit me.

I attempted to sit upright, nearly flipping the hammock, but we both had fast reflexes and managed to save ourselves from falling.

Once we were stable, I unlocked his phone and held it out. "Act like you like me for a second," I teased, sniffling.

Instead of focusing on the camera, he looked at me, a slow smile spreading across his lips, and I took the photo.

"There we go. RTBH. A new folder." I moved photos into it. Pictures from Alex's wedding, Ryder's as well, and several images of Ranger. Lastly, I saved the selfie I took of us there.

"RTBH?" He took the phone from me and began swiping through the saved images.

"Reasons to be happy." I rested my hand on his chest and angled my head, hoping he'd slant his mouth over mine for a quick kiss despite where we were.

He bent his head forward and kissed me. Zero hesitation.

"Not to be presumptuous," I whispered in post-kiss bliss, a little lightheaded from the calming effect he had on me, "but I'm hoping I can be less of a pain in your ass and someone who makes you happy instead, someone who belongs in this new folder."

His lips stretched into a wicked grin that woke up other parts of me, moving me from sad to something else entirely.

He discreetly pinched my butt. "You can be both. Make me happy and be a pain in my ass." With his free hand, he held my cheek, directing my face close to his again, on the verge of another kiss. "Because you know damn well it turns me on when you give me a hard time."

CHAPTER THIRTY-THREE

Reed

German–Switzerland border

We pulled off the autobahn in our convoy of blacked-out SUVs, following a winding road skirting vineyards and forests. The Rhine River was nearby, the Alps in view.

Hollis held my hand between our seats, and I quietly laced our fingers together as we passed a sign for Schaffhausen, making our way to the sliver of land between Switzerland and Germany—to the neutral territory where The Sapphire was located.

With the time difference, it was now Wednesday morning. It was quiet out here as we entered no-man's-land.

The Sapphire's concierge escort service was intense; they were more like guardian angels. We had two armed former military men in the front seat and a Reaper drone overhead capable of intercepting and neutralizing possible threats.

We were also boxed in with Ryder and Alex in the front vehicle and another two-man team of security personnel in the SUV behind us. We were about as safe as we could be as we approached the hotel.

"What's the deal with this place? I know Carter and that League guy, Sebastian, own it, but why is it so safe? Why would my paranoid brother be willing to come here?" It was the first time Hollis had mentioned anything related to the operation since we'd left my house.

She *also* hadn't brought up what she'd read and seen on my phone, which I appreciated. We'd need to talk about it eventually, and I could fill in a few details, but now didn't feel like the right time.

Her thoughtful gesture to create a new photo folder had been what I never knew I needed. It *also* scared the hell out of me, if I was being honest, because there were no guarantees for our future. And if I ever had to open that folder and she was no longer in my life, so help me . . .

But I couldn't let myself think like that. I had to stop with the pessimistic shit if this was going to work like I prayed it would.

It was also time to switch gears, given where we were.

The driver spoke since I'd yet to do so. "During the Cold War, a billionaire acquired the land and turned it into a safe haven. Mostly for criminals to do business without fear of bloodshed due to their extreme security measures and no weapons on premises by guests. Our bosses bought the hotel when it went on sale, and now it's used by people like us, not criminals."

"Ah, gotcha," she whispered, and I squeezed her hand.

"Everything will be okay." *Sure as hell hope so, at least.* "We have a lot of people on our side, and if your brother wants to meet us in person, my guess is, he learned something that might shed some light on what's going on. He can't risk discussing it over the phone."

She twisted on her seat, facing me. "I just hope I can trust what he has to say. I can't text Lyra and ask her to give me a heads-up, either, because we destroyed the phone my brother gave me. I don't know her number."

I'd forgotten about that. A lot had happened since yesterday, like making out with her in the shower and my hand winding up between her legs. Not to mention her learning about my past on the plane.

We stayed quiet until we made it through the rest of the checkpoints, the weight of reality hammering down on me.

The security team walked the four of us inside. The place had marble floors, hushed acoustics, and more than likely reinforced walls beneath the luxury. There was no staff to greet us, and we didn't need to check in.

"You all have the sixth floor to yourself, as requested," our driver said, offering two old-school room keys to Ryder while providing the room numbers. "You need the key and an access code to get into your rooms. Boss said you already gave Gwen your preferred four-digit one for the keypads."

"I did," Ryder confirmed.

"Those codes will also work for the elevators, the doors, and so on," he continued before tipping his head as a goodbye and taking off.

"I guess Carter and the others will meet us upstairs." Ryder started to hand me a key, only to retract it. "Are you two sharing a room? Or are you bunking with Alex and me?"

About that. I turned to face Hollis, unsure what the plan was. We hadn't discussed it. Gideon would be arriving and staying on the same floor as us. While I trusted Carter and Sebastian and their safety protocols for the hotel, I wasn't ready to trust Gideon. The idea of sharing a bed with her, though . . . *Shit.*

"Maybe there are two bedrooms in the suites?" She lifted her brows, and I knew she wasn't being modest in front of my teammates to hide what was happening between us. She was trying to be respectful of me. She knew I wasn't ready to cross the sex line with her; I'd already pushed the limits with what had happened in the shower as it was. She just didn't know why.

"One way to find out," I said with a tight nod, then ignored the curious looks from my teammates and picked up our suitcases where the guards had dropped them.

No one spoke until we made it to floor six and inside our first designated suite.

I set our luggage aside and took in the sight of the sprawling corner suite. It was a mix of old-world Alpine and modern precision. Warm woods, one stone wall, and heavy rugs. But in sharp contrast to the old was the new with all the smart technology. What a metaphor for what we were going through now. Old versions of ourselves colliding with the new. Mine by choice, hers because she had none.

Hollis walked around, checking if there were two bedrooms. Thankfully, there were, separated by a living room and small kitchen area.

"You think Gideon will have a coronary if he discovers you two are staying here together?" Alex asked, resting his back to the door, propping his booted foot up to it. He partially tucked his hands in his pockets as he stared at me, and I could read his mind. He was probably torn between being happy and worried about what was obviously happening between Hollis and me.

Yeah, well, you and me both.

"I definitely don't care what Gideon thinks. Didn't when I asked to stay with Jason in Charleston." She went to the French doors and opened them, taking in the view of the Rhine with the backdrop of the distant Alps. "Don't care here, either."

"Jason, huh?" Ryder picked up on that before Alex did. "We supposed to call you that now, too?"

I shot him down fast. "Nope."

Hollis stayed out on the balcony, mindlessly fidgeting with the potted plant at her side, smoothing her fingers over a large glossy leaf.

I opened my mouth, prepared to ask the guys to bail so Hollis and I could have a moment alone, when there was a knock.

Alex checked the peephole, then opened up. Gwen was alongside a pilot who'd flown one of the helos for Carter on our op in February. We'd never had a chance to formally meet.

Hollis closed the balcony doors and came over, and Gwen gave her an awkward smile and introduced herself. "My first time meeting you in person."

Hollis blinked, then straightened, polite but reserved. "Right. Thank you for helping Audrey before, and thanks for helping me now."

"Of course." Gwen tipped her head toward the pilot quietly lingering at her side. "You were with them in New Zealand, yeah?" When he remained oddly quiet, she went on, "This is Easton. My brooding, overprotective shadow, assigned by my father to babysit me like I'm five."

Easton rolled his eyes. "I'm slightly more than a *manny*. Thanks for the kind intro, though." His focus shifted to Hollis. "My brother-in-law is Constantine Costa," he tossed out as if he'd rather claim allegiance to the Italians than to the Brit.

I almost forgot about that relationship. While I crossed paths with a lot of people, I wasn't one to draw family trees in my head.

"So that means your nephew is the one who helped with the rave tip?" Hollis asked him.

Easton smirked, obvious pride in his eyes. "That's right." He unwrapped a stick of spearmint gum. "And I know you from before New Zealand as well. We operated together a few times back in the day before Falcon Falls formed, when Carter—" He faltered, jaw tight, then shoved the stick of gum in his mouth.

"—was searching for his late wife's killers," Gwen finished for him.

"My condolences to him," Hollis said softly. She stepped closer, sliding between Alex and me. "How'd I help him?"

Easton rubbed his jaw with his knuckles, gaze lowering to the carpet. "We needed intel on smugglers. Traffickers of antiquities and shit like that. You gave us leads."

"Why are you being so weird?" Gwen asked him, and apparently, we were on the same concerned page even though I barely knew the guy.

"I'm not." Easton dropped his hand, chewing harder, eyes darting anywhere but to any of ours. "Just trying to be careful with what I say. It's gotta be rough, learning about yourself from people who feel like strangers."

"Tell me about it," Hollis muttered. Her fingers skimmed my arm like she needed an anchor.

Easton noticed and edged a step back.

Not suspect at all.

"What's really going on?" I asked, unable to stop myself.

"Nothing." He shoved another piece of gum into his mouth.

"Two sticks to shut yourself up? Now I'm really worried." Gwen folded her arms, leveling him with a glare.

"What aren't you telling me?" Hollis pressed, arms crossing.

"Nothing you'd want to learn from me." Easton shifted toward the door, but Gwen caught his arm.

"Oh my God, E. Did you two sleep together?" Gwen asked in a low voice as if we couldn't hear her whisper.

"What?" Easton winced. "No!"

Gwen let go of his arm and cringed toward Hollis. "Sorry, no bloody filter. Meant that to remain in my head."

Too late now. My pulse spiked, and every emotion crossed Hollis's face, warring for control. She settled on disturbed.

Easton pierced Gwen with a hard look, like she'd just set the room on fire.

I forced my pulse to chill out, telling myself not to be a hypocrite. That didn't stop me from imagining ten different ways to kill him if he admitted they'd had sex.

There had to be a shovel on the property.

A tomato garden somewhere already full of dead bodies. What was one more?

Also . . . was this jealousy? I didn't *actually* want to murder Easton or the guy she *may* have been with in Rome last week, but damn.

"I'd rather not share this." Easton chewed on his gum like his life depended on it.

"Rip off the Band-Aid," Hollis requested, reaching for my hand.

Easton clocked the movement, then caught my eyes. His regret was plain. That wasn't helping. Wouldn't save him from me, either.

Hypocrite. That was me. The dark part of my mind countered, *And I don't give a flying—*

"We'll take our stuff to the suite next door," Ryder cut in, breaking through my thoughts and the tension. "Where's Carter? Sebastian?"

"On a call," Gwen answered. "They'll meet us at the bar upstairs in fifteen. It's not open, so it's reserved for us. Food is being prepped for brunch."

"We'll see you up there." Ryder picked up the other bags and glanced at me before he and Alex disappeared from the suite.

The door clicked shut, leaving the four of us and an elephant in the room.

"We went on a few dates back in 2021," Easton shared quickly.

"And?" Hollis prompted.

"You sure you don't want to just remember on your own? Your memories are bound to come back soon."

"At this rate, I'm beginning to wonder." Her voice broke. "Just tell me."

I squeezed her hand, letting her know I wasn't moving. But it was a coin toss if someone was about to get strangled to death. *Hypocrite.* I lightly shook my head. *I know, I know.*

"This is my fault. I'm sorry." Gwen waved her hands in the air like a ref calling out a foul. "Maybe Easton is right."

"Too late now." Hollis stood her ground.

"Fine." Easton pinched the bridge of his nose. "We made it to a fourth date, and then you broke it off." He squinted, and I had to look away from him so I stopped visualizing his murder. "You said you weren't the relationship type. You said you preferred dating jerks. They always disappointed you and cut out before anything got serious, saving you the trouble of ending things. You said I wasn't an asshole, so that made me dangerous to your mission of staying single."

"Annnnd that's our cue to go." Gwen hooked Easton's arm and dragged him toward the door. "We'll see you upstairs when you're ready."

I peeled my focus their way, and Easton shot me an apologetic look, clearly recognizing I had feelings for Hollis, and not only because we were holding hands.

The door thudded shut, and Hollis twisted around to face me. "This doesn't change anything," she said firmly, knowing exactly where my head was about to go. "The past won't dictate the now. I didn't want a relationship then, but I do now, and I choose you." Tears built up in her eyes. "*And* those three kids I want to have one of these days."

I stared at her, trying to process what she was saying, clinging to the hope her feelings wouldn't vanish when her memories returned. All I'd have left was that RTBH folder; I'd have to rename it, too.

"I'm not your mom, you hear me?" she went on when I refused to speak. "I won't . . . I won't hurt you." Her voice trembled as she dug her heels in. "I need you to trust me. To believe I feel the same as you. It's *not* fake."

She was going to break me.

Get me to shed a tear if she kept up with this and brought up my messed-up childhood that no one else knew about outside my parents, a police officer, and two CPS social workers (story for another day, or never).

She was peeling back my layers one by one, but with a machete.

Too hard. Too fast. Too *real*. That was the part I couldn't deny. It was real. It had to be.

"I believe you," I forced out, my voice raw. I leaned in, brushing my lips across hers, my mind made up. "I'll be sure to order that fifth chair we'll be needing for the kitchen table, then."

CHAPTER THIRTY-FOUR

Hollis

The elevator doors sighed open with a light groan, releasing us into a corridor. I was trembling on the inside. It never got easier, learning pieces of my past like they were secondhand gifts no one wanted.

My sweaty palm slipped against Jason's grip, and he gave my hand a squeeze, anchoring me back to the moment as we walked into the bar. Dark wood, amber lighting, and a wall of windows framed the Alps off in the distance.

The low murmur of voices, the clink of a glass, and muffled wind against the windows hit me as we walked in—right along with the smell of roasted meats, the tang of olives, and sweetness from baked goods.

Two men were posted up at a table near the glass, with Gwen and Easton standing by them. I wasn't exactly itching to chat with Easton after that awkward talk we'd had in the suite. He shot me a subtle glance over his shoulder and turned away. Same boat of discomfort as me, clearly.

Ryder and Alex had also beat us here, and Alex was snacking on some of the food set out.

Jason murmured as we walked, "You okay?"

I looked up at him and nodded. "*You* good?" I mouthed. "Not going to take out Easton, are ya?" I did my best to lighten the mood, only partially joking.

He gave me a wicked grin. "The thought may have crossed my mind."

"Mm-hmm," I said as we finally joined the others.

The introductions with Carter and Sebastian went by quick. They not only gave off the same vibes, but they also resembled one another. If it wasn't for Sebastian's Irish accent compared to Carter's American one (Texas, maybe?), I'd swear they were brothers.

Carter gave a hesitant smile and politely gestured for everyone to have a seat at a ten-person table, where a massive spread of food had been set out. Steam curled off a platter of bacon and sausage, the scent of oil thick, but it only churned my stomach.

The two hotel owners took their seats at each end of the rectangular table, and the rest of us filled in the seats between.

"Is it just us? Are any of your other people here on standby to help if need be for a last-minute op?" Ryder asked.

"Two men from Falcon Falls are here in the hotel now. They're ready if we need them," Carter confirmed, then Sebastian shared that he had men from The League there. "If we have more time and need additional reinforcements, we can call in POTUS's SEAL teams as well. Or the rest of Falcon."

That was something.

Sebastian leaned back in his chair, the lazy stance not diminishing the air of authority he wielded. "Your brother declined a security escort. He should be arriving at the gates any minute, though."

Of course he did. "Julian with him?"

Sebastian quietly nodded before Gwen jumped right into things, announcing, "I was able to locate where Gideon was when he called you yesterday." She focused on me. "Any idea why he'd have gone to Peru after he'd been in Rome interrogating the Putcheski kid who threw the rave?"

"South America? Not that I—" *Ohhh.* I held the underside of my chair and sat taller. I couldn't remember whether this conversation had happened in front of Delta Shield or not, but yeah, I did know why. Full-body chills slammed into me. "My family's protectors are there, doing some type of training. My brothers thought I chose to go to Rome when I did because my personal protector wouldn't know what I was up to, since he'd be off-grid."

The room fell quiet as everyone processed, as *I* processed what my brother's trip there might mean.

Gwen tucked her wavy blonde hair behind her ears. She looked to be in her mid to late twenties. Smart, young, British, and beautiful. "What if your protector learned what you planned to do in Rome, and he didn't go to South America as planned?" she suggested. "What if he was the one with you in Rome? People assumed you were together intimately at the rave, but instead, he was just having your back. Your protector had to be the one who helped you escape, but then . . ."

"Then I was captured somewhere on the street level after I left that crypt." I peered at Jason, knowing exactly what this meant. "What if he died so I could live?" *Oh God.* I let go of the chair, fisting my hands on my lap. "I went there in secret. I was reckless for doing that, and someone may have died because of me."

Yesterday, I'd known there was a possibility that whoever I was with at the rave could be in danger, or even worse off . . . but I'd been so focused on my feelings for Jason I'd put blinders on.

I stood, and the chair legs screeched against the polished stone, the sound sharp as nausea climbed my throat. The room tilted like the ground had given away beneath me.

"You don't know that for sure," Jason said in a firm voice, rising when I did. "And if it was him, he could still be alive. *You* are. We don't know anything yet." The edge of tension in his shoulders moved up his neck and into his face.

"Well, your brothers are pulling in now," Carter announced. "We can ask Gideon ourselves."

If my pulse wasn't skyrocketing before, it was through the roof now.

Over the phone, Sebastian instructed, "Escort them up." He cracked his neck, rolling his shoulders back as if preparing for a possible fight.

Jeez, I hope not.

"What's the play?" Carter asked, eyes on Ryder. "How do you want to do this? This is your op."

Ryder remained seated alongside Alex, resting his hand on his jaw as he stared at his plate. "He needs us, or he wouldn't be here. The fact he hopped on a flight to Peru after showing that photo . . . he's not our guy. He's not behind this. It'd make no sense for him to be." He surveyed everyone at the table before shooting Jason, then me, a questioning look.

"I'm in agreement," Jason said steadily.

"And I need Julian's help if we're going to pull off the impossible and undo what's not supposed to be undoable with his source code." Gwen stood. "I need to see what the bloody hell happened in Rome that night."

"What do you think?" Jason circled my wrist, not caring who witnessed this side of him.

"I think we have to work together like we probably should have done from the beginning." I swallowed. "I'm so sorry."

Jason brought his free hand beneath my chin; his calloused fingers were a steady force against my skin, his thumb grazing just enough to make my pulse trip. "Don't be. Everything happens for a reason." Gone was any sign of pessimism from this man, and I needed that. "We'll get through this."

At the throat clears by a few someones from the table, signaling we weren't alone, Jason let go of me, and we turned toward the entranceway.

Julian met my eyes first, a million apologies written in his expression, like he was devastated he hadn't fought harder to keep me in his orbit with what was going on. His fingers were restless, like he was still half in the digital world.

For the first time since last week, I wanted to hug him.

Even the broody brother, too.

I slowly lifted my eyes to Gideon, and I'd swear the man looked like he'd been to hell and back. His suit was rumpled, and he had shadows carved under his eyes.

Unable to stop myself, I slowly approached them, and they met me halfway.

"Hi," I whispered, fighting back tears.

Gideon stopped in front of me and set his hand on my shoulder. "I'm sorry," he said in a hoarse voice, shaking his head. "I'm so fucking sorry."

"Me too." An ache built in my throat as I hugged him.

Julian gathered me in his arms next. "Don't you leave me again, got it?" he said into my ear before pulling away.

I blinked back tears and turned toward the room.

"Carter," Gideon greeted with a slight bite to his voice. "Sebastian," he said next.

"Gideon," both Carter and Sebastian responded in unison, and whether they knew each other from the past or not didn't change the fact they didn't seem ready to lower their guards this morning.

Carter's index finger skimmed his fork handle, as if a utensil was as good as a 9mm. Across from him, Sebastian's chair creaked as he leaned back, watching my brothers like a patient predator.

"Was my protector with me in Rome?" I didn't even know the name of my protector yet. "Was he the guy I was with before I went missing?" I faced my brothers again.

"He was. Kylo told his family he found out at the last minute you were going on a trip, and he was worried about you. They had no idea he's been missing since they've been in Peru off-grid," Gideon explained in a somber voice.

Kylo? I let the name roll around, searching for familiarity. Nothing came, like usual. Just a roadblock to my past.

"I found a flight manifest. He arrived in Rome a day after you did. I never thought to check . . ." Gideon grimaced, clearly upset with himself for missing that. In his defense, he'd assumed my protector was in Peru. "Where Kylo went after, I don't know, since we can't track him outside the airport because of the corrupted CCTV footage in the city. And as to where he was taken after you went missing . . . ? All we know is, his phone was shut off when yours was before the blackout, and it hasn't pinged since."

Julian stepped forward, his gaze laser focused on the table, and I twisted around to see who he was staring at. Gwen, of course. "Looks like it's time for us to finally meet in person," he said to her.

I couldn't help but notice Easton carefully watching Gwen's every movement as she approached my brother.

"Julian." He offered her his hand. "Nice to officially meet you."

"You know, Central Intelligence has you listed as deceased." She slipped her hand into his.

A wolfish smirk crossed my brother's lips. "Slight misunderstanding."

She smiled back. "You don't say?" I noticed a twitch of her fingers against his, and the room's hum dulled to a silence so sharp I swore I could hear the catch of her breath before she asked, "You're him, aren't you?"

"Him who?" He let go of her hand and dragged his knuckles along his jawline.

Why'd I get the feeling we were invading their privacy right now?

"You're the anonymous hacker, the one who's been . . . the one who saved Falcon Falls from dying on that plane when we were up against The Collective. The one who saved us over and over again with your tips," she sputtered, eyes going wide. "I can just feel it."

I had no idea what she was talking about, but based on the uneasy way my brother was standing and avoiding eye contact with her, *he* did.

Easton abruptly stood from the table. "*You're* him?" A hint of jealousy boomed through his voice. So, not just a shadow, huh? Also, I clearly didn't need to worry that the guy had any kind of lingering feelings for me based on how he was looking at Gwen. That was something.

"Well?" Gwen folded her arms, waiting for my brother to talk.

From the sounds of it, Julian was a pretty damn-good guy if he'd helped her and Falcon Falls out so many times without taking credit for it.

Julian side-eyed Gideon, and Gideon gave him a slight nod of what I read as permission. "You've been bugging me over DMs for a while now to know who I really am." He let go of a deep breath. "Looks like now's the time. And I need a favor returned . . . Help me find who the hell did this to my sister so we can find an antidote to get her memories back."

CHAPTER THIRTY-FIVE

Hollis

"As much as I'm sure you two would love to chat about your computer foreplay, that's not why we're here." Gideon's voice carried a rough edge, and it earned him a sharp look from Julian and a death stare from Easton.

Well, okay then.

"We need to talk, yes?" Gideon's dark, shadowed eyes flicked upward, lingering on the ceiling before methodically sweeping the room.

"The cameras are off," Sebastian said calmly, waving us back toward the table. "Safe to speak. You know who *I* am, I know who *you* are. We either trust each other, or—"

"Fine." Gideon crossed the room, and while his back was to me, something in the hard line of Jason's jaw told me they were locked in a silent glare.

I elbowed Julian, snapping him out of his staring contest with the genius Brit.

Gwen rolled her lips inward, color high in her cheeks, her eyes still carrying a stunned kind of recognition.

Jason pulled out my chair, and I mouthed a quiet thanks as I slid into the seat before he scooted me in. He held my hand under the table as Gideon settled across from Alex.

Julian took the only spot left, which was next to Carter and right beside Gwen—leaving her wedged between my brother and Easton. Not a triangle I wanted to be solving tonight. I shoved the math away. We had bigger variables, like whether Kylo was alive.

I braced myself, waiting for Gideon to open up. Instead, he poured a bottle of water into a glass with steady precision, then took a measured sip. As he set it down, his gaze locked on the black dome camera overhead. No visible light, indicating it was inactive, just as Sebastian had claimed.

Gideon leaned forward, elbows on the table as he set his attention on me. "I don't know how Kylo found out you were in Rome, but you must have left a clue or a trail for him to follow. But when I showed a witness his photo, he confirmed he was the one there with you. He said four or five men attacked you and Kylo. Kylo must've covered you so you could escape."

What kind of warrior was I that I couldn't even handle hearing about a situation I'd been in myself?

"Any chance Putcheski's father was involved in what happened that night and he's covering his ass?" Ryder asked. "His boat was docked in Naples. Constantine couldn't confirm if he was in Rome, though."

"We found evidence to prove Benjamin was at the rave. We also have visual confirmation from inside the rave that my sister and Kylo were there as well," Gideon said in a low voice, fingers lightly drumming the table.

"We tried to get ahold of phones, but we didn't have any luck. I'm guessing you did?" Gwen locked on to Julian, and he shifted uncomfortably in his seat, like he was trying to lean away from her, preferring to take his chances with the growly-looking Carter guy instead. "I could only scour through social media for posts and videos, and came up empty."

Julian lifted a shoulder, giving off a casual *Don't blame yourself* look. He produced his phone and slid it over to Ryder. "Putcheski's dad knew what went down that night. He lied to us—probably to your people, too. Not a surprise. Benjamin tried to confiscate all phones from the ravers. *But* he missed a few guests, and we got lucky. We have a video that proves the men who attacked you were with Benjamin. You had to have been there for him."

"We've had our ups and downs with the Putcheskis for years," Gideon picked up, tone bitter. "They walk a fine line between good and evil, making it hard to legally take them out." He opened something on his phone, then passed it to me.

I zoomed in on a video and let it play. I was there, like he said. I had on a red wig, and there was a guy with me. He had his arm banded around my midsection for a brief moment, eyes scanning the crowd. Watchful and protective. "That's Kylo?"

"It is," Julian said as I watched the video again, a harsh pain building in my chest seeing myself go for a weapon just before the video cut out.

"My guess is, Benjamin spotted you, and then that's when all hell broke loose," Gideon noted, his tone remaining calm and resolute.

"Did I think Benjamin had the book? I don't understand."

"We still don't know if that book is tied to this." Julian shook his head—and why was he so adamantly against that being a possibility?

I passed the phone back. "If Putcheski's men caught up with me even though Kylo tried holding them off, how would they know about my tracker?" With my free hand, I thumbed the chain. "And know to put this on me?"

"Unless someone from your family or team sold you out?" Alex suggested the only thing that, I supposed, made sense.

"What do we need to know about Tristan *and* the book that our mother doesn't want me to know? There has to be something I'm missing here. The pieces aren't adding up." My gaze volleyed between my two brothers as I waited for the truth. "Wait," I blurted out before they could speak as a recent memory slammed into me. "I was in France this month." I glanced at Jason. "I told you over text I was with my brother, working on something there."

Jason squinted, like he was doing a mental scroll through our text conversations to play catch-up.

"I wasn't with you in France," Gideon let me know.

"Neither was I," Julian quickly added.

"Tristan, then. I was working with him privately. Did he double-cross me?"

Gideon checked the security camera on the ceiling again. "What I say here never leaves this room, am I clear?" I could hear the *Or I'll kill ya* embedded in his icy tone.

Agreeable but hesitant nods from everyone happened one by one.

"After you left Surrey, I demanded Mum talk and tell me what she was keeping back about the book," Gideon shared, eyes on me.

And? I asked in my head.

"We're required by our oaths to keep records of whatever we do, right down to who we kill and why. It's meant to keep us honest and servants to the truth. All those records were housed in vault seven before the fire," Gideon explained, and I remembered Julian telling me something similar in Surrey. "*Mum* is the arsonist. *She* burnt the place down in '92, which is why she always refused to talk about it. She couldn't destroy the one archive she was after without drawing attention to herself, so she took down the whole place to bury the truth."

Shock sent me back from the table yet again, but I remained seated as I waited for the rest of the story.

But then it came to me on my own.

Not a memory.

Just an *oh shit* moment.

"The mission where she got pregnant with Tristan," I whispered. "She didn't want any evidence to exist about him. That's why she burnt the place down, right?"

Gideon nodded. "Aside from Tristan himself, that was the only proof that he existed, *and* who his father was. He doesn't even know who his dad is, and believe me, he's asked. His dad could be alive or dead, for all I know. Mum won't tell us anything about that."

"So she was willing to destroy the entire library to protect her son." Part of me understood that. She truly loved him, even though it was too risky to raise him herself.

"There was an investigation into the fire. No blame was assigned to anyone, and the case was closed," Gideon continued. "Did our grandfather remove the book from the library before the fire . . . ?" He shook his head. "Maybe?"

I'm living proof he saved it.

"Why'd she wait until '92 to burn it down?" Jason asked, and there was a subtle *something* poised in his expression I couldn't quite decipher.

"Something had to have set her off to do it then and not when he was born, but she wouldn't tell us." Julian gestured toward the window. "Pops lived in Meiringen, a Swiss town at the base of the Reichenbach Falls. To outsiders, he was an eccentric aristocrat with a retreat in the Bernese Alps. In truth, he was a recluse to keep Tristan hidden, and the vault was housed on the property. It was on the back end of the—"

"Mountainside," I remembered, drawing up an image of the before-and-after paintings Julian had shown me in Surrey. "The manor survived, just the library was burned."

Jason took hold of my hand and asked, "Another reason why you chose to meet us here?"

Gideon nodded. "It's a thirty-minute helicopter ride away. Also, Benjamin Putcheski is currently at his home in Austria. We may need to pay him a visit together. Get the truth of what happened directly from him; he's the only one who can currently provide us answers. But he'll have an army of guards, so we'll need to be a united front to approach his property."

"I figured a few of us could go look around Pop's place with a fresh set of eyes first. We still own the property, but no one has lived there since he passed," Julian added before I could digest everything. "We can divide and conquer. If the Putcheskis are holding Kylo, and he's still alive, I doubt he has much time left."

"Would Tristan really hurt him?" My stomach somersaulted from his betrayal. "Does he have a protector, too?"

"Tristan does, but he ditches him quite often," Gideon confirmed. "He's always been a lone wolf."

"Because we did that to him by separating him from us," I said somberly. "At least, our parents did, since we didn't even know he was our brother until we were all eighteen."

"I still refuse to believe Tristan is tied to this." Julian stood. "It has to be someone else. Dad vouched for his brothers and sister. Our cousins and protectors have alibis. But I suppose if any of them have my source code, it's possible their alibis are bullshit."

"Another reason you need to work with us now. You can't trust your own family," Carter said while rising, focusing on Easton. "Can you pilot the bird to Meiringen?"

Easton glanced at Gwen as if uncomfortable with the idea of leaving her here with Julian, but he nodded. "I'll go prepare. Looks like a storm is on the horizon. We'll need to leave soon." He stood, shot Gwen one last look, then took off.

The air in the room barely had a chance to settle before Jason took me by surprise by asking, "Any chance you happen to know why whoever did this to Hollis would plant a false, dreamlike memory into her brain like a reset point?"

Julian's eyes snapped to mine. "Wait, *what*?"

"I've had the same recurring dream ever since I woke up in that coffin. Even when I try to remember something while I'm awake, my brain always pushes the same fake memory to the surface to block me from doing so. It's always Jason in the dream."

Gideon joined Julian in his somber look before hanging his head. Eyes closed, a gruff breath filled the quiet.

"What is it?" Jason asked before I could get it out.

Julian tore his hands through his hair, disheveling it even more. "You just confirmed it was great-grandfather's drug that was used. You didn't mention this to us before. Now we know for sure the book wasn't destroyed in that fire, and I was *really* hoping it was."

Gideon slowly lifted his head. "There's a fail-safe with the formula, a way to prevent anyone from trying to use any mind control substances or hypnosis to undo the effects of the drug. Once the substance is injected, and while it's flowing through you, you're supposed to picture a safe place." He zeroed in on Jason, jaw tight. "You're supposed to think of something that gives you peace and someone you love."

CHAPTER THIRTY-SIX

Reed

I wasn't sure what to think or believe, and yet, if Julian was saying what I think he was . . .

"But I didn't inject myself. I wouldn't know to think that . . ."

"Exactly, which means someone has the book and gave you instructions to do that after they drugged you," Julian finished for Hollis.

My heart was racing, because while this was horrible, it was also—

"I chose you before." Hollis spun toward me. "I created that dream myself." She launched herself into my arms.

Gideon stared at me over her shoulder as I rubbed her back, giving her a moment. I'd expected his silence to press like a threat, but it never did. Instead, he almost looked *relieved* to see his sister in my arms.

"Why do you seem so bloody worried it was that drug specifically?" Sebastian must have picked up on something I missed; I was too focused on Hollis and the fact she'd created that picture of us married with kids all on her own.

"Because," Gideon began as Hollis left the comfort of my arms to face him, "it's irreversible. It was designed to be that way, to protect and safeguard whatever secret was worth drugging oneself in the first place. That's why we hoped it wasn't that drug."

Now their sketchiness about it made sense, but . . . "No." The word came out like a gutshot reaction. "I refuse to accept that." I pointed at Julian. "If you two can work together to save the footage that is supposed to be deader than dead, then you can create an antidote for this damn drug."

"I'm not a scientist, I'm sorry." Julian covered a hand over his heart as mine tried to break free from my chest. "The only one who took after our great-grandfather was . . ."

"Fucking A," Ryder cursed. "You're going to say Tristan, aren't you?"

Neither Gideon nor Julian confirmed Ryder's question, but their silence *was* an answer.

"Diana," Carter said, stroking his jawline almost absentmindedly. "If anyone can come up with a cure, it's my wife. But she'll need the book to see the original math for it."

Gideon nodded. "The sooner we get to work, the better. Kylo's family is returning to their home base in England tonight, and they'll begin searching for him as well. If Kylo's not with the Putcheskis, and he's still out there, we'll find him." He gestured to his brother. "We need the footage from both Rome and České Budějovice to expedite the search."

Julian turned to Gwen. "Where do you want to set up?" His words were calm and flat, unlike earlier.

Gwen didn't answer right away. There was a slight shift in the temperature of the room as she quietly stared at him, like she was on the trust fence and uncertain.

"I'm sorry I kept my identity hidden from you," Julian said in a near grunt, like the words were being ripped from his mouth against his free will. "There. Better?"

"Hardly." Gwen picked up a key from the table and dropped it into his palm. "We can go to your suite. It's two doors down from your sister's."

Julian curled his fingers around the key. "And do you plan on ripping into me when we're alone? It'll fuck with my focus."

"We wouldn't want to do that, now, would we?" Gwen shook her head, then looked around the room as if remembering she had eyes on her, then abruptly started for the exit.

Gideon slapped a hand over his brother's shoulder, stopping his pursuit, whispered something in his ear, and then Julian left.

"You have room on that bird for Alex and me to join you?" Ryder asked, his question clearing some of the tension left behind by Gwen and Julian.

"There is." Carter glanced at Sebastian. "You go with them, I'll stay back and call my wife. She's in Dubai right now. I'll update her on the situation." He had his phone in his hand and was already leaving before anyone could respond.

"What about me?" Hollis asked her brother.

Alex tapped my shoulder before he and Ryder left, a quiet *good luck* in that pat, leaving the three of us in a room full of untouched food with the Alps, a storm rolling through, as a backdrop for this awkward confrontation with Gideon.

"You can work on the Putcheski files to see if I missed something. Fresh set of eyes might be good. I'll have someone bring my laptop to your suite. Are you two staying together?"

Hollis flicked her French braid to her back like a nervous tell before boldly placing her hand on my chest. "We are. Separate bedrooms, though."

Gideon's eyes flicked to me briefly, and I braced for impact. Shockingly, no swing or lecture came.

"Lyra's worried about you." He handed Hollis a new phone. "Call her later, will ya? I programmed our numbers. Just don't mention Tristan this time when you chat."

Based on Hollis's reaction, she was as confused as I was. "Okay, um, thank you."

Gideon gave her a tight nod, a look that suggested he was tolerating me—at least for now—and then started for the exit.

"Wait," Hollis called, spinning toward the door in one fast motion. "I think I need to go with you." She rested her hand against her stomach as he turned around. "If our grandfather trusted me about the book, and I spent a lot of time learning from him . . . maybe I can muscle-memory my way through his estate and find something that'll help?"

He quietly held her eyes before stealing a quick look out the window, as if unsure, given the storm, whether she should fly. But then he surprised me by nodding. "Yeah, okay."

I had to keep in mind he knew his sister was the kind of woman who faced danger like it was her job on a regular basis (and it was), so he wasn't about to treat her with kid gloves.

"Now that we know the book is part of this, I'll have Julian check if you paid our grandfather's place a visit in recent months. I assume you went there at some point." Gideon looked at me next. "You joining, too, I assume?"

"Of course."

"I'll have Alex and Ryder stay behind and give them my laptop instead. They can come up with an infil plan if we need to drop into Putcheski's estate." He checked his watch. "Meet me at the helo pad in five?"

"Yeah, okay. Thank you," she answered for both of us, and once he left, she set aside the phone and looped her arms over my shoulders, linking her wrists behind my neck. "The world is spinning."

"I think it's supposed to."

She smiled, and it was nice to see after what she'd just endured. "Kylo. Tristan. My grandfather. Benjamin Putcheski. The book. It's a lot. And I couldn't get through any of this without you. Thank you for putting up with me for so long, back then and now. For being someone I felt safe with even when we fake-hated each other."

I brought my hands between us and cupped her cheeks, catching a few tears with my thumbs. "You imagined having kids with me." I was going out on a limb here, but I'd already mentally bought that fifth chair. "You really think I could be a good dad even after I had such a bad example of one?"

"We can either follow in our parents' footsteps or learn how to walk on our own and do the opposite. And from where I'm standing, it looks like you've already been walking your own path for quite some time."

I closed my eyes and dropped my forehead to hers.

"You're upset with your father, and with *more* than good reason, but I also know that hasn't stopped you from trying to help him. So maybe after all of this, Carter's wife can somehow use the antidote on him, too?"

I lifted my head and exhaled, my heart both heavy and also full at the same time.

"Don't you dare feel bad if I was looking for that book to help him, either." She pushed up on her toes and kissed me. "I clearly can't help but be a stubborn pain in the ass, and my decisions are mine to own. Okay?"

I wasn't ready to say yes when it came to her helping my father; guilt still hit me brick by brick over the fact she was potentially in this mess because of her pursuit for a cure. So, for now, all I could do was nod and let her interpret that however she wanted.

"And if someone in my family is a traitor," she continued, her voice breaking, "it was bound to come out at some point. I did what I had to."

"A high price to pay for—"

"I'd do anything for the people I love. That's one of those innate feelings, but it's true." Her long lashes fluttered. "I'd sacrifice myself for the greater good. For truth. For what I believe in."

A tear slid down her cheek, and I held her gaze, knowing damn well those weren't just words. That mindset and feelings came from her soul, and who was I to try to change her?

The thought of her throwing herself into the fire, though—of losing her the way I'd buried brothers draped in flags—had my chest caving in.

I drew her tighter against me as my throat burned. "I know," I admitted, the words scraping out raw on my tongue. "You'll always join the fight for what's right."

I could feel her heartbeat drumming against mine, beat for beat. Outside, thunder rolled low across the Alps like an ominous reminder that this was far from over. There'd always be a cause, a mission, a *something*, that would place her in harm's way, and I had to accept that.

"*But* anyone who tries to take you from me will have to go through me first, and I won't fall easily."

CHAPTER THIRTY-SEVEN

Hollis

Meiringen, Switzerland

"Closing in on the place now," Easton announced over the headsets from behind the yoke. He and Jason seemed okay, despite the fact Easton had shared we'd gone on a few dates that thankfully hadn't ended in sex.

My brother was sitting up front by him, and from what I'd gathered, they'd never operated together, even though we had.

It was just Jason and me in the back, because Sebastian had opted to stay at the hotel, working leads with the others.

"Land over there. The helo pad's covered up, but . . ." Gideon kept talking to Easton, but I wound up tuning them out, too awestruck as the estate came into view.

The manor rose against the Alps like a relic. Stone walls weathered by neglect, shutters sagging on rusted hinges, ivy clawing its way across the front, softening what had probably once been all sharp edges of wealth and power. Now it looked like a forgotten treasure.

The sky growled overhead, thunder rolling like a lion's warning. Not ideal flying conditions, but what choice did we have? We needed answers, and I prayed we'd find something here while Julian and Gwen worked their miracle at the hotel with the footage.

Jason held my hand, quiet strength in his touch. He wasn't at all the man he'd pretended to be over text, trying to keep me at arm's length. He was kind, patient, and wicked smart, too. He was full of knowledge I kept discovering at every turn. Even as we'd walked to the helo earlier, he'd casually mentioned that Meiringen had also been the setting for one of Sir Arthur Conan Doyle's *Sherlock Holmes* stories.

The helo slowly touched down, and once it was safe, Jason helped me out and Gideon moved ahead, leading us to the manor. "I had the power turned back on," he said while unlocking the front door.

A gust of stale air hit us the second he opened up. Were we walking into my past, or a haunted house?

My brother flicked on the lights. Our footsteps echoed across the wide entry hall, bouncing off parquet floors dulled by dust. Portraits glared down from gilt frames, their painted eyes sharp and eerie in the dim light, as though clocking us as intruders.

My fingers trailed the carved banister. I had no idea when I'd last been here, but my body seemed to remember. "Anything from Julian yet about whether I came here recently?"

"He texted en route here. The closest airport where one of our planes landed in recent months was in Germany six weeks ago. You flew to Munich alone," Gideon shared. "You arrived on a Tuesday afternoon and left on Thursday. No CCTV footage exists of you outside the airport, though. It was scrubbed. So it looks like whoever destroyed the footage in Rome and the Czech Republic covered your tracks here, too. They didn't want anyone to know you came here."

"Wait." I held up my hand. "Timeline issue here, right? If it really was Tristan who stole Julian's source code, I came here *before* you suspected he took it. So either Tristan's innocent, he stole it at a different time, or—"

"Whoever has the source code can alter CCTV footage anywhere at any point, they don't have to do it in real time," Gideon cut in. "They tossed your hotel in Rome, your places in London and France, to cover up for what or *who* you were after. I'm sure they didn't know you spoke to Julian about the book, or they wouldn't have worked so hard to hide the fact you were looking for it."

"Almost everyone in our family believed the book burned in that fire." Chills dusted over my skin. "Not me. Doubtfully Tristan."

Gideon slowly faced me, a harsh breath settling from his lips. "The formula can't be activated without our blood, and it *only* interacts with our blood." He motioned for us to follow him, and I assumed he had evidence to back up his theory somewhere.

A restless energy sparked in my veins. The air grew colder as we moved down a long hallway, the scent of mildew and damp stone intensifying with each step. Our footsteps stirred dust motes that shimmered beneath the lantern-style lights lining our path.

The door groaned as Gideon opened it, and he turned on the lights before we joined him inside what looked like a laboratory frozen in time. "Tristan's probably had the book this whole time."

I looked around the large space. Tables sagged beneath the weight of abandoned glassware, cloudy flasks, and tarnished instruments. Rust had eaten into metal clamps, and an acrid tang of old chemicals lingered in the air.

An immense chalkboard stretched across one wall, streaked with faded equations and scribbled diagrams that still clung in ghostly white.

I continued to walk around, Jason protectively behind me as I took in the sight of a corkboard above a desk. The pictures must have been of my grandfather and the child he raised.

Tristan had aged in each photo, going from boy to man.

"So I talked to Julian first, and he didn't have answers, so I flew under the radar, knowing you didn't believe it was true, but then I got here and realized Tristan's had it the whole time." The words left a bitter taste on my tongue. "But why was I with him in France?"

Easton interjected his two cents. "Tristan probably lied to you when you asked him about it. Pretended to help you find it to keep an eye on you. Ensure you didn't find the truth. He clearly didn't want you to know he had it, for some reason. Then you got too close, and he set you up in Rome, maybe even with the Putcheskis."

I skimmed my finger along dusty notebooks, their edges furled and yellowed. "You really think he baited me to Rome with the book? Could Tristan be so evil to do such a thing to me?"

"It's sure as hell how it *looks*, at least. Maybe he even baited the Putcheskis, too. Or was working with them for some reason," Jason said before Gideon could respond, reaching for my hand. His jaw flexed, and his hand was the steady weight I needed in this storm.

"Tristan didn't want you to die, he just needed you to forget you found out the truth," my brother remarked in a low, haunted voice as he stopped by the chalkboard. "He probably convinced you to keep your search from us, selling you on the idea it was to protect us—or he put it in your head it was one of us who had it."

"And Kylo wasn't supposed to be with me. Now . . ." I cupped my mouth, the guilt hitting hard again. "Tristan may not have had it in him to kill me, but what about Kylo?"

"He can't use the drug on Kylo. It wouldn't work," Gideon reminded me. "But take his life?" He pocketed his hands. "I don't know, because as much of a loner as Tristan is, he's still our brother, and I'm having a hard time believing he did this." The faint edge of doubt prickled through his tone like static. "I honestly don't know what to think anymore."

Jason remained alongside me as the lights flickered, gripping my hand firmly.

"Based on how bad it's sounding out there, we're going to have to ride out this storm before we head back to the hotel." Easton hiked a thumb over his shoulder. "I'm going to check it out."

Gideon nodded. "We can't wait too long. We need to talk to Benjamin later."

"If he's holding Kylo *for* Tristan, so help me if he's hurt." I didn't remember my protector, but he'd sacrificed himself to let me escape, not knowing I'd be walking into a trap anyway, one set by my own flesh and blood.

"I'll take a look around the house and see if we missed anything, but I'm sure Tristan's already paid the place a visit. He'd know the manor inside and out, much more than us." Gideon's dark eyes slipped from me over to Jason, a silent directive written into his expression: *Keep her close.*

Once it was just the two of us, he brought our clasped palms to his mouth and pressed his lips to my knuckles. "I'd prefer not to stay here. It's giving *Frankenstein* vibes."

I wasn't sure which emotion I was feeling, so I split the difference and laugh-cried. "Right there with you."

I turned off the light behind us and closed the door, feeling as though I was saying goodbye to the past one last time.

CHAPTER THIRTY-EIGHT

Hollis

The storm broke over the house. Rain lashed the shutters, a relentless drumbeat, and the lights continued to flicker, buzzing with each surge.

Jason kept his arm around me, my head on his shoulder as we sat on the floor, our backs to the wall, waiting out the weather. It was just the two of us in there for now, and his presence was heat in itself in the drafty room.

I brought my hand to his chest, hooking my stretched-out leg over his to draw even closer to him. "Well, um, since we're going to be here a bit longer, and the last thing I want to do is think about my family, any chance you want to talk about—"

"Mine?" Thunder punctuated the word.

"No pressure. We just haven't . . . you know, since the plane . . ."

He was quiet for a few minutes, and I took that silence as his request to drop it, so I didn't expect him to begin filling in the blanks about his past.

He revealed heartbreaking stories, one after another. Quick and fast, like he wanted to skip through them to avoid me taking a moment to offer compassion or sympathy.

"I stole something once," he said, switching gears. "I was thirteen." Guilt thickened his tone. "I hadn't eaten in days, and my parents were MIA, and nothing was in the house, and as the clerk was yelling out 'Stop him,' I ran right into a cop, smashing the sandwich I hadn't paid for against his chest. The officer felt sorry for me, paid for it, then took me home and waited until my parents came back. He laid into them both and had CPS check in on me regularly. You'd think they'd have cleaned up their act after that, but they didn't."

"I'm just so—"

"Don't be. Please. And there's one more thing I should tell you. It's not exactly the time or place to do this, but if I don't share this soon, I feel like it's going to break me." Pain seared his tone, bleeding into me.

I looked up at him, our mouths close enough for him to pass the truth to me in a whisper. "Tell me, please."

"And if you hate me for it?" He closed his eyes, resting the back of his skull against the wall.

"I could never. Well, not unless it's fake hate," I reminded him. "Also, we're not going anywhere until this storm weakens, and Gwen and my brother are still working on the source code. So now sounds like a good time to unburden yourself of whatever is bothering you."

His jaw and neck visibly tensed, but he slowly tilted his head to catch my eyes. "The tattoo."

"Genesis 2:24," I remembered.

"*A man shall leave his father and his mother and hold fast to his wife, and they shall become one flesh.*" He set my palm to his rib, and I had to believe he chose that spot for biblical and symbolic reasons as well.

"It's a reminder to wait to have sex until I'm married." He closed his eyes. "I had it tattooed because I kept messing up. I kept failing. And on November twenty-fifth, 2021, I got the tattoo and promised myself never to fall again in that way."

In that *way?*

Oh.

Ohhh.

His reset point. The passcode for his phone: 11-25-21.

"I haven't had sex since the twenty-fourth of that month and year. I haven't crossed the line. And I told myself the next time I had sex would be my wedding night, and I'd change my passcode to my anniversary."

Tears filled my eyes, and I blinked a few free. "That's noble and amazing. W-why would I hate you for that?" I sniffled, trying to understand.

He shut his eyes. "Because of who I was before. I had *issues*." His Adam's apple rolled, and he expelled another deep breath. "My parents had their vices, their addictions. Mine was sex. It became meaningless. Hollow and empty. I kept trying to find a way to feel something, if you get what I mean . . ."

I thought back to his hand around my throat in the kitchen, and how bad he'd felt after. *Dominance?*

"One morning, I broke down. I was dead on the inside. And I found myself wandering down the street and wound up in front of a church. A priest was inside—like he knew I'd be coming. I'd never even been to church before." His dark lashes fluttered, and he opened his eyes. "I'd also never experienced anything so real as when I fell to my knees and put my life in God's hands instead of my own. Not even when I was downrange risking my neck in war."

A tear skated down his cheek, and I rolled my lips inward, trying not to sob, because then he'd try to comfort me instead, and that was the last thing I wanted.

"I'm not a good man just because of this. I'll never be perfect. I'm grumpy and moody, mad at the world and all the evil I see in it." He quietly stared at me before professing, "But then I met you, and my feelings for you terrified me. I tried to lie to myself that it wasn't real. I never thought you'd be with a man like me, so I did my best to push you away, worried I'd lose control and mess up."

I shifted around, unable to stop myself, and climbed on his lap. In hindsight, sitting on him like this was probably not the best idea, but I needed to hug him.

"I'm safe, I promise. I was always careful."

"That thought didn't cross my mind." I straddled him and threaded my fingers into his hair, resting my forehead against his. "I'm not mad at you, and I don't hate you. I'm so happy you found peace." I sat upright, cupping his cheeks, tears streaming down both our faces.

Guilt clawed deep in my chest at the memory of stripping and inviting him into my shower, not knowing all that he'd endured before to get to where he was now.

"No, don't you dare feel bad. I can read your thoughts right now." His brows slashed together as he held my wrists, pulling my hands away from his face. "You didn't know. I didn't tell you."

"You told me enough, and I didn't listen. I—I tried," I sputtered, "but the connection with you is so strong, and I just wanted you." I tugged one wrist free of his hold and leaned back to reach beneath his T-shirt, skimming his flesh. "I want to be your missing rib," I ugly-cried.

He dropped his mouth over mine and kissed me softly, rain hammering the windows like a celebratory applause.

The thunder boomed, rattling the frames on the wall as our kiss intensified.

The fragile moment shattered when my phone vibrated in my pocket—the new phone Gideon had given me. Why would that be ringing? Lyra?

I hated to break away, but after the third attempt to ignore the ringing to stay locked in the moment with the man beneath me, the vibrations became unnervingly loud.

"Who is it?" he asked as I brought the phone between us and showed it to him.

Julian. "Hello?" I answered, holding the phone close to Jason so he could listen in.

"Am I on speaker?" Julian asked.

"No."

"Where's Gideon?"

A chill swept up my spine as I whispered, "I don't know. Not here."

"Listen very carefully to what I'm about to say," my brother began in a steady voice, "and don't react. Gwen and I restored the original footage." The weight of the world stabbed me like a knife in the back as he rasped, "*Gideon* carried your limp body out of that store above the crypt with three other men in Rome." He paused, his breath catching over the line. "It was him. It—it was Gideon who did this to you."

CHAPTER THIRTY-NINE

Reed

"He was with us in Rome when your chain was removed and your tracker went back online. It doesn't make sense, but I'm looking at him on camera with my own damn eyes," Julian said, his voice taut, strung like a wire ready to snap.

"What's going on?" Gideon filled the doorway. Worst timing imaginable. For one, Hollis was perched on my lap. And the more obvious reason, Julian just confirmed the unthinkable: Gideon had drugged his own sister.

Hollis froze, her breath catching.

"Don't let him know you know. Just get back here safely," Julian said before the line went dead.

Rage surged through me like a blowtorch. My fists clenched, resting at her sides where I'd been holding her. The weight of my Glock pressed hot and insistent against my back, urging me to draw.

I'd walked a fine line since proclaiming my faith years ago. It'd been a tough balance to seek justice without taking it into my own hands unless it was on a mission or in self-defense, but I'd managed. Maybe there'd been a few questionable gray areas, but overall, I knew vengeance wasn't supposed to be mine to take. So I couldn't slit Gideon's throat for what he'd done to her.

I might have to keep reminding myself of that, though. Because every second we stood here, I could feel myself falling off the cliff. I even went so far as to turn down the volume on my conscience so I could push outside the gray into the dark and tell myself it was okay to take this man's life.

"Well?" Gideon's short question punched through my thoughts as Hollis brought the phone between our bodies.

"That was Julian, just checking on me. No update yet." She quickly slid off my lap. I steadied her, though my own balance was shaky with fury.

My face burned as I locked eyes with Gideon, forcing myself not to go for my gun.

The enemy—no longer her brother in my eyes—leaned against the doorframe, arms folded, eyes sharp as the scalpels I wanted to use to peel back his flesh.

I'd been angry with Tristan before, with whoever had done this to her . . . but having the enemy in plain sight flipped a switch in me.

"And you were on his lap, because?" he pivoted, not pushing back on the call like I'd have expected of someone who'd kidnap their own sister and erase her memories.

"I think it's fairly obvious at this point why." Hollis's calm delivery was a blade sheathed in silk. No tremor, no hesitation. "Tell me it's safe to fly." She linked her arm through mine, chin tipped up with bravery.

Gideon's gaze lingered, dissecting me as though he could chip away my layers and read my intent with his sister. "It is." He pushed off the doorframe, nodding.

Her poise continued to impress me, but I could feel the air shift, like static before a storm. Gideon had to have sensed it, too.

"I thought you didn't like my sister. That you barely tolerated her. What happened these last few days? I didn't ask before, but I'm asking now." His steady, even tone about sent me over the edge. How the hell could he stand there like he hadn't just lied, hadn't betrayed every kind of oath imaginable?

"Looks can be deceiving," I said like a reflex. "So can words." I bit down hard, keeping myself from leveling my 9mm at him.

Easton came up behind Gideon, meeting my eyes, delivering a silent message: *I know.* "We should move. Window's tight before shit blows up again."

Tell me about it.

"You find anything useful searching the rest of the house?" Hollis asked, slicing through the tension.

Gideon shook his head once, then stepped aside, letting us pass first. Nothing like having to turn my back to him. Betrayal always did cut the deepest when it came from blood.

The flight back was rough, the helicopter pitching and bucking in the crosswinds. Rain peppered the glass, a steady drumming that kept my nerves wound up. The cabin shuddered with every gust. I didn't let go of Hollis's hand, hers cool against mine, and my other never strayed far from the cold steel at my spine.

Only when we touched down behind the hotel did my lungs unclench and the storm take a break.

Rain slicked our path, carrying the tang of wet asphalt and fuel as we walked, Easton leading the way since he lived here.

I hadn't been expecting Ryder, Carter, and Sebastian to be waiting for us by a side door like judges at an execution.

We stopped in front of them and Gideon cut to his questions first. "Did my brother and Gwen uncover something?"

Carter remained quiet, his hand drifting to his weapon first. Ryder and Sebastian followed suit, shifting into formation like wolves boxing in prey with Easton and myself.

"What the hell is going on?" Gideon hissed, his hand sliding toward his weapon.

I'd been prepared for this moment. My barrel pressed against his temple in a single motion, stopping him from drawing his weapon.

His chest heaved, his eyes cutting sideways to me. "What the fuck do you think you're doing?" he growled low.

The door behind us opened. Julian came out with his laptop open. He didn't speak, and he probably had no words, given what he'd found out. He spun the screen around and hit play.

On-screen, Gideon carried Hollis's limp body into a black windowless van. Her head lolled against his shoulder.

The footage was crystal clear, not blurred. It was him.

Gideon's arms dropped, his whole frame going rigid. He was either a hell of an actor or truly shocked. "That can't be me."

Julian zoomed in, frame tight on Gideon's face to confirm the truth.

"There's no way. This has to be AI deepfake shit. Someone planted it for you to find, knowing you'd try to undo your own source code. You of all people should know it's bullshit." Gideon's voice cracked, but his eyes stayed hard on the screen.

"It's not fake," Julian shared, nostrils flaring, eyes on his brother.

Gideon let go of a deep breath and raised his palms slowly, forehead tightening. He stared at Hollis, then back to the damning video. Finally, he sank to his knees.

She'd surely seen her brother standing unflinching before kings and killers—not that she could currently remember that—but something told me she'd never witnessed him bowing to the ground in submission.

I kept my gun trained, finger hovering near the trigger, every nerve alive to his slightest movement.

"Lock me up." Gideon slowly interlaced his hands behind his head. *"In tempore veritas,"* he added under his breath.

Tears spilled down Hollis's cheeks as she translated: "In time, there is truth."

"Find out who the hell *made* me do that," Gideon said, his voice rough. "Because if that's really me, the only way I'd *ever* do that is if someone else was in control of my own damn mind."

CHAPTER FORTY

Hollis

My brother was locked in a windowless suite on the service level, built for this very purpose: a holding cell. Soundproofed walls and a reinforced steel door. Security inside and outside keeping tabs on him.

It'd gutted me to watch such a strong man walk himself into a cage, when I knew deep down in my soul he was innocent.

Jason was giving me time to process what had happened, and I was taking that moment with Julian before regrouping with the others. Outside on the balcony of Ryder and Alex's suite, Julian hugged me.

"I believe him," he said into my ear. "If he says someone made him do it, then he's telling the truth. He clearly doesn't remember it happening."

"They stole only his memory of being there that night with me in Rome. How?" I stepped out of his embrace, swiping away tears. "How could they selectively delete just a certain memory?" I thought back to Trevor's cousin, Tessa . . . *I guess it is possible. She's proof of that. But not with this drug. This one only works on us, so it couldn't have been used on her.*

"I don't know, but I do know there were other experiments in that book, not just the identity-wipe one that only works on our bloodline." Julian rested his back against the railing, eyes set on the room, and I looked back to see where his focus was: Gwen and Easton talking.

"Why didn't you bring this up before?"

"I sort of told you, didn't I?"

Honestly, everything was becoming a blur at this point. Not good, since I didn't have that many memories to hang on to. "You said he created weapons during the Cold War. I think?"

"Yeah, the kind used to get people to 'conform,' and do shit," he said with air quotes. "I'd always thought it was the same weird science shit as the memory drug and didn't believe it. But that stuff was never my thing. Just"—he winced—"Tristan's."

Which brought us back to the brother who was probably truly guilty. He'd used an innocent man and set him up. "Where was Gideon before you two flew to Charleston, when you called to tell him my tracker went offline in Rome?"

"I checked the flight logs on your way back here. I never thought to ask him, because why would I?" He shook his head. "But he was in Monaco, which is a short plane ride to Italy. I met him in Charleston since I was already Stateside, then we flew with Delta Shield to Rome."

My stomach pitched, cold and sour. "Gideon is the one who talked to all the ravers and Putcheski's son. You were with him for that?"

"Yeah." He kept his eyes on the damp pavement. "None of the ravers seemed to recognize Gideon when we talked to them. They only ID'd you and Kylo, but . . ." He looked up at me. "Weird thing is, now that we have the street footage outside the library where the ravers took off after, I can see Benjamin and his security making a run for it, but they didn't have Kylo with them."

"Then where the hell is he? Who has him? He wasn't on that video with me when Gideon put me in that van."

"There had to be a second side exit or another tunnel system aside from the one Constantine found, since there was only one set of footprints back there. Kylo had to get out and come up top somewhere else."

"Does that mean . . ." I didn't even know how to finish that thought; the battle of who'd done this raged loud in my head with uncertainty.

"We're working on running Kylo's face through our software to try to get a hit on where he was between the time his flight landed and the rave. Retrace his steps that way." He jerked his chin toward the suite. "We're also running facial recognition on the three men with Gideon as well. No hits yet, but something will come up."

"What about the Czech Republic?"

"There's no CCTV footage near the monastery since it's abandoned. They covered their tracks for a reason, which means whoever brought you there had to be on a camera at some point. Flight records don't indicate shit, though."

"So all we know is that someone's moving us like pawns in their game. If they used Gideon to attack me, then what'd they want with me? Why'd they change their pattern and drop me off in that coffin? Why erase all of my memories?"

"Because you were onto them." He blinked, then dragged his knuckles along his jawline, seemingly lost in thought before he startled his head upright. "If this was used on Gideon, who's to say it wasn't used on me? Or Mum? Dad's in the clear, since the memory drug wouldn't work on him, but . . . I've, uh, been forgetful lately, and I just thought it was from a lack of sleep, but what if it's something else? What if no one mirrored my rig to steal the source code, but I willingly gave it away and explained how to use it myself?"

"Rig?"

"That's just what I call my laptop, sorry."

Before I had a chance to voice my thoughts about everything, Gwen yelled, "I found something."

Julian caught my arm, guiding me into the suite to hear her out.

Ryder, Alex, Carter, Sebastian, and Easton lingered near the doorway, a solid wall of muscle and suspicion behind Gwen, who sat with her laptop balanced on her thighs. My brother dropped next to her, leaning in to study her screen.

Easton wasted no time in joining them. He slid onto the cushion on her other side, completing the triangle that always seemed to form around her.

Jason cut across the room to join me, anchoring himself at my side.

"Your source code's been active in other places." Gwen's fingers flew across the keys before she angled the laptop toward Julian. "Every time it's used, it leaves your anonymous signature."

Julian's mouth curved at the edges. "What can I say? Gotta mark my territory."

Easton rolled his eyes. Didn't blame him there.

"That ego of yours worked in our favor. I traced seventeen instances in the last year alone. You've been a busy boy. Were all of these you? Well, aside from Rome, the Czech Republic, and Hollis's trip to her grandfather's?"

Julian's eyes narrowed as he pulled the laptop closer. "Nope. And definitely not . . ." He went still, then looked at me, his tone weighted. "I know where you were while you were missing."

A cold ripple ran down my spine. "Just tell me I didn't kill someone."

"No." He spun the screen toward me, showcasing an image of a sprawling medieval-looking estate under gray skies. "You were in Florence. Probably to get something from our vault."

"Why use me for that? If whoever's been pulling our strings—"

"Only two members of our family at a time are allowed access to it. Dad, and he chose you as the other." Julian handed the laptop to Gwen and stood. "Everything in that vault is bound to Dad's line. The drug wouldn't—"

"Work on him since it's tied to Mum's side." Was that the first time I'd called her that? I wasn't sure why that realization even hit me. "Did they just knock me out in the crypt and drug me later then? How else would I have . . ." I shook my head. "Muscle memory. They kept my skills and all that intact, because then I could open it under the power of suggestion without any pushback. Stole my memories, not my mind." It had to be in that order; I'd have resisted otherwise. Then again, Gideon and Julian had also been used without losing all their memories, so I wasn't sure what to think at this point. "Can we recover the footage from there? See who was with me and find out what they had me steal?"

"Working on it now," Gwen said, eyes never leaving the glow of her screen.

Jason brought his hand to my back, his thumb sweeping in small circles, steadying me.

"Are we leaving Gideon locked up?" My voice dropped as I shared, "He was drugged, too."

"He was?" Jason side-eyed me, and I forgot that Julian and I had come to that conclusion alone on the balcony.

I quickly explained everything, then waited for them to process my sci-fi-ish remarks. "It's not so wild, is it? Mind control."

Julian jumped in to defend me, reading their unsure looks. "It's already happening naturally and organically because of the internet. The power of suggestion." He opened his palms, surveying the room. "You see and hear something over and over again, even if it's a lie, and people quickly believe it to be the truth. Trust me when I say some governments and agencies are already weaponizing that strategy to use against people to divide them. Throw in a drug on top of it . . ."

"He's not wrong," Easton said, as if it pained him to agree with my brother on anything.

"Regardless," Ryder interjected, "Gideon said he didn't trust himself. I don't blame him for that. I'd feel the same, and he's not exactly in a prison cell. Maybe we hold off for now on letting him out?"

"I still need to talk to him," Julian muttered. "Also, call my parents. Warn Mum and Lyra they're at risk. Let them know the drugs from that book are real, and they're clearly effective."

"Make it fast," Carter said to Julian while removing his phone from his pocket.

"You and Gwen need to stay locked in on this source code and go through the raw footage," Ryder added. "Whoever's behind this doesn't realize you found a way to see where it's been used and *when* it's being used. The second they try again—"

"I'll pick up on it, and we'll have their location. That's bloody brilliant." Gwen smirked.

"Coming from you, I'll take that as a compliment," Ryder said wryly.

Julian gave me a quick *Everything will be okay* nod, then took off from the suite.

"Did you all come up with an infil plan to go after the Putcheskis?" I asked at the memory. "I assume that's still on the agenda tonight?"

"We'll talk to Benjamin on the phone. Give him a chance that way first. Plus, we're short on time," Carter said steadily. "He can tell us what we need to know the easy way." He shifted toward Sebastian. "And if he doesn't, or he lies, then I guess that means your wife is putting you in time-out when you're back in Dublin."

"And that's supposed to mean?" Alex asked, cracking a smile.

Sebastian casually adjusted his red tie. "Translation: I might have to kill people if he doesn't cooperate. My wife hates when I do that. Carter finds it feckin' hilarious when I get in trouble."

I had no clue whether this was true or some inside joke, but both men seemed equally intimidating and about a hundred shades of morally gray.

Carter's grin came and went fast before he recalibrated, mission-focused again. "Pull up Benjamin's house in Austria. Access his security feeds."

"Give me a minute." Gwen's fingers moved fast.

Everything was suddenly moving quickly now that we were working as one united front. The enemy had tried to divide us, to turn us on each other, because we're stronger together. *That's how the devil operates,* my subconscious whispered in my ear.

Jason mouthed, "I got you, don't worry."

Before I had a chance to say the same, Gwen announced, "We're about to go live. They'll be able to hear you, but we won't be able to hear them." She blocked the lens with her palm, scanning the room. "Who's talking?"

Carter tipped his chin at Sebastian. "You run these parts. He'll recognize you." He unlocked his phone and handed it to him. "Already programmed Putcheski's number in it if he's willing to take the call."

Sebastian stepped into the frame as Ryder and Alex shifted back, aligning with Jason and me just out of camera range. Gwen angled the laptop to capture only him and hit a button to show our camera and unmute the screen.

"You know who I am. Sebastian Renaud, League leader," he began, his voice low and commanding. "We can speak like civil men about what happened in Rome at the rave last week"—he held up the phone, his expression hardening—"or you can imagine what happens if I have to come to your house myself."

CHAPTER FORTY-ONE

Reed

Sebastian set the phone on the table in the dining area and hit the speaker button as we all gathered around. Julian was still MIA, but Hollis could fill him in afterward.

I stared at the black rectangle between all of us like it might explode if the wrong word was said, then took Hollis's hand in my own once again. She grounded me in a way I didn't know how to put into words.

I still couldn't believe I'd wanted to kill her brother not even thirty minutes ago, and now it was looking like he was innocent. I wasn't so sure I'd ever believe my own eyes about anything going forward.

"Carter Dominick is also with me," Sebastian announced, knowing that would hopefully seal the deal on getting Benjamin to talk. The two men weren't known for using butter knives when it came to peeling back information.

My team was lucky we had their assistance. Then again, was it really luck? More like the Almighty had our backs and had brought us here together for a reason.

"What do you want to know? You've already sent the Costas after my son to question him. The Wyndham d'Aragons, too," Benjamin responded, his voice notably shaky.

"The men who attacked Gideon's sister, Celeste, were with you. You were at the rave. It was a cover for something. What for?" Sebastian asked, locking his arms over his chest.

Gwen shifted her laptop aside but kept it open, and the blinking cursor on her last line of code caught my eye as I waited for the answer. She was probably two keystrokes away from digging into Benjamin's whole damn life if Carter or Sebastian gave the word.

"I need promises. Immunity from you all. Protection from anyone coming after me before I'll speak," he finally responded, and good, we were getting somewhere. He had to know something if he was shitting his pants and wanting *us* to save him.

Carter spoke up. "That depends on what you have to say. If you're holding anyone hostage or had anything to do with Celeste getting taken, then—"

"Celeste is missing?" Benjamin cut him off.

"I've been found," Hollis said in a low voice, not correcting the use of her other name. I had to assume most of the world knew her as Celeste, which was why they'd gone with that one.

"What happened to the man who was with me?" she pressed. "Your men fired at him, but he didn't leave with you."

"I don't know. Seems to me we were both set up. Used as bait to be drawn together for some reason." The line crackled from a deep breath. "A man messaged me claiming he had something of value that belonged to your family. He offered to sell it to me. Pages from a book. I didn't believe him or think it was worth my time, but then he sent me two encrypted pages. The original in Aramaic and the translated version in English, so I could make sense of it."

"And?" Hollis edged closer to the table.

"It proved to be of value, like he said."

"How so?" I asked before anyone else could, tightening my hold of her hand, my pulse racing.

"It was an experimental drug. A truth serum on steroids. I tested it on a few subjects, and it worked."

I leaned in and whispered in her ear, "Thought the drugs only worked on your mom's side of the family?"

"Only the memory-loss one," she clarified.

Great. This damn book really was dangerous in the wrong hands. Maybe it should have been destroyed in that fire.

"I was offered five more pages at a steep price," Putcheski continued. "He sent the location for the transaction to take place. He already knew my son was throwing a rave. I didn't even know about that beforehand. I was in Naples at the time, so I discreetly made my way to Rome that night. But then I showed up, and the second I saw Celeste, I realized it was a trap. I ordered my men not to kill you, just to scare you off. I knew what would happen if we . . ." He let his words go for a moment. "When Constantine and Gideon began asking my son questions and poking around, I knew something was fucked up, but I told my son to keep his mouth shut to protect him."

"I think I believe you," Hollis said, remaining even-toned and steady. "And you have no idea who sent you the pages and offered to sell you more?"

"No, but I can forward you the encrypted messages if I have your word my family is safe from being hunted by you all," he responded a few quiet moments later.

Carter exchanged a quick look with Sebastian, then Ryder, before turning toward the phone. "That fine line between good and evil you've been walking lately . . ." The threat was loud and clear. "I need you to find your way back over to the side of good if you don't want to make an enemy of us. And destroy that drug, ensure it's never used again by you or anyone."

The man cleared his throat. "I can do that."

"I believe in redemption. Everyone can be saved, even the worst of us. I'm a living testament to that." I wasn't sure why Carter's words hit so damn hard, but they slammed into me.

Gwen joined in without introducing herself. "Texting you the email to send us the information."

"I'd strongly advise you to stay put until this situation is resolved, am I clear?" Carter ordered, then didn't wait for confirmation and killed the call.

For a moment, no one moved. The air became heavier, like Benjamin's admission (and semi-innocence) had dropped a new weight onto all of us.

Hollis broke the quiet first as Gwen pulled her laptop in front of her to begin working. "Putcheski was manipulated and used for one purpose: to draw me out. I clearly thought he was there to buy or sell the book, because that's what I was after. Someone expected it to go down exactly as it did. Kylo would protect me, and I'd attempt to escape using our preplanned exit route."

"Does this mean what I think it means?" she whispered. "Kylo set me up that night—right down to my escape plan into those tunnels—didn't he?"

CHAPTER FORTY-TWO

Reed

Julian reentered the suite, his eyes sharp as he swept the room like he could taste the tension in the air. "What's going on?"

Ryder filled him in while Gwen's fingers raced over her keyboard.

I forced myself to take a moment to breathe. I'd already gone down the wrong road once with Gideon, assuming guilt before proof. I couldn't make the same mistake with Kylo.

"We don't know anything yet," I said out loud, more so to try to convince myself to chill out. "Kylo may have also been manipulated. He'd know about your tracker, right?"

Hollis nodded, her body remaining stiff as she stared at me.

"If he was your shadow and always with you, he'd have figured out you were after the book," Alex commented, and I wasn't sure if that helped or hurt Kylo's case for innocence.

"I wouldn't have suspected he had the book if I let him come to the rave, right? I must've believed it was someone else betraying us. I doubt I'd ever accuse anyone on my team without proof. That has to be why I went to Rome without my family."

"You stumbled into something you weren't meant to find." *All because you were trying to help my dad.* I didn't voice the rest, but she knew.

"My identity was wiped clean while my brothers' memories were only punched with holes. I was too close to the truth because I was chasing the very thing someone was using to control us."

Julian slid into the chair beside Gwen with his laptop. "We'll get to the bottom of this, I promise."

"You talk to Gideon? Mum and the others?"

Julian glanced back at Hollis. "Gideon feels horrible that someone was able to control him like that, but he says that's the only thing that makes sense. You know he'd never . . . I, uh, shouldn't have doubted him. I'm mad at myself that I did." He faced his screen again. "Mum, Dad, and Lyra are still in Surrey. Heavily secured and protected. They're safe. Mum doesn't believe Tristan has anything to do with this, but I don't blame her for not wanting to accept it. I still don't." He pulled out his phone. "Giving them a heads-up now about our protectors, too."

"Gideon mentioned your protectors were flying back tonight. Do we know where they are now? Were all of them in Peru when you two visited?" Ryder asked, remaining standing on the other side of the eight-person table.

"We only spoke to Kylo's parents. We didn't do a head count, no." Julian grimaced, pocketing his phone. "And their flight isn't due back to London for another hour."

Ryder turned toward Carter and Sebastian, who were hanging back, letting our team take the lead since this was our op. "We should split up. Maybe go to Gideon and have him give you a list of names for the protectors to run through facial ID while Julian focuses on the source code?"

"Go easy on him, please," Hollis said softly. "Not his fault."

Carter tipped his head as a silent okay, then he flicked his wrist, gesturing to Easton to roll out with him, and Sebastian quietly left as well.

Ryder slapped my shoulder twice, then he and Alex also decided to take off to run down more leads and prep for, well, whatever was going to happen next. Who the hell knew at this point. The situation was fluid and changing by the second.

I shifted closer to Hollis, standing behind where both Gwen and Julian worked as if racing with each other to see who could type faster without burning up their keyboards.

"I've got the raw footage from the vault in Florence," Gwen shared a few moments later. "Oh, hell." She shifted her laptop around so we could all view it.

The screen filled with grainy black-and-white footage, time-stamped *Thursday, 05:14.*

"That's more than enough time to go from Rome to Florence," I noted.

At the sight of Hollis appearing on the screen, my stomach turned. Two masked men were surrounding her, each gripping an arm like she was a broken marionette. Her head lolled, her steps dragging, but she was awake.

My emotions hit hard, pulling like barbed wire wound through my lungs. "They clearly drugged you with something."

"My eyes are open, but I'm gone. How do I not remember I was there if they gave me the identity-wipe drug before that?"

"It's probably equivalent to when someone roofies a drink. Conscious, but don't recall what happened during the time. Maybe my memories and Gideon's weren't wiped after we were controlled—we were just roofied," Julian suggested.

One man let go of her and quickly drew his sidearm, verbally fighting with the other one, from the looks of it, though the ski masks covered their mouths.

The first guy raised his weapon at Hollis, and the other one shoved Hollis behind him, putting himself between her and the gun.

A scuffle followed, fast and messy. The original asshole who'd tried to shoot Hollis went down. I wasn't sure whether he was dead or just knocked out, but he was dragged over to the SUV and thrown into the back while Hollis stood like a statue, watching the scene unfold.

The man returned to Hollis's side and pricked her with a needle. She slowly collapsed, and he caught her in his arms and gently placed her inside the back seat of the SUV before closing the door. Then he rounded the vehicle and stopped by the driver's side, setting his eyes on the camera positioned above the garage. He brought three gloved fingers to his temple and offered a slight salute as if sending someone on the other side of the screen a message.

Hollis spoke her thoughts out loud as Gwen rewound the footage so we could watch it again. "I don't understand. If he helped take me from Rome and set up Gideon, why'd he just protect me?"

"A double-cross?" Gwen suggested. "He had to have been the one that took your chain off so your tracker would go back online. Left you in the Czech Republic so we could find you. But in doing so, he also—"

"Saved my life," Hollis responded.

"Any chance you recognize the three-finger salute?" Gwen asked Julian.

"No," he responded, "but maybe Gideon might?"

"Let me call Carter to see if he'll bring him up here." Gwen shot Julian a polite smile. "Better chance he'll listen to me than you."

We waited for Gwen to make the call, and within a few minutes, Carter returned to the room with Gideon.

Gideon's dark eyes were fixed with regret on Hollis as she approached him.

"I know you didn't mean to do it." She crushed herself against him, forcing a hug, but he didn't return the gesture. He was full of guilt and shame, eyes pointed at me over her shoulder.

"Hug me back," Hollis cry-ordered as Carter gave them space and came over to the table.

"Here." Carter slid a half sheet of paper over alongside Gwen. "Gideon gave me a list of his family's protectors."

Gwen poked Carter's side. "Maybe you could stop giving me more errands before I catch up on the ones I already have?" she teased him.

I reached for the paper. "I can look into them for you," I offered as Gideon and Hollis came back over to the table.

Gideon braced against the back of his brother's chair and studied Gwen's screen. "The hand gesture . . ." He cursed low under his breath. "That signal wasn't for whoever he's working with. That was for me." He let go of the chair. "He must have assumed Julian would find a way to undo the footage and I'd see this."

"What are you saying?" Hollis asked him, voice soft.

"That's *my* protector, Kylo's brother." Gideon closed his eyes. "I know that sign. It means *traitor among you*."

CHAPTER FORTY-THREE

Hollis

In the air

The jet engines roared as we cut through a sheet of rain, nose pointed toward Surrey. Julian had already warned our parents that our protectors might be compromised, so the decision was made among all of us—get to where my parents were immediately.

No one really knew what the hell had happened or why, and it seemed that was part of the design for whoever was behind this. If the very people sworn to protect us were traitors, then did that make us sitting ducks no matter where we were?

They'd know our every movement. They probably wrote the handbook on our fighting techniques, for all I knew. They could easily be five steps ahead of us, which didn't sit well with me. We'd trusted them, placed our lives in their hands, and now this?

Mum and Dad had refused to involve the police or MI6 when Julian asked them to. They'd claimed this was a personal matter and they didn't need anyone finding out there was a crack in our *literal* armor.

Dad alleged our enemies would smell blood and strike all at once, which would only make things a hundred times worse. Thank God for Delta Shield, Carter, and the others, or we'd have been completely screwed.

"Almost there," Jason murmured in my ear, his hand firm around mine. "Lucky your family's got a private airstrip five klicks from their estate."

Nausea twisted my stomach. "That also means whoever is behind this will see us coming from a mile away." Not that we had a choice. Time was of the essence, and we couldn't risk diverting to a farther airport.

"I've got your back, I promise," he reassured me, remaining a steady force so I could be the one to spin out, and I knew he'd catch me.

I scanned the cabin, working my ass off to be the warrior I'd been trained to be.

Gwen and Julian sat shoulder to shoulder, eyes glued to their laptops, sitting across from Ryder and Alex, as they combed through hours of footage in Rome to see if Kylo—or any other protector, for that matter—had made an appearance after the rave.

Alpha Team, Carter and Sebastian's unit, were currently on board Carter's personal jet, shadowing us.

"It's a dead lead on the men with Gideon in Rome." Julian interrupted my thoughts with his shit news.

"What do you mean?" Alex asked, elbows braced on the table.

"I found them. In a morgue outside Rome. They were Italian mercenaries, more than likely hired for a single job. Doubtfully without any ties to whoever's pulling the strings." Julian glanced sideways at Gideon on the couch to his left. "Someone tied up loose ends."

Gideon met his eyes, shaking his head. He had to be assuming that someone was him.

"I'm sure you didn't," Gwen said softly, and my brother sent her a slight nod, a *thanks* embedded in that dark, broody expression of his.

"It was more than likely my protector with him who shot those men," Julian added, voice flat. "Or at least, my protector is also part of this. I bet he's how my source code was acquired."

"Then Kylo must really be involved, too. A family affair," I noted. "Kylo set the trap for me in Rome with the Putcheskis. All of the protectors betrayed us, but why? How would they even know about the book in the first place?" Panic pressed in on my lungs when it clicked. I pulled my hand away from Jason's to bury my fingertips into my chest at the pain there. "They found out about the book because I was searching for it, and they quickly realized they could use the drugs against us for whatever reason."

Jason's hand closed around my jeaned thigh, grounding me. "You don't know that. Tristan might have—"

"No, I put the spotlight on my brother." I faced Jason, eyes blurring. "I went to Switzerland and realized if the book was still out there, Tristan would have it. I confronted him about it, and somehow, his protector or mine discovered the truth."

Ryder shook his head. "If Tristan had the book and told you, then you'd never have been in Rome at the rave. Doesn't add up."

I shut my eyes, hating the blank spot in my mind. My memories were another enemy right now.

"What if the formulas weren't just words on paper? Clearly, that one sent to Putcheski worked. What if Tristan had already tested them at some point in the past, maybe even before you contacted him?" Gideon suggested. "And when you started digging, you stirred something up." He rose, fists in his pockets. "But that isn't on you. Someone played *all* of us."

"Because your bighearted sister was trying to help the dad of someone she thought didn't even like her," Jason cut in, voice low.

"What are you talking about?" Gideon asked, eyes sharp on him. "Julian told me you were after the book, but you were searching for it because of his dad?"

"Jason had no idea. I did this behind his back." The weight of that admission filled the cabin. "Seems to me if only I'd been honest with everyone, then maybe we wouldn't be in this situation." *Just like my mother said.*

"I'm sorry to interrupt," Gwen cut in, "but I finally found Kylo on camera after the rave." She spun her laptop to the side so we could all view it.

On screen, there was a clip of Kylo being dragged unconscious by a masked man over to a windowless black van.

"That's me," Gideon muttered, pointing at himself on camera as he climbed out of the back to help load Kylo inside it.

The driver lowered his window and gave a three-finger salute right at the camera.

"That's gotta be my protector," Gideon rasped. "He has to be undercover—but if he's on the inside and helping us, then why didn't he get word to us yet?"

"And where the hell is he and Kylo now?" Jason removed a piece of paper from his pocket, and I looked on. It was a list I'd forgotten Carter had asked Gideon to make back at the hotel, pairing up our protectors with our names:

Rowan—Gideon
Kylo—Celeste Hollis
Orson—Julian
Cassian—Lyra
Waylen—Tristan

The list also included my parents' protectors and so on, but I stopped paying attention to it when Jason got up and passed it to Alex. Something told me he'd already memorized every name on it and didn't need it anymore.

"Our protectors have two bases of operations," Gideon continued as Jason returned to his seat. "A remote location outside Surrey and another site in Montana."

"If Tristan's innocent, maybe he's being held at their compound in Surrey," Julian commented, closing his laptop. "It was probably Tristan's blood that activated the memory-wipe formula." He dragged a hand down his face, sitting back in his seat. "They used the mind control shit on him, too."

Gideon stiffened. "But how would they know the formula would work on Tristan, because not even our protectors know he's our . . ." His words trailed off as he fumbled for his phone, made a call, then cursed a few seconds later.

"What is it?" I asked, attempting to stand, but turbulence knocked me back down into my seat.

"Mum. I can't reach her." Gideon dropped onto the couch. "If Tristan truly isn't in on this, that means these assholes found out at some point he's our brother, because Mum hid her pregnancy from everyone, including the protectors back then."

"If they believe we've been corrupted or our bloodline is," Julian went on, his tone as dark as the skies outside, "then in their minds, they think they have the right to take over themselves or pass on the so-called crown to someone else."

Gideon tried the call again, but it clearly failed, because he slapped the phone against his leg. "My protector must've broken with them, or he wouldn't have saved you."

The jet bucked as we descended. Rain streaked the windows, lightning flashing, forcing me to grip the chair's arms. "If they planned to kill me, they didn't need to wipe my memories, right? Couldn't they have just controlled me like they did with you two? And for that matter, why let you all live, but—"

"Bloody hell," Gwen hissed. "The source code was just used in Surrey." She looked up at me. "They're at your parents' house now."

CHAPTER FORTY-FOUR

Reed

The hangar doors rattled in the wind, rain blowing sideways across the tarmac and soaking us, even under the awning. The two planes sat dark and silent behind us, engines cooling. Gear was spread out across two folding tables: vests, mags, comms and more, all lit by a single buzzing lamp.

Sebastian's two League operators and Carter's Falcon Falls teammates were loading the two Black Hawks, prepping the helos.

Hollis fixed her French braid to her back, then slipped a plated vest over her head, and something in my chest pulled at the sight of her wearing it. She was going into battle with us. No stopping her. Hell, this was who she was.

I took over for her, and she quietly stared at me as I finished the job, my pulse pounding. Never thought I'd see the day where I'd go downrange with a woman I was . . .

Actually, scratch that.

I never thought I'd see the day I'd fall in love.

"They must be monitoring us somehow and figured out we all linked up at the hotel. Not sure how, but it's the only thing that makes sense. I was careful to cover our tracks where we went after South America," Gideon said, slamming a mag into his rifle. "My parents' home was our bait, and they turned all of us against each other . . . not sure who we could trust, but—"

"Well, we're finally two steps ahead of these bloody bastards and know where they're holed up now," Gwen interjected, earning her a small smile from Julian at her nine o'clock.

"Thanks mostly to you." He winked.

Easton grumbled something under his breath and left, clearly not in the mood to third-wheel any exchanges between them.

"It's time." Ryder shot me a quick look, then brought his phone to his ear and walked away. Probably a call to his wife before we spun up.

Hollis exchanged a few words with her brothers before redirecting to me as everyone began heading for our rides. "Are you going to ask me if I'm sure I want to do this?" She draped her arms over my shoulders, our ammo-packed vests wedged between us.

"I know better than that." I forced a smile. "But no dying on me, got it?"

"Because Audrey wouldn't like it?" She raised her brows.

"No, because I'd have to chase after you to the other side and bring you back." I leaned in and dropped my mouth over hers.

The taste of her was still on my tongue as we neared go-time from up in the air.

The storm churned black overhead, lightning throwing jagged light across the treetops. The rotor wash hammered rain sideways as the helo hovered above the clearing.

"Thirty seconds," the pilot's voice crackled over comms.

Delta and Foxtrot stacked tight at the doors, gloves ready on the ropes. Alpha mirrored us in the second bird, helmets down, every man coiled to drop.

"Now," Ryder barked. He and Alex went first, disappearing into the storm.

Gideon and Julian exchanged a sign with Hollis—silent words between siblings—before dropping after them.

I glanced at the second bird, Easton steady behind the yoke, Gwen up front with her laptop and headphones on. She'd be staying airborne and out of harm's way.

Four more operators from Alpha dropped fast behind Carter and Sebastian, including two men from Falcon Falls we'd operated with before, along with two of Sebastian's League operatives who never shared their names, but if they worked for him, then I knew they were solid.

"Ready?" I mouthed to Hollis.

She gave me a sharp nod. I tapped the top of her helmet, and she knocked down her NVGs, then slid down the rope smoothly. Good. Muscle memory remained intact.

I followed after her, boots burning on the wet nylon, rifle clamped tight to my chest.

The ground rushed up, and a flash of lightning revealed Hankley's pine forest. Beyond it, the outline of the protectors' compound: concrete, steel, and fencing topped with razor wire.

Hollis landed clean, and I went down a beat later, mud splashing under my boots as I released and dropped to a knee beside her.

The first bird peeled off to avoid radar. The second swooped wide, Easton flying like an angel fearlessly right into the storm.

"Alpha Team, advance," Carter announced.

"Stack up," Ryder ordered, his words cutting through the thunder. "Delta left, Foxtrot right."

We pushed through the trees, shadows bleeding in and out as the sky lit up like a war was overhead. Floodlights along the compound flickered with the storm, stuttering between dark and bright.

"Delta Two, heading to the northwest side to infil," Alex transmitted, then vanished from my periphery, doing what he did best: becoming a ghost.

"Roger," Ryder answered.

We waited in our positions for Alex to discreetly get inside unnoticed—his specialty, thanks to his Houdini-ish father. We had to have eyes and ears in the compound before we breached, first ensuring their protectors weren't also innocent pawns in all this before we opened fire and engaged.

"Foxtrot Two, status?" Ryder asked Julian, then went down the line, ensuring everyone from all three units were good to go. The seconds dragged by as we answered, comms hissing with the storm.

My glove slipped on the rifle grip, breath fogging inside my night vision goggles. Visibility was already shit in this storm.

Finally, Alex came back online. "Visual confirmation. Four packages inside and alive in the basement: the king, queen, prince, and princess. All detained, but the queen and prince are isolated and in a separate room."

I knew what that meant. Hollis's mother was about to be drugged. The "prince" was Tristan, and if he was bound inside, he wasn't a traitor.

"Delta Two, can you get me a visual so I can see who's with the queen and prince?" Gideon requested.

A beat later, an image pinged every handset.

"Can you ID the tango?" Alex asked, continuing to remain an undetected ghost inside.

"Yes," Gideon replied. "My sister's protector."

Kylo? My chest clenched.

"The princess's protector," he amended, referring to Lyra.

"Any sight of mine?" Gideon pressed.

Static. Fragments of words, and then . . . gunfire.

"Delta Two's burned," Ryder snapped. "All teams, snipers up to prepare for our breach. Go, go!"

The thought of losing Alex lit a fire inside me. I'd seen him on death's doorstep once before, and I wasn't about to watch it happen again. He had a family to return home to.

"This is Alpha One. My team, you're clear to take the towers now."

"Roger," came in unison from the three designated snipers for our mission.

"This is Foxtrot Two. Tower one clear," Julian confirmed.

"Alpha Three. Tower four clear," Griffin from Falcon Falls added.

"Alpha Four here," Jesse from Falcon spoke up. "Towers two and three are down. Seven tangos exiting the main property, moving fast."

"This is Alpha Three. We'll intercept and handle them. Go ahead and breach."

"Roger," we transmitted back.

Explosives thudded, rattling the ground. Lightning flared white-hot as Sebastian's League operators blew the wall.

"Stack," Ryder ordered, and we slid into position. Me up front, Hollis at my six, and Ryder covering flank.

The wall went inward with a muffled crack, smoke and rain sweeping through the gap.

They want a legit fight. It's who they are. It turned my stomach, fighting men who'd once been guardians for good, now corrupted by oaths and bloodline bullshit. Proof enough why no one should wield mind control drugs. Neither presidents, nor kings. No one.

"Move!" Ryder commanded, and I nodded to Hollis. She tapped my shoulder, locked in, covering my six as we flowed through the breach. "Delta Two, do you copy?" he tried again.

Static hissed back.

I scanned the grounds, thankful we had three sniper angels overhead now in those towers to cover us. Through the green hue of my night vision, I identified a few of the bodies they'd already dropped to clear our path.

I went still when catching a shadow by one of the garages. I went to one knee, yanking Hollis with me, and fired.

Tango down.

Glass shattered above, and Hollis pivoted. One clean headshot to the guy in the window. The man toppled, rifle clattering.

Carter nodded a quick thanks to Hollis for saving his ass since the barrel had been aimed at him, then he breached the side door before Ryder and Sebastian cleared ahead of us.

Once Hollis and I made our way inside, the world remained green under my NVGs. The lights were out, corridors narrow.

Ryder and Carter announced they'd be pushing to the basement, and Sebastian and Gideon joined them.

Over comms, Sebastian directed his two other men to the second floor to clear it, which left Hollis and me to sweep the first-floor halls, my trigger finger poised.

Not even thirty seconds later, two hostiles burst from the left. I drove one back with a controlled burst to the chest.

Lightning spilt through high windows, momentarily flooding the hall in white, revealing blood on the tile.

Hollis pivoted, boot snapping into the other one's knee. He went down hard, her muzzle pressed to his visor as the guy begged, "Don't shoot."

"I have visual confirmation on Delta Two," Julian shared. "He's alive and being dragged out the rear door."

"This is Alpha Four. Eyes on Delta Two," Jesse let us know. "Taking out the marks now."

Gunfire barked from all around, and my pulse picked up as I waited for news.

"Delta Two here." Alex popped over comms, and I'd never been so grateful to hear that man's voice before. "I had to get grabbed to buy you time. Offer a distraction."

Of-fucking-course. Typical of him. I owed him an ass kicking for that once we made it out alive.

"Where's my family?" Hollis demanded, fury bleeding through as she pressed her knee into the throat of the man she had beneath her while I swept the hall to cover her.

The man gagged. "It's Kylo."

"What?" She shoved up his NVGs, staring at his face. Searching for a truth she couldn't remember.

"I'm not one of them. Not involved in this. I just escaped when your friends showed up in the basement, and this asshole"—he nodded with his head toward the body I'd dropped—"was trying to take me out. I wasn't expecting to run into you." He held his hands out and open at his sides. "I'd *never* hurt you. I love you like family."

"Did you know in Rome—"

"No," he cut her off. "My cousins told me they found out you'd be in Rome alone and I should ditch training to go with you. I never thought to question them. I showed up to have your six the afternoon of the rave. You were surprised to see me and wouldn't tell me the real reason you were there." He paused for a breath. "Thankfully, you let me go with you that night, though, because I held off Putcheski's men. I was knocked out by someone after and woke up in a van with three men I didn't know, along with two of my cousins."

At sudden movement down the hall, I readied my rifle, only to relax when I realized it was Alex. I gave him the heads-up. "It's Delta Three."

Alex joined us as backup as Hollis focused back on Kylo, and I remained protectively at her side, letting her handle this how she needed to even if we were short on time. "Does that mean it was Julian's protector who took out those three men in the van? Or was it Gideon's protector, Rowan?"

"It was Orson who killed them. Orson told me what was going on and to pick a side: our family or yours. He said Rowan chose smartly, so I should as well. He believed your family had been corrupted, which I didn't accept, but Rowan discreetly signaled to me to go along with what Orson was saying. So I did, because Orson had you and Gideon in some zombielike state."

She hesitantly freed Kylo from being pinned down.

"Orson ordered me to take Gideon back to Monaco and stay off-grid and await orders from him. From there, Orson went with you and Rowan to Florence."

"And that's when Orson tried to kill me?"

Kylo nodded, then shifted upright, sitting against the wall while returning his NVGs in place. "Rowan didn't have the antidote to give you like I had to give Gideon, so he improvised. He removed your chain and waited in the Czech Republic for your family to get you, but when he took off, they caught up with him. They scrubbed the video footage. They assumed I was on his side, not theirs, so they locked me up after that."

"Wait, did you say *antidote?*" I rasped, lowering my rifle, chills flying up my spine and into my tense shoulders.

"Yeah, the mind control drugs apparently don't work on their bloodline, not without them being administered the memory-loss one first. They're too strong-willed." He focused back on Hollis. "From what I overheard them say, they had to wipe your identity first so you'd forget, and then they could—"

A blast rocked the building, cutting him off, and I grabbed hold of Hollis's waist to keep her steady as the walls shook.

"What's going on? Was that us?" I transmitted.

"That's not us," Julian responded. "It's coming from under the ground somewhere. We can feel it and hear it, but we don't see anything."

"I'm sure that's my cousins. They're clearing an escape path. Opening up one of our old emergency tunnels that were previously sealed off underground," Kylo explained. "It's probably their backup plan if they overplayed their hand with you all."

I swapped my M4 for my 9mm and offered Kylo my free hand to help him stand. He took it and rose while sharing where he believed his cousins would be going from here.

I relayed the information to my team, hoping he was truly on our side.

"This is Alpha One. The king is alive and secure. Lost track of the other packages."

"That's a good copy," Alex transmitted back. "They have to be in that escape tunnel now."

"Foxtrot and Delta, pursue," Carter ordered. "Alpha Team will hold the ground here and cover you."

"Orson's two brothers, Cassian and Waylen, are the ones now running the show with their father." Kylo looked at me and clarified, "Lyra and Tristan's protectors."

They must have been the traitors Rowan had signaled to Gideon about.

"Tristan's innocent," Kylo let us know before Hollis could even ask him. "It was Orson who used the drugs on Julian to get his source code. And Waylen's the one who stole the book from Tristan."

I may have had the list of names in my head for all these fuckers, but they were about to become A, B, and C in a second. Too damn many of them to keep track of. "And they just told you all this?" I scoffed.

"They didn't plan to let me walk, and I can be a persistent pain when trying to get information out of people." He started to reach for Hollis, but hesitated, clearly realizing that'd be a shit idea. I wasn't prepared to trust him yet. "Tristan's been a prisoner, right here along with me. They must've brought him here before they got to us in Rome that night."

If he was telling the truth, at least Hollis's brother was innocent. That was something, I supposed. We still had to put an end to this now and get the antidote for Hollis. But thank God, there already was an antidote.

"I can't go out there with you," Kylo rushed out. "I have to find Rowan and my parents. They buried them alive somewhere on the property. I was next, but then you showed up."

"Why'd your parents lie to Gideon when he visited them in Peru?" I couldn't help but ask, even though we needed to roll out. Then it dawned on me before he could answer. "To keep their sons alive." *Of course.*

"The four of us are the only ones who didn't go along with my cousin's plan to overthrow your family. I had no idea any of them were so power hungry. We should have seen it coming, though, I'm so damn sorry." Kylo crouched and picked up the fallen weapon from the man

I'd killed, and I clocked his every movement in case he was yet another traitor hiding behind a mask.

"Delta Three, come in. What's your status? I'm still tracking you on level one," Ryder asked over comms.

Before I could respond, a female voice called out, "Don't shoot."

I raised my 9mm, not seeing anyone through the night vision.

A few seconds later, a figure emerged from the shadows. She had a weapon down at her side and a helmet with night vision in place.

Who the hell was that?

"It's me," she whispered. "Hollis, are you there?"

"Lyra?" Hollis called out, faltering at my side. "Are you okay?" She started to sidestep me to get to her, but I hooked her arm, stopping her.

"I'm so sorry," Lyra cried out, her voice shaking. "Cassian promised me everything would be okay. He said no one would get hurt." And then she raised her handgun and fired off a round.

CHAPTER FORTY-FIVE

Hollis

Jason yanked me behind him, his body a shield. The shot cracked past us, punching into the wall.

"I know what you're doing," Jason said steadily, remaining in front of me. "You're trying to draw our fire, get us to kill you. We're not going to do that." He slowly secured his sidearm and shifted his rifle on its sling around to his back before raising his gloved hands. "You're under the influence—"

"I'm not," Lyra shot back. "No drugs. This is me, that's the problem." She fired another round, hitting the floor, narrowly missing Jason.

So help me if she hit him. He had a chest plate, but that wouldn't do any good if she caught him in the face or neck.

"I broke the rules," Lyra said through a mess of what sounded like tears. She tossed her helmet and night vision but kept her weapon aimed at us, so we couldn't move in yet. "I—I fell in love with my protector. A-and Cassian learned about Tristan this year. Waylen overheard Tristan arguing with Mum about his father months ago, and he figured out he's our half brother, and they felt betrayed."

"Whatever Cassian said to you, whatever you did—"

"I've always been so jealous of you. Everyone loves you," Lyra interrupted me. "Mum. Dad. You're probably even Cassian's first choice, really." Her voice trembled. "And y-you didn't even want this life anymore. You kept choosing to be with Audrey and her friends, and . . ."

"Do it," I whispered to Jason. "Rush her now."

He sprang forward, knocking her arm high. The round tore into the ceiling, and her pistol clattered to the floor as he slammed her against the wall.

She stopped fighting and slowly dropped to the floor.

Jason kicked her weapon to the side and let me take over and go to her. "You okay?" he asked me. "Not hit?"

"No, I'm fine." *Physically, at least.* I let my sling catch my rifle and squatted before my sister, unable to wrap my head around how the "innocent" one had betrayed us.

Jason began communicating to the teams over comms to catch them up as I knocked my NVGs to the top of my helmet, doing my best to adjust to the dark hallway and get a look at my sister that wasn't tainted by a green glow.

It also occurred to me there were no more gunshots coming from anywhere. The fight here was over, but where was Mum? Tristan?

"Waylen found out about that book sometime after that fight he overheard. You came asking Tristan about it, and that's when the three of them came up with a plan. Cassian convinced me that I was living in your shadow, just like his family was for all of us, but without the rewards—a-and he said it should be the two of us that control everything. We could be married. Start a life together."

So, this had nothing to do with Cassian's oath and everything to do with being a power-hungry monster. He'd have found another reason to do this had he not learned the truth about Tristan or how to manipulate us with the book, I was sure of it.

"You were only supposed to be drugged, never hurt. He lied to me. U-used me," Lyra said, hiccupping, but I wasn't sure how much was an act so I'd feel sorry for her.

I wasn't remotely ready to feel pity for her. I also had a million more questions to ask and a dozen versions of *how could you* to get out, but we didn't have time, because the man my sister had fallen in love with had our mother and brother out there somewhere.

"Was there a tracker in the suitcase you lent me?" I asked at the memory of her offer to use her RIMOWA. Then again, my brothers probably kept Lyra in the loop about where we were. No need to sneak around when your main enemy came from within the circle of trust. "Is anyone else in our family involved?" I asked when she remained quiet. "Cousins?"

"No. I'm the only one w-who really betrayed you all," she cried.

"Along with the men who devoted their lives to protect us." I did my best not to lose my shit and shifted my night vision in front of my eyes. "I have to go. I'll deal with you later."

"I got her," an Irishman said from behind me, and I twisted around to see another operator there with us, his NVGs in place. I had to assume it was Sebastian.

"I'm so sorry." Lyra reached for me, but I pulled my arm free of her touch and slowly stood with Jason's help.

"Find your family," I told Kylo. "Stay safe." I nodded my thanks to Sebastian and the other operator with him, then took off with Jason and Alex, ready to take out the traitors who'd started this chain reaction of betrayal.

Once we were back outside, the storm had eased up, but it was still raining. There was a pair of ATVs waiting for us alongside the Falcon Falls operators, Jesse and Griffin.

I flung my rifle behind me in preparation for the ride, and Jason wasted no time, swinging me onto the vehicle behind him.

He shifted his rifle to his chest so it wouldn't press up against me and drew my arms around his waist to hang on tight.

"Ryder, Julian, and Gideon tried to pursue behind them in the tunnel, but they were cut off. Part of the tunnel blew up, blocking their path. They're working their way back up top now," Jesse informed us. "No casualties."

Thank God.

"I have the coordinates Kylo gave us," Jason began, the rain still pouring, "but I'm not sure—"

"Gwen hacked a satellite overhead," Jesse interrupted with what I hoped would be good news.

"She found the exact location Kylo mentioned. There are two SUVs parked in a clearing in the woods where Cassian and the others should be coming out up top. Easton will do a flyover of the area once you're closer and spotlight it for you," Griffin shared. "Gideon's pilot is coming back for us. We'll be right behind you."

"Thank you," I said just before we started forward, kicking up mud with the tires as we pulled out.

The ride was rough and bumpy, and rain continued to fall as he drove us along a muddy trail in the woods.

Since Kylo's cousins were going on foot with two hostages, we had a shot at getting to their SUVs when they did.

I straddled closer to Jason as the rain picked up, hammering our helmets and goggles. Branches clawed at us, lightning painting the forest in violent strobes.

Every second that passed, it was like we were racing death itself, the ground beneath the tires slippery, the path uneven.

We broke into the clearing just as Gwen came over comms, announcing, "We've got you in our sights." She and Easton had to be within range if they could join our frequency.

I couldn't hear the blades of the helo with the storm violently raging, but light poured down as promised. We knocked our night vision up the second it made contact and lit up the ground. It also exposed multiple figures near the two SUVs.

Jason and Alex took a hard turn and shifted as gunfire sprayed at us. They killed the engines, and we hopped off and took cover to engage.

"This is Foxtrot One," my brother came in over comms. "We're about to drop in out of view from the spotlight."

"Roger," I confirmed before squeezing off a round, taking down a hostile.

Jason tapped my shoulder and slipped by me, dropping two tangos before I could even track his rifle.

I tried to put eyes on my mother and Tristan out there beneath the light. Someone was currently shoving her in the back of an SUV. She had to still be drugged. But Tristan? He was fighting back, trying to break free and help her.

"We have friendlies in the mix," I warned over comms to Gideon and the others before they joined the fight. "The prince is working to get free," I shared at the sight. "The queen is inside an SUV and drugged."

"This is Foxtrot One, that's a good copy."

"Delta One here, we're coming up on your flanks. We see you," Ryder transmitted a minute later as Alex took out the man Tristan was still battling, now enabling my brother to get a weapon.

I stayed tight behind Jason, rifle steady, as he took a knee by Alex, forcing me to duck behind them.

"This is Delta One. On my mark . . ."

I tuned out Ryder and the orders he was giving, because all I could focus on was the woods, knowing someone was out there watching me.

I didn't want to distract Jason or Alex as they continued to pick off each target one by one, so I twisted around as quietly as possible and stood. That was when a figure stepped into my line of sight from the tree line.

You must be Cassian.

He came close enough I could make out his face. He gave me the kind of smile meant to unnerve me, and the knife in his hand glinted when lightning split the sky.

Rage poured hot into my veins, and I removed the heavy weight of my rifle, then tossed my helmet with my night vision.

"He's mine," I whispered, letting Jason know not to engage when he heard what was about to take place.

"Hollis," Jason hissed as I walked before a man who was supposed to protect my sister, not seduce and trick her.

I lunged at Cassian, knocking his blade wide.

He countered, his elbow slamming into my vest. I absorbed the hit and drove a knee into his ribs. He staggered but twisted, catching me in a choke hold. I was slippery and soaked, hard to hold on to in the storm.

The gunfire died down around us to dead silence.

We'd won the war.

One battle left to go.

I stomped on Cassian's shin, twisted free, and drove an elbow into his jaw. His head snapped sideways, but he used the momentum to hook my arm, dragging me down into the mud with him. We hit hard, rolling, grappling in the storm's fury.

He went for his blade, but Jason kicked it from his reach without intervening, knowing I wanted this piece of shit for myself.

I shoved my forearm into Cassian's throat, cutting off his airway, but he clawed at my wrist until my grip slipped.

"I got it," I promised Jason so he wouldn't try to save me. Well, not unless I truly needed it.

Rain blurred my vision, and Cassian flipped me over against a fallen tree and bark scraped my shoulders. He pressed his weight into me, whispering in my ear, "I corrupted the good little angel. The innocent one. Got her to do whatever I—" He was ripped off me in one fluid motion, and I was grateful Jason had ignored my pleas to stay out of it.

Jason was still snarling as he helped me rise, but then he stepped off to the side, letting me finish what this bastard had started.

Adrenaline burned through me, and I forced Cassian back up only to slam my knee into his ribs. A sharp crack followed that rattled his breath.

He stumbled back, and my hand went instinctively to my holster at my thigh. Fingers slick, I yanked the Glock clear in one motion.

He spat blood off to his side, then gestured with his wrist to bring it on.

I closed the space between us and pressed the Glock to his forehead, finger hovering on the trigger.

He held open his arms at his side, a dark laugh falling from his bloody mouth. "You don't have it in you." He abruptly grabbed my wrist, steadying my hand, and shoved the muzzle more forcefully against his forehead, baring his teeth. "Go ahead," he provoked. "Do it."

"Hollis," Jason said in warning from behind.

I trembled, my eyelashes fluttering from the mix of tears and rain as thunder and lightning crowded the night sky.

I didn't need my memories to know I'd never taken a life in cold blood, and was I going to start now?

I thought back to the family crest. "In time, there is truth." My voice caught as I tore my wrist free from his grip and stepped back, lowering my weapon. "You'll rot in a cell for what you did."

"I knew you couldn't—"

A gunshot cracked the night. Jason's hand went to my waist, dragging me close as Cassian's head snapped to the side and vanished in the spray.

"No, you won't." Tristan dropped the 9mm into the mud. "You'll rot in hell instead." He turned toward me, the spotlight burning at his back. "Hollis," he murmured.

My chest ached as I remembered the boy in those photos from our grandfather's house. "You were helping me all this time, weren't you?"

Jason gave me a small nod, a quiet signal he'd step aside. He melted into the shadows but remained nearby as Alex moved in with the others to secure the field.

Off near the SUVs, Jesse and Griffin guided my mother to safety, her steps unsteady.

"You came to me asking if I had the book," Tristan said on approach. "When I admitted I did, you requested I come up with a way to reverse engineer the memory-wipe drug to help others."

"And did you?" I whispered.

"I had to first make it work for our bloodline before I could extrapolate the data to see if I could use it on other people. And I, uh, tried both drugs on myself, and that's how my protector found out about it. I trusted Waylen. I asked him to inject me. Gave him the instructions. You're a stubborn pain in the ass"—he half smiled—"and I knew you'd have insisted on testing the drugs on yourself, so I had to beat you to it. I never had the chance to work on it further, because the book and all my research was stolen. We met at your place in France a few weeks ago, assuming there was a traitor among us."

That's why they tossed my place in France. London. The hotel. They were searching for any evidence I may have gathered.

I hung my head, guilt taking hold of me.

In a way, I truly did trigger all this, but ultimately, Cassian clearly had an evil side and so did his brothers, and they were bound to betray us eventually.

"Waylen told me the truth while I was here as a prisoner." Tristan twisted around and pointed toward the dead bodies, and I took that to mean Waylen was now one of them. He faced me, shaking his head. "After the first experiment, Waylen realized I didn't recall anything that happened during the time between when the first drug was administered and the antidote. That gave him and his brothers the idea to use the mind control drugs from the book on us in that in-between time period, to get us to do what they wanted. We'd never know about it. But we screwed up their plans before they could even start by closing in on who the hell stole my book in the first place, forcing them to rush and change things up."

"Wait, rewind." I stared at him in the downpour, trying to make sense of what he'd just said. "Do you mean that I'm going to forget—" I let go of my words as thunder cracked, shaking the earth, and the spotlight above us spun wild.

"We've been hit," Easton barked out over comms, voice strained. "Brace!"

A screech cut through the storm, followed by a burst of fire overhead.

The world pitched sideways, and before I could react, Jason slammed me and Tristan to the ground, shielding us from the falling sky.

CHAPTER FORTY-SIX

Hollis

Jason's weight crushed me down until the last chunk of debris hissed out in the rain. The metallic tang of jet fuel burned my nose; branches cracked under boots and shouts tore through the storm—calls for Gwen, for Easton.

The clearing was chaos. Flames licked at twisted metal, rotor blades stuck in the muck. I caught the faint sound of coughing over static in my comms.

Jason hauled Tristan and me upright, and we sprinted toward the wreckage. The helo had taken out one of the SUVs, but my mother was alive, lying on the wet ground off to the side of the crash.

We clawed through smoke and splintered branches, the world redacted to static, until we reached the team fighting to pull Easton and Gwen free.

Please be okay. Please, God, please.

Jason kept me from collapsing at the sight of Jesse and Griffin pulling Gwen out, her body bloodied and limp. He banded his arm across my chest, an iron bar against the shaking, as Gideon and Ryder helped Easton out next.

Easton had one arm hanging at the wrong angle, blood streaking down his temple, but he was making sounds, trying to lift his good arm as though to reach for Gwen. Then his head dropped forward like he'd had a delayed knockout, and his body went limp, nearly pulling the two men down with him.

"Gwen has a pulse, but it's weak," Jesse said, and Alex swapped places with him to help with CPR as Jesse called to the second pilot for an immediate medevac assist.

I covered my mouth and watched as both Gwen and Easton received CPR, and Jason kept me pinned against him.

"You get the son of a bitch?" someone yelled out.

"He's down. It was Cassian's dad. An RPG," another voice hollered back.

The next movements bled together—sirens, stretchers, oxygen masks, a blur of faces and wet ground littered with traitors—until somehow Jason got me out of those woods and up to the seventh floor of a hospital.

One call from my father to the prime minister had the entire wing cleared out for only our family.

Forty-five minutes had crawled by since Gwen and Easton disappeared behind closed doors into surgery. No updates yet.

My mother was in the next room, unconscious, waiting for Tristan's antidote. Dad hadn't left her side. Julian paced the hall with the rest of Falcon Falls. Even Carter was wearing down the floors.

Jason and my father had insisted I stay in bed until I also received the antidote, though I was perfectly fine aside from a few scratches and bruises.

As for Lyra? Gideon and Sebastian were handling her. I couldn't face that betrayal yet. Not until I knew Gwen and Easton were fine.

"Is Kylo almost here with his family?" I asked when Jason checked a notification on his phone. He had his hand propped up on the window by my bed as he read a message.

"They just pulled up. Kylo needs to get his brother and parents help first, then he'll stop in to see you." He pushed off the window and turned toward me, a solemn look on his face.

"I'm so glad he got to his family in time. I can't handle any more bad news." I also refused to believe Easton and Gwen would die.

Carter had been the one to call Gwen's father, Wyatt, as well as Easton's brother-in-law, Constantine. Both men were already heading to their respective airports to fly here.

A soft knock pulled my attention to the doorway. Tristan stood there, cleaned up, but shadows still darkened his face. "Am I interrupting?"

I gripped Jason's wrist, silently requesting he stay as my steady rock in the storm while I motioned to my brother to join us.

Julian slipped in behind Tristan, and then my father walked in as well.

The air thickened, tension crowding the small room.

My stomach knotted as my dad closed the door with deliberate finality, leaning his back against it. Tristan and Julian moved closer, one on either side of the bed.

"What is it?" I slid my hand from Jason's wrist, lacing our fingers together.

I thought Tristan was pulling the syringe with my cure from his pocket; instead, he produced a ring. He stepped forward and set it in my palm. "This is what they had you take from our vault in Florence. I recovered it from Cassian after you left for the hospital. The Ring of Solomon. Most believe it's a myth."

The gold was dulled with age, the signet etched with strange markings. Power hummed beneath its weight, like it was alive. "Wait, are you saying this actually belonged to the real Solomon?"

Dad stepped forward, his tone low and measured as he shared, "Whether or not that's true, I don't know, but my great-great-*great*-grandmother got hold of it, and it's been with my bloodline ever since. Whoever has it is considered the legitimate leader of our family." The words sank in like stones in water. "I chose you to be the one to inherit it and all that comes with it."

"That's why I had the second code to the vault in Florence." My fingers locked around Jason's hand like a lifeline. "Cassian needed us gone so only Lyra would be left to take over." I shoved the ring back into Tristan's hand. "What if I don't want this?"

Tristan passed the ring over to Dad, and he slid it on his finger.

"You will when you remember who you are," my father said without meeting my eyes.

"Speaking of your memories," Tristan started, "I have the antidote. Just gave Mum hers as well before heading in here."

"Did they ask Mum who your dad is? Do you know the truth?" I couldn't help but wonder.

Tristan glanced back at my dad, then over at Julian. "They did, which is why I couldn't leave anyone alive out there."

So you know who your dad is. Something told me he wasn't going to do a name reveal anytime soon. Maybe never.

Tristan removed a small vial from his pocket and opened the cabinets, searching for a syringe.

"Did Kylo and Rowan overhear who your father is? Their parents?" Jason asked.

"No. They weren't in the room with us when they drugged Mum." Tristan filled the syringe with a clear substance.

I lifted my hand, a request to keep it away from me, when a memory surfaced like a knife cutting through fog. "You said something in the woods about forgetting the in-between . . . ?"

Tristan gave me a hesitant nod. "The by-product of the treatment is that you won't recall anything from when you were drugged the first time up until now. You'll lose the week. The last thing you'll remember is being at the rave."

My heart landed in my throat, and a wave of blistering chills cut across my skin.

Jason's hand went slack in mine. He pulled away and turned toward the window, bracing his palm against the glass yet again, shoulders caving like the weight of the news had broken him.

Every moment we'd shared—our tangled, impossible week together—was about to be erased.

No, no, this isn't fair. Panic spiked as my gaze ricocheted between my family. "Find another way. Don't let me forget."

"I don't know if I can." Tristan's mouth tightened as if he didn't want to say more before adding, "And it's already been a week since you were given the first drug. I don't think we should risk waiting any longer to give you the antidote."

"Don't give it to me," I decided. "I'd rather keep this week than regain my other memories."

Jason spun around, anguish warring in his expression. He snatched my hand, threading our fingers together. "Absolutely not. Don't you dare choose me over your entire life." His eyes, fierce and burning, pinned me hard. "I'll never forgive myself if you do that."

Everything inside me hurt as I stared back at him, unsure what to do or say. "After Gwen and Easton are out of surgery and okay, I'll, um, give you all my answer then." That was the best I could offer for now.

My dad surprised me by not arguing, and my family quietly filed out of my room.

Jason sat on the edge of the bed and held my hand. "I won't let you do this." His chest rose with a heavy breath he kept caged for too long before letting it go. "You've fallen for me, I know you have. And it can happen again." His mouth tugged into the faintest smile. "I'm being presumptuous, but—"

"I am falling," I admitted, the words trembling out of me. "You brought me back to life, even without my memories. And I know this week did the same for you."

He gathered me in his arms, pressing my cheek to his chest. His heartbeat thundered steady and strong beneath my ear, the only anchor in a world unraveling.

"I can't forget," I begged, clutching him, digging my nails into his back. "Please."

A ragged breath tore from him. He held me tighter, hiding his face in my hair. "You *will* find your way back to me. You're stronger than any drug." His voice wavered as he rasped, "And you can be sure I'll be a pain in your ass until you remember us."

CHAPTER FORTY-SEVEN

Reed

Ten hours later, the seventh floor of the hospital continued to hold its collective breath. The low hum of the fluorescent lights, the footsteps echoing down the hall, and the steady rhythm of beeping from screens in the nurses' station were the only constants. Everything else remained suspended as we waited for Gwen to open her eyes.

I rested my back against the wall in the hall, keeping my distance from where Easton hovered outside Gwen's room alongside his sister, Juliette. His face was battered, mottled with bruises, his arm in a sling, crutches tucked underneath him to take the weight off his bad leg. *But* he'd survived, and he'd heal with a few months of PT.

Now we needed Gwen to wake up and for the doctors to deliver good news, preferably before her father, Wyatt Pierson, arrived, which would be soon.

I'd been with Hollis all night and morning, sleeping in the bed with her at her insistence.

Her brothers had shown up about fifteen minutes ago, *fortunately* when I was sitting next to her and not in her bed, so I'd wandered into the hall to give them privacy. I assumed they planned to talk to her about Lyra.

I swiveled my ball cap backward and shoved away from the wall at the sight of Constantine returning with our coffees. His son balanced the tray while Constantine pushed a baby stroller.

I stole a look at Illiana asleep as Constantine handed me my coffee. "She's—"

"A gift from God," Constantine finished for me while freeing a cup from the tray for himself.

"I'll take these two over to Mom and Uncle E." Colin, who was practically a copy-and-paste version of his dad, gave me a tight smile, then took off.

With one hand, Constantine pushed the stroller back and forth, just enough to keep his daughter asleep, while sipping his coffee. "Easton's never going to forgive himself for this."

"It wasn't his fault. He couldn't make a controlled landing in the middle of the forest after taking a direct hit, and—"

"His skill is the only reason they didn't die on impact," he cut me off, setting his coffee in the stroller's cupholder. "But he's not going to listen, not with Gwen in that room fighting for her life."

Those last words burrowed under my skin like an itch I couldn't scratch. *Fighting for her life.* I barely knew her, but the thought of losing her hit harder than I expected.

"Juliette's got everyone she knows all over the world praying for her. She'll make it out okay. She has to," he said with conviction.

I focused on Easton with his sister and nephew. Juliette was clearly trying to calm Easton down and reassure him everything would be okay and that this wasn't his fault. He should've been in bed, but he'd ignored the doctors to be out there waiting by Gwen's room.

"Is Carter almost here with Wyatt and the others?" I asked.

Carter, Jesse, and Griffin had gone to the airport to pick everyone up. I wasn't sure who was on the plane with Wyatt, but I had a feeling quite a few worried people had traveled with him.

"Yeah," he breathed out. "And I have a feeling Wyatt's going to misplace his anger on someone the second he gets here."

Easton. I finally remembered to take a sip of the shitty hospital coffee, and quickly confirmed it was, in fact, shit. "If anything, it's my team's fault we let Cassian's father escape to send off that RP—"

"Don't." He killed that line of thought fast.

Needing a reprieve from my dark thoughts, I glanced at Illiana. Her dark lashes fluttered, and I expected her to open her eyes, but she must've only been dreaming.

Constantine lifted up a shade to block the harsh overhead lights from hitting her face.

"Should've done that before," he grumbled, probably still getting the hang of being a dad to a newborn, since he hadn't been in Colin's life until recently. Hell, he hadn't even known he had a son until not that long ago.

I opened my mouth, about to say something—no idea what—when I stopped myself at the realization the hall was even more crowded.

A terrified father stood at the center of a group; he was holding his chest as he slowly started down the hall.

I twisted around, catching sight of Easton using his crutches to turn in Wyatt's direction.

Wyatt's wife, Natasha, was at his side, holding their youngest daughter, Emory, in her arms. His brother-in-law, Gray Chandler, who co-ran Falcon Falls, was at his left with his daughter in his arms. Gray's wife, Tessa—Trevor's cousin—was there as well. Carter, Jesse, and the others were just behind them.

The group moved as one, their silence heavier than the air. It looked less like a family arriving at a hospital and more like mourners walking behind a coffin.

Not a visual I wanted right now.

But Gwen's not gone, and she'll be okay. I'd glass-half-full my way through this if I had to.

Wyatt broke away from his wife and the others and headed for his target: his daughter's room. His body was stiff, face unreadable, as he passed by Easton without a word or even a passing glance.

Natasha nodded a quiet hello to the two of us as Emory held out her little hand and palmed my cheek. I forced myself to smile and then waited to exhale until they were out of sight.

Natasha kept hold of Emory, leaned in, and rested her forehead on Easton's shoulder for a brief moment. I couldn't read her lips, but she said something before joining her husband in Gwen's room. While Gwen wasn't Natasha's daughter, I knew she loved her like one.

Easton didn't look around at anyone else after that, just wordlessly started toward his room on his crutches, and Juliette and Colin trailed after him.

"Any updates?" Carter asked, joining us as the others filtered into one of the nearby waiting rooms reserved for our people.

Constantine gave Carter a grim expression while shaking his head.

Carter stole a look around the shade at Illiana, then rested his hand against the wall and hung his head. "Diana and my son are on their way. I'm sure she'd like to see your family when she gets here with Matteo."

Constantine nodded, slapped a hand on his shoulder twice, then let us know he was going to check on his family, leaving the two of us out there.

Helpless wasn't a feeling I knew how to wear. I cleared my throat, searching for the right words. "All loose ends tied up at the compound?"

"It's as if nothing ever happened," Carter confirmed. "Everything's been cleaned up per Secretary Chandler and the prime minister's orders."

"Learn anything new before you picked them up from the airport?"

"Just that we were right. Cassian, Orson, Waylen, and their father were the architects behind the betrayal," he said flatly.

Their father was the bastard who took down the helo, vengeance for killing his sons, and Ryder hadn't hesitated and put two in his head right after.

"What else did Gideon's protector have to say? How'd Rowan wind up undercover in the first place? Why not give Gideon a heads-up beforehand?" I couldn't help but ask.

"Rowan's cousin called and told him to bail on the training plans because he needed help in Rome. Rowan already knew Kylo had gone there for Hollis, so he assumed it was about her. When he showed up, his cousin gave him a choice the night of the rave. Pick a side."

At least his story tracked with his brother's.

"Orson had already drugged Gideon at that point, stealing his memories. So Rowan did what he could to protect Gideon by agreeing to his cousin's plans." Carter pushed away from the wall. "Gideon was brainwashed with that mind control shit, making him believe he was protecting his sister in trouble when he drugged her."

"Tell me you destroyed all the research related to those drugs."

He slowly looked up at me. "I watched Tristan do it myself," he said firmly. "Aside from the antidotes, at least."

"Any chance your wife can turn that antidote into a cure for anyone with memory loss issues?"

"Maybe. Probably take some time. But between her and Tristan, it's possible. Maybe one day." He nodded, letting a few quiet moments pass before he changed gears. "It looks like the only thing we didn't see coming was Lyra. Hollis's cousins and everyone else in her family were cleared. No idea how they'll forgive her after what she did."

The idea of forgiveness sat like glass in my throat, jagged and slicing when I tried to swallow.

"Gideon and Sebastian brought Lyra to a mental health facility in Dublin. It'll be up to her family to decide how long to keep her there." I barely had a chance to absorb that news before he shared, "I have to head back to the airport and pick up my wife and son." He gestured down the hall, and for a split second, I caught the strain in his jawline, the exhaustion riding his shoulders.

I turned to see the woman I had no idea how I'd live without on her way over.

"Reach out if Gwen wakes up before I'm back," he said before parting ways.

I tossed my coffee in the trash as Hollis joined me. "You okay?"

She lifted one shoulder. "My brothers told me about Lyra and where she's at. I, um, just . . ." Her voice cracked. "I can't help but blame her for what happened to Gwen, even if it's not directly her fault."

Understandable.

"I was wondering if you'd come somewhere with me?"

I held her hand, drawing her knuckles to my mouth, kissing them. "Anywhere."

She quietly led the way down the hall, into the elevator, and all the way outside the doors of a chapel.

I froze, boots rooted in place, my palm slipping against hers as my heart rate spiked. "I actually haven't been back . . . well, since that day."

Reasons why I didn't belong here rose, pulling me under like quicksand. The enemy's voice slithered in, whispering I'd never be good enough, never live up to the expectations of—

"I thought we could pray for Gwen." Her words pierced the noise in my head. "Juliette seems to think it'll help."

Chills rushed beneath my clothes, goose bumps standing sharp on my arms, and the hair at the nape of my neck lifted. Something unseen pulled me forward. So I did it. Took one step. Then another. With this woman at my side, I crossed the threshold.

It was empty. A nondenominational space, welcoming all faiths to worship, hushed and still. The faint smell of candle wax lingered with the sterile tang of disinfectant, a strange mix of holy and hospital.

We walked down the narrow aisle to the front. She kept hold of my hand as she lowered to her knees, and with my free hand, I removed my hat and mirrored her. The last time I'd been in this position, I'd been braced in battle, rifle in hand, ending lives. Now here I was, about to make a plea to save one.

I bowed my head, forced the images of war from my mind, and closed my eyes. A deep, shaky breath left my mouth.

Hollis tightened her grip on my hand and began to pray, voice soft, almost hesitant at first. Then steadier, like muscle memory carried her through. Each word echoed faintly off the chapel walls, finding me in the quiet.

And with every syllable she whispered, the vise around my chest loosened. My fists unclenched. My jaw softened. A lifetime of trauma I hadn't realized I still carried began to slide free.

It was in that moment that I knew something had shifted, and I'd truly never be the same again.

CHAPTER FORTY-EIGHT

Reed

Eighteen hours later

I couldn't wrap my head around it, and neither could anyone else, especially Gwen's team of doctors.

From the hall, I watched through the window as they finished their last round of tests. Everyone pressed in behind me, breaths shallow, waiting for the word that had already been passed around: *miracle*.

Gwen had been intubated with a severe concussion, internal bleeding, a collapsed lung, broken ribs, and a spinal fracture doctors believed would paralyze her. Yet she was not only alive, but she'd also already stood, walked, and spoken.

Walking. Talking. Fine. Impossible.

If I hadn't seen it with my own eyes, I wouldn't have believed it.

Wyatt helped Gwen back to bed and remained alongside her while holding her hand, not bothering to hide his tears.

"It really is a miracle," I overheard Constantine's wife say. "No other way to explain it."

"Why won't Easton come out here?" Colin asked his mom. I shifted away from the window to look at him as his gaze sharpened past me. "He needs to stop blaming himself."

I followed his line of sight to see Wyatt now joining us. "She needs a few months of PT, but she's going to be fine." He swiped a trembling hand down his face as if he could erase the worry with one motion. He searched the hall, voice low and rough as he said, "Gwen's asking for him."

Colin went around me to confront Wyatt. "It's not his fault what happened. Don't hate him."

Easton was carrying the wreckage like it was strapped to his back, like he'd shot the RPG himself. Every time I'd seen him since, his eyes had a thousand-yard stare, like he was still up in that storm, gripping the stick and replaying the moment they went down.

It could have ended much differently, like with them both dying, and Easton needed to see that. *Hear* it from everyone, too, especially Wyatt.

Wyatt's eyes narrowed into slits as grief crowded his face. "She should never have been up there in the bloody first place." He exhaled hard, chest shaking. "I'm not ready to talk to him. I don't know how *not* to yell." His jaw flexed. "Just get him for her." He turned, pushing back into Gwen's room without another word.

Constantine slung an arm around his son's shoulders, quietly leading his family away to find Easton.

I slipped away from those gathered there. Hollis was waiting for the final word. She'd been too nervous to come out here herself.

Her door was cracked, and Julian was alongside her bed, hands on his hips, eyes expectantly on me. "Is it true? She's really okay?"

"She's going to be fine," I confirmed, relieved to give them something bright after everything.

Hollis slapped a hand over her chest, closing her eyes, and Julian's expression eased with the same fragile relief. Whatever else he thought of Gwen, I respected him for never blaming Easton once.

"You can take the antidote now," Julian reminded her. "Tristan insists we get it over with. You *need* to do it." He tipped his head toward the door, letting us know he was going to give us a moment alone first.

Once he was gone, I pulled out my phone, opened the camera, and slid onto the bed beside her. We shared the pillow, her warmth soaking into me. I held out the camera and took a photo of us, then quietly added it to the RTBH folder. "You're going to come back to me, I promise," I said, refusing to give her a choice about this antidote.

She was on top of the covers, and she hooked her leg around mine, anchoring me. "I'm not ready to let go of this life."

"It's the same one." I pocketed my phone and tangled my fingers into her hair. "We need you back, though. *I* need you."

"You already have me." A tear slid to her temple, and I caught it with my thumb. "I'm worried I won't be the same."

"You'll be exactly who you're supposed to be," I rasped, my throat tight, fear digging claws into my chest.

"You promise you won't give up on me if I forget what we have?"

My smile probably came out crooked, shaky at best. "I promise."

Her lashes were wet with tears as she squeezed her eyes shut. "Let's get it over with, then. Julian said Mum went a little wild after her injection. She had to be restrained."

Her mother had also panicked when learning she'd revealed the truth about Tristan's father, not that she remembered doing it.

I brushed my knuckles over her arm. "We'll hold your hands and be right here with you while you're going through it."

Her eyes open now, a touch of fear flickered there I hated to see.

We lingered in the quiet for a few minutes, kissing like it'd be our last time. Though I knew damn well it wouldn't be.

My throat burned as my nerves tried to fight their way forward once her brothers joined us.

"Don't let me forget, okay?" she whispered, and I couldn't answer. Not with the syringe glinting in Tristan's hand. Not with her wearing one of my shirts like it belonged to her (and it did now, as far as I was concerned).

I stood alongside her and held her hand. Her grip crushed mine, desperate. Gideon clasped her other hand, and Julian laid his palm on her shoulder.

"Close your eyes. Go to that place of peace you created," Tristan told her.

"Wait," she blurted out a moment later, then angled her head to get the chain off. "I don't want this on." She tossed it over to one of her brothers. Eyes back on me, she murmured, "Just in case you ever need to find me."

God, I hope not.

She finally shut her eyes, and the needle slid in, and her grip of my hand slackened. Her body arched next, seizing hard enough to shake the bed. Sweat broke on her brow. Her cry burrowed into me when we had to pin her down.

"You sure this is normal?" I bit out, dying on the inside seeing her like this.

"Yeah, she's just fighting it more than Mum did," Tristan said, helping us hold her down. "The drug is moving through her system. Waking up the dormant pathways that were blocked off."

My pulse pounded like a drum, sixty seconds stretching into a lifetime before she finally settled down and went still.

Her eyes parted, wide and frantic. She scanned us one by one.

"You." She focused on Gideon, breathing hard. "You did this to me, how could you?"

Gideon let go of her and staggered back, wrecked with guilt for something that wasn't his fault.

Her gaze slid to Tristan next. "What's going on? Where am I?" Then to me, she whispered, "Reed?"

Hearing that name on her lips shredded me more than I'd ever admit.

"Why are you holding me?" She yanked her hand free, and that was the final blow to my ability to keep my shit together. I backed into the chair.

"Wait," she called out as I turned for the door. "Your dad. I was looking for something to help him. I—I think. I read the letter you hid, and . . ."

Letter? Oh shit. In my bookcase. Now it all made sense.

Her fists pressed against her forehead. "It hurts. I'm s-so confused."

I turned, torn apart watching her break, knowing I couldn't reach for her.

"Why don't you step out, get some air?" Julian urged.

Her brothers gathered closer to her as I left the room, finding Ryder and Alex out there waiting for me.

"Don't do something ridiculous like try and hug me," I warned. The only arms I wanted didn't remember ever holding me. "How's Easton?" I deflected.

"He just stood by Gwen's bed for a minute and looked at her like she was a ghost. He barely said a word and didn't stay long," Alex shared, voice tense. "He's still shouldering the blame. He told Carter out in the hall he was quitting, then he went back to his room."

My stomach clenched. "He saved their lives. He'll change his mind." *Things change. People change.*

I looked through the window into Hollis's room. Her brothers were still near her, and she had her hands over her face. She was about to learn everything, and it would break her all over again.

Needing something solid to hold on to, I went for my phone and to the last photo we took before she was taken from me.

"She'll remember," Alex said, remaining steady and even-toned for my sake. "And if she doesn't, I have no doubt you'll make that woman fall in love with you a second time."

CHAPTER FORTY-NINE

Reed

Charleston, South Carolina; six days later

Wyatt should've been the one leading Echo, but he was still in England with Gwen, staying close to her even though she was out of danger. But Echo Team needed an assist on a quick op, so Secretary Chandler spun us up and plugged Delta in alongside the rest of the team. Our boots had barely hit the ground after coming home before we'd had to leave, bringing Trevor with us this time.

We'd deployed to the Balkans, mountains sharp as broken glass, pine air heavy and wet.

Insert, clear, snatch the HVT, exfil. Nothing fancy.

I'd covered Alex's flank and cleared buildings with Echo Four, but my head had stayed back in Charleston, mentally awaiting a text from Julian to give me the green light to reach out to Hollis's new number.

Every op break, every comms lull, I'd checked for Julian's go-ahead. Every minute of silence had been a betrayal of my promise to her that I'd fight for her. For us.

By the time we returned Stateside, mission complete without complication, I was exhausted, stinking of cordite and sweat and in need of a shower, when *finally* his message hit my phone.

Julian: You're good to text her now.

I stared at his words, thumb hovering and heart racing. In a daze, I shoved my phone into my pocket and went inside.

Chase had already dropped Ranger off, so my Maligator was there to greet me by the door, tail wagging hard and clearly searching for Hollis.

"Not here," I told him while flicking on the light. I tossed my bag on the floor, locked up, then made my way to my room for a shower.

I stripped, turned on the water, and went still at the memory of her being in there with me last week.

I managed to pull myself together, then hurried to my bedroom to grab my phone from the pocket of my jeans.

Naked, with a dog next to me and my phone in hand, I probably looked like a guy about to lose it, but I sent the text anyway.

Me: It's Jason. Julian gave me your new number. How are you?

I tossed the phone on the bed and showered in under sixty seconds. Towel wrapped around my hips, water still dripping down my body, I went back into my room, praying for a response.

Hollis: I thought you hated being called by your first name. 🙄

I cracked an honest-to-God smile, the first one I'd had in a long damn time, and brought my hand to my rib and over the tattoo.

Me: I do. Unless it's by you.

Bubbles. Then gone. Then back.

After a few minutes and no answer, I set the phone aside and wandered into my closet in search of clothes. At the sight of the present she'd left there for Audrey's baby shower, I abandoned my mission for clothes, about to go for the blue box mocking me, but Ranger's barking stopped me.

He was in my doorway, up on his hind legs. "What is it?"

I tightened the towel and followed Ranger to see what was wrong, anxious to get back to my conversation with Hollis, hoping she'd text soon.

Once in the living room, Ranger barreled past me and jumped straight at her standing by my couch.

The her. *My* her. A woman who'd quickly become my everything.

Hollis took a knee and nuzzled his nose with her face, and I may have died, because was this real? Did she break in and was now petting my dog?

She slowly lifted her head, her green eyes lighting a match inside me as they locked on to my face. "Hi," she mouthed. "Figured I'd just answer you this way instead, if that's okay?" Her gaze worked slowly up my naked torso before finding my face. "I fondly remember the last time I broke in to find you in only a towel." Her lips twitched into a slight smile. She stood, and Ranger ran happy circles around her as my heart exploded. "I have something outside I need your help with, do you mind?"

Her dark hair was down and wavy over her shoulders, and it only just now registered that she had on my old PT shirt, loosely tucked into her jeans.

A shy blush worked up her neck and into her cheeks; I'd never witnessed Hollis shy in the past before her memories were stolen, and this was the "real" her, so I wasn't sure what to make of it.

Still remaining quiet, I stepped forward, arm falling to my side. I wasn't prepared to get my hopes up. Not yet. But she was here, so . . .

I ordered Ranger to stay put, and I quietly followed her outside to an SUV parked in the driveway.

Hollis popped open the back, and I rounded the Escalade to see what she had to show me. "How handy are you? Chair-building handy? It's from IKEA, so it might—"

"Hollis," I rasped, my heart battling against my rib cage.

She turned to face me, eyes glossy. "I remember," she blurted out as if unable to hide the secret any longer.

She opened her palm and held it between us, and I hesitantly rested mine on top of hers. A tear fell down her cheek, disappearing beneath her jawline.

"I remembered my place of peace. You. Our kids."

I froze, worried I'd passed out in the shower and was dreaming.

She sniffled, swiping away tears with her free hand. "Then it all came back to me," she cried. "And, I, um, heard you were operating, so I wanted to wait until you'd be back and surprise you."

I about keeled over. Instead, I snatched her in my arms and hauled her against me, crushing my lips over hers.

She tangled her hands in my hair, then ran her nails over my back as I made love to her with my mouth. I was fully aware I was on my driveway in only a towel, and couldn't give two shits about it because she'd found her way back to me.

Ranger howled with excitement as I continued to ravish this woman, my heart stitching back together in real time as my world tilted.

"Your towel," she said against my mouth, her fast reflexes saving me from exposing myself in public.

"Maybe we continue this inside," I said, my voice husky, as I stepped back and fixed the towel.

I shut the back door, then took her hand in mine.

Once in my kitchen, she went still the second she peered at the table. "You already got the fifth chair." She whirled around toward me, her hands landing on my chest.

"Of course I did. I knew you'd be back."

"Guess we'll have to amend that dream to four kids to fill the other seat."

I pulled her back into my arms, and this time, when the towel slipped, she didn't save it from falling as we kissed.

A few dog howls later, her lips broke from mine, and she dipped her chin between us, catching her lip at the side of her mouth as she took in the size of me. "How, um, long until we make my dream a reality?"

"Is the courthouse open now?" I was only partially joking. I curled my mouth back to hers, laughing against the kiss, and she melted into me.

My hands slid over her hips, lifting her tight to my erection. I pressed her back against the closest wall, and she hooked one leg around me. "We'll wait until we're married. I want that for both of us," she whispered, shaky but certain.

"Whatever you want," I promised, resting my forehead against hers.

"There is something else I want, though." Shit, that sounded heavy.

She slung her arms over my shoulders, clasping her hands at the base of my neck. "I'm still processing everything. Lyra. People we trusted betraying us for power to claw out of the shadows." Her long, dark lashes fluttered shut. "And Lyra, she needs a lot of help. I visited her before I came here and forgave her, but those are just words. I still need time to actually feel the weight of forgiveness, if that makes sense."

I understood that a little too much. Though I'd yet to do the actual words part of that equation when it came to forgiving my parents.

"My family has to reevaluate everything and reorganize. No more protectors, only teammates. Stuff like that. Gideon will take over when Dad and Mum step aside. I've made up my mind that I don't want to be in charge. In fact . . . I don't want to be part of it at all. No ring. No power. None of it."

My heart thundered wildly against my ribs as I absorbed what she was saying.

"I want to be a mother. A wife. Not a human weapon. I—I want some peace. I'm going to have my tattoo removed, too. No more tracking me." She pointed her green eyes at me, and they shimmered with resolve. "That vision when I was drugged came to me for a reason, and it's because it's what my heart wants. My *soul.* I'm allowed to change my mind. I made a choice once, and now I'm making the choice to do something different," she whispered, her voice catching from emotion. "I want to be here with you. *This* is where I'm most myself and happy."

"Are you sure? I mean, nothing is set in stone. If you change your mind again, you—"

"I'm certain. Gideon is more than capable of leading everything, and if I get the operator itch, I can convince POTUS to let me spin up with you here and there like Trevor does. Heck, I can be part of the attachment unit, even. You know, maybe later, *if* I want to be."

"I support you, whatever you want. Always," I said firmly, meaning every word.

"I should apologize for violating your privacy. I promise I didn't mean to find that letter from the hospital about your dad. I was checking out your books, and it fell out."

"I could never be mad at you. Only fake hate, remember?" I smirked. "And as for a cure . . . maybe one day there will be one."

For the first time in weeks, my chest became light.

She was here. She chose me. *Us.* And I'd never be letting go.

I guess people really could change and happily-ever-afters existed even for people like me after all.

"Now." I cleared my throat, and she lowered her eyes between us down to my cock that'd yet to behave. "Back to the whole marrying thing . . ."

She slid her tongue along the seam of her mouth. "How soon is too soon? We talking years or months? Four kids to have and all, so."

"Fuck years," I choked out. "Maybe months." I kissed her. "But if you really want to make a guy happy, how about *weeks*?"

CHAPTER FIFTY

Hollis

Five and a half weeks later

I gripped the ivory-draped railing of the terrace Jason had rented for us. Below, the French manor spilled into the water's edge, a painting come to life. Gas lanterns flickered along the curved stone path, their glow brushing the jasmine climbing the walls.

Beneath strings of tiny lights swaying in the coastal wind, the world fell away to just the water and the weight of my husband's hands as they framed my waist. He pressed his chest to my back, steady and warm, anchoring me.

Less than an hour ago we'd married at the church where Trevor worked security, officially becoming one like his tattoo promised. Only our closest family and friends were in attendance. Although I'd met his parents in Houston two weeks ago, he'd decided not to invite them, and there was no way I could handle having Lyra at my side tonight. At some point, we'd have a bigger reception to celebrate, but this moment was for us.

"Peaceful here," he murmured, his voice sending anticipation shivering up my spine. "You could've picked anywhere in the world for our honeymoon, but you wanted to stay local. Why?"

"Mm. Easy. It's the home I've always wanted. Why go anywhere else?" I angled my head back to meet his eyes. "Plus, no way was I waiting a whole plane flight to"—I playfully lifted my brows twice—"you know."

He smiled against my mouth, breathing, "My wife," and I swallowed the words.

"Husband," I returned, kissing him before facing forward, leaning into him. "You know, you could've married me on my birthday last month. One date to remember both."

"I would never take the easy way out like that." His grin curved against my skin, and his laugh slipped down my neck.

"You thought about it, though."

"Only because it meant we'd be married sooner." He swept my braid over my shoulder and lowered his mouth to my ear. "But I'll never forget either date. You have my word."

I heard the promise beneath the tease, the shadow of his father's condition threading through it. Maybe one day Tristan or Diana would find a cure and we could add another miracle to our list.

We'd waited forever to be together, but the wait would be more than worth it. That thought sparked another, and I slid my hands into his pockets, searching.

"Not what I was hoping you'd reach for," he said darkly, catching my wrist as I tugged his phone free.

Holding it between us, I smiled. "Time to change your reset point."

He took the phone and placed it on the small table. "After," he said, voice low. "I plan to make love to you first."

I stepped back against the railing to better look at my husband. The tuxedo fit him like a second skin, broad shoulders tapering into a frame that looked both lethal and devastatingly refined. A man who could move mountains, and tonight, he'd be moving mine.

His eyes drifted over my dress—simple silk, elegant and timeless, slipping against my skin with every movement and light enough to sway in the breeze.

He closed the space between us and went for my braid, tugging loose the pins until the woven strands unraveled into waves. His fingers combed through until my hair spilled free over my shoulders. He framed my face with both hands, tilting my head just enough to kiss me like we owned the moment.

When his mouth broke from mine, his eyes were still closed, lashes dark against his skin. "I love you." The words settled over me, warming me up.

"I love you, too. So much." My palm slid up his chest, catching the glint of the diamond on my finger. My grandmother's ring. She'd died young in battle before Tristan was even born. Though I'd never met her, I knew how deeply she'd loved my grandfather, and he'd set it aside for his future granddaughter.

He'd saved the book for Tristan.

The love of his life's ring for me.

While I hadn't wanted Solomon's ring, this one was a symbol of grace and happiness. I could carry my family forward with me in this way and on my terms.

Jason caught my hand and kissed my palm, his lips tickling my sensitive skin. He lifted me easily, carrying me inside.

The lantern light followed us through the open doors as he set me on the edge of the bed and lowered himself to his knees in front of me. His hands moved under the skirt of my dress, to my calves, my thighs. His eyes locked on mine with a heat that made my pulse stumble.

He ducked beneath the dress, and his mouth replaced his hands, a slow burn up the inside of my leg that had me trembling. My fingers buried into his shoulders as he slipped my panties aside and pressed a tender kiss to me there, my breath stuttering.

Panties back in place, he retreated, then rose over me, loosening his bow tie.

"Tease," I protested.

"Only for you," he said huskily, unbuttoning his shirt.

"Damn right, only for me." A soft laugh escaped me, filling the quiet.

His eyes darkened as he undressed with precision, like this was the mission he'd been born for.

The tuxedo fell away piece by piece.

I stood and slipped my dress from my shoulders and let it pool at my feet. I kept on my white lingerie, and he pulled me against him, our vows echoing in the night.

I kissed his neck, and he angled it to give me better access as his hands dragged along my silhouette.

Every touch from him was calculated to unravel me, every kiss deeper, hungrier, until his control slipped.

He moved aside the silk between my legs and pushed two fingers inside me. A gasp ripped from my mouth, caught by his tongue.

He cursed under his breath while pumping his fingers, then dropped to his knees, sliding my panties off completely. His fingertips sank into my thighs as he tasted me like a man starved. He licked and sucked, flicking his tongue, pushing me to the edge without letting me fall.

"I want . . ." I panted, clutching him, " . . . our first time to be together."

He gave me one last, slow sweep of his tongue before working his way up my body, taking the time to shift my bra cup over to draw my nipple into his mouth before moving to my neck.

I reached between us and wrapped my hand around him. He swore and fisted my hair gently, tugging my head back as his other hand found my throat.

"I wouldn't do that. I'll explode," he growled before kissing me.

His hand went from my throat to my jawline, his lips following. I forced myself to let go so he wouldn't come yet.

He lifted me and laid me out on the bed, covering me with his body as his mouth crashed over mine. The kiss was desperate and consuming. The kind that stole the air and returned it as heat.

Impatient hands slowed to skim along my body, racing over my curves, mapping me with calloused palms and reverent touches.

"Be with me," I pleaded.

He lifted his head, and his brows knitted together as I clung to him, nails raking his shoulders. Finally, he gave us both what we wanted and needed.

My body opened for him, tightening around him as we joined as one flesh. Once I adjusted to his thickness and length, we began to move together with purpose, every thrust threaded with love and months of tension breaking apart in one fierce, shattering release.

Pleasure tore through me, a rush of heat that left me crying out, shaking, undone. He followed with a groan that vibrated against my mouth, his body pressing me deeper into the mattress as he gave himself over completely.

When it was over, he collapsed against me, chest heaving, skin slick. I wrapped my arms around him, holding him as tightly as he held me.

We stayed like that for a few quiet minutes before he got up to fetch a warm, wet towel to clean me up. He took his time, eyes blazing as they swept over my body.

"My wife," he murmured, voice trembling. "I don't know what I did to deserve you, but I'll be the man you need, every day of my life."

I whispered my own promises back to him, then stole the towel and tossed it so I could draw him closer—flesh to flesh, heartbeat to heartbeat. No drug, no *anything*, would ever take these memories from us. I knew that deep in my soul.

Emotional, teary-eyed, I urged him on top of me. On my forearms, I pressed up to find his lips. "Let me know when you're ready to go again. I miss you already."

He laughed against my mouth. "I'm only just getting started, darlin'. You have no idea how much I have planned for us tonight." He licked my lips open before setting his mouth to my ear. "Can you handle that?"

I bucked against him in anticipation, greedy for more of him. "Mmm. Bring it on. Give me everything you have."

"I've already given you my heart to keep," he whispered. "Now I'll give you the family we both want."

EPILOGUE

Hollis

Two months later; December

The first notes of "Not Mine to Keep" from Callie Costa's hit single drifted through the speakers, the melody soft at first, then swelling like a promise you could feel in your bones. Earlier, she'd debuted and personally sung her new hit with Audrey at the piano—you'd never guess she'd just had a baby. They hadn't gone with my suggestion for a song name, but I had to admit "Into the Deep" had a nice ring to it.

Jason's palm was currently warm against my waist as we danced beneath a canopy of white lights strung under the tent. Lanterns glowed on every table, softening the edges of the night. Our friends helped pull the entire thing together for us because party-planning was not my strong suit.

He spun me, then caught me in his arms, a grin tugging at his lips. I knew exactly what was on my husband's mind: baby-making. After holding Audrey and Alex's newborn daughter in our arms at the hospital three weeks ago, we were even more ready to have our own children.

Jason drew me closer and set his mouth to my ear. "I know what's on your mind."

I smirked. "Only because I read yours first."

He arched into me, letting me feel the weight of his erection pressing against his dress pants. "We're on a crowded dance floor, and I'm hard as a rock."

"Maybe we can ditch our party for a few minutes and—"

"Mind if I cut in?" Mum interrupted.

Seriously?

Jason tried to protest, but with his current problem, he shut his eyes, probably conjuring up the most unsexy thoughts possible before surrendering to her.

"Traitor," he mouthed with a smile before I disappeared into the packed crowd of mostly operators and their wives.

Almost everyone had shown up to our delayed reception. From Secretary Chandler and his SEAL teams to the Costas and Falcon Falls. Even Kylo and Rowan were there, but no longer as our protectors.

Heck, Jason's parents were in attendance, too. He'd forgiven them a couple of weeks ago. That hadn't been an easy decision to make, but I respected his choice. Didn't change the fact I still wanted to plant a heel in his father's ass for hurting him in the first place.

The only notably absent people tonight: Easton and Lyra. One had an invitation and declined, the other never received one.

While I may have forgiven her, I wasn't ready for her to leave the center she was at and be here with us. My brothers and I were still sorting out how to pick up the pieces of the mess she'd left behind with Cassian and the others.

Everything will be okay, I told myself. *One day.* It had to be.

I stole a look at Julian on the dance floor with Gwen. He had to use an alias to even be here since the world believed he was dead. Thankfully, the majority of our guests were covert operatives and knew the truth, so he was mostly safe from scrutiny.

As for Gwen, months of recovery and PT had given back her glow. She was a living miracle on two feet. She tossed her head back, laughing at something my brother whispered in her ear. Part of me wondered whether they might become something more. Another part believed she belonged with the man who hadn't shown up. *But* it wasn't my business. I just wanted everyone to be as happy as Jason and me.

I started for the bar, where Tristan was sitting alone, when a tug at my dress stopped me.

"Dance with me, Auntie Hollis?" Chase stood there in his tiny tux, absolutely adorable. How could I say no?

"So," I asked while taking hold of his little hands, "how does it feel to be a big brother?"

"Baby Katiya makes stinky diapers"—he scrunched his nose—"but nothing I can't handle." He shrugged.

"You're a real trouper." I winked, then twirled him around, which had him giggling.

After the dance and the song ended, Chase bowed like a perfect gentleman, just before Gideon stole me away next.

"Hey you." Gideon's lopsided smile wasn't his usual one. "We've missed you. Heard you just operated with Delta. Almost late to your own party."

Yeah, about that. I shrugged, glancing at Trevor dancing with a dark-haired guest I didn't recognize. "They haven't hired two more recruits for Trevor's unit yet, so they needed help, and I couldn't resist."

"Rumor has it, you went up against a drug lord and—"

"Like that isn't just another Tuesday for you?"

He shook his head, unamused. "If you have the itch to operate, why not run missions with us again?"

I had felt that coming a mile away. "Because I want to get pregnant and have kids, and only scratch that itch when I'm, well, feeling itchy," I said with a laugh. "And it should be you running things. You were always going to take over regardless of a ring and tradition, and we both know that. You were born for this. Me?" Worried how that may have sounded, I quickly amended, "That doesn't mean you can't have a family, too."

"I don't think I'm the commitment type."

"I wasn't, either, before Jason, so never say never," I reminded him.

He tilted his head toward Gwen and Julian. "Don't think a family is in the cards for him, either. Don't get your hopes up about Gwen—that's not happening. They're way too alike for it to work out."

"So the idea of them together crossed your mind, too?"

A dark laugh sat between us. "Hell no. That's just what Julian told me last week after a few too many drinks."

"Which means he's actually into her, and . . ." My words trailed off when I spotted a man at the edge of the tent.

Easton Holloway in a dark suit, and his crutches were clearly a distant memory. His eyes were fixed on Gwen and Julian dancing.

I let go of my brother when Easton turned and went back outside. I started to chase after him, only to have Gwen catch my wrist mid-pursuit.

She looked back and forth between where she'd left my brother on the dance floor and the direction Easton had gone. "Let me," she whispered, then let go of me and took off.

"Was that Easton?" Jason asked on approach, pulling me close to him.

"It was." I swallowed. "How was the dance with Mum?"

"She apologized for some things she said," he casually tossed out, and I knew he really didn't give a damn about my mum's opinion of him, but *I* cared about her treating him right, so. "How was the dance with your brother? He trying to win you back to the dark side?"

"I think he accepts I'm where I belong." He hadn't said that, but I believed it. "I'm still worried about Tristan, though." I looked around for him, and found him still at the bar, alone, a drink in hand. "Not sure yet what he plans to do with the knowledge about his father. I mean, maybe his dad's not even alive."

"He's not." Jason stopped dancing, letting a curse settle between us as he winced. "I don't think so, at least."

I arched my brow. "You have something to tell me?"

"You know how I know too much about a lot of random things?"

I nodded.

"Well, I remembered something. An event that happened in 1992. Did some digging."

Mum burned down the vault that year, right.

"Do you actually want to know who I think it is? It's felt like a lie to keep this from you, but . . ."

"I'm not ready to carry that burden. Your instincts are spot on." I gulped. "Mind holding that secret for me a little longer?"

"Of course."

I rose on my toes and kissed him, hard enough to silence every lingering thought. He tasted like bourbon and a bright future.

When the kiss ended, the world faded back in. "Can we please ditch the party and steal a few minutes for ourselves?"

He laced our fingers together and led me toward the edge of the tent past the swirl of our family and friends. Kylo, no longer my shadow, caught my eye and offered me a small smile. Maybe now he could have that family he'd always wanted, too.

Jason and I slipped outside into the crisp night air. We wandered through the gardens, about to stop and kiss, when voices reached us. Easton and Gwen?

I gave Jason's backside a slap, signaling to duck away unseen and find another spot.

Within minutes, he had me tangled in his arms inside a gazebo at the back of the property my father had rented. Whatever secrets still haunted us, and whatever truths still ran deep in my family, none of it mattered right now.

His grin was dangerous and familiar as he pulled out his phone. While we technically didn't need photo folders as happy reminders now that we had each other, we kept them anyway and added new memories all the time.

"Come here before I give you what you need." His rough order made my already damp panties wetter.

He patted his leg, and I sat on his lap, hooking my arm around his back.

"Look at you, being the selfie king now," I teased.

He rolled his eyes. "Such a pain in my ass." He bucked his hips, letting me feel him hard beneath me. Stretching out his arm, he angled the camera at us, a handsome smile stealing across his lips as he demanded in a husky voice, "Now, be a good girl and act like you like me."

AUTHOR'S NOTE

One of my favorite things to do is to have characters from other series cross over into new books to keep them "alive." Delta Shield Security has quite a few cameos from three different series.

The Costa Family—Italian American "vigilantes" (in private security) who are former military: Enzo (*Let Me Love You*), Alessandro (*Not Mine to Keep*), Hudson / Isabella Costa (*The Art of You*), Constantine (*The Best of Us*).

Stealth Ops—Navy SEALs working covert ops for the president of the United States.

- **Stealth Ops: Bravo Team**
- *Finding His Mark* (Luke, Bravo One)
- *Finding Justice* (Owen, Bravo Two)
- *Finding the Fight* (Asher, Bravo Three)
- *Finding Her Chance* (Liam, Bravo Four)
- *Finding the Way Back* (Knox, POTUS's son, Bravo Five)

- **Stealth Ops: Echo Team**
- *Chasing the Knight* (Wyatt, Echo One)—where we first meet his daughter Gwen
- *Chasing Daylight* (A.J., Echo Two)
- *Chasing Fortune* (Chris, Echo Three)

- *Chasing Shadows* (Roman, Echo Four)
- *Chasing the Storm* (Finn, Echo Five)

Falcon Falls Security—features former army operators who work private security. This series is a direct spin-off from the Stealth Ops series. Carter Dominick (*The Fallen One*) co-runs Falcon with Grayson Chandler (*The Taken One*).
- Book 1 is *The Hunted One (Griffin)*
- In the last book of the series, *The Wrecked One*, Carter acquires The Sapphire Hotel with The League leader Sebastian Renaud (from the Dublin Nights series). Sebastian's book is *The Real Deal*.
- We also first meet Julian (as the mystery hacker) in *The Wrecked One*.
- Gwen's book releases September 2026.

ABOUT THE AUTHOR

Brittney Sahin is the *Wall Street Journal* bestselling author of numerous series, including Delta Shield Security, the Costa Family, Falcon Falls Security, Dublin Nights, and many other novels of romantic suspense. She began writing at an early age with the dream to be a published author before the age of eighteen. Although academic pursuits (and later, a teaching career) interrupted her aspirations, she never stopped writing or imagining. It wasn't until her students encouraged her to follow her dreams that Brittney said goodbye to upstate New York to start a new adventure in the place she was raised: Charlotte, North Carolina. Here, she decided to take her students' advice and begin to write again. When she's not working on upcoming novels, she spends time with her family. Brittney is the proud mother of two boys, and a lover of suspense novels, coffee, and the outdoors. For more information, visit www.brittneysahin.com.